BAD GUYS DON'T ALWAYS LOSE

BAD GUYS DON'T ALWAYS LOSE

a work of
fiction

MICHELLE THOMPSON

Published 2025
by Michelle Thompson

ISBN 978-0-473-76262-9 (International Edition)

© Copyright Michelle Thompson 2025

All rights reserved.

COPYPRESS

Designed and distributed in New Zealand by CopyPress, Nelson, New Zealand.

www.copypress.co.nz

Dedicated to my husband and biggest fan, Simon

PART ONE

Ben

It was the year 2009. Ben stood on the lot at 9 am that Monday looking at all the trucks for sale. He was only going to drive it twice, once away from here and the second time to complete the job of killing Mellissa. He didn't care about the colour or the state of the interior. It just had to be big and mechanically it had to be in tip-top working order. He could not afford it to break down at a critical moment; he didn't fancy spending the rest of his life in prison.

A lot of planning had gone into this. He had been having private heavy rig lessons and gained his HT licence. He'd had to hire a large warehouse to store the truck in until he needed to use it, and he had paid the rent in advance in cash; the people he was dealing with didn't ask questions.

No one knew what he was about to do. He'd had good advice from a lawyer years ago who said, "If you don't want to get busted for a crime, don't tell even one person." He couldn't afford to have a weak link on this one, so he had done exactly that, kept it to himself. The only person that he would have ever trusted was dead, and he still held himself responsible for not preventing it.

He was surprisingly nervous, he had to control his emotions, walk around a bit and take some deep breaths, shake it off. He was used to being in more control than this. Now he was out of his comfort zone. He was about to cross a lot of boundaries.

Ed, the truck salesman, eyed Ben up from behind the window in his office. What a fuckin loser, Ed thought. Hadn't that mullet look died with Elvis? Rode in on that big Harley-Davidson; walked around like a hero with tennis balls under his arms. Tyre-kicker – probably come in with a broken-arse story about starting a business for himself. You heard every story in this gig.

Well, thought Ed as he rolled a cigarette, showtime. Put on the best mate act. Convince himself this punter was the best customer of the day. Kill some time talking shit with this guy; after all, he was the first customer of the day. Wasn't that meant to be good luck? Ed had his routine well-rehearsed after years in the trade. He'd pat this guy's ego, talk about his hog.

"See one you like, young fella? We got a special this week. Throw in a fifty-inch telly if you pay cash." He laughed at his own joke.

Ben held back the urge to laugh or show any emotion. Here was your classic Aussie car salesman – smooth, slicked-back hair, possibly dyed, yellow nicotine stain on his index finger, overweight, shirt gaping between the buttons and something spilt down the front. Was that coffee or food?

"As a matter of fact, I have, sir. The big blue one over there in the corner, the one with the big kangaroo bars. I'd like to buy it. Are we able to go for a test drive please?"

Ed was taken aback; he'd thought he could read this guy. He hadn't predicted the quietly spoken voice and good manners. He quickly started to rethink his approach. This biker guy might just have a brain.

The blue truck was a beast, a Western Star six-by-four Sleeper Cab. The asking price was $149,500. Deceased estate, high mileage on the clock – Ed knew it was a hefty price. It had been on the lot for a while and the widow was desperate to sell. Might be room to negotiate. Could be the sale he needed to keep this joint afloat.

"I'll just check your licence if you don't mind, son, and I'll go inside and get the keys."

The licence was in the name of Benjamin Wallace. The photo matched but he hadn't picked him for a Benjamin. Who cares if he buys the bloody thing; and Ed would get his commission.

The test drive was relatively short. Ben didn't want to hang around this guy too long, didn't want a thousand nosey questions. Ben's cover story was that he had come into an inheritance and always wanted to be an owner-driver and start doing long hauls up to the Northern Territory. Needed the right truck for the job.

He was careful today to dress so his tattoos were covered, and he kept his glasses on. And he was definitely going to cut this ridiculous hair after he finished this job.

When they got back to the office Ed was surprised again by Ben's softly spoken voice and manners.

"Sir, I'm going to make you a one-time cash offer of $120 thousand. It's all the money I have. I have the money on me now, in cash. Would you be able to contact the seller on my behalf please, sir?"

Ben had done his homework. He knew this truck had been on the lot for more than a month and before that, it had been well maintained by all accounts.

According to the deceased husband's colleagues, he had been a good sort, knew his trucks well. The widow was a bitch, selling everything that wasn't nailed down to support a gambling habit. The bank was about to foreclose on her house. $120k cash – she'd take it. Ben was sure of that.

Ed returned from his office after fifteen minutes, face flushed. He'd obviously had a battle on his hands. Either that, or he had been having a quick swig of whisky from his hip flask to celebrate. But his hand was out; he wanted to shake on the deal. Ed quickly reminded Ben they were all out of fifty-inch TVs.

Ben picked the truck up later that evening, just going on dark. He had arranged with Ed to have an updated vehicle safety compliance certification done on the truck that day.

As he drove to his warehouse, sitting high up in the truck, a sense of relief washed over him. Step one over. He was buzzing with adrenaline and could hardly keep still. Was that adrenaline, or that hit of methamphetamine he'd just sucked into his lungs? Who cares, in a couple of weeks it would all be over, he could move on.

Doug

It was 1984. Robert Henderson and his son, Doug, had shifted eight times in ten years. Doug's father was a bank manager, and they had transferred nearly every year so Robert could move up the corporate ladder.

Doug's mother had abandoned the family when Doug was five. What little memory Doug did have of her was never pleasant. She had drifted back and forth occasionally in the beginning, always with her hand out for money, always drunk, and the fights with Doug's father left Doug frightened so he'd hide in his room under the bed.

She picked him up from school once when he was about seven, only to abandon him in a shopping centre after she had gone off with some bloke she met in a bar. First Bob Henderson knew was the police turning up at his work with a scared and very sad little boy. Doug had been found cold and hungry, crying in the gents' toilet. His father had never been able to forgive her over that incident and had taken the necessary legal steps to stop her from having access to the child.

She was found dead several years later from a drug overdose, but Bob didn't even bother going to the funeral. He dealt with it the only way he knew how shifting again and starting a fresh life in a new part of the country.

Bob had always been awkward around women so when he finally got one, he married her instantly. He was a pushover, did whatever he could to make his wife happy so she wouldn't leave him. His wife saw him as boring and weak and walked all over him. She would get drunk at staff functions and become abusive and emotionally expressive. He always felt he had been publicly embarrassed after every incident and found it difficult to hold his head up at work. He would apply for a transfer just to save face. He was just happy he had his son; he probably would have committed suicide if he hadn't had Doug to come home to every night.

Doug had spent a life in kinder and after-school care. His father loved him, but Bob's brain was fixated on providing a financial legacy for Doug, an only child, so he spent long hours at work and often picked Doug up late and dropped him off early.

Bob had been a little concerned with some of the antisocial behaviours Doug exhibited at kinder-care and school. He would frequently get calls from the teacher. Complaints always centred on Doug's tendency to show unreasonable acts of aggression towards other children at the centre. The teachers had recommended counselling, and the consensus was that the possible early childhood trauma Doug experienced with his mother's behaviour had had a negative effect on him.

Bob didn't need a counsellor to tell him what he already knew. The kid was smart, and at home what little time they did spend together was always the best time of Bob's day and life; they always laughed and talked. He was sure it was a stage, and Doug would grow out of it.

Bob thought the truth was that he was probably the one who needed the counsellor. He was the one with the problems.

Doug was resilient, he'd had to be. He didn't like babysitters so when he'd got a bit older, he had convinced his father that from age nine he could manage himself in the afternoon at home alone. But he didn't mind Maria, his father's lady friend who occasionally came to visit. She was a funny Spanish woman who stayed over a few times a week. She taught him how to cook and how to speak Spanish, and she always had an endless supply of cigarettes for Doug to smoke.

He was easily able to provide himself with a reasonable meal at night if his father was late home. Might not have always been a healthy option, but it filled his belly, and he was quite proud of his creations. He just had to put up with Maria telling him off for making a mess of the kitchen from time to time.

Doug and his father had travelled extensively on annual overseas holidays. His father felt Doug needed to see the world, and they had always had the privilege of travelling business class. When Doug was only ten, he could boast that he had been to more countries than the prime minister. He often got to practise his Spanish, and many times was trusted to do the negotiations for his father when conversations overseas had been lost in translation.

Doug didn't have any friends, largely because they never stayed in one place long enough to bond with anyone, but mostly because of all the fighting he was forced to do to defend himself at every school he attended.

As a child, Doug had suffered severely from a staphylococcus bacterial infection on his face. It was complicated by Doug not keeping up with regular medical applications advised by the doctors. He kept playing with the skin surface rather than giving it time to heal and this caused his face to react. When the skin was cut open or provoked by injury from fighting, it made the infection ten times worse, and over time this eventually caused deep, red-coloured scarring.

To add to his woes, at age ten he was nearly twice as tall as all his other peers, so he always walked with a stoop and his face down, which made his arms look too long for his body. They could never get clothes to fit him, let alone school uniforms, and he was already in a size eleven men's shoe. People literally drew breath when they saw him. He learnt to avert his gaze and not to make eye contact with anyone. It wasn't the look of shock on people's faces that he was avoiding, it was more the looks of sympathy that he hated the most.

Not only the children at school were cruel, he'd even heard adults calling him names when he walked in the streets or the shopping malls. Doug had heard all the jokes at his expense, he knew them all by heart: Frankenstein, Quasimodo, Freddie Krueger, Face Ache, Pus Boy, you name it. The names and the taunts, followed by the group laughter, always made him lash out and punch the nearest boy in the face.

On the odd occasion he'd wanted to punch a girl in the face, but he had another plan for them. He'd resorted to carrying a little vial of urine on him and when they would start their nasty little tirade of name-calling or exaggerated laughter, he'd retrieve the vial from his shorts pocket and pour his urine all over their heads and face to shut them up. What he loved the most about doing this was the look on their faces when they worked out it was his piss, and it was in their hair and on their clothing, and they'd start crying, thinking if they brushed it with their hands, they could somehow wipe it off. He usually only needed to do that trick once at a new school and all the girls just screamed and ran away from him after that.

So here he was, Bob was dropping him off at yet another new school, going through the polite introductions with the headmaster, hoping that Doug would last the day at this school without a phone call about his behaviour after a couple of hours. Bob never disciplined Doug, he just kept thinking it would sort itself out eventually. He didn't have the heart to tell the boy off, ever.

So once again, Doug was about to be led into another class by another head teacher and be introduced as Doug Henderson, the new boy – how original. He

   MICHELLE THOMPSON

could sense the laughter before the door even opened. His face was starting to itch, and sweat was running down his temples even though it was a cool day.

The class was full. Everyone was sitting in rows across the room, with an aisle down the middle separating the two sides. As usual, the more popular kids clustered down the back, the alfa males and the football heroes and their bitches. He had no respect for bitches; they were all cunts.

By now he was used to it – same old, same old. It would be a first week of shit until they all settled on a mutually agreed nickname: nothing pleasant, nothing original. At least two punch-ups in the first week, and the highlight – his smelly urine attack. He always used urine from the first piss in the morning, which was the worst and the strongest smelling. They usually left him alone after that. And he could go about the rest of the year in the library reading books.

Take a deep breath, suck it in.

Mellissa

Mellissa was already startlingly beautiful from an early age. People always wanted to stare at her or even touch her. Long blonde hair, slightly olive complexion, piercing dark blue eyes, perfect skin, slim athletic build. Her looks were not just skin deep; she was a lovely caring person. She would light up a room with her big smile and she always had something pleasant to say. She was no shrinking violet; she called a spade a spade. She had a wild sense of humour, an adult sense of humour. And she appeared to not be afraid of anything. Her father called her a tuff little rooster.

Mellissa's parents, Don and Andrea Robertson, were cattle farmers and had a big ranch on the other side of town. They were motorbike enthusiasts and very social people. Their house was always full of friends and visitors. Her father believed in giving everyone a chance, and he was forever hiring no-hopers and friends of friends to work on the farm; everyone always had a job. If you worked hard, you got fed, that was his simple philosophy.

Their social events were legendary, a party with a band turned into a concert. A simple barbecue would end up with at least fifty guests and her parents would be the life of the party. It was an environment surrounded by love and constant laughter. Bikers from all over Australia were always welcome, as well as selected locals, and staff were treated like part of the family.

Mellissa was an only child; her mother had had her when she was twenty years old. It was a difficult birth, and they had decided not to try for any more – they never regretted their decision.

Mellissa had horses, her cats and a naughty little terrier. From an early age, she'd been taught to ride a small farm bike so she could accompany her parents out on the farm. She had fallen off heaps of times, but just like with the horse, her parents had encouraged her to get back on and stop whingeing. They were acutely aware that she was a beautiful little girl, but they taught her manners, and they never hid any of life's lessons from her. She had to pull her weight around the farm just like everyone else. Everyone liked her, and much like her parents, she was a perfect host and made everyone feel part of her extended family.

　　MICHELLE THOMPSON

Doug and Mellissa

It came as no surprise to anyone that the new boy was given to Mellissa to look after on his first day at the new school. She got all the new kids. She sat up the front of the class, not because she was a goody-two-shoes, but because she was easily distracted, daydreaming about her pets and things she enjoyed doing at home on her parents' farm. Sitting up front was what she decided she needed to do to concentrate on the lesson, it was her choice.

She had grown up in the area and had always gone to the same school. She knew everyone, and everyone knew her.

Her sparkling blue eyes looked up at Doug and their gazes met for a second. She instantly saw the fear in his eyes as he was being prodded into the room from behind, it was as if the teacher was afraid his skin was catching. She'd seen worse-looking guys. A friend of her dad's had been badly burnt in a fire, and this was on a par with that. He was introduced as Doug Henderson, the new boy. She always found that amusing; of course he was the new boy, who else was he going to be?

She stood up and came forward confidently and immediately took his hand firmly. She pulled him alongside her to his seat and patted the chair beneath him, prompting him to sit down. "Sit here, beside me." It was almost an order.

In her mind, the quicker he got to sit down with his back to the rabble behind him the less time they had to look at his face. She needed time to gather her thoughts and calm the situation down. She could feel his fear through his hand; he was like a scared rabbit caught in a trap. That was when she realised she was still gripping his hand. She relaxed her grip but didn't let go. She could hear the murmur building behind them; this was going to be a tough day for him.

The teacher tapped the board and called everyone to settle down and carried on with the lesson. Everyone went quiet for now.

Doug was staring ahead, still in a state of shock. This was his worst nightmare, even worse than he had predicted. Why had they put him with the pretty girl, and why was she still holding his hand? He had his free hand firmly gripping his vial of urine. One smart word and this bitch was going to get it.

He didn't want to look in her direction, no eye contact was always best. He could feel small objects pelting off his back and off his head, as the back row was using him for target practice with bits of paper and erasers and probably rolled-up balls of snot.

To his surprise and fear, she was now moving closer to him. She had written him a note which she slid in front of him. As he read, he was expecting some vicious comment, but instead, it read, 'Morning tea at ten and I'm starving. I'll show you around.' She remained sitting close to him and continued holding his hand till the bell rang.

At morning tea, she had dragged him around at a pace, given him the quick school tour and shown him a couple of key areas around the school that he needed to know.

Then the bell rang, and they made their way back into the same class and sat at the same seats. She had let go of his hand by now, but she was still sitting closer than any girl had ever sat to him before. Her leg was touching his, he could smell the perfume from her hair and her breath didn't smell at all. He still didn't want to make eye contact.

Although she had been genuinely nice to him, he was still waiting suspiciously and preparing for the catch – there had to be one, no one was ever this nice to him. In his experience, the joke would come out soon and the whole class would be laughing.

At lunch break, Mellissa deliberately sat them away from the other students. Oddly enough, and to Doug's surprise and confusion, she wanted to see what he had for lunch and was busy pulling her lunch out of her bag to negotiate what he was prepared to share or swap. He wasn't hungry, but he was prepared to give her all his lunch just to stop her from talking. In fact, he felt like throwing up.

She wasn't asking any questions about his past, or his life, or where he came from or how he got such a bad face. She was upbeat and kept smiling at him and talked about her dog and her pets. He was trying to work out if he hated her or not; she was confusing him.

Doug was used to eating alone and sitting alone at lunchtime and he was feeling uncomfortable having someone so close in his space. He was a loner through survival and necessity, and he wasn't used to a girl, of all things, being this nice to him. Plus, he was busting for a leak and a cigarette, one of the unhealthy habits he had picked up being home alone so often and sharing cigarettes with Maria.

   MICHELLE THOMPSON

The pressure was too much; he made an excuse and made his way to the toilet block, leaving her sitting on the bench alone. He'd find a place to have a cigarette after he'd had a piss.

Mellissa understood Doug was scared, he couldn't even string a sentence together and she thought that if she was in his boots, she'd be bawling by now. She really felt sorry for him. She didn't want to pry and ask him personal questions; he'd tell her when he was ready. She just tried to keep the conversation light and neutral. Her dog and her other pets were an easy subject, and she could talk all day about them; he was such a naughty but cool dog.

After a short while, Mellissa's sixth sense told her something was wrong. Doug wasn't back and there didn't seem to be any boys in immediate view on the playground. She almost expected what happened next.

She headed off to the toilet block at a brisk pace and was within ten feet of the building when it became clear from the noise that something far more interesting was going on behind the structure. As she rounded the corner there were two boys with bloody noses and four more were in the circle, jeering at the ringleader to 'smash him'. Poor old Doug, covered in blood, was up against it. They were calling for Gordon Maxwell, the school bully and resident self-imposed hero who was also covered in blood, to finish the 'Elephant Boy' off.

Before anyone had time to react, Mellissa instinctively flew into the circle and launched her left foot directly into Gordon Maxwell's crotch, connecting on target with his ball sacks with great force, the metal buckle on the top of her shoe causing extra discomfort.

The crowd of boys went quiet. Everyone just stood there, even Doug stood there, fists still up in the air with his bleeding mouth gaping open, drawing deep breaths. It was like time stood still; everything went in slow motion.

It took only a few seconds for Gordon Maxwell to register in his mind that the frightening pain he was experiencing was coming from his crotch, possibly from a split or ruptured testicle, as he dropped to the ground in the foetal position clutching his battered ball sack. All the other boys grimaced and moaned in unison going white in the face, clutching their genitals in case they were next, viewing the whole scene in stunned silence.

Once again, Mellissa acted instantly and seized the opportunity, grabbing Doug's hand. As he was in as much shock as everyone else, he followed without resistance. She dragged him away, and she reminded him sternly, "Smoking is bad for your health, so that's the last bloody cigarette you're ever going to have, Doug Henderson!!" And it was, he never smoked a cigarette again after that day.

From that day onwards they were inseparable.

Doug went home that night and cried himself to sleep. He was exhausted trying to get his head around everything that had happened in the last twelve hours. He just couldn't explain it. It was the first time anyone else had had his back. The gratitude for acceptance, the act of violence which was meant as kindness; all these strange feelings were rushing through him and aroused him in a strange way. And a girl, not just any girl, the prettiest girl he had ever seen in his life. He didn't know how to act: this was unfamiliar territory. Was it going to be awkward tomorrow at school? Note to self: better take a better lunch to share.

Bob had sat with him for a while that night till Doug fell asleep. He had listened to the whole story of the day's events. Today was the first time that a school had not rung to complain about Doug. Perhaps this was the turning point. This might be their last move.

When Mellissa got home, she told her parents everything. Her father was more worried that she'd injured her foot and made a comical show of checking it for a sprain or a fracture. He was secretly proud of her; they had always stuck up for the underdog in his household and she had learnt this from them. She couldn't stop talking about this new boy Doug, she was so excited to have a new project.

Don decided to arrange to meet Doug's father, invite him for a beer. If this boy was going to turn out to be some sort of weirdo, he'd best find out early, before he became one of Mellissa's animal rescues.

They were having a BBQ that weekend, just a small affair, only a hundred people or so. He instructed Mellissa to find out where they lived. He would call around and invite them personally. He was going to insist the boy and his father had to attend. They were new in town, and, after all, his daughter had saved the boy's life. And at least if he went to their house first, he could assess them, see how they lived, work out if they were lowlifes or not, and tell the son to fuck off then and there if he didn't like what he saw.

The meeting went better than he expected. The father, Bob, was a bit of a nerd, but he was keen to meet some new people, "As I'm planning to live here for the next year or so, I had better try and make friends for Doug's sake as well."

  MICHELLE THOMPSON

"No need to bring anything to eat or drink. Just bring a couple of sleeping bags so you don't have to worry about drinking and driving if you decide to stay late. You can stay over," invited Don.

The BBQ was a tremendous success. Bob was a bit stiff and formal until he got a few beers in him, then he relaxed and had to confess later that he enjoyed himself. He was so busy working he'd forgotten about himself along the way.

Don was an absolute hoot. Bob had a sore belly from laughing so much. It surprised him how well he got on with the other visitors attending the party, as they were not the sort of people he normally socialised with. And Don kept bringing women up to him, telling him he was looking for a root for him. No one in the bank ever spoke like this; thank God no one from the bank was invited.

What's more, it was the first time Bob had ever seen Doug so happy. All the kids at the party seemed to accept him; he didn't detect any name-calling or segregation once. It would be such a shame if that pretty little girl broke his heart. She had been so good to Doug. Don and Bob had told everyone at the party the story about Mellissa kicking that boy in the balls to defend Doug! Bob watched Mellissa dragging Doug everywhere by the hand, almost a bit bossy, but Doug wasn't resisting, he was smiling and laughing.

Mellissa was teaching Doug to ride a trail bike; he was so tall he could ride her father's farm bike. He caught on quickly and before long he was able to join the other kids as they were having races around a course of tyres and jumps that Don had created for them in a paddock. There were plenty of minor accidents and Mellissa's mother was kept busy with the iodine, but they all went back for more.

In the wee small hours, all the kids had gone to bed in different rooms around the house. Mellissa had made a bed for Doug on the floor of her room. They talked until the parents reminded them it was extremely late and told them to go to sleep which just made them giggle for another hour before they both fell asleep.

Their parents were still up, debating the state of the economy until the sun rose.

Earlier that evening, Don had given Doug a drunken word of advice and told him, in front of his dad, "You're welcome to hang out here after school every day until your dad picks you up after work on two conditions. One, you help out with jobs on the farm, which you'll get paid for. Maybe you could save up and buy your own bike with the money, and two, don't ever show Mellissa your penis."

Doug was really embarrassed by this statement. She was his friend, and he'd never considered showing anyone his penis, let alone his friend. "Yes, sir, I promise," stammered Doug. They shook hands on the deal and the two dads rolled off in another direction, laughing their guts out.

This was possibly the happiest day of Doug's life that he could remember.

—

As the years went by Doug spent most of his childhood with this new, large extended family and he finally felt like he had real love and acceptance. Mellissa's mother kissed him on the forehead every day and fluffed his hair when she met them off the bus. He laughed every day, and he was big and strong, so he did his best to help on the farm in any way he could. Mellissa never let him down; she was as close to a sister as he assumed you would be, except they didn't ever fight.

Doug and Mellissa

It was 1994 and Mellissa was away at university studying to be a naturopath. She only came back to the farm on term breaks. She was doing well. She had met a young man called Danny, who was studying to be a criminal lawyer. He was what her father called a nerd; he was on the debating team, the university campus committee, and the student union. He wasn't a physical person due to a rare, recurring blood infection which often left him sick and hospitalised for long spells. His parents were well-off, and they were always researching overseas cures to find a way to cure Danny's condition.

Mellissa had a crush on him and at least Daddy hadn't given this one a lecture about showing her his penis. They had talked about getting a flat together. She even knew he would be the one she was going to marry, but she kept that to herself.

Doug had ridden down on his bike on several occasions to check Danny out. He didn't see Danny as a threat. He was a sickly-looking fella, and Doug could see Danny was another one of Mellissa's rescue projects and he approved.

Doug and Danny really connected and got on well. Danny always joked that Doug was going to need a good lawyer one day. How true that would become.

Danny loved to hear the stories of Doug's life. It was never a life he was cut out for himself, especially due to his long-term illness, slim physical stature, and of course his moral values. Doug had a good sense of humour and entertained Danny with his stories. At times he wished some of the stories weren't true, but he knew instinctively to never repeat them to Mellissa, or anyone else for that matter.

Doug had taken a different path. Mellissa's dad had got him a job as an electrician's apprentice. He was good at it and progressed into IT, fixing and programming computers, and was just about to go out on his own and start a small business when he opted for what he saw as a more exciting opportunity.

In his eyes, he had the privilege of being accepted into an outlaw motorcycle club. It came about when Mellissa's father had taken him away with him one weekend on a motorcycle run to a convention that the gang organised annually. It started out as a normal ride with a couple of Don's mates, and along the highway, a few more bikes joined the group. They came up to a car park just out of the suburbs where there looked to Doug to be about a hundred other bikes and gang members. Doug didn't know what the exact protocol was here, so he just followed the lead from Mellissa's father. He was a little bit intimidated and, at first, he didn't recognise any of these leather-clad men, all with wrap-around shades or bandanas on. They looked more menacing than he remembered at Don's parties, but he thought they looked really cool.

Mellissa's father was well received and there was a lot of handshaking and back-slapping. A couple of the men acknowledged Doug as they had met him at gatherings at Don's house in the past and made him feel welcome.

Doug was totally impressed with the organisation and the execution of the ride. The road captain told Doug where he had to ride in the formation, which was nearly at the back until they could assess his experience.

As he was riding along with the wind in his face and the noise of all those bikes, he occasionally caught the looks on other motorists' and pedestrians' faces. Some gave them the thumbs-up or waved, others looked at them with disgust. Some called them wankers, but it seemed everyone stopped to look. It was exciting to all of Doug's senses. At this point, he didn't want it to end, he felt a million dollars.

The venue for the convention had bands, food, alcohol, questionable ladies with their tits and other things out, tattooists and merchandise. Doug wanted this lifestyle permanently. He'd ask Don to introduce him to the right people. He knew there would be a lengthy probation time when he would have to prospect and earn a place in the gang. He was prepared to do whatever it took. He had the time and the guts.

When Don introduced him to the president of the gang, the first thing he said to Doug, with a big grin on his face was, "Fuck you're an ugly cunt!" as he put his big paw out and shook Doug's hand. Most people thought it; this guy just came out and said it. Doug instantly saw this as unconditional honesty.

The gang had become his new family. They accepted him and he was happy with the social life and the opportunities that he could see being involved in a large club.

Doug was the 'club rat' for years. He worked the bar at the club, ran errands and generally did all the jobs no one else wanted to do; he never complained and followed orders. He progressed to crimes that generated income for the club, leading up to bigger crimes, including rival gang shootings and armed robberies. He was well respected and making a name for himself as someone not to be messed with.

Mellissa always accepted whatever Doug decided to do and supported him, although she was sure this club might be more trouble than Doug was letting on. But he was happy and that was the main thing.

On the few occasions that Doug picked her up and took her to meet his friends, they were all very nice to her, and Doug was as proud as punch showing her off. And what's more, it always meant taking her for a ride on the back of his bike, the only time he would put a sissy bar on it. Riding was one of her favourite things and one of the things she had missed after going off to university. They would spend many hours on the road, stopping for beers and lunches at times. Danny didn't mind. He hated motorbikes and always joked it was cheaper than buying her a horse.

In the coming years, both Mellissa and Danny graduated into their chosen professions. Mellissa's father financed her into a health food shop and Danny got accepted into a well-respected law practice. Danny was working his way up to be a partner in the firm and, eventually, the plan was to go out on his own.

The timing was right, so Danny and Mellissa decided to get married. The wedding, of course, was a memorable occasion with all of Mellissa's parents' friends, all of Doug's friends and all of Danny's friends and family. The after-party lasted for three days on the farm and a fun time was had by all. Years later, Mellissa found out that Doug had paid for the whole thing; it was his wedding gift.

That was the last time Mellissa heard directly from Doug for five years. He had gone to jail and didn't want her to know, but her parents had told her and sworn her to secrecy. She agreed to pretend she had no idea, although it killed her to think he might be suffering while incarcerated.

Mellissa and Danny had been caught up in their careers and travel and buying and selling houses. They were doing all right, and time just went by. Every time she asked her parents for an update on Doug or if they had heard from him, they reported back that they heard from him often and that he was healthy and getting three meals a day and had lots of friends.

It was 3 am one morning in 2004 when the police rang.

Doug

Doug's employer, who was putting him through his electrical apprenticeship, was a friend of Mellissa's father. He was also a patched member of an outlaw motorcycle club, and this man had sponsored Doug into the club and cleared his path to be a prospect for the club. Doug was well-liked and he enjoyed the brotherhood he received from the other members. He'd always been rejected from other male bonding circles growing up, he'd just never felt comfortable or that he belonged, but these guys treated him like family. Some of the members were childhood friends he had met growing up on Mellissa's parents' farm.

He was a real grafter and had quickly worked his way up the club's order of importance and was now, years later, allegedly running his own chapter. He was reluctant to call himself president in front of Mellissa but, according to the newspapers, this was his title, and he was also allegedly the kingpin of an international drug ring, owning strip joints and tattoo parlours. He was heavily involved in violence and extortion. He always laughed at the newspapers and their slight exaggerations and played it down if Mellissa asked.

Doug had been off the radar for a few years; he'd been in prison. He had a crew who were robbing jewellery stores and jewellery manufacturers' premises. Doug's knowledge of electrics and security systems came into full use during this time when disengaging the alarms, but they foolishly made a mistake one night and got the vehicle jammed in an alley. Doug took the rap for the crime to save the rest of his crew, pleaded guilty and went to jail.

Jail wasn't that bad. He had plenty of contacts inside and put his head down and did his time. The hardest part was keeping it secret from Mellissa. Her parents knew and they all agreed to not tell her. She was busy setting her life up and pulling shifts at the hospital when Danny was sick, and it was decided to cross that bridge later. One day he would tell her. Anyway, he didn't want her coming to visit and have the thought of a couple of hundred men masturbating over her in their cells at night. He'd already had to have a couple of good fights to assert his dominance in his wing.

Doug was relieved that Mellissa's parents never gave up on him and visited regularly, updating him on news of Mellissa at every visit. His own father was apprehensive at first but came to visit on a couple of occasions with Mellissa's father and he could accept it for the time being and be as supportive as he could. But like every parent, they heard the terrible stories of prison life, and Doug told him it was all true and at times worse. Bob was terrified that prison, or the gang life, would result in Doug's early death, but he buried his head in the sand and tried not to think about it.

Doug had been out of prison for only a week when the police phoned Mellissa as next of kin. Doug was seriously ill in hospital with stab wounds to his chest after an altercation, allegedly over a drug deal that had gone wrong. He had a guard stationed outside his room and, unofficially, he was under arrest. There was also a chance of rival gang retaliation, so there was a heavy police presence at the hospital. The police were convinced they had their man. They had had a long-term surveillance operation in progress and had been clamping down on motorcycle gang activity across the state.

When Mellissa got the call, she decided not to wake any of the parents till the next morning; no need to alarm them at this hour.

Doug was just out of surgery when she and Danny got there. He was in intensive care in the recovery room hooked up to every machine possible and she was permitted to sit by his bed.

When he started to return to consciousness, he was dreaming he was back at school, with Mellissa holding his hand. Was it a dream? But, as his vision cleared, he could see those pretty blue eyes looking at him. He couldn't speak; he had some sort of contraption on his face, so he just stared at her. He had forgotten how beautiful she was. He had missed her, and he felt like crying; must be the effects of the morphine. He knew she would come. He could always count on her to rescue him. Thank God she had married a lawyer. He was going to need a good one this time. He was really in the shit.

Mellissa and Danny arranged for Doug to be transferred to a private hospital at a secret location away from the media attention. The police had charged him with several drug-related offences, but Danny had argued that the witness could not properly identify him and somehow brilliantly turned it around on the Middle Eastern crime syndicate network. Some carefully planted evidence and a tip-off to the police led to another series of arrests and some key members of the Middle Eastern crime syndicate were off to jail for a very long time.

Doug recovered over time and went about the normal management of his club and his businesses. The only one who really benefited from all this was Danny, as he suddenly had more work than he could throw a stick at defending Doug's new family in court. He became an overnight sensation and was on the front page of the *Sydney Morning Herald* with photos of him and Doug leaving the courthouse and subsequently made the front page of every newspaper in Australia after that. They nicknamed him the 'lawyer of the gangs'. He made enough money to start his own practice, and everyone wanted to interview him and do editorials about him. He was on the front page of the *Justinian,* the *National Enquirer*, and other well-known tabloids.

Angela

Angela hung around all the different biker clubrooms whenever she could. Financially, she struggled. She had no real education and got by working for tips and wages at a bar and restaurant on Kings Cross. She had no family to speak of and had spent her childhood going from one foster home to another, often under abusive conditions. She had always fancied having a biker for a boyfriend and was determined to do whatever it took to get one. She was attracted to the roar and excitement of the bikes as they cruised up the strip with the noise of the big motors from the Harley-Davidsons as they went by. To her, these guys always looked cool.

She was a pretty girl with short black hair, although her major asset was her large tits. She kept herself tidy and fit and always dressed in black – the genuine Aussie Bogan.

Doug and his mate Ben had been coming to the restaurant where she worked every Thursday night for a steak dinner and a few drinks for a couple of months. They would pull up outside the restaurant on their bikes and frighten the punters who weren't used to them. Angela was working up the courage to invite herself to one of their parties.

Ben was the better-looking of the two, he had a nice smile. But she had her heart set on the big ugly one – he was the president – she wanted him. She didn't want to settle for a lesser-ranked member.

She had to admit, he was really ugly. She laughed to herself about an old saying. She'd have to lie back and think of England if he was having sex with her.

To begin with, Doug wasn't interested in her at all. He made it quite clear by his complete lack of response towards her. In Angela's mind, she would have to try harder. She had never seen him with a woman, except the girls that he managed out of the gentlemen's club that he owned further down the strip. She'd have to give him a couple of free meals and get his attention. Damn it, she would just come right out and ask him for a date next time she saw him. Surely, he'd be flattered.

The following week, after she finally built up the courage and asked him out, to her surprise he said, "Okay, I'll pick you up after your shift tonight."

Later that evening he arrived in a nice V8 Holden car. He was on time, and he had a bunch of flowers for her.

They drove across town in awkward silence. She was the happiest woman in the world. She had finally cracked it. He didn't speak a lot, didn't ask her any questions, just muttered about traffic now and then. She thought it best not to speak either, trying to play it cool.

They eventually pulled up at a house in the suburbs, entered through an electric gate that he had a remote in his car for, and drove into an internal garage. She didn't expect to be taken back to his house on the first date, but she was good with it. She was up for anything. It was all going according to her plan, her fantasy.

Bizarrely, the lounge and bedroom walls were covered with framed photos of a blonde girl. She had the most beautiful blue eyes that gazed at you from every corner of the room. Everywhere you looked there were pictures of her, of the girl and Doug. Must be his sister.

She couldn't resist and asked, "Who's the girl in the photos?" That was the last time she ever asked about the pictures. She knew instantly she had made a mistake in asking. His face suddenly contorted and turned flaming red, almost purple. At that point, he looked uglier and scarier than ever. She suddenly felt fear course through her veins and her arms prickled as he lunged towards her.

Doug grabbed her by the hair. He'd treat her like he treated all the others. Nosy, jealous bitches was his opinion of all the women he had had anything to do with. He ripped her top off; her fat tits escaped. He could see she was shocked and frightened, but this only heightened his arousal. He forced her head down on his cock. "Let's see how good you are at blowjobs."

For the next hour, the things he did to her were not pleasant and were at times extremely painful. If she cried out, he seemed to concentrate on making the pain worse. She thought he must have been on something to make him last, as he maintained an erection throughout the whole encounter.

After the ordeal was over, he gave her an old T-shirt of his to put on to cover her tits. No words were spoken throughout the whole sexual onslaught, then he simply ordered her to get her things.

The next time he spoke, was to ask her where she lived. He ordered her back into the vehicle, and he drove her home. When he dropped her off, she thought she would never see him again but to her surprise, he said he would pick her up the next night after work if she was into it. And she willingly agreed. If this is what it takes to be the president's missus, she would have to put up with it.

Their arrangement went on like this, on and off, for a couple of months. Then, to her surprise, one day he asked her to shift into his house with him. Angela was over the moon. Finally, she had got to the next stage. If she was living there full-time, she could concentrate on healing him and mould him into a better person. Perhaps give him some pointers on sex.

On the day he arranged to collect her and her meagre possessions from her flat, he turned up in a Holden Ute and parked outside with the motor running. He yelled at her to hurry up, not bothering to get out and help with any of her belongings.

On the way back to his house, he presented her with a neatly typed-out one-page list of rules that he had prepared earlier. He told her if she could stick to these rules, she could stay. The list went as follows:

Never change or remove any of the photos on the walls.
Do not bring visitors, this includes your family, to the house under any
    circumstances.
Do not repeat anything you hear inside this house.
Do not mention anything that could incriminate us if the police are listening
    through listening devices.
Keep the house and the garden clean and tidy so the neighbours think we are
    respectable.
Do not talk to the neighbours, they might be police informants.
No loud music.
No pets.
Never, never talk about our relationship to anyone else.

He went on to say, "And you can give up work immediately. No cunt of mine is going to work at a restaurant. You won't need any money to live here; I'll give you money. I'll give you cash every week for housekeeping and spending money and if you need more money for anything else, just ask. Just operate on the cash I give you. Don't use your bank account, the police will be tracking that and if you want drugs, tell me what you need.

"There will always be a couple of cars in the garage, you can drive either one. There is a spare remote for the gate in one of the other cars.

"And remember this, I will never love you, so get any ideas of babies or getting married out of your head right now. That will never happen.

"And if you're feeling hard done by or you're not happy here or with me, or you don't like the rules, you're free to go. Just take your things and fuck off. But never come back. That would be a mistake."

As time wore on, or the novelty of abusing her wore off – she wasn't sure which – she saw less and less of Doug. He was always busy, preoccupied with something else. He left early in the morning and was home late if he was home at all. He was never gentle or affectionate and would often leave the bed after his interpretation of sex and sleep in another room. It was always rough, painful sex and he always wore a condom. If she had her period, he would either stay away till it was over or make her sleep in the spare room. And she wasn't permitted to keep any of her sanitary products in the bathroom where he might see them.

Angela was too ashamed to tell anyone that she'd made a terrible mistake.

Doug seldom took her anywhere in public and if he did, it was in the car, never on the bike. His excuse was that he didn't like taking pillion passengers as it was too dangerous.

The only visitor she ever saw was one of the boys from the club, Ben, who wasn't yet a patched member and who had been coming to the restaurant with Doug when she first met him. Ben was always concerned about her well-being. It was Ben who told her who the blonde girl was; some childhood friend called Mellissa with a flash lawyer husband who was always in the paper. They both decided that Doug obviously had some freaky obsession with Mellissa and wondered if she knew that he had the house plastered in hundreds of photos, which they made private jokes about at Doug's expense.

Angela looked forward to Ben's visits; she wished she had chosen him now instead of Doug. They decided to keep his visits secret, no use making the situation more complicated. Ben had the advantage of knowing where Doug was, so he could pick his moments to visit.

In Angela's mind, she was the president's missus, and at least she had money, drugs and nice cars to drive around in. Best she shut up and be grateful.

 MICHELLE THOMPSON

Danny and Doug

Doug looked at his phone's caller ID. He didn't answer it these days unless he knew he had a secure line. Doug had many phones; he frequently threw them away or destroyed them. He kept a clean phone for immediate family and was careful what conversations, if any, he had on this phone. The last person Doug was expecting a call from today was his lawyer and friend Danny. He wasn't due to appear in court, nor did he have any current charges pending; he instantly broke into a cold sweat. Had something happened to Mellissa?

Doug's hand was shaking as he answered the call, but he kept his voice steady. "What's up, buddy?"

Danny didn't make small talk. "I need a big favour, Doug. It's personal. I need to see you as soon as possible. Can we meet up today? My office. Mellissa's not in any harm, but I needed your help, you're the only one I can trust."

An hour later Doug was sitting across the desk from his friend Danny in a flash office in the city overlooking the harbour. He no longer recognised Danny. It had been a month since he had last seen him, and he looked as if he had aged ten years in that time. His hair was gone. He resembled a prisoner from a concentration camp.

"I know, I've looked better, right?" Danny could see the shock on Doug's face. "I'm dying, Doug. The cancer's finally won. The doctors have said I've got months, possibly weeks, to live. It's aggressive: the chemotherapy, all the modern drugs haven't worked."

It was 2007, and they were researching new drugs all the time. Danny was on the waiting list for any trials that might save his life. He had been sick for a while, but they thought they had it beat. Then it came back with a vengeance.

"The doctors told me to go home and get my affairs in order."

Doug had a few mates who had died of cancer, and he saw the effect it had on the families. He always wondered how they coped after. He suddenly had a feeling of complete loss for Danny. He liked Danny, and Danny had saved his arse so many times.

He never thought about Danny fucking Mellissa, which was too much for him to get worked up about. If he went down that track, he'd probably want to put Danny in a mincer at the pet food factory.

"I want you to take care of Mellissa for me when I'm gone. I've left you a considerable amount of money and this place will continue to support Mellissa with an income. I've done this so you'll not need to spend as much time with your other interests. She's tough, you know that better than most, but this has hit her hard and she's going to need someone to hold her hand for a while. She's always loved you, we both know that, and perhaps it's time you took the next step and followed your heart.

"Don't get me wrong, I've never had a problem with her affection for you, but I know there's more there to give and we both love her more than life itself. You're the only one I trust to protect her and take care of her.

"And, before you argue with me, don't be silly about the money. I know you have your own money, and so does she, but you both may as well retire in style."

They talked for a couple of hours about life and death. Doug was reluctant to leave his friend that day.

"One more thing," said Danny. "Just make sure you give me a good send-off, aye mate. Bring the house down."

Doug got up to leave then Danny waved him back.

"Oh, I almost forgot. That matter you had me investigate for you." He opened a locked drawer in his desk and handed Doug a thick folder in a sealed envelope.

"You better read that," he said as he slid a hefty file marked Private and Confidential across the desk.

"It's serious. They have polished this turd and I'm afraid I'm not going to be around to sort this one out. Best you sort it out before it turns into national headlines. You can't be looking after Mellissa from behind bars."

The funeral was a huge event; Doug had spread the word far and wide. The police had to put up roadblocks on the main road into the city as the cavalcade of over a thousand motorcycles made its way to the funeral home.

Danny had requested a closed coffin; said he didn't want everyone looking at his scrawny body – he'd lost so much weight from the cancer. He had been a reasonable-looking man, and he wanted people to remember him as he was.

    MICHELLE THOMPSON

Mellissa was sitting quietly beside the coffin in the room next to the chapel, unable to face the other hundreds of mourners who had already turned up early and come to pay their respects. Danny had been a popular man in all walks of life, and he was going to be missed by a lot of people, including Mellissa. She was no longer able to hold his hand and reassure him everything was going to be all right.

It had been over a year of pain and suffering for Danny, and everyone said it was a blessing it was over. She didn't think so, Danny didn't want to die. He even went to Germany for special cancer treatment to try and beat it. The hardest thing was keeping it a secret; he hadn't wanted to alarm anyone. He always thought he would come out the other end OK and joke about it later.

She knew Doug was coming, but it was as if time stood still, and he was taking ages. She resisted the urge to ring him and see what was taking so long. She knew that would be pointless. He'd be on his bike; he wouldn't hear the phone ring.

She felt the ground rumble before she heard them. She could also hear the Channel 9 News helicopter overhead – mind you this was Doug's crowd, and it was probably more likely the police helicopter. She resisted the urge to run outside and watch them coming down the road. Someone would video it and it was sure to be on the six o'clock news tonight. She almost googled on her phone to see if it was being broadcast live. She waited patiently until she heard the last motor turn its engine off. "Not long now, Danny boy," she said as she patted the coffin.

Doug took over from this point, ordering the pallbearers to carry the coffin from the room Mellissa was in into the main chapel. He had organised everything with Danny before he got too sick to communicate, including the music, the flowers, the video clips of good times gone by with outdoor video screens for those that couldn't fit in the chapel, and he'd taken care of the after-match function as they called it. He had contacted all Danny's old schoolmates, professional acquaintances and ex-clients.

Doug sat next to Mellissa in the front row the whole time, holding her hand. It was the first time he had ever seen her cry; his heart hurt for her. He only left her side briefly to stand at the front and give a eulogy, which at times reduced the whole audience to tears and, likewise, laughter. Danny would have been pleased.

For a change, Doug had his road captain working with the police organising the funeral procession to the gravesite. He had men stationed along the way at every intersection to block the traffic from pulling out as they went past; no use having one of his own men killed at Danny's funeral.

It was a long day. After the obligatory sausage rolls and club sandwiches, Doug took Mellissa and all the parents back to Mellissa and Danny's place in a minivan he had hired. They were all exhausted. They needed some quiet time to reflect on the day, and Mellissa had nagged him to watch the video of all the bikes coming down the road.

Doug stayed with the family for a while and made sure they were all locked in for the night then went back to the party, promising to come back first thing in the morning.

He couldn't wipe the grin off his face as he drove back to the party and the band he had organised for the mourners. Now was the time for his plan to really come to fruition. Bring it on. Tonight was going to be a good night. The beginning of the next stage of his life.

Doug

The way Doug saw it, he had one year to get all his ducks in a row. In that space, Mellissa would have enough time to mourn the loss of her husband. So, if he asked her to marry him at the end of the year, fingers crossed it wouldn't be a no or an awkward silence and hopefully, it wouldn't seem inappropriate or disrespectful in her eyes. He was still nervous that it might not work; he had to get the chemistry right leading up to the day.

Of course, first, he would have to ask her father if it was OK now to show Mellissa his penis if they got married. He'd never stopped laughing at that request. Both his dad and Mellissa's dad brought it up every time they saw him. Cheeky bastards.

He was currently in negotiation, with the help of Mellissa's dad, to purchase a couple of thousand acres next door to her parents' property. He planned to build a big kick-arse mansion on this property and ask Mellissa to help design it. After all, it was going to be a palace for his princess.

They could both be near their parents, who weren't getting any younger, and the time would come when they would need a bit more support. And if Doug and Mellissa had children, they would need support also. He was going to surprise Mellissa with all this when he took her out to visit the property when the time was right. At this stage, the hardest thing was getting the parents to keep it a secret.

Doug had been calling in on Mellissa every day since the funeral. She looked weak and vulnerable still, but the light in her eyes was slowly coming back. She lit up at the suggestion they go for a ride on the bike, so every day the weather was nice they would spend a couple of hours on the road. He loved the feeling of her body snuggled up against him; he felt like one with her when they were out riding.

All his crew loved her. He didn't get jealous because he knew she wasn't interested, and she didn't flirt or act all crazy around them. She'd grown up with some of them, and their parents were friends of her parents. It was the good old Aussie two degrees of separation.

As he got closer to the shift, he would let Angela think they were moving to a new house. That way she'd be keen to pack all their belongings into itemised boxes. He would give her a list of exactly what was to go in each box. Then he'd drop her and put the fear of the devil in her, so she'd fuck off for good; she had served her purpose.

The day had come to surprise Mellissa with the new property purchase. Her parents and his father had insisted on a ribbon-cutting ceremony across the gate and of course, any excuse for a party to celebrate. Miraculously no one had spilt the beans, and it had been kept a secret from Mellissa so far. She could be quite perceptive, and she had asked a few tricky questions, so she knew something was up.

If the time felt right, he'd ask her to marry him when they were alone later that evening. He had taken a chance and purchased a huge diamond ring to knock her off her feet. He had designed it himself, so he had also had to factor into the equation that she would like the ring if she did say yes. He was used to getting what he wanted through fear and intimidation but that would not work with Mellissa. She'd tell him straight, black or white, no in-between.

He'd picked her up earlier in the day and they'd gone to lunch at a favourite roadside bar. He'd told her they were going to end up at a vineyard out of town later in the day. Eventually, they rode in the direction of the estate with a group of friends, deliberately late to allow all the other partygoers to get to the farm before them.

Doug was sweating despite only wearing a half jacket and T-shirt. He was going to be so embarrassed if this went pear-shaped.

As they got closer it was hard to hide the crowd that had gathered, and Mellissa punched him in the side of his ribs when she clicked that something was happening.

Mellissa was bursting with life; this was the boost she needed. Doug's suggestion that she help design the house was met with, "Try and stop me!" She instantly started pointing out to him where everything was going to be; he didn't argue. She was even talking about benchtops, swimming pools and wheelchair access for their parents when they hit eighty. She took photos on her phone so they could show the architect the light from every angle. So far, the plan Doug had was coming along nicely.

They joined the party and worked the room among the guests.

     MICHELLE THOMPSON

Now Doug was forced to approach Mellissa's dad about his intentions. To complicate the matter Don and his father were together and when he approached them, they were having a very in-depth discussion about a game of golf.

Once he got them to be serious for five minutes the words wouldn't come out of his mouth. He was so nervous he was stuttering but he managed to blurt out what he wanted to do and instead of giving him an answer or sound advice, they both told him they would think about it and come back to him in one hour if they approved. Just like those two old comedians to make him suffer more. He was completely lost; this wasn't part of the plan.

He was about to walk away when they burst out laughing and called him back. They were already planning the engagement party. They wanted all the details: did he have the ring, how much did it cost, could they see it, could Don tell Mellissa's mother yet, when was he going to do it, was his penis still OK?

He swore them to secrecy and begged them not to alert the crowd but left them rolling around on the ground in gales of laughter. He'd better find Mellissa and distract her.

He shuffled around nervously when he caught up with her talking to a group of friends. As if she read his mind, she said, "Let's go back to the building site and take more photos with the sun setting in the distance to gauge a different perspective of the lighting."

They jumped on a quad bike and took the shortcut across the paddocks.

They walked around for a bit looking at angles of light while Mellissa took photos. Doug's palms were sweating. He wanted to throw up.

She looked cold and he detected a shiver as an evening wind briefly blew up from the south. Doug put his arm around her, and she leant back into him. He felt her take a deep breath and relax into his body. Her head was tilted to the side and Doug was looking down at her exposed neck. It just felt natural as he leant down and kissed it gently, left his face there for a minute and breathed into her ear. He felt her legs falter a little, so he held her tighter.

At this point, he had no control over the actions of his penis. She pressed back onto his erection which was now straining through his jeans. His head started to swim; he'd never been this intimate with a woman before. He was embarrassed he couldn't control his erection. He could hardly get away with dragging this one around by the hair as he did to all the others taking his anger out on every woman he met for all the laughter from his childhood. He was now in unfamiliar territory, frozen in time willing for something more than just his now embarrassingly large bulge to happen between them.

Mellissa was the first to speak. "Is that a gun in your pocket, or are you pleased to see me?"

That broke the silence and they both burst out laughing and he had to confess to her it was both. She turned to face him and kissed him on the lips for what seemed an eternity. When she drew back for breath she looked up into his eyes and said, "Well, where is it? Aren't you going to make an honest woman out of me finally?"

This was the bossy Mellissa he knew.

She had known all along that this was leading up to him popping the question. She had finally put it together when she saw Doug approach their two dads earlier that evening. She had been watching their expressions from across the crowd and the handshake gave it away. Mellissa was too impatient to wait any longer and she knew Doug well enough to know he was going to struggle with crossing the line with intimacy so that's why she suggested they cross the paddock to the building site alone.

Doug got down on one knee.

Mellissa didn't hesitate. She said, "Yes," and kissed him again.

The ring was magnificent; a chandelier was what she nicknamed it. It was terribly impractical because it was so large, but it was the most beautiful ring she had ever set her eyes upon. She hated to think what it cost: she was never going to take it off.

They went back to the party to tell everyone the good news, but the surprise was on them. The two dads had been watching the whole event unfold through binoculars and had been giving the crowd a running commentary. They were met with cheers and whistles from the partygoers.

They partied into the night, and Doug and Mellissa held hands and cuddled each other all night. Everyone was stunned by the size and the magnificence of the ring. They endured embarrassing stories of their childhood that the two fathers shared with anyone who would listen.

It was around 5 am when Mellissa suggested they head back into town to her house to finally finish what they started over at the building site.

Mellissa took control once they got back to her place. She gently guided him through the awkward spots and they both felt it was the best sex they had ever encountered. They were in perfect unison. Everything fitted just right, and they seemed to be fully synchronised for every movement and every position.

They slept well into the next day and didn't hurry to move far from each other for the next twenty-four hours. They were so comfortable in each other's company; it just seemed natural that they be together. They talked for hours and hours about everything that had happened in their lives. Doug didn't leave anything out.

Mellissa told him of the many times she nearly asked him to marry her and confessed to falling in love with him back when they were teenagers. He was shocked by the revelation but added his own misery of loving her but not being able to do anything about it.

It was decided that Doug would collect his things and shift in immediately. They did not want to spend another day apart for the rest of their lives, which was one thing they both knew for sure.

Angela

Doug drove to his house early that day. Angela was in a shitty when he got there. He couldn't be bothered fighting with her for a change. Her mood was understandable because he hadn't been home for about three days.

He had to hand it to her: she'd done an excellent job packing the house up. She had followed his instructions to the letter; everything was labelled and boxed as he requested. He settled her down by suggesting he make it up to her by taking her out to lunch. "I'm sorry, I shouldn't have put work before you. It won't happen again."

Doug had recently bought a four-by-four vehicle capable of going off-road and as a treat, he was going to take her for a drive in it. It was a serious-looking vehicle: bull bars on the front, black tinted windows, big chunky tyres. They'd go out of town to a winery for lunch.

As they got further and further out of town, Angela was sure she didn't know of any wineries out this way, but he'd been nice for a change, and she didn't want to start an argument by asking questions.

Finally, they stopped at the end of a bush trail in a remote area of hot, barren land. No cars and no buildings, nothing for miles, just some rocks, some scruffy trees and lots of dirt, and definitely no grapevines. She couldn't help but have that prickly nerve-ending feeling in her veins and arms again.

"Why did you bring us way out here, Doug? There's nothing here."

"I've always fantasised about having sex in the wilderness. I want to experience that fantasy out here, with you."

Doug seemed to know exactly where to go. He stopped by some big rocks which were protected from view by some scrub.

They both got out of the SUV.

"Take your pants off and bend over the rock with your arse facing me. I want to fuck you on the rock." He'd unzipped his jeans, and he showed her he was ready.

Angela never sensed danger for one minute and willingly removed her pants and spread them down on the rock to reduce the chance of getting dirt on her front; she didn't want to go to lunch with a dirty top.

She proceeded to lay down over the rock, spreading her legs slightly apart to make it easier for him to enter her. She waited in expectation – they had never done anything like this before, and she was aroused at the thought.

She never saw him remove the gun from his jeans. Never heard him unlock the safety. Never realised that it was the cold gun barrel pressed up against the back of her head. It was all over before she could blink.

Doug had planned the execution weeks in advance. He had already prepared a deep hole for the body as he'd have to be sure no dingoes or foxes dug her up.

He wiped the gun clean and threw it into the pit with the body; the skull was unrecognisable which gave him some small satisfaction.

His day was only getting better. He started to fill the hole with dirt. He'd use the four-by-four to push a big rock over the hole after he had replaced the soil.

He must remember to buy a big bunch of flowers on his way home for Mellissa.

Mellissa

Mellissa was under no illusions about Doug or his connections. None of which gave her cause for concern. She knew one thing for sure and that was that he was her soulmate.

She had loved Danny and had a lot of laughs and good times with him, but she had never truly felt one with him. She had never wanted to have children with Danny because of his childhood illnesses, and when he became sick and started having chemotherapy that option was taken away from them anyway.

She knew she loved Doug on the very first day at school.

She had secretly followed Doug via the media and stories from Danny when he was saving him from another prosecution or incarceration.

Mellissa had also volunteered at the homeless and prostitutes centre for a few years because of her need to satisfy her urge to rescue everyone and had encountered several females over the years with serious vaginal and anal tears and facial bruising caused by violent sexual encounters with a man who often fitted Doug's description. These women were reluctant to talk at first, but Mellissa promised them confidentiality, and they confessed the events leading up to the injuries. All injuries were consistent with these women frequenting a local motorcycle club and consenting to casual sex with the assailant. None of these women was willing to report the crime to the police for fear of retribution.

Mellissa could see clearly why Doug had no respect for them, but it gave her an insight into his lack of intimacy and perhaps his skills around making love to a woman. He had been hurt so many times by females in his youth; it had turned him into a sexual predator set on revenge.

She never doubted for one minute that she would not have the same problem. Her relationship with him was based on unconditional love.

Then there was the story Doug told her himself about a girl called Angela who he had had a brief relationship with. In his words, he'd ended the relationship suddenly to protect himself from probable future criminal charges. It was the safest option for all.

 MICHELLE THOMPSON

Now that she was about to marry him and live the rest of her life with him, she was thinking of the children they were yet to have, the new house and shifting back to the farm. She couldn't be happier.

Doug and Mellissa

The house was nearly finished except for a few cosmetic details. Mellissa had spent as much time as she could on-site as project manager, subtly cracking the whip. Doug had business obligations that only he could take care of, but he found time to turn up when required or summonsed by Mellissa.

It was 2008, the wedding was almost upon them and things had taken an unexpected turn when Mellissa broke the news that they were going to have a baby. She would want to walk down the aisle before she got too fat for her dress. Doug was over the moon and was desperate to know the sex of the child as soon as possible. For them both it was a fairy tale come true; they were planning to have a big family. They were both only children and didn't want that for their own offspring.

And now they could finally dodge the pressure from the grandparents to be. Jokes from the two fathers like, "We finally let you use your penis, and it doesn't work!" or "When are you going to make some babies?" – which of course they found funnier than anyone else.

Mellissa never asked questions about Doug's business – didn't want to know – but she wasn't surprised that he insisted that a panic room be built into the house and that the interior and exterior of the house and property was fitted out with the latest high-tech security system. If they were going to have children, they would need to take precautions.

Doug was starting to wind down his commitments to the club. Younger, smarter guys had shown they had the calibre to take over and he trusted them. Now that he was starting a family, he was letting everyone know he wanted to spend as much time at home as he could. Every day he felt blessed that he could wake up to his beautiful wife. He wanted to look after her, and look after his children, and protect them from everything.

The wedding was held on Mellissa's parents' farm. They brought in a professional wedding planner who organised everything from the celebrant to the flowers, right down to the guest list, RSVP, the caterers and things they didn't think of. Her parents were guests, so didn't need all the stress associated with organising such a big event. They had all decided that they wouldn't complicate the day by taking care of proceedings themselves; it was their day to relax also. This gave them all more time to mingle with the guests. They made a point of requesting no gifts but instead, if guests felt like it, they could donate to a cancer research fund they had set up in honour of Danny.

At the wedding, when it was time for Doug to give a speech, he relived the first day he met Mellissa on his first day at her school and how she had held his hand. He gave a funny rendition of the story about the boy she kicked in the balls and how she cured him of smoking cigarettes. He had the whole reception in stitches, but he got the greatest laugh when he confessed it was actually Mellissa who taught him to ride a motorcycle, so it was her fault he became a biker.

His voice was full of emotion as he went on to say, "I have loved Mellissa unconditionally since day one and I don't think I would be here today if she hadn't saved me that day at school and given me the will to live."

He finished the speech, proposed a toast and thanked the guests for coming.

Of course, to lighten the mood, the two fathers got up and told the story about Doug's penis! That never got old, and they had everyone crying with laughter with other stories about Doug and Mellissa's youth.

The wedding planner had organised a couple of shuttle buses to commute between the farm and the city to save people driving drunk. They had also set up a huge area with 'glamping tents' erected for guests who wanted to stay on for a couple of days.

But it was a dry wedding for Mellissa. She was pregnant and couldn't drink and Doug had decided to support her by also not drinking. He wasn't a big drinker, so he could spare a night of not drinking and besides, he had other ways of getting out of it if required. The worst part was all the ribbing from his mates calling him a soft cock.

Doug and Mellissa went home early across the paddock to their newly finished home to technically consummate the marriage and just to be alone together. It had been a long day, and they were both exhausted.

Somehow Doug had arranged to fill the house with red roses without Mellissa knowing. When they got to the house, he carried her across the threshold and carried her to the bedroom. They both could not have been happier at this moment; their whole life journey, the immense, deep love they felt for each other, just didn't need words. They communicated through feelings and a sixth sense. They both just wished they could live a long life together.

Later that night Doug lay next to Mellissa with her securely in his arms and when he was sure she was sound asleep he cried himself to sleep; he was always fighting his demons.

He only had one more job left to do then he felt he could retire.

 MICHELLE THOMPSON

Ben

Ben had been deep undercover for so long now the lines had been blurred. He wasn't meant to get emotionally involved. He wasn't meant to have developed a meth habit either, but drugs went with the territory. As his father used to say, "If you sit in the barber's chair long enough, you're bound to get a haircut!"

The original objective, brought about by the Anti-Criminal Gang Laws for NSW, was to get as close as he could to the target, Douglas Henderson, who was considered the ring leader, and get enough dirt overall on the organisation that they could close it down and stop the biggest organised crime distributor of drugs across Australia in its tracks. But these people were smarter than the force anticipated. It was 2009, and it was taking Ben longer than he expected.

It had been an effortless process to start hanging out with a few of the lesser-ranking members. Firstly, he got a job working with one of the members at a plastics factory, convincing his workmate he went to school with him all those years ago. The key was remembering names from the yearbook and events that the school held at that time. It was easy enough to find all these things out on Google and where, in relation to houses, they both lived in the same suburb.

He had kept his real first name. That way he wouldn't blow it if he forgot the alias he was meant to be using. But another reason was in case someone from his past recognised him and called out to him in public and called him Ben. He could easily pull them aside if necessary to eliminate suspicion.

Then he ended up needing a place to stay. His story was that his missus had left him and run off to be a lesbian, and that's when his work buddy put him up. And of course, he had a Harley-Davidson motorcycle and a few tattoos; it was a recipe for acceptance.

He purposely kept on the fringe for a while; made out like he wasn't too eager to get involved but chose a couple of key events to attend to get noticed.

When he first met Doug, he instantly knew why this guy was so successful – he was a born leader. His physical stature was menacing, to say the least. He was a giant of a man, with huge hands and he was as strong as an ox. His face was extensively scarred, and you felt sorry for him. He would have had a difficult childhood dealing with that shit. When he spoke, he captivated the room. He mentored his younger foot soldiers, helped them out financially, and set them up in legitimate and not-so-legitimate business ventures, keeping a major shareholding for himself and the club, of course.

He was a shrewd businessman and carefully dissected every new business proposal he put his money behind.

The club had their fingers in lots of ventures: tourism, storage facilities, working farms that employed youth – they had spread the net wide and it wasn't all drugs and violence. They were businessmen now, with lawyers and accountants.

Doug treated every one of his men as if they were the most important person he was dealing with at the time. He had what he called an open-door policy, and you could go to him at any time with a problem or a question and he'd sort it out for you.

Occasionally one of his boys would fuck up and he'd ask them what they'd learnt from the experience then tell them how he was going to fix it. You couldn't help but like the guy.

The organisation was so large that to be involved in the really hard-core operations was something only trusted to his high-ranking and long-term associates. Ben's assignment was to get near that level at the least, connect the dots between the gang and the drugs and take this monster down for good.

There were occasions where people just simply went missing. No one talked about that, and Ben was a long way off finding out that part of the process. There were rumours that you ended up in the pet food factory somewhere. He wasn't keen to find out personally.

From early encounters, Ben witnessed Doug's appalling treatment of the women who dared to frequent the clubrooms who weren't invited guests. You had to have your head read if you were a chick and thought you fancied this guy. He was, to say the least, brutal. He would drag girls he didn't like, or girls that made comments about his face or laughed at him, off into a back room and moments later you would hear them screaming and crying and begging him to get away. Someone always turned the stereo up to drown out the noise. Then these poor unfortunate souls were dumped outside the gates of the clubrooms and threatened to have the pet food experience for their whole family if they dared to complain to the authorities and told never to come back. Some did

   MICHELLE THOMPSON

of course, desperate to have a gang member for a boyfriend. Ben could never work that one out. Probably no use telling the police with no witnesses to back the story up.

Doug would return from each encounter full of adrenaline and revitalised and he'd hunt down his next victim from the bevvy of sluts dancing and gyrating on the dance floor or up at the bar hinting for drugs.

What was more surprising was one day Ben witnessed Doug turn up with a beautiful blonde woman. She had a wedding ring on. Was this his wife? He treated her like a queen; you could tell they were close. Everyone liked her; she just had that aura about her. They'd come for a quick drink, and he'd grab a couple of boys, and they'd all go off for a ride. Ben was never invited, that was reserved for the inner circle only. He asked his flatmate about her and found out she was an old school friend, and her husband was the famous lawyer for the gangs. The way Doug was with her, was in vast contrast to his behaviour around other women. It was creepy.

In the early days Doug never spoke to Ben, just watched him from across the room, observing him. These were tense times as Ben had to play it cool and not slip up. If Doug suspected anything at this point it could end very badly for him. Doug had a stare that went right through you. Stories of the crimes he had committed were legendary.

The turning point for Ben came when someone from another gang blew up the front of their clubrooms and, in retaliation, a few of the boys, including Ben, planned a revenge attack and shot three of the rival gang members they held responsible outside the opposition gang's headquarters a week later. Ben pulled the trigger and shot two of the so-called enemy. He was suddenly branded a hero and elevated to a level of respect.

Doug took him aside and gave him a courier job running parcels across town. They would meet every Thursday night at a local restaurant up at The Cross and have dinner together and Doug would give him the delivery itinerary. Ben didn't ask any questions, and he never looked in the parcels in the initial stages. This could be a test and he'd taken too long to get this far to blow it now. He would do his time and wait patiently for the next job.

He made sure he was never late, never taking too long from pick-up to delivery and kept everything as per the plan set out in the itinerary. The cars were always nondescript little white hatchbacks. Orders were that you were never to speed or commit any road rage; never draw attention to yourself so you didn't get pulled over.

One of the main rules was for any club member, or up-and-coming, not to partake in the use of methamphetamine. Doug apparently hated the stuff and what it did to people's minds.

Ben didn't ask any questions at the pick-up or drop-off points. Someone just handed him a square parcel, and he'd hand one back. Every week the order of the parcels would change, but there were no new parcels.

Ben hadn't expected to fall in love with Angela. She was the waitress at the restaurant they met at every Thursday night. He was into big tits, so he was instantly taken by her little elf face and her big tits.

He told Doug he was planning to ask her out and asked Doug what he thought his chances were. Doug laughed and told him he didn't have a shit show in hell. Couldn't he see she was gagging at the bit to fuck Doug? He rather arrogantly made it plain that he'd have the first crack at her, and Ben could have his cast-offs. Ben had planned to bite the bullet and ask her out the following Thursday but to everyone's surprise, she asked Doug out herself, and as she did, Doug looked at Ben and said, "I told you so!"

Ben replied, "Yes," with a big grin on his face. If this was just to piss Ben off it worked.

Ben was determined to send Doug to jail out of sheer hatred, now. In Doug's own words, "She's no good for you boy, she's a dumb slut!"

Once again it just astounded Ben how desperate these women were and the lengths they would go to, to get near Doug. What was it? It certainly couldn't be the looks.

Part of his assignment was to get close enough to attach tracking devices to all of Doug's private vehicles and put listening devices inside every room of his home. They already had a GPS tracker on his phone but that hadn't been as successful as they hoped. Doug didn't like using phones and often gave them away, left the phone behind, or destroyed them.

Ben had been shifting parcels for over a month now and could work out on most occasions where Doug would be so if he thought it was safe, and he thought he would have enough time in the house to monitor and plant his listening devices, he'd call around to Doug's house and visit Angela. The safest times were when Doug was out riding with the blonde bit of fluff. Ben knew he would have a couple of hours up his sleeve on those occasions.

It was extremely hard going at first as Angela was petrified Doug would find out or worse still, arrive unexpectedly at the house while Ben was there. She had already been subjected to his insane sexual behaviour and wasn't prepared to give Doug any more cause to assault her more than he already did, so she was hardly going to agree to let Ben walk around the house and plant listening devices.

Ben persisted. "I know exactly where Doug is and how long he's going be. You know you can trust me. I won't harm you."

After a couple of visits they had built up a friendship and she talked a little bit more about her childhood, and she started to open up about her relationship with Doug. Nothing she told Ben surprised him and together they made a secret plan to get her out safely.

"You have to trust me," urged Ben. "I promise you I'll make sure it's safe when it comes time to get you out. But we need to be bloody careful, if we get caught together it's going to end badly for us both."

There was an electric chemistry between them, and Ben fantasised about having sex with Angela.

It was on one of these visits that she accidentally brushed up against him in the kitchen while making him a coffee. He'd deliberately tried to get in her space. He couldn't help himself. He put his arms around her and kissed her, feeling her tits pressed up against him.

It was suddenly as if they were two sex-starved animals. They tore at each other's clothes with urgency, made their way hurriedly to the bedroom and completed the act of intercourse. In what seemed like seconds it was over.

Out of breath, they both laughed about it afterwards. It was the first time in a long time he had been with anyone, and it was the first time in a long time she wasn't forced to perform oral or anal sex, or that someone knew where her nipples were. They decided they'd get better with practice, and he promised her he'd be back the following week and hopefully, they'd both last a bit longer. But the fear right now of getting caught by Doug outweighed the option of trying again straight away.

They met weekly after that, sometimes twice weekly, if he was sure it was safe. This gave Ben an opportunity to bug the house and the vehicles in the garage as well as give Angela the confidence to prepare to leave. He had a safe house on the other side of Australia; they could shift there, to begin with, and then relocate to wherever he got a transfer. He was ready to settle down and commit to someone full-time and he felt real love for her. He could see a future together.

She had no idea who he really was but once he got her out safely, he planned to tell her. She might be able to give valuable evidence if she knew she was going to be protected.

He'd been kept unusually busy in the last couple of weeks. The package transfers had picked up for some reason, so he was shocked and confused to go around to the house on one of his planned safe visits to find the house completely empty, not a stick of furniture anywhere, no rubbish, and the house and grounds completely cleaned from head to toe.

Ben noticed the elderly neighbour next door. "Excuse me, do you know what happened to the couple who lived here?"

"A couple of big trucks came in the night and cleaned out everything. As far as I know, it was all donated to hospice. The nice man with the motorbikes even gave me a matching pair of armchairs for free – genuine leather," responded the elderly man with obvious delight.

The old guy next door was more concerned with who the new tenants might be as it was going to be up for rent, and he'd been lucky with the last owner – no barking dogs or noisy children.

The elderly neighbour also didn't know what had happened to the lady who lived there. He never saw her helping with the truck. He was no fool, he didn't want to get involved. The nice man with the motorbikes looked like he could cut up rough if he was provoked.

Angela had completely disappeared. Her bank accounts hadn't been touched for a long time as Doug gave her cash for all her household and spending needs so there was no way of tracing her through her transactions.

Doug had bought a brand new four-by-four and Ben hadn't had time to put a GPS on it, so tracking its whereabouts in the last week was out. She hadn't left the country – he was able to check that – and he knew she didn't have any family to speak of to visit. She had his phone number and hadn't rung or left a message, and her phone was no longer in service. She had no vehicle of her own. Ben could only think the worst. There was no way of proving anything so all he could do was lodge a missing person report. He didn't even know her full real name. The bank account had been opened back in the day when you

     MICHELLE THOMPSON

didn't have to provide evidence of ID. Even he didn't have any faith in the police turning up anything. It gave Ben even more reason to get revenge on Doug.

He weighed up asking Doug how Angela was at his next Thursday meeting. He wasn't sure if that was the right move, but he'd have to risk it, see if he could read Doug's expression.

When Ben asked Doug how she was, Doug sounded genuinely hurt. "She left me, dumped me. Ran off with some of my money and left no forwarding address. I can't understand it. I gave her everything; treated her like a queen."

Ben wanted to smash him in the face; shut the lying bastard up. He was good at lying, that was for sure. All that practice in court no doubt. He could feel his face going red with fury; he struggled to control it.

Ben left the meeting completely shattered. He had dropped the ball and let Angela disappear because he wasn't vigilant enough to read the writing on the wall. Had Doug found out about them? Paranoia was setting in now.

Ben's superior was recalling him back into a normal nine-to-five routine – nice little desk job up-state, or even relocation to East Timor or Papua New Guinea. Somewhere there weren't any bikies to kill him. He had been unsuccessful in his assignment and the force had lost faith in his ability to get enough evidence to see a conviction through to a sentence. Everything was spiralling out of his control.

He'd started opening the packages he was couriering and found they contained cash but no drugs. He just couldn't work it out. Was he as useless as his superior was suggesting? Had he let the methamphetamine cloud his judgment? He was going to be the laughingstock of the Anti-Gang Criminal Investigation Unit – that's if he wasn't already.

He turned it over in his mind and decided to make Doug pay. He'd taken it personally and no ugly biker cunt was going to get the better of him. He'd hurt him where it really hurts; show him who the biggest legalised gang in Australia really was.

Ben formulated a plan and started following Mellissa. He spent weeks watching her every move. He'd see how consistent her routine was, know where she was every day of the week, what car she drove, where she shopped, who her friends were. He'd kill the bitch. He'd buy a big truck and mow her down in the street. He'd make sure they'd have to scrape her off the radiator by the time he was finished.

Then he'd disappear into the crowd and watch the carnage from a distance, watch that ugly, big giant suffer. The police would cover for him; boil it down to the stress of the job and a drug habit. Maybe plead temporary insanity.

He knew he'd only have one chance. He would run her off the road, smash her face in with an iron bar if she survived the crash. Or wait till she got out of her car to do some shopping and run her over or crush her up against a building or other vehicle. He was working on every possible scenario. He'd steal some money from the packages and buy the truck with Doug's own money; how ironic. He'd write him a letter later and tell him it was for Angela.

Weeks went by and he finally saw his window of opportunity. There was an open stretch of highway coming into town from the farm with a 100 km speed limit. Mellissa came this way every Wednesday when she volunteered at the hospice. The bonus for Ben was he had found out she was pregnant, so he had the satisfaction of knowing that he wasn't just killing her, but he'd be killing Doug's unborn child in the process. He was smug with satisfaction.

He'd have to time it right. Pick up enough speed to cross the centre line at the last minute and give her no time to react. Hit her head-on, hopefully, run right over the top of her, or crush the car up against the median barrier. As an extra precaution, he had managed to obtain a hot pistol. If there was a chance she survived the collision, he'd put a bullet between her blue eyes.

Wednesday morning came around quickly. He had been hard out on the meth pipe for a couple of days now and he was completely wired. He'd gone to the storage shed early because he'd wanted to start the truck up and have the engine nice and warm before he set off. He'd packed a bag and brought some things along just in case he had to hide out in the shed for a couple of days until things settled down. He'd bought a new phone which he'd leave at the shed so he could ring his superior and get an extraction if he needed one.

He climbed up into the cab of the truck.

The second he turned the key in the ignition a couple of things flashed through his mind instantaneously: he thought he heard Angela call his name then there was an unfamiliar smell.

The explosion was so large that it was heard, and the seismic wave was felt, ten blocks away. The building and the truck were completely vaporised by the amount of plastic explosives packed into and under the truck and packed into the walls of the building.

     MICHELLE THOMPSON

Doug: 2009

When Danny had handed him the top-secret file, he hadn't expected it to contain the details of a major undercover operation against his club, and more so him. Danny couldn't disclose where or who he had received the information from, but it was so detailed and so well planned and researched that it left Doug noticeably shocked as he read the contents.

It took Doug a few days to absorb the potential ramifications if the undercover operation reached a successful conclusion. He knew he had a rat in his network but finding out now who it was and stopping them before they brought his empire down was going to be the difficult part. Danny was right, he couldn't protect Mellissa from behind bars. And he was the main target of the operation.

His lucky break came by chance when he decided to take a detour past his own house one day and noticed Ben's courier car parked outside.

He decided to start following Ben and discovered that Ben's visits to his house were weekly. On one of these occasions, Doug parked around the block and snuck into his own house through the garage to listen in to the conversation. Perhaps they were both in on it.

He wasn't surprised to find that Ben and Angela were fucking in his bed. He was sure then he'd found the rat. His gut told him he was right.

He didn't confront them; he had to make sure he had all the pieces of the puzzle before he reacted. He was adrenalized with the prospect of putting this all together and hurting them both.

Killing Angela was the only way to be sure she couldn't give evidence if the undercover operation was successful. Plus, he had some quiet satisfaction knowing that little Benny-boy would be looking for her. He'd like to have seen the look on Ben's face once he turned up at the house for his weekly fuck to find it completely empty. He also relished the rush he personally got from planning someone's demise.

Doug spread his network of trusted informants wide to uncover any more information they could on Ben, and through this process, he discovered the truck and the warehouse.

He took more precautions. He made sure all the courier packages only contained money, and he had Ben running around all day delivering the same parcels.

He also arranged for one of his associates to make sure Ben also had a healthy supply of meth to keep him going; the word was he already had a habit.

Doug put some of his crew on a roster following Ben day and night. He knew something was seriously wrong when some of the boys came back visually upset and almost afraid to tell him that it was Mellissa that they discovered Ben had been following.

Doug's blood ran cold. Ben was obviously going to get revenge for Angela's disappearance. He knew what he had to do.

Doug packed every available space in the truck with plastic explosive and wired it to detonate when the ignition was turned on. To make sure this didn't fail he also packed the building with plastic explosives and detonated them remotely. He'd always been a fan of fireworks. He might even take Mellissa to brunch that morning. A restaurant high up so he could witness the explosion; it was sure to be spectacular.

Now he could retire. Well, that was the plan.

2014

Doug's life had changed dramatically in the last five years. He now had a five-year-old daughter who he absolutely idolised. They had called her Edith after Edith Piaf, the singer – he'd always been mesmerised by her voice for some reason. Then, to everyone's surprise, a couple of years later Mellissa announced that she was having twins. To anyone's knowledge, no other sets of twins had been born in the history of either family, so it was a very pleasant surprise when they came two months early. The twin boys, Joseph and Kane, were now aged three. They were a handful at the best of times. They were real boys who loved trucks and snails and dirt. Doug could sit for hours watching all three children playing in the back yard. It never got boring watching the two boys work things out or solve logistical problems in the sandpit.

The prospect of having more children after the twins were born was on hold for the time being as both parents found it all very tiring, even with the support of grandparents and friends. And Doug didn't want to put Mellissa's body through that ordeal again. He wanted to return to taking her out at night to nice restaurants for dinner and other little surprises. They hadn't been for a ride together for months and he knew that was one of her favourite things. He loved his children, but a small part of him hated sharing his wife with anyone.

Doug had both sets of grandparents living on the old property now so there was no shortage of doting grandparents who were always complaining that Doug and Mellissa didn't go out enough and let them look after the children. Although, Doug joked, they would only say that once about the twins. Those boys woke up running and didn't stop till it was time to go to sleep at night.

Doug's love for his wife and family had taken on an obsessive quality verging on unreasonable. On the odd occasion, Mellissa had to tell Doug he could relax a bit more and let children be children. He knew what she meant, but he was always so worried they would hurt themselves, and every time they fell over and skinned a knee or a toe, he felt completely helpless that he could not have prevented it or that he had to hear them cry.

He did have the ability to laugh at himself when he and Mellissa were alone, and he could clearly see the times he had gone over the top.

The one thing Doug refused to give up was dropping off and picking up Edith from kinder or day school. She was a quiet, nervous child and they shared a special bond. He'd read too many stories about children getting snatched and he was always suspicious about men hanging around the school. He was often scaring the living daylights out of innocent strangers who happened to be in the vicinity. It wasn't safe to be a paedophile in his neighbourhood.

It took the teachers a while to get used to Doug at first. They told him later, at drunken parent-teacher BBQs, they'd had their fingers poised to dial 000 to call the police when he first started turning up. But they soon found him extremely helpful in organising working bees and a lucrative source of funds when new equipment was required for the school. They had heard rumours about him and read things in the paper but if concerned new parents ever broached the subject, they instantly defended him and reminded them about all the lovely equipment they had at times when traditional funding had been cut back. As a result, the school had a massive waiting list for new entrants. They nicknamed him the Tomato Guy, and they told him this to his face. He'd been called much worse, and he appreciated their honesty.

And they couldn't deny witnessing the genuine displays of affection he showed where his kids were concerned.

Doug had handed over most of his club duties. He was developing the two farms and as Mellissa's parents had handed over the reins to him now, he'd had to find alternative ways to make both farms a profitable business.

With the fluctuations in cattle prices, he'd diversified into hothouses and was growing tomatoes commercially. He was currently supplying two major supermarket chains and was about to expand into bell peppers. He'd become one of the main employers in the vicinity where they lived and offered cadetships for members of his club who showed an interest in farming and agriculture. He also needed staff for the hothouses, the farm and general maintenance. He'd appointed a full-time manager but oversaw most of the development of both farms himself.

The local area had had a few problems with cattle rustling in the past, so he was busy project-managing the erection of new perimeter fencing around the entire property to keep would-be rustlers out or at least deter them. Well, that

     MICHELLE THOMPSON

was the story he spread around. Doug was really more concerned with home security and was quite happy turning his little oasis into a fortified zone. He'd stopped short of razor wire but was seriously looking for an opportunity to introduce it at some stage. In the meantime, he'd let everyone think he might be going into deer farming and was busy talking his neighbours into undertaking a similar project purely so he could contract out the fencing business with his own crew.

Luckily, the neighbours saw him as the guy who could fix everything. They were fully aware of his connections and often came to him with all sorts of problems, thinking he could wave a magic wand and make everything all right. At times, when he felt the cause was worth the challenge, he would agree to get involved, but always if there was a benefit to him in some way. But he did repeatedly remind them that he was retired now, and his interests rested in tomatoes and cattle.

Doug had also made it clear to all his neighbours that, given the opportunity, he would like first right of refusal to buy their properties if they decided to sell. None had come up yet.

One morning, Doug had dropped Edith off at school as usual. He'd parked right outside the school office and run in with a couple of bags of tomato seconds for the staff. He'd only left his truck for less than two minutes but returned to find a typed note and a mobile phone on the seat. He was hesitant to get into the truck at first and looked around to see if he could see anyone nearby. The car park was bare; no kids playing games. His anger flared a little. He yelled out to the office lady and asked if she had seen anyone near his truck. He didn't tell her why he asked. She shook her head.

Doug sat in the truck and read the note. *I need your help. After I ring you on this phone, throw it away.'*

He was halfway home when the phone rang. He pulled over and cut the engine. He had the feeling he needed to hear all this conversation and if he could, he'd listen for background noise from the caller.

It was a woman's voice. "I need help. My husband has gone missing, disappeared without a trace, and I think something bad has happened to him."

"Call the fuckin police," Doug said roughly. "I'm not the missing person's man." He was a little annoyed with this drama, he was a busy man and didn't need this shit.

"I can't call the police. He was doing something illegal when he went missing."

"Well lady, if it was bad shit then he's probably dead by now so I hope you had him insured."

There was a drawn-out silence, and then the female voice said, "He was bringing three hundred and seventy million dollars' worth of pure cocaine into the country two days ago. That's why I can't go to the police!"

They were both silent now. She spoke first. "If you find the cocaine, you can have half. I'll be in touch in two days to see if you're interested in finding my husband, dead or alive. Make sure you throw the phone away."

The phone went dead. Doug got out of the truck and smashed the phone under his boot till it was just shattered plastic pieces.

He went home after the phone call and took Mellissa into the panic room, sealed the door and told her about the events that had just unfolded. He kept nothing secret from her these days; it helped him sleep better at night. Doug very seldom left the farm these days, but they decided he would have to go into the city himself. "I'll ask around and see if anyone has just won the cocaine lottery. A haul that big will be being talked about all over the streets by now."

He knew his crew had nothing to do with it, nothing that big would be passed without his knowledge. And, of course, what if this was a massive set-up? The police would surely still be looking for revenge for the death of one of their own. He'd have to tread carefully. And how did this strange woman think she was going to contact him again? Was he going to leave his truck open again?

Doug spent all day in the city, but every avenue drew a blank. If the underworld didn't know about it, had the missing husband been successful? How was he going to shift it when he got it here? And how was he getting it here? Such a huge amount; you couldn't hide that up your arse. He was either a take-a-chance amateur or his other thought about a police sting was the more obvious conclusion.

The next day an envelope arrived in the mailbox with a picture of a yacht called *Stacey's Escape* and directions to the Balmain Marine Centre. It had been hand-delivered.

Doug and Mellissa talked about the photo and the events of the previous day long into the night. It was decided that the next day they'd both drive out to Balmain Marine Centre and look for this boat. They also decided that this mysterious lady, if she was real, must know them or know of them. "She was at the school to drop off the phone and the first note, and she rang you when you were halfway home," Melissa pointed out.

Had she previously timed his travel distance? He was reasonably consistent these days.

"She also delivered the envelope to our mailbox, so she knows where we live," replied Doug. "She has to know she was taking a real chance if she is a fake and I catch up with her."

Would she be watching them when they got to the boat or the marina?

"We'll take the car, so we don't draw too much attention to ourselves. If we take the bike, everyone will be looking. We can have lunch and make a day of it. Finally cut the apron strings and leave the grandparents in charge of the madhouse. Good luck with that," laughed Doug.

Doug and Mellissa dropped Edith off at school on their way to the marina. They drove in silence most of the way, thinking heavily about the notes and possibly finding the boat. They held hands and every so often, Mellissa would lean across and kiss him, which Doug pretended to complain about, "You'll cause us to have an accident, woman."

It had been a while since they had been alone together on an outing, and they really enjoyed each other's company. Mellissa spied a couple of restaurants they could decide on later on their way back.

The marina was nice, not too large, with some nice boats attached at berths on the floating docks and more boats secured to moorings out in the harbour.

It wasn't hard to find the yacht; it was tied up on one of the floating berths. Mellissa took photos of it on her phone and if anyone asked, they were going to say they were interested in buying one like it. They both concluded that this must have been the way the cocaine had been smuggled into the country. Why else would she have sent a photo of it and directions to the marina?

The yacht was unlocked so Mellissa kept lookout while Doug went aboard. He looked all through the boat. It was spotless and he couldn't help but think it had just been cleaned or given a coat of paint. Doug found no loose internal panels, and nothing seemed out of place. There was absolutely no paperwork, maps or electronic equipment on board. There wasn't even any toilet paper; someone had done an excellent job of cleaning this boat. Something just wasn't adding up.

They found a lovely place for lunch nearby at the Riverview Hotel which turned out to be a glorious gastronomic and romantic experience in the upstairs restaurant, and the beer was nice and cold. Over lunch, they discussed the things that just didn't add up: the cleanliness of the yacht and considering someone had sailed across the ocean with a boat full of cocaine they would have been shit scared to stop anywhere so they would have had to have had food supplies, bedding, clothes, and a compass. Yet the boat was completely bare.

"Surely there would be shit paper," said Doug.

The external rigging was all intact. The emergency lifeboat was onboard along with the emergency locator beacon; no life jackets – but that didn't mean anything, whoever cleaned the boat could have taken those.

"The husband must have made it back to Aussie in one piece," said Doug, "or who would have docked the boat? Was he alone? If customs had caught him, it'd be all over the news by now."

They decided to make a list of questions in order of priority for when the mystery lady called back.

Before they left to pick Edith up from school Doug wanted to have one last look at the boat; something was nagging at his subconscious.

He stood on the dock and stared at the boat for a while and then it clicked – this was a different boat. He looked back at the photo. Both boats were identical – colour, life raft – but they had spelt this boat's name wrong on the bow he was looking at. This vessel they had in front of them spelt *Stacy's* without the letter 'e'. Now it was really getting interesting.

As they drove off, they didn't see the old green Hilux parked just out of view. The guy behind the wheel had a hat pulled down over his ginger brow, he wore dark glasses, and he was making a phone call.

"It's me. We got big trouble. There's been a guy looking at the boat. Nah, he's not police, he's worse. He's that big ugly bikie fulla from up at The Cross. You know, the one that's always in the papers. We're fucked if he's involved. I knew that dumb cunt was too stupid to be acting alone."

When Doug and Mellissa got home that afternoon, they were greeted by exhausted grandparents who had called one of the girls in from the hothouse to help them with the twins. The house looked like a bomb had hit it. The young girl from the hothouse was desperately trying to put it back in order

    MICHELLE THOMPSON

as Doug and Mellissa walked in. Doug couldn't help but laugh – he'd warned them that the twins were a handful.

Mellissa gave the young girl some money for her trouble although she refused to accept it. Mellissa insisted. She might turn out to be a useful backup if they needed to go out in the future.

The twins came roaring out from nowhere dressed as pirates, screaming and yelling and brandishing plastic swords. They were taking Edith hostage on their make-believe ship – Edith was so good with the twins – then they all went off to play.

The grandparents had had enough and were already holding up the bar and ordering Doug to open the drinks cabinet. "It's about time that you seriously consider hiring a nanny, even if it's part-time, just to give yourselves a break and get out more often."

The grandparents were exhausted and really didn't want to volunteer to look after the twins for any extended length of time again; a couple of hours maximum would be enough.

Doug had to admit he had had a very pleasant day, and he was always so proud to be seen in public with his beautiful wife, despite the looks from strangers trying to work out the connection of such a pretty woman with such an ugly guy.

"You know, a nanny's not a bad idea, we'll give it some serious consideration," said Doug

They all laughed as they were sure his trust issues and his obsession with the safety of the family would get in the way, but they suggested a trial for a few hours at a time and see how it went from there. Doug sort of agreed. They all laughed again and ordered him to pour more gins.

Doug and Mellissa decided to tell their parents the whole story about the day's events and get a different perspective on it. They discussed it well into the afternoon.

Next morning, Doug and Mellissa were standing outside a small farmhouse on a lifestyle block about five miles from their home. Mellissa decided to go with him in case Doug needed a witness.

The house was badly in need of repair, the fences were non-existent, and the pasture looked like it had died years ago. He could see why they might desperately need money.

It had been their parents' idea to check the parent roll at the school and see if there was a parent called Stacey. Doug had hit the jackpot. There was a Rodrigues and Stacey Mara. It only took Doug five minutes to find the address after that. He was parked in the drive when Stacey pulled up. The obvious shock on her face let him know he had the right person.

Still cautious that she might be bugged Doug asked her to step away from the vehicle and stand a little further out in the paddock. She understood completely.

She looked terrible like she'd hadn't slept for days. She was shaking with nerves – or fear – it was hard to know. Doug had that effect on people. She looked like she could collapse at any moment.

Doug was over the dramatics and wanted to punch her in the head, but he wouldn't get the answers he wanted with that approach, so he suggested that Mellissa reassure her that they weren't going to hurt her.

Doug advised her to tell him the full story and that it was important that she didn't leave any detail out.

The whole story was a disaster from the start.

"We are in too deep with the mortgage at the bank," began Stacey. "My husband doesn't speak much English; he's from Uruguay. We met at a hippy retreat in India years ago and sailed here about five years ago. I got pregnant so we decided to get married; our child goes to the same school as your daughter, Edith.

"Rod lost his job at the timber mill. I've got a part-time job at a nursery but it's not enough to even cover the basics. We're facing a mortgagee sale, and we got desperate. Rod has a family connection out of Ecuador, so he took the gamble to make a drug run alone and hoped this would answer all our problems. This isn't the first time we've taken a gamble with drugs. When we came here five years ago, we brought a small amount of cocaine with us on board our boat and got away with it. So, with no consequences and desperate times, we decided to make one large hit and retire.

"Everything went according to plan. Rod miraculously managed to hit the mild weather and nothing on board broke down in transit, so he didn't need to stop at Tahiti for emergency repairs.

"Rod phoned me when he docked at the marina – we have a secret safety word – to let me know he was safe and that everything had gone smoothly."

Rod had come in under the cover of darkness. Over the years they had got to

          MICHELLE THOMPSON

know the harbour master well and they knew what nights he was preoccupied. Rod had practised coming into the harbour at night many times so it wouldn't look suspicious if he came in at night on his own.

"After Rod called, I drove to the marina to pick him up in a van I had hired with a horse float. When I got there, Rod was missing, and the boat was completely empty. His cell phone message said his phone was switched off, or currently out of service.

"I was beside myself; I knew I couldn't go to the police. That's why we're here now, talking in the middle of a paddock. I've heard the gossip, Mr Henderson. I've heard about your reputation. I don't care about the drugs anymore; I just want my husband back. And I know if anyone can help me it's you.

"The only asset we have that we could sell is the yacht, but that would be a last resort."

Doug didn't let on that the name of the boat tied up at the marina was different from the photo she gave him – he was keeping that ace up his sleeve.

He did, however, inform her that the possibility of her husband still being alive was slim. "But, dead or alive, I will find him and get him back to you. I've asked around and whoever has the drugs, hasn't come out of hiding yet, so that's a good sign."

Doug continued, "The first thing I need is a list of names, phone numbers and addresses, if possible, of the people Rod worked with. I presume that they've also all been laid off, which could give them a motive. I'll make some enquiries at the mill. Was he involved in any sports clubs, or did he have any other friends? And as far as you know, did anyone else know about what you were doing?"

Doug wanted every bit of information he could get before he left. He didn't want to come back to this address unless he was buying the farm off them, which he could see was a strong possibility. He planned to have this sorted before too long and put the poor bitch out of her misery.

Before he left, Doug gave her $1,500 cash to cover the mortgage and minor bills. He'd arrange for some vegetables and meat to be dropped off later that day.

"One last thing. You're not to tell anyone I'm involved with this under any circumstances, is that clear? And don't come to our house, either. If whoever is involved in this is watching you, they could work out I'm tracking them down and we could lose the element of surprise."

She confirmed that she understood. "You have my word."

"And if you get any calls regarding your husband's whereabouts, be very suspicious. They could be the people who have the drugs, wanting to know if the police are involved. If they have killed your husband, they're probably prepared to also harm you and your daughter. Or it could be the police trying to set a trap.

"Most of all, try and go about your business as normally as possible. Right now, you look terrible, and that alone will draw people's attention to you.

"If anyone asks where your husband is, tell them he's been suffering from a mental illness after he was made redundant and has had a mental breakdown. He's been living rough on his boat, and you've been keeping it a secret because you were embarrassed to tell anyone.

"I presume you can speak Spanish, so make sure you only converse with your husband in his native tongue. It's important that he doesn't talk to anyone till I have this whole thing cleared up."

Doug and Mellissa were about to leave when, as an afterthought, he asked, "Out of interest, what were you going to do with the drugs once you got them into the country? Who did you think you were going to shift such a large volume of drugs to? You didn't think you were going to knock on my door and say, 'By the way, want to buy some pure cocaine'?"

Stacey laughed for the first time in a week. "Something like that!"

The Workmates

Rod's workmates Vic, Gill, Dan and Phil, who now had the cocaine, were completely out of their league and now they presumed that Doug was involved, they were shitting themselves. They had nicknamed Rod 'The Spaniel', as he spoke very little English, and Spanish was his native language. Rod had assured them that no one else knew but they all knew what a big mouth he had when he'd been drinking.

What had started as some dumb talk and a bit of a joke around the bar after work with their Spanish workmate and had been the pie-in-the-sky solution to losing their jobs, had now spiralled out of control once Rod returned to Aussie. They had thought he was full of bullshit, telling stories about sailing back from India five years ago with a kilo of cocaine on board. As Rod had become drunk and more animated, he had exaggerated who his contacts were back in South America, and they had all got caught up in the fairy tale. Then they all got caught up in greed.

What surprised them the most was that he made it back alive and didn't get stopped by customs, didn't fall overboard, and hadn't been shot by some drug cartel in Ecuador, or wherever he was going.

They had spent many a windy afternoon out in the harbour sailing with him, so they thought his ability to handle the yacht could get him through. So, when he rang them to boast that he was on his way back, they went into action with the plan they'd decided on all those months ago when he first set sail. Once they knew he was on the return trip with the cargo on board and the plan was set in motion, the nerves really set in. As he got closer, they set up a round-the-clock watch on the harbour, determined not to miss the opportunity when he returned.

They decided to wait till he docked. They had another boat prepared that was almost identical, moored alongside his berth under a huge boat cover. The plan was to kill The Spaniel and dispose of the body later. They'd tow the boat full of cocaine across to the Drummoyne Sailing Club and leave it covered for a few days on a mooring till they could be sure the dust had settled. The wife would come down in the dark, see the boat was empty, see Rod was missing and she'd be too scared to call the police and report it. The lighting was poor, and it was dark, so she probably wouldn't notice any minor differences with the swapped boat.

They watched Rod tie the boat up with very slow motions, which seemed odd. It took him a long time to do what should have been a simple task. When they approached the yacht and called out to him from the jetty and he didn't answer, they knew something was wrong.

Rod was lying motionless on the floor of the cabin; they checked his pulse. He was skinny and malnourished, covered in terribly infected sores. He had hit his head on the way down and blood was everywhere. There were no signs of life. They thought he must have died of a heart attack.

They had only moments to react and hook the yacht up to the towing vessel they had organised. Although they had rehearsed the plan over and over in the lead-up to Rod's return, everything was going in slow motion. They weren't used to the rocking motion of the boat, and they didn't factor into the equation that the boat would be so packed with bricks of cocaine that there was no room to move in the boat, not to mention tripping over Rod's body in the process. They had to get the boat across the harbour to the other mooring at Drummoyne before the wife turned up, so they decided to leave The Spaniel there on the floor of the cabin and moved a whole lot of bricks on top of him, so they didn't feel so bad when they stood on him. They could sort out dumping the body later.

Everything went smoothly. It had been like taking candy from a baby and the bonus was they hadn't had to draw straws to see who was going to kill Rod, the poor bastard had died on his own. Once the boat was securely tied up, they made sure the cover was properly tied down. There was a storm predicted to hit Sydney in the next couple of days, and they had to make sure it was secure.

They all quickly got on the towing vehicle and made it back to shore before daylight was upon them. Before they left the yacht, they decided to take a kilo of cocaine to try and bury Rod's body under a pile of more cocaine bricks and a drop sheet, so that if by chance anyone did look inside, it wouldn't be obvious at a quick glance.

—

     MICHELLE THOMPSON

Rod had collapsed with exhaustion and dehydration and his body had shut down with an infection. He hadn't eaten for days; he'd run out of food weeks ago and had been surviving on what little fish he could catch. His desalination system had broken down just past Tahiti and he didn't want to take the risk of stopping. Some rain was expected, and he was relying on what condensation he could get from the windows and some jars he had set around the boat.

Once back at the marina, when it had come to docking the boat his sea legs, so unaccustomed to walking on land for months on end, made the process almost impossible. He was relieved to see his work buddies heading down the dock to see him – he was expecting his wife with the trailer, but he'd need all the hands he could to help load it. He hadn't calculated being this weak and he was barely capable of walking. He couldn't expect his wife to load it all.

Rod had expected to bring in about ten one-kilogram blocks, but his cousin had decided to immigrate to Aussie and wanted his share, so somehow, he'd ended up with seven hundred and fifty, one-kilogram blocks. His cousin was going to fly out the following month when he gave the word that the coast was clear. Rod was sure there was more to the story about where his cousin had got the cocaine from, but he'd hurriedly left the country not wanting to ask any questions or get murdered if his cousin had ripped someone off.

The Glasshouses

The construction of the new glasshouses and the packing warehouse had started. Doug had decided to hire another manager to manage the peppers and project-manage the build in his absence.

These were going to be state-of-the-art structures covering twenty-three hectares in total. Ventilation and watering were going to be controlled by computer; one million plants with each plant capable of producing forty capsicums each, per plant, per year. If they could achieve this standard, they would be guaranteed a contract with the same major supermarket chain that took his tomatoes. The glass had to be toughened. He'd learnt this the hard way with the tomatoes as Sydney often had severe hailstorms with stones as big as golf balls, which would cause massive destruction, especially for glasshouses.

Doug's original plan was to bring in huge water tanks to support his needs, but it had been suggested to him to do two things: build a huge dam and utilise the base of the glasshouses by making a storage facility underneath that could hold water, like a huge underfloor swimming pool. It made sense and, although it was going to cost a lot more, it would be a huge saving in the long run. The dam could be big enough that they could ride jet skis on it or even water ski. Or a nice swimming area for staff functions in the summer. He had suitable terrain where he could use the dirt dug up from the glasshouses to help construct the wall at one end of the dam.

The perimeter fencing on his own property had been completed and he had two other farmers in the area who had hired him to fence their properties. Cattle rustling had been on the increase and Doug just wasn't sure if it was poor people from outside the district, or another farmer in the vicinity stealing cattle to prop up his income when finances were hard. He knew it wouldn't be long before they slipped up and he caught up with them.

With the help of Mellissa, he also hired a part-time nanny. This gave them time to go for rides during the day and stop for lunch somewhere, or just spend time alone together, which she liked, and which made her happy. And if Mellissa was happy, he was happy, and things ran smoothly.

     MICHELLE THOMPSON

It was a cold and dark stormy night when Rod's workmates went back a couple of nights later to dispose of the body and to bring the cocaine ashore. They hadn't been game enough to even try the one-kilogram block they had at home for two reasons: one, it was meant to be pure, and they had read plenty of internet stories about overdosing, and two, they were complete amateurs in this field. Except for watching a couple of *Scarface* movies, they didn't know what to do with it. Since they saw that bikie guy looking over the docked boat, they knew it would only be a matter of time before he caught up with them and they didn't want to have any missing cocaine. It was going to be hard enough to explain that Rod had died before they could kill him. If Rod was on Doug's payroll, they were almost dead themselves.

Vic called a meeting with his three workmates.

"I'm sick of this bullshit, but I have an idea. Let's get the cocaine off the boat and drop half of it off at the prick's front door and say that's all there was. Tell him Rod contacted us and panicked and dumped half overboard on the way in. I think we should draw straws to see who goes to see him, only two of us. That way two of us can at least make a new life somewhere else.

"Failing that, unless you want to be hunted down like a wild animal, whoever survives will have no choice but to go to the police and hope like hell they'll be put into witness protection."

What the other three didn't know, was that Vic was planning to rig the draw, so he was always going to be the one left with the cocaine. It was always going to be all about him.

The boat cover was hard to untie. The rain had made the rope swell, and the boat was rocking around heavily in the conditions. They had decided to fill their twenty-three-foot motorboat with as many bricks as they could and run it backwards and forwards to the shore to fill the furniture truck they had hired for the delivery. They had all worn black full-body wetsuits; if they needed to disappear into the dark or into the chilly water to get away, this could help disguise them. This whole thing had turned into a massive nightmare and until they handed the drugs back, they couldn't rest.

The men had brought some home gym weights and some tie-down straps with them for Rod's body. After they were finished unloading, they'd take the body way out to sea and throw it overboard. They brought a knife with them to puncture holes in the abdomen so it wouldn't float to the surface when it bloated – they had read this on the internet while researching how to dispose of a body at sea.

They finally managed to lift the hatch cover up on one side, expecting the smell of the body to hit them immediately when they opened the cabin door and shone their torches into the cabin. They stood there in stunned disbelief. The boat was empty. Completely. All the cocaine was gone. And the body was gone. Someone had cleaned it. Not even any of Rod's blood was on the floor.

—

Stacey was woken at 6 am the morning after Doug and Mellissa had been to her house by the sound of heavy knocking on her door. She could see two police officers through the glass in the door and the squad car with blue and red flashing lights in her driveway. Her heart instantly sank; she felt like vomiting. This would explain it. They had arrested him at the dock all those days ago and he was in custody. Now they were probably going to arrest her, and their child would go into foster care for the next ten to thirteen years. Would she be dragged away in her nightgown, or would they let her get dressed? Would child protection come and take her child today? What would the school parents' committee say about her?

She almost collapsed when the two police officers confirmed they had the correct address; her head was spinning.

Everything they said just sounded like a faraway recording. The words all jumbled together. It was like she was floating above the room, listening in to the conversation.

"Your husband is in critical care in Sydney Hospital. He was found naked and unconscious by diners at the Drummoyne Sailing Club boat ramp last night. Do you have any support or family members who can drive you to the hospital? The doctors are quite concerned that he won't survive the day. He is in hospital in an induced coma. I'm afraid, due to his extreme physical condition, we will be requiring you to come down to the station and help us with our inquiries at some stage. It looks like he has suffered a head trauma; possibly someone tried to mug him and robbed him of his personal belongings. But right now, we must insist you try and make it to the hospital immediately."

After the police left, Stacey closed the door then raced to the toilet and vomited from sheer stress. Her head was swimming, and a million questions raced through her mind. He was alive, for the meantime, which was the main thing. Whoever had left him in that condition probably has the cocaine, and they won't want him to pull through and identify them. Would they come after her and her child now? The big bikie guy is involved now, and he knows that the cocaine is somewhere out there. How could she get a message to him to tell him that they had found Rod? Would it be in the newspapers? Would he help her with protection for her and her husband? He'd want to keep his distance now that the police were involved.

She quickly dressed and bundled her sleeping child into the car. She just hoped she could make it to the hospital in time to see him before he passed.

Front page of the Sydney Morning Newspaper:

The naked body of a man was discovered by diners at the Drummoyne Sailing Club. Two diners discovered the body lying face down on the boat ramp when they went outside for a cigarette. They alerted the authorities immediately. Police were unable to release details until next of kin could be notified. The man is currently in a critical condition in Sydney Hospital and not expected to live.

A photo showed the two diners standing on the boat ramp where they had found the body, with the sailing club in the background.

One of Rod's workmates read the newspaper article out to the others while they sat there in stunned silence, listening intently to every word. No one spoke for ages; the events of the last forty-eight hours were too enormous to take in.

The men decided to write a list of all the possible scenarios that could get them out of the shit and then take a vote on the best idea. To make this work, one of them must also volunteer to take the rap to protect the identity and the safety of everyone else. But they figured Doug would want more sacrifices given the potential money he had lost.

"First of all," said Dan, "what if Rod had also phoned Doug or his wife? What if they already know how much was on the boat? If Rod dies, then our story could still stick."

"How do we find this bikie guy anyway?" asked Vic,

Gill's idea was just to drive around all the tattoo shops on the Cross. They all yelled in unison, "Shut the fuck up, Gill."

"Don't be so fuckin dumb all the time," said Vic.

Phill put in a thought. "How did Rod even get off the boat and onto the shore, wasn't he practically dead? Perhaps he heard us and was playing dead. If he's told anyone this, then we are all dead.

"Vic, someone should go to the hospital and see how much the wife knows, if she lets on anything."

"Should we just leave the country now, go to New Zealand or something? Or go to the police now?" suggested Dan.

Vic was getting agitated, he wanted the cocaine all for himself, so no talk of police. He felt he had to shut this meeting down. He said, "In the meantime, Phil, you hide the one kg of cocaine at your house; your father's some sort of God-botherer so no one will suspect you. Dan, you try and see if you can ask to see the CCTV footage at Drummoyne. I'll go home and dig out the old man's shotgun, just in case we need it."

They sat around for hours drinking and discussing every angle. The consensus was that none of them were cut out for the drug business, and they wished they had never got involved. Their get-rich-quick scheme had completely backfired. After all, the reason they got laid off was that they were hopeless at even working in a timber mill: always taking sick days, always late for work, turning up drunk. They were always looking for the easy way out and still hadn't learnt their lesson.

—

Stacey identified herself at the nurse's station at intensive care and someone from the family support unit took her daughter off to a playroom. They gowned Stacey up, gave her a face mask, and took her into the room.

At first, she was shocked by the amount of equipment, lights and alarms attached to her husband, and there was a machine helping him to breathe.

She could only hold Rod's hand and talk to him. She spent hours updating him on the farm and her job and news he had missed in Australia since he had been gone. She was careful not to mention anything about the boat or the support from the neighbours. She followed Doug's instructions and made sure she only spoke to her husband in Spanish.

The doctors took her aside and gave her a grim prognosis. "We're sorry, Mrs Mara, there's a strong chance your husband could very well be left with brain damage, if he recovers at all, judging by his physical condition – he has some major organ failure. You need to consider what will happen if you have to decide about taking him off the machine when the time comes to see if he is capable of breathing on his own."

All she could think of right now was she had him back and she had a physical body to touch. That was better than not knowing what had happened to him or not finding the body.

She hoped Doug could find the bastard that had done this and make him suffer.

Now that the cocaine was gone, who was going to pay for long-term medical care if Rod required it, and how were they going to pay for the house?

—

Gilbert was one of the mill workers. He was fat and lazy, a bachelor with no immediate prospect of acquiring a partner in the near future. His dry, springy ginger hair hadn't been cut professionally for years, and his once white singlet was now yellowed with stains from countless spilt meals and beer. He rented a one-bedroom cabin in a caravan park, but he couldn't even keep that in a clean and tidy condition, with dirty dishes that were interlocked with pizza boxes and Red Rooster cartons everywhere.

He wasn't surprised he was one of the guys the mill had let go claiming cutbacks – he didn't blame them. He'd miss the toilet paper he stole every week and drinking the milk directly out of the bottle in the canteen every day. Now he was on welfare, spending all his available funds on beer and porno magazines.

He knew one thing; they had really fucked up! This business with the drugs had turned into a disaster. He was planning to shoot through and leave the others in the shit. Get the hell out of there and go up north and see if he could get a job mining opal or something. He hoped this bikie guy didn't hunt him down, he couldn't fight his way out of a paper bag. He was a coward and running away was the best option he could see.

He liked The Spaniel; they were the closest of the group and they were always on the receiving end of the jokes because they weren't always the brightest in the group. It hadn't been his idea to kill him, it had been Vic's, but he didn't have the balls to disagree. And the others convinced him that it meant more money for him if they didn't have to split it so many ways. He could buy a house and a car and finally leave the caravan park.

Gill stumbled into his cabin, belching a big foul breath of beer as he entered through the door, suppressing a shit he'd been dying to have for the past hour. He reached for the light switch; bloody bulb was blown again.

As he groped his way across to the bench where another light switch was, he felt the rough rope of the noose tighten around his neck and he was suddenly hauled into the air, so his feet weren't touching the ground. He started to struggle and tried gyrating his huge body to gain some leverage and get his fingers under the noose. It was no use; he was too heavy, and the rope was cutting into his flesh. As his eyes adjusted to the light, he could just make out the huge physical form of a man. He knew it was the bikie. He lost consciousness as his bowels gave way, and he was covered from the waist down in his own urine and faeces. He was dead.

Doug was quietly amused by the bulging red face as it swung from the rope. He lay a chair on its side, to give the impression of a suicide.

He was disgusted at the sloth-like behaviour of Gill – he deserved to die just for the state of the cabin alone.

There was no reason to question him, he already knew all the answers. Now he just had to pick them off, one by one, and watch them sweat. Doug had missed this side of his life. He'd been quiet for a while now playing happy families. He was really enjoying himself – he loved the thrill of the kill. Probably best not to share that particular detail with Mellissa.

—

Construction of the glasshouses was at a standstill. The authorities had to sign off each stage and that seemed to be taking a long time and a lot of money. Although Doug was frustrated with the bureaucracy, he knew it was pointless fighting them.

He had refocused his attention on the dam. It was turning out slightly larger than he had originally anticipated, but it was not only going to be an innovative idea to irrigate both farms, the recreational side would be a benefit for everyone. He could see plenty of family and staff gatherings in and around this venue. He was looking forward to making effective use of it. Anyway, he wasn't happy unless it was bigger and better than everyone else's idea. He might start a mini-competition with water skis or something. His staff were extremely competitive.

—

Stacey spent every day at her husband's bedside. She had arranged for her daughter to stay with the family of a student from the same class who her daughter went to school with.

The whole community had rallied around to support her. They'd had no idea that her husband had suffered a breakdown. Now that they had found out, they had reached out to her. Doug and Mellissa had organised a makeover of the Mara's house, so that at least if Rod recovered enough to come home, the grounds and the house had been completely redesigned, allowing wheelchair access if necessary. And the gardens had been transformed so they were maintenance-free.

Doug oversaw the finishing touches to the paintwork on the house and the new fencing for the property. He thought it was the least he could do for the poor dumb bugger. He was even considering giving Rod a job on his property if he recovered. If not, he'd consider a generous cash offer on the property to help his widow out.

On the rare occasions that Stacey did leave his bedside, it was only to get something to eat or go to the bathroom. The hospital had set up a bed for her on the floor of Rod's room. He was out of intensive care now and breathing on his own, but he hadn't regained consciousness. And he was still on an intravenous drip.

It was on one of these occasions when she left the room to go outside and stretch her legs, that an elderly gentleman approached her in the car park. He had on a big coat and a hat but took his glasses off to talk with her. He had a kind face and familiar eyes.

He had a message from Doug. "Doug wanted me to remind you not to speak to anyone about this business," he said. "Continued to update Rod on what's happening but only talk to him in Spanish in case any of the nurses are listening. And even though Rod hasn't woken up yet, remind him that it's still not safe for him to speak to anyone. It's surprising what the unconscious mind can understand, so if he can hear you at all, we need him to be up to speed if he wakes up. The men who did this are still out there, so everyone must be careful."

Before the man departed, he asked her which bank she and Rod banked at, which she thought was a strange question, but she willingly told him the bank and branch. He then slipped her a large brown envelope which she tucked under her coat, and then he disappeared into the car park and out through the gardens. As quickly as he appeared, he was gone again.

As she made her way to a toilet cubicle to inspect the envelope, Stacey wondered if the elderly man was Doug's father. She had heard from her daughter and some locals about all the work being done at her property and she was extremely grateful. She didn't care about the rumours she had heard about Doug; she was his biggest fan.

Once in the safety of the toilet cubicle, Stacey looked inside the envelope only to discover it was full of cash – $100 bills. She'd have to go to the bank tomorrow and put it all on the mortgage. She was already behind and the letters and phone calls she got from the bank had got quite serious now. The words Property Law Act resonated in her ears.

　　MICHELLE THOMPSON

Vic

Victor, or 'Vic' to his mates, had worked at the mill for five years. Five of the best years of his life, he told people. Where else could you go every day, do nothing, and get paid for it? He had devised a way to always be lost in the plant for hours and never do any actual work. It was such a big site that if he walked around with a clipboard all day, nearly everyone left him alone. Most workers at the site despised him – his four like-minded buddies thought he was a hero.

He'd laugh for hours about how dumb the bosses were. That was until the retrenchment was announced. Then he was facing the redundancy list with his name on it. He had no formal qualifications; he'd got the job originally because his old man worked there before he died.

Vic's life outside his four mates at the mill was a rented house in the suburbs with his partner of seven years and their two girls. His partner and the two girls hated him. He was always drunk and aggressive, and he'd spend what little money they had on booze, cigarettes and what he called necessities for his shed, which he called the Vic cave. The shed was lined wall to wall with pornographic posters of women's breasts and vaginal openings in different states of exposure. He boasted he had a collection of over one hundred DVDs, ranging from soft porn to hard-core porn. He could sit for hours watching his movies and masturbating in his shed. His partner and daughters had never stepped foot through the door and had no desire to engage with him once he was down in his cave.

Vic had a new project on the go. He had searched the library for ways to cut down a shotgun to turn it into a 'sawn-off'. He was busy attempting to cut off the barrel.

He wasn't convinced Gill had committed suicide – he thought Gill was too dumb to think of it and too lazy to climb up on the chair. But then Gill was probably too lazy to carry on living. But just in case, if the big bikie came looking for him, he wanted to be ready. It was his father's gun. He didn't have a licence, and it had been sitting in the cupboard for years with some old cartridge shells. He'd need something a bit smaller to carry around with him;

it was a bit awkward swinging that long barrel around. This way it would be more practical if he had to use it in a hurry.

He'd tested the gun earlier in the evening while the barrel was still long to make sure it still worked and that the shells still fired. He'd thought it was funny to blow a hole in his wife's blanket on the clothesline.

Vic went up to the house to warn her that he was going to fire it again and to lock her cats up if she didn't want them killed.

She was sitting in an armchair in her sweatpants and a hoodie watching television. She didn't even look up; she was sick of his shit and his idle threats.

As he went back down to the shed, he thought about how ugly she was and what a fat slob she had turned into. No wonder he was attracted to the beautiful babes covering his walls. He had wanted some of that cocaine money to buy him a good-looking missus like that. He wondered if they should even give back the one kg at all. He could easily fuck off and leave that fat bitch behind with the kids.

He ducked into his Vic cave, feeling pretty cocky. He could live that life with a hot broad, and she'd have to have big tits.

The explosion of the gun in the small, confined space left his ears ringing for ages but it muffled the sound from outside, so it was worth it in Doug's mind.

He had been waiting for a few hours in the dark, watching and listening to this idiot from outside the walls of the shed. When Vic went up to the house, he'd left the gun out and the lights on, so Doug presumed he was coming back. Doug slipped inside the door, loaded the gun and turned the lights off to give the element of surprise. It would look like Vic had accidentally shot his own head off while testing the illegal changes he had made to the gun.

Doug shot him at point-blank range. There was a glimmer of realisation when Vic worked out what was happening as Doug stared at him with black eyes and a smile on his face as he pulled the trigger. Doug had worn forensic booties over his shoes; he had learnt that from a detective programme on TV. There was a lot of blood, so every precaution helped.

Doug was in such a good mood: two down, two more to go. He'd think of a nice gift to buy Mellissa on the way home, something sparkly.

Vic lay dead for two days before his wife and children commented on his absence. They didn't look for him or phone any of his friends. His two remaining mates from the mill had rung several times looking for him. Vic's wife told them

     MICHELLE THOMPSON

she hoped he had fucked off. It wasn't until the neighbours complained about the smell of a dead animal at the bottom of the yard that they discovered the decomposing body. She was lucky that even though they were dirt poor, she had managed to keep up the payments on his life insurance.

—

Rod was discharged from the hospital. He had regained consciousness, and it was decided that with the modifications to the house and the district nurse calling daily, he would be able to continue his rehabilitation from home. The doctors thought that being back home in familiar surroundings might jolt his brain back into some sort of normal function. He was wheelchair-bound, and he had to have his head supported, as he had no strength in his neck muscles to keep his head upright. Over time, this would get better.

Stacey was happier in their own bed and their daughter needed to be back with them. It had been too long. Their daughter had become unhappy with her host family and had developed a few behavioural issues. The sooner they could get back to a normal routine the better.

Every day Stacey discovered some new addition to the property or the house. She was constantly amazed at all the things that the community had done to help them. She explained every little detail to Rod as they came to light.

The biggest shock had come when she went to the bank to make the catch-up payments on the mortgage. Someone had paid the house off completely. She didn't have to guess who. Until she saw him in person, she'd keep to the instructions he had given her, keep a low profile, and stick to the story if anyone asked.

The police eventually contacted her and seemed to easily accept her explanation of events. They wanted to close the case and move on and that suited her.

—

Phillip and Dan sat silently in Phillip's bedroom, staring at the one-kilo block of cocaine. They had it out just sitting on the bed. They had just left Vic's funeral, and they were under no illusions that both Gill and Vic had met the same ending at the hands of the bikie called Doug.

Phil and Dan, the youngest of the four, were in their early twenties. Phil had been left in charge of holding on to the cocaine as he had a small safe fitted onto his wardrobe shelf. He lived with his parents in a nice part of town and the house had a security alarm. It seemed a logical decision and his parents were Baptist ministers, so he'd be the last person you'd expect to have a kilo of cocaine in the cupboard.

Dan had gone to school with Phil and had been working at a car yard when Phil told him about the job at the mill. They both applied and got a seasonal contract clearing up rubbish and bark scraps from around the yard and selling them for mulch. They didn't mind the work, and they really enjoyed the fooling around and the after-hours pub activity with the older men. Vic's porno collection had been a total rite of passage. The older men had shouted them their first prostitutes, so they experienced sex for the first time with a woman who knew what she was doing. They were experiencing life for the first time, and they felt grown up.

The Spaniel was a real hard case, but mostly because they could take the piss out of him all the time. He always got the English words wrong, and they cracked up laughing every time.

Now, their contract at the mill had wound up at the same time as the others were made redundant and they were both still out of work. Phil was lucky his parents could support him financially, but Dan's parents were in the process of throwing him out so he could bludge off the government and not them.

What to do now was the big dilemma. Did they go to the police and tell them the whole story? They had no faith that the police could protect them. But the other option was that they would probably be hunted down like animals and slaughtered by Doug, one by one.

Did they drive past the bikie clubrooms and throw the block of cocaine out the window, or could they just post it to them?

They decided to write Doug a letter, tell him the whole story making sure they pointed out that they hadn't wanted to kill Rod, but the others had decided that part. They would leave out their names, of course, and post back the cocaine with the letter.

According to the paper, Doug owned a tattoo parlour up in Kings Cross. They changed their minds and decided they wouldn't risk posting the parcel in case a drug dog sniffed it out in transit. Instead, Phil would go in heavily disguised and hand it over the counter. They would mark the parcel 'Private

　　　MICHELLE THOMPSON

and Confidential' and write DOUG in big letters all over it. Then Phil would run like fuck to where Dan was waiting in a car around the corner. It all sounded good, and they decided to start watching the tattoo parlour for a few days before the drop, walk the route, and make sure the car was parked in a suitable position so that it wouldn't get stuck in traffic if they were chased and had limited time to drive off.

They never factored into the plan that if Doug had murdered Gill and Vic, then Doug probably knew their names and where they lived.

A week later, Doug watched from the cameras in the office out the back of the tattoo parlour as the parcel was delivered by a scrawny kid. He'd had people keeping track of them every day for the last two weeks, watching them walk past the parlour, even coming in and asking about getting a tattoo. Today was obviously the day they made the drop. He wasn't too sure just how they were going to do it, but he knew it would be amusing, nonetheless.

He had to laugh at the amateurish execution of the delivery. Doug had purposely picked the staff he had working during the two weeks leading up to the drop. He had to have men he could trust.

In normal circumstances, one of them would have leapt over the counter, grabbed the scrawny little runt by the neck and held him until Doug arrived. They would have put the word out immediately, pulled the other little shit out of the car and dragged him back as well. But this way, Doug wanted them to think they had got away with it, for now at least. The drop went smoothly, and he was even more pleased to discover that the one kg hadn't been tampered with.

Dan

Dan had met the love of his life at their local watering hole. She was everything that you didn't tell your mother. She looked like the ladies on Vic's walls, and she knew a few tricks like those ladies as well. She was living in a nice apartment in the city, and she had a job on a tourist boat operating out of Sydney Harbour that took people out on dolphin and whale watching trips. She said she could get him work on board the boat. It wouldn't be a flash hostess job like she had, but the pay was good and if he could prove he was a grafter, they might give him a full-time position. She suggested he shift in with her, that way he could get his parents off his back. He had to pinch himself; since they had handed back the cocaine, he felt like he could live again; things were finally looking up.

His first week on the boat was a disaster. He was really seasick and was fearful he would lose his job and lose his new girlfriend. He looked like such a drip lying below deck in all the fumes out of sight of the paying clients, but the staff seemed to understand and largely he was left alone. They kept telling him he would gain his sea legs soon.

Every night his new girlfriend was so caring and considerate. She'd cook him dinner and they would go to bed early and have lots of sex. He was sure his parents never started like this.

The crew kept telling him that the owner of the company was going to call by and introduce himself any day now. He had a policy of meeting his new staff in person to find out their interests and see where they could fit into his company. They spoke highly about him, wouldn't work for anyone else, and the staff Christmas parties were legendary.

Halfway into the next week, there was a buzz about the boat. The owner was coming to inspect the boat and during that process, he'd be introduced to Dan. They were all told to bring some swimming gear; they were going to have a staff outing as a reward for good work.

Doug was waiting at the dock in the morning when the crew got there. He was a formidable form standing next to the huge catamaran. All the crew embraced him when they approached him, and he helped everyone onto the boat. The mood was cheerful and full of laughter and excitement.

He had brought his wife along; she was a beautiful, friendly woman and she knew all the staff names, and in some cases, their parents.

Dan's knees nearly gave way as his girlfriend dragged him along the dock towards Doug. He thought he was virtually going to shit his pants.

He had no doubt at all who this guy was, standing next to a shiny big Harley-Davidson. His instinct was to run in the other direction. Doug had a big smile on his face and his big paw was extended. He shook Dan's hand and nearly lifted him off the ground. He slapped him on the back and welcomed him into the company. He introduced his wife Mellissa and insisted Dan call them by their first names from now on as he was now part of the company family.

Dan had never put two and two together, never considered that the owner of the boat was the same person. He would have thought a detail like that someone would have mentioned, or was he just being paranoid?

Dan couldn't believe his luck; this guy didn't know who he was. Here he was suggesting he come to the staff Christmas party and asking him how he was finding working on the boat. Doug had heard he had been seasick, so he had some suggestions for dealing with that. Dan never detected any recognition on Doug's behalf.

Dan relaxed a bit more as everyone settled down; Doug and Mellissa had had hot ham and cheese croissants delivered. They all shared the food and laughed and joked and they all seemed to know each other well.

He tried not to stare at Doug's face; it was a mess. How had he got such a good-looking wife? She was gorgeous. Dan couldn't get over the size of the man's hands and he was tall and had big arms like he lifted weights or something.

Dan's girlfriend had got off the boat with Mellissa – they didn't like swimming or fishing. They were jumping into a taxi off on a shopping trip, and they would meet up later when the boat came back. A couple more of the crew got off. They had a commercial charter to run on the other boat, so they weren't needed today on this boat. Dan didn't recognise some of the crew today, but they all seemed to know each other. It was a big company, so he figured they probably came from another boat. Doug wanted to have a staff fishing trip to welcome the new guy.

As they headed way out to sea Dan became seasick again and was forced to apologise to Doug for his poor form.

"Why don't you go below? Lie down on one of the swabs in the galley," suggested Doug

Doug provided him with a blanket. "I find it's best to try and sleep and keep my head down to avoid vomiting. I'll wake you when we reach their destination," Doug assured him.

Dan didn't argue; he knew that lying down was the best way to avoid throwing up.

It seemed like they had travelled for a long time when Dan was woken up by Doug and told they had reached the place they were heading for. He sat up and looked out the windows of the galley – where had the land gone? He couldn't see anything on the horizon: no boats, no land, no seagulls – he didn't think he had ever been this far out to sea before.

The crew already had rods overboard and burly bombs in the water to attract baitfish. Someone was strapped into the game chair in case they got a strike. Dan wished he wasn't so ill; this looked like it would be fun. The boat was trawling at a slow idle.

Dan tried to act like he knew what he was doing and wearily hung on to the edge of the boat to stabilise himself, wishing he could go back to the swabs and lie down again. All he wanted to do was throw up. Dan tried to put some enthusiasm into his voice and asked what sort of bait they were using, which was met with loud raucous laughter from the crew. They were all staring at him with big smiles on their faces.

He didn't see Doug behind him with two giant stainless-steel hooks attached to steel traces. He felt the heat in his back but didn't register the pain as Doug drove both hooks deep into his back and with no effort at all picked Dan up and propelled him overboard. Dan suddenly found himself flying through the air into the cold choppy water, blood streaming down his back. He was a poor swimmer but that didn't matter, he was being dragged backwards behind the boat, his screams drowned out by the noise of the boat's big engines, the noise of the sea and the raucous laughter he could hear over the surge of the engines as the boat crested the swells.

It was then that he saw the big shark fin ripping through the water towards him. The white pointer showed no mercy as it tore at his flesh, then released him to get a better bite. Dan wished he could die sooner but he was alive in almost a surreal moment watching the shark and now a second shark fighting over his limbs and torso.

Doug was in such a good mood he couldn't wait to get back to port and take Mellissa to dinner.

Stacey

The last of the glasshouses had finally reached the final sign-off stage and Doug was impatient for the building inspector to arrive and extract more money from him so they could close the deal. He had every piece of the puzzle ready to action so they could start full production growing the peppers and hopefully get his first crop to market.

Doug had hired Stacey as the manager of the capsicum hothouses. She had turned out to be a most valued and loyal employee and he felt confident enough in her ability to let her have the freedom to implement any initiatives and changes without consulting him daily.

She ran a tight ship and for every shift, she was on-site to present start-up and production meetings. She fostered succession planning and made sure every staff member knew what the production bottom line was. They worked together as a team to deliver yield on time and to projected numbers. He paid her well, and the position came with a company car which she never abused. Doug often told her to take more liberties, but she wouldn't.

Stacey didn't seem scared of him and even joked with him at times. She wasn't afraid to tackle him about things that she felt strongly about changing. They always conversed in Spanish when they had employment issues to discuss, to secure confidentiality. She never brought up the past, but she did emotionally tell him once that she was so grateful for his help that she would take a bullet for him, and she considered him family. He joked with her about that one and told her that was a high possibility all things considered, and for a laugh, he bought her a Kevlar vest. She was the only female outside his wife and family that he liked, and he felt comfortable in her company.

Rod was still a long way off from being fully recovered so the logical decision was that Stacey become the breadwinner and Rod stay at home and manage the household and their daughter's schooling. Doug had other plans for his future if he ever recovered fully.

The dam that Doug had originally started as a small reservoir to irrigate both farms had turned into a huge man-made lake, requiring months of heavy machinery to shift tons of soil day and night. Doug had utilised a steep valley, which had little farming potential, and had virtually blocked one end to create a lake. He built up an area at one end for social activities, including a pétanque court constructed to international competition standards and size. He also extensively planted out the areas that weren't used, to attract birds and stabilise the sides. Besides its practical use, it looked beautiful, and guests often commented on its features. It was also fully wired and had underground lighting and electrical outlet points for bands.

The lake was big enough to irrigate both properties and the glasshouses. Doug joked that if they ever had a fire, they wouldn't have to worry about having enough water to put it out.

Phil

Phil had purposely distanced himself from Dan. He was glad it was over, and he could put the whole ugly situation behind him. His father had some contacts up in Darwin and he had a job opportunity which paid well and would get him as far away from the bikie called Doug as possible.

Dan had texted a few times inviting him to the city to meet his new flash girlfriend; Phil always found an excuse to avoid the trip and the connection.

A couple of weeks passed, and Dan texted to say he wanted to meet him at their local pub where he and the old crew hung out after the mill for a few drinks. Phil agreed; it would be a good opportunity to say goodbye properly and make sure Dan had no ideas about following him.

Phil arrived and searched the bar for Dan. Typical; he was running late.

The barman called out to him. "Mate, it's your lucky day. A pretty lady left two hundred dollars on a bar tab for you. Said to apologise that Dan was running late from a fishing trip."

Phil thought Dan must be doing well in his new job; $200 was a lot of shots, which was going to get him well drunk. He'd get a head start on Dan and drink all his money before he got here – big flash job in town; he could afford it.

He could sleep in tomorrow. It was Sunday and his parents would spend the better half of the day at church. In fact, Sundays were his favourite day. No subliminal mind games to pressure him to get out of bed or conform to the house rules.

A couple of hours passed and still no Dan. He wasn't responding to texts, so Phil guessed he must be stuck in traffic. The time was passing quickly, and Phil had already drunk $180 worth of shots and was busy making a nuisance of himself to an elderly couple at the next table. He was determined to drink the full $200 just to piss Dan off for being late. He started to mix his drinks which was making his head swim, but he wasn't the sort of guy who would have a spew; he'd just catch a taxi home and crash out. His mother always left the back door open when he went out for the night drinking – that way he could slip back in under the radar and avoid a lecture from his father.

Another half hour passed, and the barman hinted that perhaps it was time for that taxi, so Phil drunkenly agreed with some joviality that he would listen to the barman's wise words and let the staff order him a taxi and give the driver directions to Phil's parents' house.

Phil swayed in the fresh air after the taxi dropped him off outside the neighbour's house, so his father wouldn't see the taxi pull up or, worse still, watch Phil negotiate the path in his drunken state through the back gate.

Phil braced himself against the back gate while he urinated on his mother's garden. He really was drunk this time – just fumbling with his trouser fly was a mission. The sooner he crashed on that bed the better. He left his pants open so it would be easier to kick them off when he reached his room, and anyway, he was far too drunk to attempt to do them up again.

Phil felt like he was being super quiet as he let himself in. He had a couple of rhythmic bounces off the hall walls on the way to his bedroom. He could just make out the noise from the TV in the lounge that his parents were still watching. He'd better retreat to his room before his father gave him another boring lecture about wasting his money and his life.

It was times like this that he wished they had succeeded in pulling off that cocaine haul. He'd be able to slap that in his dad's face if he was rolling in money; it wouldn't matter what he spent his money on! Whether he worked or not. He'd be able to afford any car he wanted; hell, he could have his own house and not put up with the bible-bashing shit that came with the rules of this house.

Phil was asleep before his head hit the pillow. He was never consciously aware that he had been bitten. A two-metre adult eastern brown snake had found its way into his bed. Within a few minutes, his body had gone into acute deterioration, paralysis and cardiac arrest.

His parents didn't discover the body until 3 pm the following day when they returned from their parish activities and their normal Sunday routine.

They were extremely fortunate not to get bitten themselves. Phil's mother had called and called him with no response then she had gone into the room to shake him from what she presumed was a drunken stupor. It wasn't till she pulled the covers back that the huge brown monster reared its head to strike at her. She screamed and ran from the room, slamming the door behind her. She knew instinctively that her son was dead.

It was several hours before the police and emergency services located a man from animal control to come out on a Sunday and remove the snake and check for any other snakes, so they could remove the body.

The police and animal control presumed that the snake had found its way in from outside, as one of the catches on the bedroom window next to the bed was broken and, as Phil never made his bed, it was the most likely place for the snake to find a nice warm place to sleep.

The guy from animal control was extremely impressed by the size of the snake. He commented on the fact that it was possibly the largest brown he'd seen in suburbia for a while.

The Police Raid

Doug and Mellissa heard the choppers before they saw the police cars speeding up the driveway with their sirens blaring. Doug activated the fire alarm in three short bursts, which was the pre-planned signal to all staff that they were about to be raided by the Australian Federal Police: in this case, the Drug Squad. It was 10 am.

Each site manager was well-rehearsed in the drill of what action to take in this situation. In an orderly fashion, each staff member grabbed their ID and in a single file, quiet procession, made their way to the picnic evacuation area at the side of the lake.

Canteen staff had orders to transfer snack food and refreshments by golf carts to the entertainment area to give to the staff while they waited for the laborious process to run its course.

Mellissa stayed at the house with her mother, the twins and the nanny. She had already rung their lawyer.

Mellissa and Doug's fathers locked up the family dogs, so they were safe. It was their experience that police sometimes shot the dogs when they started to lose control of the situation, and dogs could be a little unpredictable when there was a lot of unusual activity around. They then made their way to the picnic area to entertain the staff.

All the staff on-site were inducted by Doug through his gang contacts and were very familiar with police procedures. They were calm and relaxed and looking forward to possibly having the rest of the day off. They were all streetwise.

Doug waited in the courtyard to greet the overzealous police sergeant in charge of the operation.

Stacey collected all the IDs and ticked the names off on the roll call, while all the staff made themselves comfortable and watched with interest.

The police sergeant looked like he was about to burst a valve. He was extremely excited and was ordering his men and the drug dogs in every direction, as he slapped a search warrant in Doug's hands with a smug grin on his face.

He looked like he had already banked his promotion. He had waited his whole career to take down someone this hated by the NSW police force, and with such a big reputation in the organised crime network.

Doug remained calm; he knew he had the upper hand here.

"How can I help you, Officer Dibble?"

Doug used a smart name referenced from a cartoon character he'd watched as a child. The police sergeant had no sense of humour and gritted his teeth. Doug really got under his skin.

"What? Police life got boring, so you decided to spend a day in the country?"

"We have intel to suggest that a very large amount of cocaine has made its way into the country and that your organisation has something to do with it. This warrant is for us to search the property, starting with the water reservoirs under your glass houses."

And, as if by magic, several police divers appeared from a van ready to investigate the water tanks. Doug didn't bother to tell him they had only proceeded with one tank in the end and, so far, it was still empty.

"Police drug dogs will also search the grounds and the buildings for any traces of narcotics or illegal weapons."

"Help yourself," said Doug. "All I ask is that you don't scare my two small boys who are in the house with my wife and mother-in-law; they are only four going on five, and this is their first police raid. They're a bit out of control at the best of times. Perhaps you could send some female police officers inside to carry out that search. I would appreciate that.

"And can my wife be excused, if you're still here at 2.30 pm, to collect my daughter from school? I'm happy for a police officer to accompany her if that's what it takes. I pick her up every day to be safe because you guys are so busy chasing dreams that you're leaving paedophiles free to prey on the community."

The police sergeant wanted to spit in his face. How dare he act like nothing was wrong – this was a strong lead. He was determined that Doug was going to pay today. If it was legal, or he thought he would get away with it, he wanted to punch Doug in the face. Not that it would affect him. Doug was a full foot and a bit taller than him and his face looked like it had had a battle with a concrete brick.

He thought wisely about the effect on the children – they couldn't help it that their father was bikie scum. He ordered the female officers inside along with one dog handler, who had children at home, so the dog was accustomed to a family setting. Anyway, it would look good in the papers tonight that the police protected the welfare of the children.

The sergeant started shouting orders and talking on the radio. He had a roadblock set up down the road to try and delay the lawyers. He had a small window of opportunity to find what he was looking for before the lawyers got there and found some loophole to close the operation down.

Mellissa looked out the window at her husband and felt a sense of pride at the way he conducted himself in these situations. How calm he was; how he thought everything out clearly almost instantly; and to see his huge stature towering over the police sergeant – she couldn't be more in love with him at this moment. He caught her glance and waved with a huge smile on his face. She knew she could relax now.

The two policewomen and the dog handler were thorough and polite. Mellissa and Doug kept a clean house so there was no chance of finding any drugs in the house. The twins had already started trying to hang off the police officers' legs. The two female officers found them delightful but did comment that they were a bit of a handful and full of life. Like everyone, they didn't know how Doug and Mellissa could tell them apart, they were virtually identical. They declared the house was clear to the sergeant and they were ordered to start on the staff facilities and the glasshouses with the others.

Stacey joined Doug at the glasshouses. She could tell Doug was enjoying this, it was a game to him. She had to suppress a laugh when she saw all the wetsuits and the dive gear. She remained silent. She gave Doug the bag with all the IDs and the roll call list for the thirty staff that were on-site today. Doug winked at her as he took the bag.

"Find out how far away the lawyer is, will you please, Stacey? Thanks. And wave that Channel Nine News chopper down onto the front paddock. May as well let them see up close what a fuck-up this is; let them see how the police waste taxpayer's money."

The Senior Sergeant had arrived now; he was an old adversary of Doug's. He'd also turned up hoping to settle some old scores himself, put this bastard behind bars once and for all.

Doug had been expecting the raid for a while now. That much cocaine coming into the country – tongues would waggle, the rumour mill would be in overdrive with everyone wondering who ended up with it. Whichever gang ended up with it was then in the prime position to control the drug trade in Australia. In this game, you not only had to contend with other rival gangs that you were at war with, jealous that they didn't get there first, but you had pillow talk and domestic revenge, and someone was always out to throw you under the bus, so to speak. People heard bits about the missing one kilo, then that story got exaggerated and you end up here, with a massive police operation. Doug wasn't worried, in fact, he was enjoying the break in routine.

The police had been on the property now for four hours and still had not uncovered any drugs or weapons. They had taken great delight in pulling everything apart and leaving a mess everywhere, not bothering if they broke anything, leaving ceiling tiles pulled down and discarded on the floor. It would be a hell of a mess to clean up after they had gone. Doug would have to pay overtime. Then there was the loss in production. He made sure the TV cameras captured the mess.

The police were convinced that the drugs were in the water reservoir under the greenhouse. They couldn't hide their disappointment; not only that the tank was empty of water, but also the lack of drugs.

The congregation of workers had now restlessly progressed into a full-on party. The police dog handlers had done a couple of circuits of the picnic area and declared it clean.

The TV crew was having a field day. Doug had them feeling sorry for him now, claimed the police were still hounding him after all these years; persecution they were calling it.

The most serious charge of the day was one staff vehicle had an expired roadworthiness certificate.

The lawyers arrived and put an end to the interviewing of all the staff and the search of the property came to a complete standstill.

The police gave an interview to the press, stating they had a strong lead and had been following the gang for weeks now and were convinced the drugs were on the property, but today's search was unsuccessful.

Likewise, Doug referred to the search for drugs on his property in comparison to finding Saddam Hussein's bombs in the desert. "This was a non-event thought up by a frustrated Senior Sergeant looking for promotion or retirement." He went on to add, "I operate a legitimate enterprise providing

   MICHELLE THOMPSON

work and internships for staff who were previously long-term unemployed. I have taken many of these workers off the street."

"Mr Henderson has also supported the community with a percentage of the finances from the glasshouses to improve the school facilities and many other community projects," added Stacey.

The front page of the *Sydney Morning Herald* showed Doug as a leading community figure trying to make a straight living but still being harassed by the police. There were photos of the police in full dive gear and jokes about them having no water to swim in.

Business As Usual

Life returned to normal after the clean-up. The twins couldn't wait to tell Edith all about it, and about the police dogs. Edith was upset that everyone had had fun without her and spent the rest of the evening glued to her father. She was a real daddy's girl, and her delicate little hand was always engulfed by her father's big paw. She was now seven years old and was a girly girl and, just like her mother at her age, she had numerous pets; a horse, cats and dogs. She had her father wrapped around her little finger and he virtually accommodated her every wish. She was going to be tall. She'd inherited her father's height, and he could only thank God that she hadn't inherited his bad skin.

The twins were a month off turning five years old and about to start school full-time. They were bright for their age, spoke well and could hold an enjoyable conversation. They were constantly up to mischief, playing games, riding their pushbikes around the farm and being cheeky to staff. They were completely identical and at times even Mellissa and Doug had to take a second look. They always had their grandparents on, and the staff just didn't stand a chance. They were close and had an uncanny way of communicating with each other and, although they had their own beds in the same room, every night they would sneak into one bed together.

Doug and Mellissa had decided not to have any more children – they were happy with three. They had decided that spending time together as a couple doing things they enjoyed was something they thought was important and had missed. Often Doug broke out into a cold sweat just contemplating a life without Mellissa, and he'd have to fight his demons to snap out of it.

Doug was comfortable leaving the farm managers to operate their own departments independently and Stacey had the overall authority to authorise payments and make crucial decisions in Doug's absence.

Doug and Mellissa's parents were Doug's next concern. They weren't getting any younger, although they looked like they could live to a hundred and were living together in Mellissa's parents' old homestead across the paddock. They were all very happy and not complaining, but their residence was far too large for three older generation people and the time had come for that residence to be refurbished and modernised. It would become accommodation for one of Doug's farm managers who had a big family and who, coincidentally, was his sergeant-of-arms in his club. And, as Doug pointed out, the parents spent more time on his side of the fence pottering around the glasshouses and Doug and Mellissa's family home.

So, it was decided that Doug would have some modern units built near the main house. Close enough that they could be on hand to look after the children if Doug and Mellissa went out for the night.

Doug wished he had never mentioned it, as the parents had strong ideas of their own and had a list of their requirements. They argued every step of the way over proposed wheelchair access and long-term health concerns, which they were sure they were never going to need. They were going to live to a right old age; no need for wheelchairs or walking frames.

It was their idea to have an extension to the main household, so the new addition wrapped around the other side of the swimming pool on the same level, with views of the pool and the courtyard. Their rationale was they could be connected to the main house, so the grandchildren had access if they needed, and they were close for childminding purposes. They also had the option of socialising in the main house – primarily at the bar. They wanted their own rooms with en suite in each room and all modern appliances, plus a separate lounge just for them, for when and if they did want to get away from the grandchildren. Doug almost got shot for suggesting an extra room for a full-time nurse when it was time. The outcome was that Doug left it up to them and directed the architect to deal with them directly, so at least he dodged the arguments.

Construction on both sites would begin almost immediately, starting with the old farmhouse, but they would wait till the twins started school in a month before they started on the extension.

And for once, there was no argument at the suggestion that all the grandparents go away on holiday together overseas on a river cruise through Europe, while the main building and construction were in progress.

Stacey

It was 3 am when Doug and his sergeant-at-arms rode home. It had been a rare club night for Doug; he'd needed to let his hair down and Mellissa could tell the signs, so she virtually ordered him off to town. As he and his sergeant-at-arms got their big bikes out of the shed and roared into town together earlier that evening, he knew she was right. He had missed the other personality that came with what he called his other life.

They rode at high speed out of the country and into the city picking up another couple of boys on the way, making for maximum noise on their big Harley-Davidsons as they arrived at their destination just before nightfall.

As the night wore on, he had to admit he was really enjoying himself. He had consumed a vast amount of cocaine, and the night was humming. It was just one of those evenings where everyone was in high spirits and full of laughter and entertainment. He actually had a sore gut from laughing. He caught up with some old friends and decided he had to get out more often.

They had the harvest for a big shipment of tomatoes looming back at the farm in a few hours, so they decided to head home.

In the dark, they came across Stacey's vehicle, parked on the side of the road leading to the farm. Doug knew instantly something was wrong. They pulled up alongside. She was already out of the vehicle and had been waiting for the sound of the bikes in the dark.

Stacey was wearing a big thick trench coat which was unusual for that time of year. Doug could smell fresh blood on her – that distinctive metallic odour. The trench coat was covering her clothing beneath, and he could see from the blood splatters on her face and her neckline that her clothing was absolutely soaked in blood. In the light from the bikes, he could dimly make out bruising to her face.

She had known not to ring him in case the call was traced so she decided to wait for him in the dark on the side of the road. That was one of the things he liked about her, she was always thinking ahead.

Quite calmly and without any emotion, she told Doug and her co-worker the story.

   MICHELLE THOMPSON

When she was on her way home from work that day Rod had rung her and told her Alfredo, his brother-in-law, had arrived in a taxi and was asking questions that Rod wasn't able to answer. Not that he was trying to hide anything, but purely due to his loss of memory from his near-death experience. Alfredo had arrived without notice from Ecuador looking for his share of the drugs.

"He wouldn't accept that the drugs had been stolen and that Rod nearly lost his life as a result. Alfredo could see all the home improvements, the new fencing and the vehicles and decided that we were lying to him; he became violent. He said he was desperate and that he had nearly lost his life to a drug cartel and had no choice now but to set up a life in Australia because he couldn't go back to South America without being killed. He started arguing with Rod and when Rod couldn't answer the questions, he beat him about the head until he was unconscious. He wouldn't stop. He kept beating and kicking Rod on the ground and stomped on his head."

Stacey had suspected that his visit wasn't going to bode well, and thank God, had arranged for their daughter to stay over at a friend's house. She told the mother that Rod had had a relapse after a change to his medication.

When Stacey jumped on Alfredo's back in an attempt to rescue Rod, he had punched her repeatedly in the face and side of the head until she fell to the ground dizzy, almost losing consciousness herself. He then pounced on her from behind and started to strangle her while forcing her onto her knees and trying to rip her pants down in what, she thought, must have been an attempt to rape her.

She fought for her life and found some inner strength and used all her force to throw herself backwards. She managed to unbalance him and clawed her way to the kitchen table with him pulling at her leg.

She'd managed to grab a knife from the table that had been set out for dinner and stabbed him in the eye first. He just didn't seem to die or slow down like they do in the movies. She had to stab him several times in the neck and the mouth. She'd just kept stabbing him blindly until she was sure he was dead.

She hadn't been able to think much past that point. She had managed to drag and lift Rod's unconscious and battered body to their bed, put him in the recovery position and cover him in blankets in case he went into shock.

She had covered Alfredo's body with a shower curtain just in case someone happened to look in the window and see the bloody form lying on the floor.

"I remembered you and Brian had gone out for the night, so I decided to wait on the road until I heard the bikes returning."

Doug was assessing the situation while she told the story; he would have to contain this, and quickly. Luckily for her, he had the experience and the network to pull it off. They decided to follow her back to her house.

When they walked in the front door Doug let out a big breath of air through his lips. What a fuckin nightmare. Blood looked to be splattered on every surface of the room and the ceiling hadn't escaped either. It looked like someone had murdered a cow. He sure had bled a lot.

Doug checked Alfredo's body for a pulse, which was pointless – Stacey had virtually severed his head from his shoulders.

"Fuck, Stacey, I've just redecorated the joint. If I'd known that you wanted a 'Jackson Pollock' paint job I could have saved you the trouble," Doug joked to lighten the mood, his big grin putting her at ease.

Brian had checked on Rod and declared that he was in a bad way and was going to need a hospital sooner rather than later.

Doug gave out a couple of orders.

"Stacey, have a shower and get cleaned up. Put your bloodied clothes in a pile on the floor, put fresh clothes on and take Rod to the hospital. You're going to have to tell the hospital that, due to his brain injury, he has been periodically experiencing more severe bouts of pain and this time he lashed out at you, and you had to have a terrible physical fight with him to contain his episode. That'll explain your own injuries. Say you were ashamed, so you didn't tell anyone that it's been going on for a while. Blame the medication.

"Brian and I will take the bikes home and come back with a wagon and some tarpaulins."

They had contacts in a pet food company and Alfredo would make a pleasant change to someone's weekly dog food menu.

Doug would make a few phone calls and get a crew down here to shift everything out of the rooms not affected by the carnage in the lounge and kitchen into a container.

They had no choice but to burn the house to the ground. Doug would make sure it looked like an electrical fault. He'd have to build Stacey a new house.

Stacey didn't complain or even comment. She was exhausted and just wanted the night to be over. She looked like she was about to burst into tears – her lip quivered as she thanked him. He gave her a bear hug and patted her back. Then ordered her to get her fuckin shit together. They both laughed.

He decided then to get Mellissa to run them to the hospital and stay with them to field any tricky questions. He reminded her to only talk to Rod in Spanish.

Doug asked for the keys to Stacey's vehicle. He'd have to burn the car in the garage connected to the house in case it had any traces of blood in it, which it was bound to have.

By the time Doug got back with a black zip-up body bag for Alfredo, Stacey was all cleaned up and didn't look too bad. She was going to have a black eye, but with all the blood cleaned off her, she'd scrubbed up better than he thought she would.

Brian stayed behind at the farm to see to the shipment that was due out that morning from the glasshouses. He would tell everyone Stacey's husband was sick and cover for her shift keeping a lid on the talk as some of them would already know Doug had an operation in progress.

A crew of Doug's boys were only minutes away with a truck and a container. It was already beginning to get light, and they might have to wait till it was dark again to start the fire. No use risking some local seeing the smoke and calling the fire brigade.

Mellissa had brought blankets and sheets to cover the back seat of the car. They lay Rod down and buckled him down flat – no use him taking another tumble on the first corner. Rod had been doing so well; this would really set him back again.

Doug gave Stacey strict orders to stay overnight the next night at the hospital. If they forced a discharge, she was to catch a taxi to a hotel and stay there until Mellissa came and got her. Everyone had to play their part for this to work properly.

—

Months passed and Xenith Homes was well underway building Stacey and Rod's new home. Doug had originally let her choose the building company, but she'd gone for a budget home, and he wanted her to have quality, so he encouraged her to look at better options and the home they were now building was beautiful. He'd also bought her a new Holden Colorado for her work vehicle.

Meanwhile, they were living in a trailer home on the property, so Rod was on hand to manage the daily activities on the build. Doug had paid for an elite private school for their daughter in the city and she was able to come home on weekends.

Rod had a series of operations to remove a blood clot from his brain, and it seemed that all this time this might have been the problem with his recovery, as his health improved remarkably after the operations.

Stacey and Doug had told Rod that his ex-brother-in-law had run off into the night, in fear of being arrested for the attack and for burning down their house.

Rod also believed later that Doug had tried to track him down and had checked the airline records and confirmed Alfredo had flown back to Chile on a LAN Chile flight.

Rod was embarrassed that his brother-in-law had caused so much trouble and was grateful for the support Doug and his family had given them.

   MICHELLE THOMPSON

The Surprise

When the house was nearly finished and daily life had returned to normal, Doug had one more surprise for Stacey and Rod. "After all the rotten things that have happened to you," he said, "this is really going to blow you away. It's a combined effort from everyone to thank Stacey for all the support she's given, not just to my family, but to the workers too. We all respect you and we want to show it."

It took a bit of organising, but he wanted to make it memorable. He asked them to keep the day free, which happened to be timed for Rod's birthday.

Stacey kept trying to find out what was happening, but no one would tell her. Her work colleague, Brian, had her on and kept hiding the knives from her at lunch in case she stabbed him for keeping a secret.

She had earnt a lot of respect from the boys for her actions and sheer toughness on that night.

So, the day of Rod's birthday came, and Doug and Mellissa picked them up from their trailer home. They drove towards the city, and all the time Doug was having them on about the restaurant they were going to have lunch in.

When they pulled up at the entrance to Balmain Marina they were still confused and thought this must be where the lunch was going to be. As they got closer to the dock, they could see lots of bikes lining both sides of the road and Stacey recognised some of the boys from her work. Everyone was clapping and cheering them on as they drove down to the jetty.

A huge tarpaulin screen was erected at the beginning of the gangway. Doug made a speech and handed Stacey a bottle of champagne. When the tarpaulin screen was dropped, there, tied up to the floating jetty, beautifully restored, was their old yacht *Stacey's Escape*. Everything had either been replaced with new or given new life. Rigging, bow rails, new sails and all new electronic equipment. Freshly painted and varnished, it looked virtually brand new. The whole interior had been freshened up and the squabs re-upholstered.

Rod hadn't even thought about the yacht since that night. Rod's memory of the journey was lost forever; it just hadn't crossed his mind to think about his yacht. Rod and Stacey just stood there with their mouths open in shocked disbelief, tears running down their faces. This was the best surprise they could ever imagine.

Stacey had thought of the yacht briefly on the odd occasion, more so when she read the obituaries in the paper. But she was so angry, she hadn't pursued it.

Doug handed Rod another bottle of champagne to break across the yacht's bow. "She's ship-shape, mate, and able to make long international voyages again. And when you're feeling better, maybe you could teach the boys to sail."

They all made their way back to the restaurant that Doug and Mellissa had found on a previous visit. Doug had hired out the second floor for Rod's birthday celebration.

The Cocaine

The afternoon of the day that Doug and Mellissa had found the yacht empty, then discovered it had a spelling mistake in the name, they had sat around the bar with their parents discussing the events of the day and the strange messages from the mystery lady leading up to that day, going over every angle for hours.

It was Mellissa's father who came up with the idea that the real yacht probably wasn't too far away. He sensed that this was a job by amateurs who were possibly in a hurry and didn't want to get caught towing a boatload of cocaine, in the dark, around the harbour, which would have been suspicious on its own. He suggested that Doug hurriedly get some of his crew together and start looking for the original yacht, and more so, its contents, and if he found it, swap it with the fake yacht and trick them at their own game.

Doug immediately swung into action that same night and in less than an hour he had got his top six club members together to help him; the only ones he could trust with his life and a secret this big.

After he briefed them, they split up into groups of two, on smaller motorboats, and began searching the surrounding boats at anchor and neighbouring marinas. They did not attempt to ring each other while the search was on, opting instead for a timed rendezvous to meet and talk, just in case the police were involved, and this was a huge set-up.

They hit the jackpot – the old man had been right on the money.

Doug was first to climb aboard, armed with a handgun in case they had put someone on watch on the yacht. Once on board, he shone a flashlight into the boat to confirm it was the right boat and that the contents he was expecting were still there. They couldn't wipe the smiles off their faces until they saw the soles of a pair of white wrinkled feet sticking out from under a pile of plastic-wrapped bricks.

Doug knew instantly who it was going to be.

At first, he thought Rod was dead, but he thought he felt a pulse in his armpit though he was ice cold to touch. He was as light as a feather as Doug scooped him up and removed his clothes in case they had traces of cocaine on them.

Although it was risky, he washed Rod's body in the sea then they had no choice but to place his emaciated body on the edge of the boat ramp.

There was a private function upstairs at the boat club so sooner or later someone was going to find him, dead or alive. Doug was true to his word about returning the body to the wife. Doug would drive by later and if he was still there, he would make a 000 call to the paramedics if he had to.

They then went about swapping the yacht with the fake one and put the cover back over the top, the way they had found it. In the dark, you wouldn't be able to tell the difference.

It took all night to unload the original yacht into several shipping containers. They used the shipping yards where they did the maintenance on their own commercial tourist boats. From this point, they simply covered up the original *Stacey's Dream* until Doug decided what he was going to do with it.

It wasn't unusual for a shipping container to be delivered to the farm, given all the construction that was in progress at the time and the deliveries of tomatoes to supermarkets they supplied. The trick was positioning the container into the hillside and deep enough on the edge of the man-made lake, as well as shifting tons of dirt on and around it so it couldn't be detected by the naked eye, metal detectors or drug dogs. Doug had planned a picnic and entertainment area for this part of the complex so the container wouldn't be required to support any weight from the pressure of the lake. The entry point to the container, for when it was going to be required to restock supplies for the club, was through a trap door that was accessed from under the pétanque court.

The club stood to make millions from the drugs, so it didn't matter that he spent a bit of money here and there on Stacey and her family.

Doug was sure that Stacey knew that the men from the mill who had worked with Rod and then tried to kill him, had come to a sticky end at his hands, but she never said anything or referred to the incident. Likewise, Doug was sure that Stacey had made sure Alfredo was well and truly dead so she could close off any loose ends and make sure the loop could not reopen. This was what he admired about her. There were very few people he could trust. She had turned out to be one of them.

As soon as Rod was well enough and when the time was right, Doug would encourage him to make another sea journey. In the meantime, he could start to teach his boys to sail.

Doug just hoped he wouldn't get too bored waiting for the next adventure.

PART TWO

The Hospital

Joseph stood looking through the window into the Intensive Care Unit at the bloodied mess of a body that should have resembled a human. It was hooked up to every lifesaving machine possible, each machine working with hisses and bells to sustain life. The sight was more than he could bear to see. He felt tears forming in the corners of his eyes. Intensive care registrars frantically adjusting buttons and silencing alarms, were visibly stressed. One of the bodies was termed critical; this was his mother's room.

In the next unit was another body, still alive, still breathing in time to the hissing and chiming of machines. There weren't so many people fussing over that body – Doug's body. Had it not been so shocking, Joseph was sure he'd be blubbering like a child. The doctors hadn't even had any time to reassure him, all they could say was, "We're doing what we can," not making eye contact – their faces told a different story.

Suddenly there was a multitude of alarms and nurses and doctors rushed into the first room. Mellissa had flat-lined again and a team of doctors and nurses were frantically trying to restart her heart.

What would Kane do if he was here? He'd have it under control, everything would be organised, and we'd all feel better even if the outcome was final. Kane was so much like Dad in that respect; he was the thinker; Joseph was the dreamer. Kane was the strong one, the brave one. Joseph was always happy to let Kane take the lead; there's always one dominant twin.

Joseph was only home to pay his respects to Uncle Rod who had passed away. He'd battled ill health ever since Joseph could remember. Rod and Stacey were virtually family and, as a sign of respect, they called them uncle and aunty. Joseph and Kane had played 'Rock, Paper, Scissors' to decide who would come back for the funeral. They were in the middle of a very lucrative charter with precious cargo and couldn't afford for them both to leave the boat.

Oh Christ, here comes the professional wailer – Edith. Fuck, that's all we need, her dramatics and bawling. Yes, it's bad, but crying isn't going to help anyone right now. Kane would probably say slap her and tell her to fuck up; save her tears for the funeral. He loved his sister, but she often brought a bit too much theatre to any event.

The hospital had rung the house less than an hour ago; he'd dropped everything. Stacey had taken over. She was so capable; she'd started making the phone calls to inform the people who needed to know and was trying to send a message to Kane who was somewhere on his way to the Arabian Sea. Brian had ridden with him to the hospital (bikes were faster in the heavy traffic), the stress clearly visible on Brian's face. Doug and Mellissa were his childhood friends.

It had only been two hours ago that his parents had left for their weekly ride. Couple of crazy old bastards, still madly in love, off to have some time together like they did every week. Have a spot of lunch and a drink in a nice restaurant or winery; meet up with some old friends; feel the wind in their hair. Mum looked natural on the pillion seat, arms around Dad, leaning into the corners. How could this have happened? Dad was a good rider – really experienced, perhaps a little too cautious.

There was a flurry of activity in one of the rooms. More hospital staff were suddenly pushing one of the gurneys down the hall at speed back into surgery trying to stop an internal bleed – the ICU surgeon firing orders as they ran.

Joseph thought it was special what these staff at the hospital did. It didn't matter about race, creed or colour. They didn't discriminate between bikers or priests; they were just conditioned to try to keep their patients alive no matter what. He made a mental note to tell Stacey to send the hospital staff a donation. If his parents lived, if Kane was here, he'd want to give the doctors a personal cash donation.

Doug and Mellissa and been flown in by the Westpac Emergency Helicopter. Had it not been for that service they would never have made it alive thus far; they would be dead on the side of the road somewhere. They would need to send a donation to the Emergency Helicopter Service as well.

Joseph thought he would have to remember to tell the hospital staff that his parents needed to be in the same room – they had never spent a night apart as long as he could remember. Separation would kill them faster than their injuries. He would shift them to a private hospital if necessary. He kept making mental notes – it was helping him cope.

Brian broke into his thoughts. "No police have turned up to give the family a briefing of the events, which seems odd. Perhaps they're rubbing their hands together to finally have Doug off their books."

He had a good point.

They would know it was Dad's bike, and they would normally be all over it by now. Even the six o'clock news would be on to it if Dad was involved. Shit, I know they hate him, but you'd think it was protocol to put at least a rookie on it and report in at the hospital to update the family. Something was up.

Edith was looking for people to cry on. Stacey would be here soon; she knew how to contain Edith and surely Gay Kenny would be getting her some tissues or smelling salts right now. Gay Kenny was usually always five paces behind Edith. To be fair, Edith would take it the hardest. She was so spoilt by Dad that she never left his side if she was home and, when she wasn't at home, she was living in the city managing Dad's empire. They shared secrets that no one wanted to know. She was a shrewd but emotional individual.

Joseph felt his face heat up; he was about to lose control of his emotions himself. A sudden sense of loss overwhelmed him when he thought of his mother, she loved him so much. Even now, as grown men, she liked to kiss the twins goodnight before they went to bed. No matter what trouble he and Kane got up to, she'd find no wrong in it. In their lifetime they had never gone to bed unhappy or worried, she'd made sure of that. Tonight, would be the first time in his life he would be worried and sad that he could remember. Perhaps she had spoilt them. He felt suddenly weak at the thought of something happening to her.

Christ here comes Edith again; she was like a cling-on if she got hold of you. Where the fuck was Stacey? He was battling his own emotions; he'd need to make a phone call and dodge her in the meantime.

Six hours had passed, and the doctors had finally called for a family group conference. They didn't seem to mind that the family included farm staff and a motorcycle gang.

"Both of your parents are still in critical care," the doctor began, "Only one is stable: your father. If they survived through the night, that will be a good omen, but they aren't out of the woods yet. The fear for both of them is internal infection."

The doctor said Doug had been shot twice in the chest at point-blank range. One of the bullets went through his shoulder and one flattened out as it passed through bone and cartilage, exited out his back then tore through Mellissa's neck and ripped through her spine.

"It appears that Mellissa has also been shot twice at point-blank range; one bullet to her chest and one up through the base of her neck. The third bullet was possibly the bullet that went through Doug's chest cavity and out his back," the doctor informed them.

"Mellissa's heart has stopped three times. Our fear is that the bullet to the base of her skull has caused permanent brain damage."

He informed them it was a foregone conclusion that she would be a quadriplegic. It was too soon to tell the outcome, but the family was told to prepare for the worst. The family's heads swam with the sudden amount of information to process.

The doctors and nurses looked buggered, there was nothing more they could do and say at this stage. They suggested that the family notify the next of kin in case Mellissa and Doug didn't make it through the night.

Joseph remembered to ask if his parents could be in the same room.

The head registrar replied, "I'll see what I can do once they're more stable." Once again, his face told a different story.

As an afterthought, the registrar added, "Apparently the police said the assailant was dead on arrival – took his own life."

Everyone looked at the doctor in stunned silence. Until that point the family had no details about the events that caused the injuries; the revelation of the gunshots slowly sinking in. The doctor could tell by the looks on their faces that this was news to the family.

He went on to say, "To my knowledge, from an eyewitness who had spoken to the paramedic, they'd pulled off the highway into a restaurant car park. A young man simply walked up to them pointing a pistol and started shooting at your mother. Your father jumped in the path to protect her from the gunfire, then the young man turned the pistol and shot himself fatally in the head."

The doctor was surprised that the police hadn't told them, and he couldn't hide his surprise when he was told that the police had still not met with the family.

They were still numb and processing the news that someone had shot their parents in an execution-style shooting in broad daylight in a public car park. It just didn't make sense. Doug had almost retired. These days he was very low-key and hardly left the farm.

It was going to be a long night.

     MICHELLE THOMPSON

Kane and Joseph

Kane and Joseph had always experienced a gilded life. They had parents and family who loved them. There was never a shortage of money, holidays overseas, toys and hobbies, and friends. They were very popular and could always be relied upon to be the life of the party. They were always up to no good, playing jokes on people and generally getting into mischief.

It had been expected that they work in the glasshouses from a very early age, learning all the intricacies involved in running the farm. Doug worked hard on the farm, and he expected nothing less from the twins. It didn't matter what day it was; when you woke up you got a job.

They were both very handsome fit young men and charmed their way into the hearts of everyone they met, including females, often leaving a string of broken hearts along the way.

Their father had made it very clear that they were under no circumstances to have sexual relations with current members of staff. Doug was adamant this was not a policy that he would approve of in the workplace, especially when you owned the company, and you could open yourself up to legal allegations. He had a saying, "Never dip your pen in the company ink."

When the twins were old enough to understand he had explained what sort of other business interests he was involved in and precautions that had to be taken to avoid conflicts with the law or authorities that could cause adverse publicity. Therefore, any allegations of sexual harassment would be on the radar, or worse still, criminal charges that might restrict their travel in the future.

The twins overcame this problem by convincing the unsuspecting female to leave her employment with the farm for the promise of a happy relationship and long-standing love outside the company. Everything was a game to the twins. And if they could avoid the disapproving looks from their father and the lectures from Aunty Stacey it was always a good day.

Their passion in life was sailing, and if it meant an excuse to get out of a job on the farm they jumped at any opportunity. It was a hobby that their father surprisingly encouraged.

From a very early age, Uncle Rod had taken them sailing at every opportunity. Rod loved to sail and didn't need any encouragement to get out on the water. In fact, he was employed by Doug as a sailing instructor. A very well-paying role and he only had two students, Joseph and Kane, so he was able to cope when his health was poor.

He was a skinny pale man; he'd suffered greatly since his brush with death from the major journey he endured coming back from South America with the drugs. But he seemed to gain a healthy glow every time he went out on the water, so everyone encouraged him to take the twins out at every opportunity.

The twins caught on quickly and advanced rapidly in their sailing skills.

They started in the P-Class division, which was a small dingy with a sail. They would practise on the man-made lake at the farm almost daily. When they went to the sailing regattas, they would outclass the other contestants every time and bring home the trophies and ribbons. Rod was always so proud of them and their parents and grandparents would make a huge deal of their success, posing with them for photos and celebrating with a party whenever possible.

They advanced to a class called Moths and then Lasers as they got older, but soon got bored, and encouraged Rod to take them to sea in his yacht. It was the one that he had sailed in from South America twice. Rod referred to the boat as a woman with attitude that you had to treat with respect. They would often catch him talking to the boat like it was alive.

They started with day trips and, as the weather permitted, they then took sailing holidays. These would extend into longer voyages around the coast of Australia. Once they even took a six-month holiday and sailed to New Zealand and back. Rod taught them how to read the stars, plot GPS, and how to navigate around tropical storms and international shipping lanes in the dead of the night. These experiences just made them hungrier to go further afield.

Doug decided that it would be a requirement that they went to a maritime school, and both sit their commercial skipper's ticket so that they had more credibility, and with extended knowledge, it would open more doors for them in the future.

On their twenty-first birthday, they were taken to what was meant to be a surprise party at the hangar on the marina in Sydney Harbour. This was where Doug did maintenance on and stored his tourist boats, yet another of Doug's lucrative businesses he had established.

On their arrival, they saw more than the usual number of vehicles in the

     MICHELLE THOMPSON

car park and a large crowd had gathered and spilt out of the entrance of the building. Mellissa made them stay in the car while she prepared the partygoers for their entrance.

Mellissa told the twins they were in for a massive surprise, and, as part of the excitement, she produced a pair of blindfolds, and they agreed to be led blindfolded into the hangar. The silence as they shuffled along was broken by the occasional giggle from the guests, it seemed a lot further blindfolded.

What they weren't expecting as the blindfolds were removed was a huge screen blocking off one end of the hangar. They knew the hangar well, and at this end, there was normally a large door leading to a shipping berth.

After a short speech, Doug readied himself to pull the drop sheets aside and raised his arm to encourage silence. He asked the crowd to count down from ten. At the count of one, he unveiled what was hidden behind the screen: a stunning sixty-foot yacht.

Everyone in the room drew breath but remained speechless.

Luckily for the boys, one of Doug's clients had run into a spot of financial trouble and Doug had helped him out by taking the yacht in exchange for the debt.

There was a flash of cameras from many mobile phones. Everyone in the hangar was mesmerised by the grandeur and the size of the boat.

Looking at the yacht you would expect it could easily travel across international oceans. It offered the occupants on board many luxury facilities like a recently upgraded interior, a layout which featured two sleeping berths and state-of-the-art galley with new appliances. She also boasted brand new navigational equipment which Doug had fitted shortly after he acquired it. He knew his boys would be travelling far and wide and wanted to give them the best chance to survive if anything went wrong. The yacht was finished in beautiful, polished wood, deep carpets and highly polished brass fittings; no finishing detail appeared to be overlooked.

If the crowd was stunned to silence, then the twins were more stunned, they even forgot to close their mouths until Doug came past to give them a hug and tapped their chins shut.

Uncle Rod was already on board beckoning them to join him for a tour of the facilities. Rod had been instrumental in helping Doug upgrade it where he felt it was needed.

The twins climbed aboard and forgot their guests for a full hour while they went through the boat tour with Rod. They had to stop themselves from going "wow" or "oh my goodness" at every new discovery.

They asked guests to remove their shoes and put down their drinks before they came aboard for a tour, they were already overprotective about the impact that so many people walking through the boat would have on keeping the surfaces pristine.

Eventually, their mother came aboard and reminded them that they needed to mingle with the guests and pay respects to some of the visitors who had brought gifts that they had not yet opened or thanked people for.

The question on everyone's lips was, "What were they going to do with the yacht?" The twins already knew the answer to that question. It had been their dream since they were children when their grandparents took them away to places like Italy and Spain, the Caribbean and the Grenadines, and they got to see the rich and famous on their super yachts.

And as they got older, they experienced the perks that came with that lifestyle: women, cocaine, fine wine, more women and lots of sex.

They were lucky enough to charter a yacht like this once and got to enjoy a couple of weeks exploring the unspoilt beauty of remote islands, hidden coves and secret diving spots.

They wanted to explore the coastlines of the world, with boundless freedom to choose their course and follow the sun without being confined to any route or schedule.

     MICHELLE THOMPSON

Edith

Edith was the brains of the family. She had a natural ability with figures and maths, and it just seemed natural that she fit into Doug's business empire. Doug had shared with her the intricacies of the organisation, and she completely understood what was always at risk. She wasn't what would be called a beautiful girl, she'd inherited her father's build and height. Edith was comfortable in her own skin; no flashy diets, or high-maintenance beauty treatments and she dressed in a very conservative manner.

She didn't know why, but she was a very emotional person, always at the wrong time: weddings, sad movies, animal programmes. She even shed a tear at some very happy moments or some good news story that came on the television. Her grandmother had told her once she was psychic, and she was crying because of the emotions she felt for those who had passed. This didn't really help. Short of advertising as a professional wailer, she didn't know how to stop it or control it. She did, however, have the ability to control it in a business situation, opting for a more ruthless approach to handling situations.

The only luxury she permitted herself and had time for was running. It would not be unusual for her to run up to ten kilometres on a tough day. She started doing this after reading an article on how to relieve stress and de-brief all the shit that came into her day dealing with her dad's companies.

As a youngster, she had spent so much time with her father at his so-called business meetings that she couldn't avoid listening in on very adult conversation. As she got older, it just naturally morphed into her being included and asked for her opinion or her father asking her to take notes and remind him later of what was said. At times she was left to make the decisions on some matters. Edith just naturally became the essential key to the equations. She studied accountancy and human resources at university. She had wanted to be a vet, but her father persuaded her to follow a line more useful to the needs of the family business. She didn't argue, he was normally right about things, and she trusted his judgement.

Edith had a major problem with relationships – any boyfriends or potential boyfriends were frightened off by Doug. Some were frightened off before they even met him. She resorted to one-night stands, but these were few and far between. Everywhere she went she felt like she was being watched, and the 'knitting group' would often nark on her to her father, completely freezing her sex life. The only other man in her life was Gay Kenny, her office assistant.

Gay Kenny

The trouble with 'Gay Kenny' was, he wasn't gay. He knew this for sure, but it suited him for many reasons to keep up the charade.

Kenny's father was one of the 'Tight 5'; five men who were life members of the motorcycle gang that Doug had been president of for many years. Now they were all old grey-beards, but still not people you would fuck around or like to meet in a dark alley.

For as long as Kenny could remember he liked bright flowery things, jewellery, extrovert clothing, and dressing up as a woman when he was a child. He'd even had a Barbie doll – he didn't care much for the Ken doll. Barbie had pointy tits, but he could hardly tell his mother that was the reason he liked her. He loved tits.

Kenny had a thin, delicate build; his features were pretty much like his mother's. He was described as a pretty boy, rather than a handsome boy.

His father was a man's man; stocky build, muscular, covered in tattoos, got into fights, rode motorcycles, drove V8 cars and liked fishing, none of the things Kenny liked at all.

Kenny would often overhear his parents talking at night when they thought he was asleep. He could hear his mother defending him, telling his father it was just a stage, and he would grow out of it.

Great arguments would erupt when it came to buying him clothes, as his father refused to give his mother money for fancy Italian suits and flamboyant shirts and man purses.

When he turned sixteen his father sat him down across the kitchen table from him and told him they needed to have a serious talk about the birds and the bees. Kenny cringed at the thought but got great enjoyment watching his father struggle with the words, sweat breaking out on his father's forehead before he bluntly asked Kenny, "You're not a fuckin homo are you, boy?"

Kenny played dumb. He liked to see his father squirm. His father was so capable with everything else he could put his hand to, but when it came to his son his emotions took over.

To antagonise his father more, Kenny, looking confused, said, "What do mean, Dad? I don't understand."

With that, his father, now with sweat running off his forehead in a steady stream, asked Kenny directly, "Kenny, son, have you ever let other men poke their cocks up your arse or have one of our relatives ever made sexual advances to you?"

To all of which Kenny replied emphatically "NO!"

His father seemed satisfied with the response and reached over and patted him on the shoulder twice, handed him a roll of money to go shopping, and left the conversation.

Later that day, Kenny looked up on the internet the topic of anal sex between men, he even tried to find a YouTube clip. The thought horrified him. Once or twice, he'd found it painful passing a hard shit, he couldn't imagine someone poking a hard cock up his arse. Let alone a pair of hairballs slapping on his arse. No wonder his father was sweating.

Then as if to accelerate the problem at home, some weeks later his father discovered Kenny's internet search history in the memory and his way of dealing with it was to drag Kenny downtown to a female prostitute to have sex.

It was obvious that this rather mature lady of the night had already been given the heads-up, and she must have felt like she was doing Kenny's dad a favour. She led Kenny into a sparsely decorated room out the back of a gentleman's club. The room had a double bed, a night table and a red lamp. It had a peculiar odour about it, partly the smell of rubber and partly the smell of cheap Kamasutra perfume.

With little or no class, she hitched her skirt up to her belly button and lay back on the bed in the room with her legs apart. She was wearing no underwear and much to Kenny's horror there was this huge hairy vagina staring up at him. She told him to get his cock out and masturbate himself, then she grabbed at her labia and pulled them apart. Kenny wasn't sure if it was the odour of an old wet sock that hit him first, assaulting his nostrils, or the heat of the room; he fainted.

Next thing he knew he woke up in the back seat of his father's car and they were driving on the way back to their house. His father sternly told him not to tell his mother about the events of the day, and the subject was never brought up again.

     MICHELLE THOMPSON

Kenny, conveniently, was sent away to a private school where he majored in computer technology. He was given a generous weekly allowance and had very little need to go home often unless it was for family events and celebrations. But when he did go home, he made sure he always wore an outlandishly extravagant outfit, just to wind his father up.

Kenny wasn't sure when he got labelled with the nickname 'Gay Kenny', but everyone called him that and he went along with it.

When he was 18, he was asked if he wanted to leave school and go and work in an office doing computer and reception work with Edith and he jumped at the chance.

He had grown up with Edith, gone to the same junior schools and spent summer holidays at her house. She was his best friend. She had even rescued him when he was being bullied at school once. A couple of big lads had tried to steal his lunch money and Edith had come around the corner and caught them in the process. She'd punched them both out; boxed them like a true professional.

He loved Edith, in more ways than one, and she had big, luscious tits!

First Colombian Invasion – Sebastian

Sebastian considered it a tremendous privilege and a position of honour to be selected by *Señor* Matias Hernandez for a special project. Señor Matias, amongst other things, was the Minister of Agriculture and Rural Development for the Colombian local government. He carried a lot of power inside and outside the government through family connections. Sebastian, as a young child, had grown up in the same neighbourhood called the Soacha slum that Matias' family had stemmed from. Sebastian's parents were respected and were looked upon as honest hard-working folk. Sebastian and his family had never known riches.

When Sebastian was only nine years old there was a family tragedy, and his father was killed in the crossfire of a turf war. He had been an innocent bystander and the sole income earner for the family. The Hernandez family took pity on them and employed his mother as a housemaid. They also paid for Sebastian's private education. Local gossip suggested that it was guilt money and that it was a shoot-out over drugs that started the conflict and ended Sebastian's father's life.

Sebastian had completed his schooling with Matias, the son of Carlos Hernandez. They had shared many years in each other's company, and he considered Matias his family and respected him, but also feared him. Everyone feared him.

It wasn't till Matias and Sebastian had left school that he was approached by the head of the Hernandez family, Carlos. Carlos had given them a villa to live in and occasionally asked them to run a few errands. Sebastian was streetsmart; he knew this was a powerful family with a lot of connections. You didn't ask questions, you just said yes, and you didn't fuck up.

Sebastian was considered a close friend of Matias as they had bonded during the survival years of private school. Before long he and Matias were managing their own crews, running guns and cocaine. He had relocated his mother to a better part of the city to provide her with a better life in her elder years. People looked up to him; he had connections now.

The Hernandez family business would one day be in the hands of the son Matias. Just like his father, Matias was well educated. His strategy was to take an aggressive approach to business. His position in the local community was used as a cover for his drug empire and his thugs to restore order when necessary.

Sebastian was very important to Matias. Matias trusted him. Matias was comfortable in his ability to manage the unsavoury parts of the family business and relieve him from getting involved in the ugly bits, which wouldn't bode well if the media connected Matias directly.

Matias called Sebastian and asked him to meet him at their usual meeting place, a little café on the edge of town that the Hernandez family sponsored. They got a table outside under the veranda overlooking the road. The noise of the traffic would drown out the conversation if they were being bugged.

Matias was furious, he always wore his emotions on his sleeve. His fingers drummed impatiently on the table; he had no tolerance for waiting. The coffee was taking longer than he thought it needed to. He felt like scolding the waitress, better still, he would invite her to his city apartment later and fuck her.

Sebastian was on time – that's what he liked about Sebastian. He never let Matias down; he knew his duty. He served the Hernandez family well. And as a result, he got chosen for the special projects.

They both knew a large amount of his father's cocaine had gone missing.

The urgency in Matias' voice was unmistakable, as was the fury in his eyes as he leant closer to Sebastian. "It's our fault the cocaine was stolen, our poor judgement. We need to get it back or get payment before my father blames us for it. You're the only one I trust, Sebastian. Retrieve the cocaine or what's owed to us. Kill whoever is responsible if you have to, I don't care."

Sebastian arrived in Sydney on the LAN Chile flight via Colombia and Santiago, Chile. He had watched all the Australian Border Control miniseries on television. His story was he was meeting up with an intrepid tourist organisation which he had pre-booked, he was only staying for a week, a seven-day tour, and he had a return ticket. Although Matias had offered him an all-expenses-paid vacation if he decided to stay on, he didn't want to stay away too long. It was more important to get back home and be rewarded for his services. He would be paid handsomely for his effort. He had flown economy so as not to draw attention to himself.

He followed the instructions that their Australian connection had given him and headed to the public car park, park number 24A. He already had the keys to the Toyota HiAce van that was waiting. He was buggered, so he decided to sleep it off in the van tonight; best he kept a clear head for the task ahead. He'd searched on the internet for a camping ground for 'freedom campers' and headed directly there. He'd make sure he only spoke Spanish; this way he would hope to avoid any conversation or human interaction. Tomorrow he would meet Rodrigues, the cousin of Alfredo and hopefully find out where Alfredo was, or at the least get the satisfaction of killing Rod and his wife because he was sure they were involved.

This would send a message to all involved about messing with the Hernandez family. He might throw in a bit of unpleasant torture while he was at it, just for good measure.

He looked up the address; it would only take him an hour and forty-five minutes to arrive at the house from the camping ground. Interesting to see if Rod remembered him from school, he would invite himself for dinner. He had heard through family connections that Rodrigues had suffered an accident which had left him with a stroke or something. Something was wrong with his brain, which was all he really knew.

He surveyed the van and found the items he had requested – just the basics: toilet paper, coffee, bedding. Everything on his list was there including a packet of 'Cherry Ripes' which he loved but couldn't buy in Colombia. It was his guilty pleasure. Meantime, the bed felt comfortable, and he could feel the effects of jetlag creeping in. He was asleep before his head hit the pillow.

When Sebastian pulled up in the driveway of Rodrigues and Stacey's home, he wasn't expecting to find Rod just sitting in the sun in a rocking chair. This skinny frail old man wasn't the boy he remembered from school back in Colombia, he also didn't fit the profile of a drug smuggler or a robber. The conversation was mildly awkward to start with. Rod clearly didn't have a lot to say but said he had sustained a brain injury. He had no memory, and he said he relied on his wife Stacey to care for him.

The state of Rod's health and inability to communicate changed things for Sebastian for the time being, but the outcome would still end the same.

Rod was welcoming enough and loved speaking in the Spanish dialect again. Sebastian just couldn't work out where this limp human fitted into the puzzle if he fitted in at all. Nevertheless, he had to kill him eventually. The house was of upmarket design and value but surprisingly the wife was still working. You

     MICHELLE THOMPSON

would think that if they had all the money from the cocaine the wife would not need to work. It was a bit of a puzzle.

Rod suggested that Sebastian visit his wife at her place of work. He would ring ahead to ensure she would be free. It was only five kilometres down the road. She was working at big commercial pepper and tomato glasshouses. You couldn't miss it. He gave him a business card just in case; it had a little map on the reverse.

This sparked Sebastian's curiosity, he wasn't getting any sense from Rod, wouldn't hurt to talk to the wife, see if he could invite himself to dinner. He'd have to tell the wife he was just looking up some old friends, schoolmates who had been emailing him and raving about how great Australia was, and it turns out one of those mates was Rod's cousin, Alfredo.

Hospital Update

When Doug regained consciousness he lay still for a short while, assessing the room and his surroundings, allowing his eyes to adjust to the light. He tried to swallow, but his throat was sore and dry, it was no use trying to talk. He knew there were probably numerous tubes and instruments attached to his body.

He was staring ahead at the weeping family members surrounding his bed. His daughter Edith was holding his hand in hers; it was soft and warm.

He didn't need to be told that Mellissa was dead, their faces told it all. Don and Andrea suddenly looked old and grey; they seemed to have aged ten years in a short number of days.

Doug did a quick headcount, someone was missing. He narrowed his eyes when he looked at Joseph, poor boy looked like he had the weight of the world on his shoulders.

He turned his head towards Edith, her face was all puffy and red, and her eyelids were swollen; she had obviously been crying for a while. He joked to himself 'professional wailer'.

His dad was in the corner, face buried in his hands. He wasn't looking at anyone, he didn't handle public displays of grief.

Doug tried to clear his throat, trying to get some moisture back in his mouth so he could speak. A doctor entered the room and checked the equipment, the nurse who followed him lifted Doug's mask and swabbed his mouth with a wet cotton swab then gave him a sip of water.

"Where is Kane?" he watched as they all stole glances at each other.

"I want to know, so tell me the truth."

They told him that Kane, and the yacht, were missing, and there was a high possibility that they had been boarded by Somalian pirates. They had lost communication with him.

"Where was the last GPS location?"

"Mogadishu, the boat is now stationary."

"Has there been any ransom demand?"

"Not yet."

"Are the media all over it?"

     MICHELLE THOMPSON

"Our family has made front-page news for the last three days."

Doug suddenly took control and started barking orders. "Get Stacey for me. Tell her I want a private jet to Iran. Find that American negotiator who brokers ransom deals with pirates.

"Andrea, you take Dad and the kids and organise the funeral. And someone locate the doctor and find out how soon I can get out of here.

"Don, can you stay behind? I need to have a private talk with you; there's something I need you to do."

An hour later, Doug was alone in his hospital room. He ran through the events of the accident in his head. He knew Mellissa was dead almost instantly. He'd felt her slump, and the light just seemed to go out of him. His heart was sore with grief. He thought of all the lonely nights to follow. Just the little things like watching television together, her blue eyes, her smile. She was his drinking buddy; she made him laugh; now she was going to make him the saddest man on earth. He loved her so much.

He knew who was behind the shooting. He'd go and rescue his son, then he'd sever the head of the snake that killed his wife.

The Colombians – Sofia

Sofia had mixed memories of her childhood. Her mother, Maria, had been a famous cabaret singer in Colombia. A very beautiful lady, the photographers would often wait outside their home, hoping to catch a friendly smile or wave. Maria sang at high-end hotels and luxury resorts.

Sofia's daily life was always full of travel and surrounded by musicians, politicians and movie stars. She was educated in a private school run by Catholic nuns.

One of her greatest joys was when her father Carlos visited. He didn't live with her mother because her mother was his mistress. Carlos always arrived with lavish gifts and carried Sofia around on his shoulders. He loved her deeply and when he could he'd tuck her in and read her a bedtime story, always making the characters come to life with different voices. When she'd got older, he'd often taken her with him on his business trips and showed her off to everyone he met. The relationship he had with her mother was a very public affair, and it just seemed to be accepted as the done thing. And besides, Carlos was a very rich man who was very generous to his charities and his donations to the Catholic Church. So, no one was prepared to point out the obvious.

Sofia matured into a very pretty young lady with light coffee-coloured skin, fine bone structure, flowing long dark brown hair; she was a natural beauty, and he would tell her so, often. They lived in a magnificent mansion, and they had house staff as well as a chauffeur.

Carlos was a shrewd businessman and a person you wouldn't cross if you had any brains. He had his fingers in a lot of business ventures. One of his main legal sources of income was his emerald mines. This was the business he was grooming Sofia to take over when he got too old to manage them himself. So, it was imperative that he show her the good side of the business, along with the vicious underbelly of his competitors and his enemies.

Sofia didn't always agree with the treatment of the labourers in the mines and wanted to make some changes to their conditions. She was often at loggerheads with her father on this subject, but he admired her spirit and was somewhat open to her suggestions. The most he ever agreed to, was the delivery of food

     MICHELLE THOMPSON

parcels to the mining camps. Later in life, Sofia would deliver these herself, to make sure the workers knew it was her that brought and approved the food. She considered it to be future insurance amongst the villagers for when she took over the family business.

Sofia's life was turned upside down when she was seventeen and her mother contracted glandular fever which affected her heart. Maria seemed to go downhill after that and wasted away until she was too weak to get out of bed and died. Carlos never left her bedside and wept openly at the loss of his mistress. He locked himself in her room after her death and stayed there for a week, only letting Sofia in to nourish him with warm soup and whisky.

After a week, he came out and called Sofia saying, "The house is to be packed up and I want you to come and live with me in Bogotá with my family. You will spend most of your time on the road with me, though. I want to teach you the other side of my business interests. I have made my decision, and that is final.

"Pack a few things now, enough for a week, and the removal men can pack the rest. Until your belongings arrive in Bogotá, if you need anything we will just buy it. Now, go and catch your cat and put it in the cat cage, he can come with us today in the limo."

He made a few phone calls, and before long some cars arrived, and they filled them with their belongings. They drove off in silence. He hugged her all the way.

The night seemed like a blur as the cars sped past the lights of the city to the airport where they boarded Carlos' private jet and flew to Bogotá, to begin Sophia's new life.

Rodrigues

Rod played up the head injury part well. Yes, there were some major blank spots in his memory, but equally, he remembered a lot more than he let on.

He knew the calibre of a man like Doug; he'd grown up with this sort of individual. It was safer to be on Doug's good side.

Doug had looked after them well, they had not wanted for anything. In fact, he was sure Doug had saved his life.

He never really made eye contact with Doug; opted instead for the vacant dreamy look, the brain injury look. He was afraid of Doug.

Rod had a genuine love for the two boys; he'd had no sons himself and his love for sailing was equalled by their love for sailing. Doug came in handy when it came to supporting their passion financially.

Stacey and Doug had a special relationship. Rod knew that when the time came for him to pass on Doug would make sure Stacey and his daughter would be taken care of.

Rod had been resting on the front deck in the warm sun when the white van pulled up in the driveway. As if it was some kind of spiritual warning, Rod's blood ran cold; he sensed immediate danger.

Before the visitor opened his mouth, Rod knew he was from Colombia. He looked vaguely familiar – it was Sebastian. He had gone to school with him, and he would be here to kill him if he didn't get what he wanted. It was times like this that Rod felt like he held the trump card. He'd soon meet Doug; Rod suddenly felt safe.

The safest option now was to redirect him to Stacey and ring ahead and warn Doug.

Sebastian was fishing for information about Rod's cousin Alfredo. Rod genuinely didn't know where he was, so he felt confident that he wasn't lying. He didn't give anything away by blushing or getting a nervous tremor in his hands, he clenched his fists just in case and he played the head injury card.

When Sebastian drove away Rod rang the preloaded phone number in his phone for Doug. All he managed to say was, "There has been a strange overseas visitor here asking questions about my cousin Alfredo."

     MICHELLE THOMPSON

Doug thanked him and then the phone went dead.

Rod felt like vomiting. He raced to the bathroom and vomited then evacuated his bowels. Afterwards, he went and lay down on his bed. The stress exhausted him; it was going to be a long night.

Invitation to Dinner

Stacey watched the van through the window as it slowly rolled up the driveway towards the office. She checked her pulse and controlled her breathing. Doug sat behind her in an office chair; he was silent, motionless. Just before the van pulled up to a stop in the visitor's car park, Doug jumped up with a big grin on his face and announced, "Showtime." He had a little spring in his step.

They welcomed Sebastian with open arms and both Stacey and Doug spoke fluent Spanish with him; they were very welcoming.

Sebastian cut to the chase and enquired about Alfredo.

Stacey played her role to perfection. "I know, why don't you both come for a family dinner tonight? I'll ring Alfredo at work and leave a message for him to come. Alfredo is hanging out up the road at a pet food factory. It will be a nice surprise for him to see his old friend from Colombia. I won't tell him who the guest is, it'll be a big surprise for him.

"Doug, why don't you and Mellissa come as well? We can give Sebastian a real Australian welcome."

Doug declined the invite. "Sorry Stace, me and Mellissa have a previous engagement which I can't postpone."

They suggested a couple of tourist spots he could visit while he was waiting for Stacey to finish work and go home and prepare for dinner.

"There's a nice winery down the road which is famous for its award-winning wines. You could buy some bottles as gifts to take back home, or a nice wine for dinner." Doug suggested a dessert wine.

Doug was fascinated with the camper van; he loved the unique features which they had packed into such a small place. He joked that he wouldn't fit in it himself, as he was too tall. He looked it over, measuring it with his eyes.

They watched Sebastian drive off down the drive. They had a very tight time frame to prepare for dinner.

     MICHELLE THOMPSON

Sebastian Prepares for Dinner

Sebastian felt sure he knew who had the cocaine now. It changed his plans slightly. The first thing he would do would be to ring Matias and update him on his findings.

It still wouldn't change his plans to kill Rod and Stacey tonight, but the revelation that Alfredo was just up the road – it was too easy. His instincts were jaded with jetlag, but he couldn't help but think that this lot was really dumb. But he would be sure that he would kill them all in their sleep tonight. He'd insist on sleeping in his van and wait till they were all asleep and go back inside and kill them. He would inflict a bit of pain first before he killed them; it was all falling into place, almost too easy, dumb bloody Australians.

For now, he'd take their advice and visit a winery to pass a little time, perhaps even get a boxed wine gift to take back home as they suggested.

His mind kept returning to tonight's plan. Alfredo wasn't a fool; he would know that payment for the cocaine was required. Would he even turn up? He might bolt. He'd have to think of a strategy around Alfredo's reaction when he saw him. It would be a good ploy to let him think he also was on the run from Matias. What he couldn't work out was if Alfredo had the cocaine what was he doing at the pet food factory? He couldn't work that part out – unless he had bought the business with the money. It just made him all the more sure that Doug must have intercepted the cocaine at some stage, and they were all linked somehow – it was a puzzle.

The hairs on the back of his neck stood up. That Doug was one big ugly bastard. He looked tough but he had taken on tougher men than him. Doug would soon learn a lesson.

Sebastian pulled up in the hardware store car park; he loved hardware stores. He'd be able to buy all the things he needed for tonight. A pair of sturdy garden shears that could handle cutting off fingers, wooden skewers used for kababs that he could insert in the eye of Alfredo's penis once he was tied up and pleading for his life. And the best thing he had found was a thing the Australians called gaffer tape; he was sure he would find this very useful; it was amazing stuff. He found a Sauber saw to cut their heads off and an industrial staple gun so he could staple their eyelids open to their foreheads; the least they could do is watch him carry out his handiwork. He wanted some razor wire to tie their heads back like a gag through their mouths but that was taking it a bit too far in the hardware shop.

Once they were all tied up, he'd make each one of his victims watch the others being murdered. It was the way they did things back at home, this was the part he enjoyed the most.

Lastly, he purchased a pair of disposable overalls, gloves, safety glasses and a mask – the mask was for when their bowels evacuated; the stench was overpowering.

Mediterranean Sea

The Mediterranean, the playground of the rich and famous. The twins' original plan was to hang out at the hot spots like the Dalmatian Coast, the Greek Islands or Monaco and just simply have fun. There wasn't any pressure from their father to get involved in anything illegal yet, but they were sure it was a subject that would be brought up soon. Up until now, they had been given a healthy allowance, so finances hadn't been a problem. Except for the odd visit from their sister and their grandparents, they hadn't had to conform to any rules or schedules.

They didn't like to stay in one place for too long. It could get a bit awkward with female relationships. The twins were in it for the variety, not the commitment. And it was a bachelor yacht and a bloody mess inside, but it was home, and they liked it the way it was.

Occasionally they would hook up with another Australian or a New Zealander and they would help crew the yacht to the next port. They were always meeting new people and expanding their network; they were welcomed wherever they sailed.

Since they left their last port, Malta, Kane and Joseph were pretty sure they had a stowaway on board. First, it was the missing food, then the wet footprints inside the cabin, and someone appeared to be cleaning up! They set up a couple of traps but never followed through so the plan to catch the stowaway always fell short due to their lack of commitment to do anything for too long. There were so many places you could hide on the yacht. They searched a few of the most obvious places but gave up. They had surveillance cameras on board which they never had a need to use but now seemed like a good time to turn them on again. As an added precaution they would make sure the locker the equipment was stored in was always kept locked.

It took them a couple more nights before they discovered that their stowaway was a small child, possibly a boy. They made a concerted effort to catch the child, which involved an elaborate exaggerated act of drunkenness, lots of yawning and saying out loud how tired they were, then leaving nice cheese and cold meats out on the galley table and going to bed, a bit like catching a mouse.

They locked the external door to the cabin so, if they cornered the stowaway, he or she couldn't make their escape by diving overboard.

They lay silently for what seemed like hours, then they heard the creaking of the teak floorboards and the cheese plate being shifted. They gave it a few more minutes before they sprung out into the cabin with a baseball bat and a number nine golf iron, making "raaa" noises like they were herding a bunch of cattle into a pen.

There sitting at the galley table was a small boy, he looked barely fazed by their lightning charge. He continued eating and with a wide grin on his face said, "You could have left bread."

Orhan was a refugee from Syria. He was lucky he wasn't one of the 34,361 migrants who had already died trying to get into Europe. He had no living family, his only relative, his sister, had been too weak to survive the trip over in the boat they were smuggled to Italy on. They'd had no food and poor sanitation on board.

Orhan was seven years old but looked about six years in size and build. He spoke good English, French, Italian and his native tongue, Arabic. He was wise beyond his years; his mother and father were killed when the rebel fighting descended on Aleppo. Orhan and his sister and eleven million others were forced to leave their homes. He'd witnessed things no seven-year-old should ever experience. If they had stayed, they risked rape, torture and murder. They had no access to food or water and the constant threat of rockets filled with the nerve agent sarin being fired into their suburb forced them to escape the conflict.

He'd been watching the twins for a while at the Port of Licata, Sicily. He had observed that they were a little lax on security; they often had multiple people coming and going from their berth in various states of intoxication. Once he had snuck onto the yacht, he had found plentiful supplies of food and drink. It was warm and dry, and he didn't face the prospect of getting murdered in his sleep by other desperate refugees or caught by authorities and sent back to a refugee camp. A couple of times he had even saved the twins' life. They had gone to bed on two occasions and left a pot cooking on the stove, and once they had left the gas on. He would use these stories to negotiate his permanent passage on the boat if he needed to.

The one thing he had worked out about Kane and Joseph was that they had big hearts, they were just a couple of nice Australian boys. Obviously spoilt rotten, so he was gambling that they wouldn't throw him out to survive on his own.

He launched into his pitch. "I'll be no trouble; you will never see me. I've been living on the boat for a month, and you didn't notice until now. I'll cook and clean, do the shopping and tend to the guests' needs, like a multi-skilled butler. I can keep the boat maintenance up and do the washing, whatever you need me to do."

He drew breath and tried to look cute and sad at the same time. And in a perfect Australian accent he said, "Whaddaya reckon, mate?"

Kane and Joseph burst out laughing, he had them at cooking and cleaning. They slapped him on the back and shook his small sparrow-like hand energetically.

The first thing was to give the poor little bastard a proper bed to sleep in, up until now he had been sleeping under a bench seat in secret. They liked Orhan and they had no trouble with him staying, he would come in handy.

As an afterthought, they showed him a photo of their father and warned him not to piss him off if he was ever to visit.

Dinner is Served to Sebastian

Sebastian felt a tingle of excitement when he pulled up in the driveway. He always had butterflies before he dispatched someone. He'd brought dessert as an offering of thanks; it was also laced with finely crushed sleeping pills that his doctor had given him for the long flight. He also had another container of sleeping pills in his jacket pocket that he had crushed to a fine powder and a bottle of wine laced with powdered pills to wash it down. If that didn't work out, either way, he would get the job done tonight.

Stacey met him at the front door and welcomed him with a kiss on both cheeks. First, she showed him the amenities. She had even made up a room for him if he decided to stay inside the house rather than the van. She gave him a brief tour of the house and told him a little story about the community and how they rallied around after Rod received his head injury in a farming accident.

The tour ended at the kitchen server where Rod was waiting on a bar stool. Stacey got on the kitchen side and continued preparing a cocktail for each of them.

"I almost didn't make it to dinner," Sebastian said. "When I left Stacey's work today, I was confronted by not one but two large black spiders in my van – they nearly made me drive off the road. I don't know how they got in there." Although he had his suspicion that Doug had put them in the van.

"At the winery, they told me that they were probably Huntsman spiders, and I was lucky not to get bitten."

They chatted about other dangerous spiders and snakes, then politics and life in general while Stacey continued the finishing touches to dinner. She thanked him for the wine that they would have with dinner, placed the dessert in the fridge and thanked him again. She sounded genuine; Sebastian made a mental note to kill her first.

Stacey explained that Alfredo was running late, as she made another cocktail for Sebastian and Rod. She sipped hers between checking pots on the stove. She assured Sebastian that she would try the wine once she had dinner under control.

It crossed Sebastian's mind briefly that the cocktails might be drugged because that was what he would do, but all three of them were drinking so he dismissed the thought.

Sebastian was looking into the light; he could make out shadows passing through it, he couldn't hear voices, more the sound of a scratchy radio on a bad channel. He tried to make sense of it all. The back of his head was numb. He knew he was being moved; he felt like he was floating. He became vaguely aware that he was now outside in the dark and the cold. He tried to fight it, but his body was unresponsive, he was paralysed.

Through vacant eyes he saw a big figure pass in front of him, he knew it was Doug, he was placing him on the bed in the van. Sebastian tried to talk but no words came out. The cocktails must have been drugged!

The big grey outline of Doug's body came into view standing over him on the van bed. Doug came closer so his face was by Sebastian's ear. He could smell garlic on Doug's breath. The last words that Sebastian heard were, "Take that, mother fucker." Doug pulled back the hammer on the pistol and shot him at point-blank range in the forehead.

Doug unloaded the shipping container from the truck and opened the doors. Before they pushed the van into the container Stacey and Doug had made sure everything that Sebastian had brought with him was put back in the van, including the wine and the dodgy dessert.

Doug got to work and started to weld shut all the doors and Stacey spray-painted all the inside of the windows with black paint. They removed the number plates.

Doug had made sure with his connections that this container would be on the next ship leaving Australia bound for nowhere. It could circle the oceans and ports for years before it was finally noticed and either opened or sold at some storage auction on a US reality show. Either way, someone would get a surprise. He had the urge to post it back to bloody Colombia, but that fight could wait. They would know before long that something had happened to their man. Doug was sure more men would be coming; it was only a matter of time.

Rod once again had been a casualty of tonight's events. They'd had no choice but to drug him as well; they couldn't afford for Sebastian to become suspicious. Rod would sleep it off and they would tell him he'd had another one of his turns. Stacey would explain that Sebastian had to leave, he had a ship to catch. She knew Rod well enough to know that he would not actually care; he didn't like visitors in any case.

Earlier that day they'd had Sebastian followed by Edith and Gay Kenny. They had witnessed him purchase the goods from the hardware shop. They knew then that it was 'game on'. They would have to be alert from now on.

When they had finished packaging up Sebastian, Doug gave Stacey a friendly hug, he knew they made a good team.

He did salvage the unopened gift box of wine. He'd take that home for Mellissa, a nice little present for his lovely wife.

Doug was happy about today's events – he felt alive.

Hugo

Hugo had left Colombia when he was twenty-one, with only one change of clothes, a backpack and a one-way plane ticket to Germany, he was off to experience what the world had to offer. He chose Germany to start with, just to say he had experienced a beer festival. Life was good, he was a cool-looking dude, toned and tanned, slicked-back hair, open shirt, gold chains; he fancied himself in the mirror. He was a chick magnet, and he was proud of it. He had big plans to travel, work in bars and cafés when he got low on funds, and he wanted to fuck his way around Europe. He had savings but he didn't want to dig into them, he would need that money to set himself up when he settled down.

He had left Colombia and vowed never to return. Sure, he had friends and family there, but he was sick of the politics on the street, the danger around every corner and the odds of staying alive were always slim. Sure, he knew the right people, but you could never count on them to always be in power, new cartels were formed all the time.

He didn't fancy bringing up children in his homeland. He planned to permanently immigrate to another country, set himself up in a small business and send money so his parents could come and live with him. That was the plan.

It was love at first sight. He spotted Maggie across the tables at the beer festival, she was everything he had ever dreamed of, long blonde hair, lovely long legs, ample bust, beautiful smile and a fantastic Australian accent. He followed her around like a dog on heat. She stopped traffic when she crossed the road, she was so beautiful. She was everything a good Catholic girl wasn't his mother wouldn't approve.

Together they toured Europe, Great Britain and Asia. They would get odd jobs cleaning bars, waiting on tables, gardening – anything that got them a place to sleep, a party and a meal.

Somehow, they managed this for a year, living on a shoestring and making great discoveries together. They were totally in love and the sex was fantastic. Everyone they met enjoyed their company.

Maggie fell pregnant the following year and Hugo couldn't have been happier. They decided to head to Australia and live with her parents until they could get a place of their own. They would get married and start a family. This was everything Hugo had ever wanted.

The first child arrived, and Maggie had put on an extra ten kilograms and never lost it. Then she proceeded to eat her way through as many hamburgers and doughnuts that she could stuff down her throat and put on another ten kilograms. She turned into a fat argumentative cunt. Sex dried up completely and she took to wearing bland grey sweatpants and a hoodie. There was no sign of the beauty he had arrived in the country with. Hugo felt like he had been tricked.

He suggested it might be some sort of post-natal issue. That comment was met with a firm, "Fuck off." His work friends suggested he should have sized up the mother-in-law's big fat arse before he got her pregnant.

He had one consolation; he had a beautiful baby daughter so he concentrated on her and all the activities he could do with her.

He bought the camper with the view to spending as much time as he could travelling around Australia on holidays with his daughter. It was a great little camper; it had everything he needed.

When he got the overseas phone call from an old associate to borrow a vehicle, the van was all he had to lend that wasn't in full-time use and he was reluctant to help. He loved his little van, and he wanted no part of the plans they had for it. The caller assured him it was only going to be for a couple of weeks. He told his wife it had gone in for repairs but that had been over a month ago; he was going to face some questioning soon. She'd be like a dog with a bone; she wouldn't let it go.

He knew better than to get involved with that Colombia cartel again. If something bad was going down, he'd have to distance himself from the problem if he could. His mood went from pissed off and angry at his own stupidity to a sweating fear. He remembered now why he left Colombia in the first place.

It was 3 am. There was crashing and the sound of breaking glass as the front door got smashed off its hinges. Then he heard his wife screaming. He was in a funnel of light and haze; big angry hands were ripping him out of bed, and he was pinned down painfully in the middle of his back with a knee. Someone was putting handcuffs on him and reading him his rights. Amidst the confusion he realised he was being busted by the police; they were saying

     MICHELLE THOMPSON

something about a terrorist. It took a few more minutes before he realised it was him they were referring to.

The property was surrounded, flashing lights, orders shouted, Hugo was even sure he could hear a helicopter. Police tape was being erected around the perimeter of the property, men in chemical suits and masks were walking around the back of the house and an officer had a police dog inside the house.

Hugo and his wife were separated and put in different rooms. His daughter was with his wife; Maggie looked like she was already hungry. She was being questioned.

He could see the men in the back yard lifting a large blue tarpaulin, and below it were gun barrels that Hugo had never seen before. He didn't know how they got there; they weren't there before he went to bed last night.

Suddenly the policeman with the dog was shouting that he had found something in his daughter's room. There was a cachet of guns, including a rocket launcher under her bed. They also found a laptop with links to a radical extremist group and an Al-Qaeda flag. The whole thing was surreal; Hugo's head was swimming.

As he was being dragged out to the front yard, in the white paper suit the police gave him to wear, towards a police van, he could see all the neighbours with shocked expressions, some covering their mouths in shock, others taking pictures. Someone yelled an obscenity at him. It was just breaking daylight, the sun was coming out, and as he looked back at his house for the last time, he thought he saw the number plates of his van in his front yard!

Sofia Meets Her New Family

Sofia's new family could only be explained as a living hell.

The house staff, on the other hand, were delightful. They were all lined up in a row for Sofia to meet and as time went on you would always find Sofia in the staff wing laughing and being spoilt.

Sofia was introduced to her own personal maid, Camilla; she had been assigned to be at her side twenty-four hours a day if required and would become her closest friend. Her father had chosen her specifically not only for her domestic duties but as a personal bodyguard for his daughter. Camilla had been expertly trained in the Colombian elite operations unit.

Carlos's wife, Amanda, and her son Matias were another story, they were clearly disappointed with the situation. How had Carlos had the audacity to bring his bastard child into their family home? The wife's face was strained, and her lips pinched, she looked flushed, and her eyes were red from crying. Matias stepped forward and shook Sofia's hand then stepped back in the line, his face gave away no emotion.

Carlos went through the formalities and explained to everyone that Sofia was here to stay permanently. He had a word of warning to everyone. "If I ever discover that her happiness is compromised in any way someone will pay dearly, and I will deal with them directly."

Sofia lived in a different part of the estate to Amanda and Matias and although she seldom had to interact with them, she knew instinctively, and wisely, to avoid them at all costs.

She had everything she needed, and she would spend hours with her father in his office while he explained the intricacies of his business interests. At times Matias would be there also, he needed to know what his duties were to keep the family interests alive and profitable.

Sofia and Matias had little in common. She was always polite and tried to be friendly, but it wasn't reciprocated. She would often hear her father scold him for his behaviour and ask him to try harder. Matias never did.

—

Sofia returned from a business trip to her emerald mines in the eastern portion of the Andes, between the Boyacá and Cundinamarca regions; she was tired and travel weary. It had been a tough trip with the weather conditions hampering access.

She knew instantly that something was wrong, the staff were not at the car to greet them. Camilla had taken a phone call earlier and she had become silent and deep in thought.

Her father was waiting in her room; he had sad news. Her cat had been killed. The details were never revealed to her, and she had not been permitted to see the body.

"I am sorry, Sophia," Carlos began gently. "It appears that Matias has murdered your cat out of spite. He tortured the poor animal to death. I think it would be unwise to get another cat," Carlos continued. "I suggest you make friends with the stray cats that frequent the courtyard."

Sofia cried herself to sleep that night and all the staff came to see her and cried with her. They had never seen her unhappy and the event moved them all.

Matias Pays the Price

Matias had tried to catch the cat for weeks, but the cat was on to him and managed to avoid him. In the end, his mother helped him, and they lured it with food. They hated Sofia and all the attention she got from everyone.

Matias was about to pay the ultimate price. Carlos had gone very quiet over the matter and refused to speak to him, so he knew punishment was brewing. He instinctively perceived that it was going to be different than in the past, but he could not guess what the punishment would be.

Two mornings after he had been caught red-handed torturing the cat by one of his father's bodyguards, his father came into his room and ordered him to pack several bags of clothing. All he would tell him was that he would not be coming back to the house for a very long time, so make sure he took everything he might need. When he was finished, he was to go downstairs and wait at the front of the house for the car to pick him up.

He stood in the courtyard for some time before several SUVs with black tinted windows appeared. The bodyguard that had caught him got out and ordered him into the back seat and placed his bags in the back. To his surprise, his mother was also in the SUV. She had been crying. She hugged him close and kissed him on his forehead twice. They drove in silence for hours, with the other two vehicles behind them. He had no idea who was in the other vehicles.

They eventually reached a remote location well into the jungle. They were ordered out of the vehicle. Matias and Amanda stood together holding hands.

Carlos stepped out of the second vehicle with a pistol in his hands. He didn't hesitate. He marched from his vehicle, placed the gun up against Amanda's temple and shot her dead. Her skull exploded and her brains and blood sprayed all over Matias' face. Her body slumped to the ground like a plastic toy that had lost all its air. Carlos ordered Matias back into the SUV. The third SUV stayed behind to take care of the body.

Matias sat in the vehicle in silence; he was still in shock. They drove into the night. The journey ended at a privately-run university where they were met by the head of the school. His father got out of his vehicle and shook hands with him and after a brief discussion, Carlos handed him a large envelope. He nodded at the driver of the SUV that Matias was in, who started to unload the bags from the back. Carlos ordered Matias out of the vehicle and pushed him towards the headmaster of the school.

The days and weeks that followed were a hard adjustment for Matias. He was stripped of his allowance, and he had to adjust to daily life at the school. He was fortunate to have his own room but that was his only luxury. He wrote to his father regularly to plead for forgiveness and even wrote to Sofia and told her how sorry he was. But he never got a reply or acknowledgement. If he managed to phone the house his calls were never put through, or they were cut off immediately.

He decided that the least he could do was prove himself to his father, prove that he could be responsible and study hard, and be of future value to his father's empire.

He still hated that little bitch, and he would one day find a way to make her pay for his mother's death.

Precious Cargo

Kane thought he detected a bearded gentleman following him through the market. He had gone ashore with a list from Orhan for food supplies. They were about to set sail again.

He went into a shop and hid for a while, peeking out through the shop windows to see if he had stopped the man from following him. He decided to be more vigilant and made a couple of quick fake moves to see if he was keeping up. He was right, the man was keeping his distance, but he was definitely being followed.

Kane did not continue his shopping but returned to the boat and told Joseph. Kane went out again and Joseph followed from a safe distance. The least that they could do was confuse the follower with a different twin and play a bit of cat and mouse with him.

Kane returned to the last spot in the market where he had seen the bearded man but could not see him. He walked around for a while, but it got too hot, and he gave up. He caught up with Joseph and returned to the boat.

As they got close to the boat, they saw a warning signal that Orhan had placed on the deck, it was a yellow plastic 'Slippery When Wet' sign. This had been one of Kane's ideas to warn the others if something was about to turn to shit. They were to place it in full sight on deck. It was a similar idea that the banks use, to place a rubbish bin or a card somewhere in the doorway to alert other staff whether it was safe to enter the building or not. It was a great idea, but now that it was actually in practice, they didn't know what to do next; they hadn't thought that part out during one of their drunken great-idea sessions.

Kane decided to go on the boat first and assess the situation. Joseph would wait on the pier for a signal. Kane suddenly felt a twinge of fear for Orhan, hoping the poor little bugger was okay. If he had time to put the sign out, he must have some control of the situation.

Kane boarded the boat and ducked down to enter the cabin. He had thought ahead and grabbed a screwdriver from the deck and tucked it into the back of his pants just in case he needed to protect himself or Orhan.

The visitor and Orhan were drinking apple tea and speaking Arabic. Orhan stood up and introduced the gentleman in English. His name was Hakim. Hakim was wearing a cheesy pale blue linen suit, white open shirt and terrible white slip-on mules – it was definitely the man from the market and, although he wasn't prepared to say who he worked for just yet, he said he had a financial proposition for them.

Kane signalled Joseph to board the yacht.

"I have a wealthy client who is willing to pay a substantial amount of money for services rendered," said Hakim. "My client needs to be transported from Araxos in Greece to Bandar Abbas in Iran, no questions asked. My client's identity needs to remain confidential at this stage until I am sure a deal can be brokered. Given the risks involved in sailing through the Suez Canal of attacks by Somalian pirates, we are prepared to pay one million US dollars, and your passenger will be accompanied by a bodyguard."

Kane asked Hakim a blunt question. "How do you know that we won't go to the authorities, and have you investigated?"

To which Hakim replied, "My organisation has done their research thoroughly." He then proceeded to give a quick history lesson on their father and a detailed report on all the boys' stops and activities since they had been in the Mediterranean.

"I will give you until tomorrow to confirm if you are in, but after that, the deal will be off and there will be no more contact."

One million US dollars was a lot of money, and it sounded easier than drug smuggling. They had always planned to pay their father back for the boat and this seemed like a good opportunity. There was a lot of speculation about who the passenger was.

Orhan was shitting himself. He said repeatedly that it was a bad idea to get involved with these sorts of people.

The twins talked long into the night. They agreed to do the job, just for the adventure as well as the money; they were excited. They worked out that if it was good weather, they were looking at seventeen to twenty days at sea if everything went okay.

Hakim arrived early the next day and confirmed the arrangements. "Your passengers will be boarding just on dark tonight. Any problems with sailing into Iranian waters are already taken care of.

"You are not to converse with the passengers unless it is an emergency, and a life needs to be saved.

"Orhan will be given a list of dietary requirements and enough food and supplies for the voyage will be dropped off later today."

"As my client's cabin is fully self-contained, they will have no reason to exit the room. The bodyguard will make up a bed outside my client's room but will otherwise be stationed in the main cabin at all times."

Hakim handed over a large suitcase with pistols, ammunition and hand grenades in it. "This is in case you encounter pirates."

He also handed over an attaché case with documents relating to a bank account in Geneva in their full names, complete with sign-in details to activate the account; the statement showed that half of the one million dollars was already deposited.

"You will get another twenty-five thousand dollars once you reach the end of the Suez Canal, and the rest when you meet our contact at Bandar Abbas. The code word for the contact is Didgeridoo." Kane and Joseph thought this was hilarious, but Hakim wasn't smiling. It was like something out of a movie scene – they loved it.

Shortly after sunset several carts were wheeled down the pier and all sorts of wonderful delicacies and fresh vegetables were unloaded, including beautiful blankets and pillows and several bags of clothing.

Just on dark, three figures made their way down the pier – one was Hakim still in the ridiculous shoes. The bodyguard was a well-built muscle-bound guy who was obviously carrying a couple of pistols in holsters around his shoulders and waist under his jacket. The third was a smaller slightly built person, in a full niqab with eye veil, but not traditional black; it was made of fine, beautiful blue silk and had jewels around the neck, hem and sleeves – this was obviously a woman. She was ushered into her room by Hakim and the bodyguard closed the door and assumed position in front of the door. Hakim shook their hands and blessed them and left the boat. The journey had begun.

It all seemed too easy. The weather was great, the sailing was smooth, they had good winds, and the food that Hakim had dropped off was even better. They never saw their passenger the entire trip, and the bodyguard had no sense of humour. Orhan communicated with him on the odd occasion, mainly when he was preparing a meal or about to serve it.

     MICHELLE THOMPSON

As they sailed into the Gulf of Iran, they were met by a smaller launch from which two armed men boarded their yacht, talked to the bodyguard and directed them to a superyacht that was anchored just ahead of them. It all happened rather quickly from there; the passenger suddenly appeared, and people seemed to emerge from everywhere. They helped her aboard the superyacht and then they were handed confirmation of final payment and waved off. The case with the guns and ammunition was handed back to them and they were told they might need it to pass back through the entrance of the Suez, a common place for pirates.

It all seemed a bit final, and they were disappointed the handover didn't have more drama but a little relieved it was all over.

They checked their account, and the rest of the money had already been deposited.

It was Orhan who broke the silence. "Let's do some sightseeing on the way back to the Mediterranean and make the most of the food that's left over."

Once again, they were lucky with the weather, and it was plain sailing. They were back on the Amalfi Coast before they knew it.

Sofia Meets Her Match

There was a big gap between mining and environmental concerns. Sofia was constantly paying off some official or another. She eased her guilt by supporting the villages with medical and educational programmes. Just when she thought everything had settled down, she would be blindsided by yet another planning consent or greedy local body official. She didn't know what was worse. Either way, at times she felt like she was haemorrhaging money. She paid her workers more than the other mines and she built schools and flew in medical supplies on a regular basis.

So, when she got the phone call to say there was a white man chained to the entrance gates of one of her mines, she almost asked her father to dispose of him. She was sick of it. But he had a few broken-arse supporters with him, and they had placards and an amateur film crew. It had the potential to reach national or even international news. He was making a documentary – that is what was being reported back to her. Sophia ordered her foreman to create a new entrance and ignore him. Now she would have to travel to the mine and talk to him face to face. Her father's solution would be to just shoot him, but Sofia was trying to be more diplomatic at this stage. Shooting would be an option later if they couldn't come to an amicable solution.

Environmentally it was well known that for years runoff from the mines had caused high levels of pollution to local rivers, which was leading to the extinction of rare fish species, and there was also an endangered palm, of all things, which grew on the shores of the river. What annoyed Sofia more was that she had made huge changes to traditional mining practices and her business had been awarded for its innovative ideas to reduce pollution because it is a manual process and no polluting substances such as mercury or cyanide are required, and it was well publicised. She couldn't work out why now this dickhead was targeting her.

Gerald McIntosh was not what she expected. He was a good-looking man for a ginger. He had degrees up the yin-yang in environmental studies. He wore T-shirts with whales on, and you couldn't shut him up if it was a subject, he was passionate about. He met her with his hand out and a beaming smile that she

     MICHELLE THOMPSON

would never forget. He was very engaging, and they both agreed to disagree.

He caught her by surprise by immediately asking her out to dinner so he could pitch his case. Her knee-jerk reaction was to instantly say no, but he had asked in front of a large audience of workers and Camilla, and they all seemed to have an opinion and told her she should go. Camilla had been in a relationship with Carlos for several months now and had been encouraging Sofia to find someone special to share downtime with. So, it was arranged, but only on one condition – Sofia chose the location for dinner; she was very fussy. Gerald didn't argue, he looked like he had won the lottery and promised to be a fair negotiator but joked, and promised, to not let her get a word in the conversation all night.

Sofia was completely out of her depth and nerves got the better of her. She tried to cancel several times before dinner, but Camilla told her to keep a level head and stick to the business plan. Her father even rang and encouraged the meeting. It was beginning to look like a 'set-up'.

Gerald was easy to talk to; he was interesting and knowledgeable about his passion for saving the planet. A bit of a weirdo her father would call him. Above all he was extremely funny – she laughed until her stomach hurt. They ended the night with Sofia agreeing to spend the next day with him going up the river in a boat, so he could show her the rare palms that her mines were killing.

The next morning, they met as arranged. Gerald was a bit taken aback by the number of people who had invited themselves and suggested they reduce numbers based on the size of the boat.

In the end, only Camilla and the mine foreman boarded their boat. The rest of the entourage decided to take another boat. Sofia explained that this was normal practice when she went anywhere – it was something that her father insisted upon.

The rest of the trip went without a hitch, and it was obvious that Gerald had done his homework based on the environmental damage along the banks of the river. He pointed out rare birds and knew all about their breeding patterns, what they ate and how the flow-on effect was resulting in their possible extinction, every now and then stopping to hold her arm and getting right in her personal space, which she was slowly adjusting to, but she was like the Queen of England, no one dared to touch her normally. It was protocol. It felt awkward. This was not completely new information to Sofia, but it was hard to not get caught up in Gerald's beliefs. She did notice that Camilla and the foreman kept their distance at the back of the boat all day, and she knew that they were trying the old match-making trick.

When they returned to the dock Sofia hit Gerald with a blunt question. "Mr McIntosh, what do you want, or what do you expect from me? I suggest you put your demands in writing. Send me an email and I will give it my consideration. I can promise you I will be reasonable if you're demands aren't ridiculous." She shook his hand and bid him a safe journey then left him standing at the dock. She never looked back.

Gerald didn't send an email but arrived unannounced at her father's mansion with an attaché case. Before Sofia was informed of his presence he was having late afternoon coffee with her father on the terrace. They were laughing and talking about the history of the city. She felt mildly annoyed that he was muscling in on her privacy but at the same time she was excited to see him – she just hated not having full control.

Sophia made her presence known and both men stood up when she entered the terrace. She suddenly wished she had dressed better.

Her father suggested that Sofia give Gerald a tour of the gardens and informed her that he had invited him to dinner. She was furious with her father's suggestion but proceeded to lead Gerald away determined to not let him off the hook about turning up unannounced.

As they walked through the garden, Gerald pointed out the names of the trees and shrubs and exotic species of plants in all their commonly known names and their botanical names, which ones would poison you if you ingested them and which ones just kill you outright. He was nervous for two reasons; one, he had googled one of the biggest crime families in Colombia and he was currently in their backyard and still alive. And two, because he was madly in love with the most beautiful woman he had ever seen in his life, and she was standing beside him. He could look into her beautiful brown eyes, see her perfect teeth and smell her perfume. Everything about her fascinated him. He felt quietly confident that her father liked him, after all, he had been invited to dinner. He had been running out of ideas to see her.

Sofia took the opportunity to tell Gerald she was disappointed that he had just arrived without her permission.

Gerald laughed and said, "Carlos rang and invited me. Look, I know we are being set up by him, but I was delighted to have the opportunity to see you again so jumped at the chance."

Sofia blushed and for a change was stuck for something to say. She made a mental note to have words with her father later.

As they rounded the corner of the courtyard Gerald couldn't help but notice how much Sofia lit up at the sight of several wild cats that she had been feeding. They all looked a bit worse for wear and ran away, except for one she called Mr Biggles. He was a big ginger boy and had a tatty ear from fighting, but as soon as he saw her, he rolled on his back and exposed his belly for a rub. He was cautious of Gerald, and she asked him to stand back while she scratched the cat behind his ears. She produced some cat biscuits like magic from her pocket and fed him by hand. She confessed that she spent hours out here with the cats when she was home. She changed the subject rapidly and he didn't push for more of the story. He had a feeling it was a taboo subject.

A little later one of the security guards came and got them. "Miss Sofia, your father requests you and your guest meet him in the main dining room for pre-dinner drinks."

When they entered the room, her father was loud and welcoming with his arm stretched out to shake Gerald's hand vigorously again.

"How is Mr Biggles today, Sofia?"

"He's fine, Daddy, getting fat."

Camilla was also present as well as a local politician and his wife and a quartet of musicians playing in the background. The meal included five courses with matching wines which Carlos chose from his own cellar. Conversation was light; no one wanted to get into a subject that would be controversial. Carlos was a bit of a comedian and told hilarious stories about his travels. The room was filled with laughter which helped Gerald to relax a little. Sofia laughed till she had tears running down her face at one point. What was obvious to Gerald was that Sofia meant the world to Carlos.

As the evening ended Carlos suggested Gerald be taken home by one of the chauffeurs and come back for his own vehicle the next day and winked at him. Gerald took the hint and graciously accepted, it also gave him an opportunity to see Sofia again the next day.

They all politely shook hands, and Carlos ushered his guests into a limo, and they all left together. Gerald looked back but could not see Sofia on the step waving with the rest of the family but then he caught a quick glimpse of her from a second-floor window and his heart skipped a beat.

Gerald wasn't surprised that the driver already knew his address, and although it was a paranoid thought, he knew his accommodation had been expertly searched in his absence.

The following day he arrived at the estate late morning, anxious to see Sofia again. He was asked to wait in the study while Carlos was located. They left him waiting for some time before Carlos appeared. He was friendly and genuine in his greeting and apologised for the delay and offered Gerald a whisky, which he declined – he wasn't a big drinker, and it was far too early in the day.

Gerald's heart sank when Carlos informed him that Sofia had to attend to an urgent business matter up north and would not be present today. Carlos wasn't sure when she would return. Gerald tried to hide his disappointment but, as if Carlos had read his mind, he asked him to sit down. "I would like to talk with you about your intentions regarding Sofia," Carlos said. "In case you are wondering, I like you Gerald, and I approve of you having a relationship with my daughter, if that is your intention. I'm sure you will not be surprised that I admit I had an investigator look into your past. He went deep into your family's history and left no stone unturned. Luckily for you, nothing came up that caused me any alarm."

Carlos smiled, as if to make light of the unspoken consequences had the search found otherwise. "I make no apology for the intrusion into your privacy," he continued, "because I know that you are aware of who you are dealing with. I know this because my people also investigated your Google search history."

Gerald wasn't too shocked, after all, he was trying to date the only daughter of the head of the biggest drug cartel in South America. Carlos slapped him on the back in a jovial manner and asked him if he had any questions.

"Yes," said Gerald. "How do you think I should go about this? She'll be a tough nut to crack." With that, they both laughed.

Easy Money Two

The funny man in the blue suit boarded the yacht again just out of Cypress. He seemed to appear from nowhere. He still had the appalling white shoes. He had clearly been watching too many bad movies.

His proposition was very much the same as last time: same journey, one passenger and cargo but two guards this time. He would give them till the next day at noon to decide if they were in or out. The boys figured that if there were two guards this time then the cargo was obviously more valuable. Therefore, the price should go up, so they figured that they would ask for two million this time. The twins had built up an element of trust after the first delivery. They had nothing to lose. So, when the little blue man returned the next day at precisely noon, they told him that the price had gone up to two million and they would be ready to leave as soon as the passenger and the cargo arrived. He didn't argue or barter, one and a half million dollars was in their Swiss account within thirty minutes.

As arranged, just after sunset, three heavily robed men with head wraps boarded the boat. Along with them, several cases with metal trim were loaded which were locked shut with radioactive symbols transferred on them. More guns and grenades and a rocket launcher that fired grenades plus a large quantity of food were carried aboard.

One of the guards was the same bodyguard from last time. Smiler, they called him, because he didn't smile. The new guard was called Mohammad, and the passenger was also called Mohammad, and they looked the same. It was going to be confusing to start with until they identified a personality trait.

Both Mohammads conversed with the twins but the one who was in charge conversed more; they called him Little Mohammad. In fact, he was quite interesting and spoke very good English. He asked if they minded if he helped out with the sails, and once they set out, he got changed into European clothing – shorts and a T-shirt. For the rest of the trip, he spent most of his time on deck and turned out to be a keen sailor and was willing to learn.

Mohammad, the guard, was a keen cook and helped Orhan prepare meals, and except for Smiler, they all got on and the seventeen days passed without incident.

Little Mohammad suggested that they board his father's superyacht and be his guest for a couple of days. Kane and Joseph clicked then that it was possibly his father they had been working for. He'd even arrange for a private tour of the city. The twins jumped at the chance. They felt comfortable in Mohammad's presence; he had become a friend. Orhan chose to stay on their yacht.

On land, they were driven to a huge mansion just out of the city. They walked around with their mouths open at all the household's rich furnishings, the gold furniture and exotic rugs. They lost count of the fountains and swimming pools. Staff fussed over them. Kane and Joseph met Mohammad's parents and his sister; they realised that she must have been their first passenger. The family was relaxed and friendly, and very down-to-earth. Although it wasn't planned, they ended up staying for a week. Mohammad assured them that Orhan had been checked on and was coping on his own.

When it was time for the twins to leave and go back to their boat, it was a genuine heartfelt departure and Mohammad vowed to catch up with them again in the future. He connected with them on Facebook but under a different name. The boys never questioned him about this or asked any other personal questions. They figured when the time was right, he would tell them. The twins never asked what he did or why he needed passage back to Iran, but they understood that the cargo could not be sent on a public flight. All they did know for sure was that the job paid well, and the superyacht they connected with in the harbour off Iran was extremely large and very expensive.

On the return journey this time, they agreed to take Smiler back with them as there were reportedly growing concerns about pirates. This was highly recommended by Mohammad, as Smiler's skill with firearms would come in handy if they encountered any trouble. Smiler wasn't any trouble; he didn't talk much and kept to himself.

The arrangement to transport people became a regular gig and it averaged out to once every two months. Occasionally Mohammad would appear out of nowhere and join them on the boat. They enjoyed these trips the most, as they were all similar ages and had similar interests, which always led to mayhem accompanied by disapproving looks from Orhan.

Unplanned Business Trip

Sofia often got last-minute assignments from her father. She seldom complained as it was all part of running the business. She arrived off her father's private jet at Furatena Airport in Muzo. It was late in the evening, and her father had arranged for her airport transfer ahead of her arrival to take her to their private villa. Carlos had been busy before she departed and had told her little about what to expect when she got there. All he said was that her instructions would be with the driver.

She didn't recognise the driver at first, he had his chauffeur's hat pulled down over his eyes, a cheap black suit and a large sign that simply read 'Miss Sofia'. It was a little unusual that he was also wearing Nike runners. She thought fleetingly that her father would rip him a new arse if he was here.

He put his hand out to take her case and as his head rose to meet her gaze, his broad white smile gave the charade away. Gerald was flushed with a combination of fear and embarrassment. He was instantly put at ease when Sofia took his hand and kissed him on both cheeks. He escorted her to the car, where the real chauffeur was waiting. On the way to the villa, he told her how he had asked her father for advice, and between him, Carlos and Camilla, they came up with this plan.

Sofia's skin was alive like pins and needles, blood rushing to her face and her nipples were strangely itchy, almost like they needed to be rubbed; she thought her heart would burst at any second. She had run scenarios repeatedly in her head on how she would progress things with Gerald, but none of the scenarios had worked out like this one. This was the ideal location to be discreet and there was so much to do here. She could show him the mine, and they could relax by the pool at the villa and get to know each other better. She would have to play ladies and remain in separate rooms, as she knew for sure that the servants would be ordered to spy on her and give her father regular updates.

Sofia couldn't remember a week that she had had so much fun. It all seemed such a whirlwind – every day they did something new. If it wasn't tramping about in the jungle and the rivers looking for exotic animal species and plants, then it was visiting the mines or the mining villages taking care parcels to the families. At night they ate like kings and Gerald told stories long into the night about his hometown and his travel adventures. Tomorrow night it would all be over, and they would have to return to their normal lives – Sofia just couldn't imagine a day without Gerald now. They both made a promise to see each other every day if possible or Skype each other if location and work meant they couldn't be together.

Gerald had one more trick up his sleeve that he had prearranged with Carlos and Camilla. As a surprise, on the last night, he would ask Sofia to marry him. He realised that he was moving a bit fast, but it just seemed right and honourable for a good Catholic girl. They were so much in love, their hearts hurt when they were apart.

Carlos had given him a ring which had been his mother's. It was a magnificent emerald set within a circle of diamonds. Gerald's pride fought within him that financially he couldn't provide a ring of such grandeur himself, but he soon got over it. When he found out its history and, as Carlos so eloquently put it, "Let's face it, she owns five emerald mines, she's only going to change it later if it's not good enough." Gerald could see the sense and accepted it gratefully.

Sofia smelt a rat earlier in the day. Gerald was acting differently – a bit more stress had crept into his mannerisms. She knew a surprise was coming and although she didn't want to presume anything, she secretly hoped it would be an engagement announcement. They had talked about marriage and children. She knew her instincts were on track when the staff started arriving from Bogotá and began rushing around cleaning, then boxes of food and champagne arrived. She knew then that her father and Camilla were about to appear like magic.

Gerald felt confident that Sofia would say yes, and to help matters he had her father's blessing. Carlos and Camilla would arrive later in the day to help celebrate. He had rehearsed the words in his head all night. The traditional one-knee proposal was essential. Gerald had fixed views on how to propose but he was also constantly aware of the carbon footprint. And it just wouldn't be him if he caused pollution on what was meant to be the most significant day of both their lives. So, he had struggled with a way to make it memorable. Eventually, with a little help from Camilla, they came up with a brilliant plan.

When Gerald suggested to Sofia they go out for lunch, Sofia had visions of a restaurant terrace proposal, instead, they arrived at an animal shelter where she was handed a pair of overalls. Together they cleaned cages and walked and

     MICHELLE THOMPSON

fed the dogs. Sofia got to help in the infirmary with the dogs and puppies that needed extra support due to injury and neglect. She was exhausted but was having a great time, a very rewarding experience, and she felt like she was supporting a good cause.

She had completely forgotten about the proposal idea when she was asked by the shelter manager to get some medicine out of the brown fridge. She found two white fridges and eventually found the brown fridge. She did a double-take when she first opened it, as it was empty except for a sign that said, "Will you marry me?" and an open ring box with the most beautiful ring that she had ever seen.

She was shaking when she pulled the ring from the fridge. She turned around to see the entire shelter staff watching her, all holding their breath. In the middle was poor Gerald, who had gone whiter than white and was down on one knee. Sofia held her face and cried. "Yes! Yes! Yes!" She was shaking too much to put the ring on, so Gerald helped her – it was a perfect fit.

Someone filmed it so later that night they relived the event for her father and Camilla and laughed every time they saw her cry. They tried to Skype Gerald's parents, but they couldn't make a connection. Gerald would have liked to have told them first.

Everyone was in agreement that they made a perfect couple. Now great plans were underway for a grand wedding.

The celebrations were interrupted when a servant came in from the main reception to inform them that some unexpected guests had arrived. As an extra surprise for both Gerald and Sophia, Carlos had secretly arranged for Gerald's parents to be flown over from Ireland. Apart from the shock on Gerald's face and his near heart failure, it couldn't have worked out better, although he would have some explaining to do once his parents worked out who Carlos was.

Sibling Rivalry

Matias sat reading with a frown on his face. Everyone in the room knew to keep away from him when he sat quietly with this particular frown; he was known for his short temper and aggressive outbursts. He was reading the front page of the *EL Espectador* which featured a huge colour photo of his father, Camilla, Sofia and her fiancé and his parents. The article was celebrating the engagement news and there was a superimposed insert of the ring. To add salt to the wound, the ring was his late grandmother's, to be left to the eldest grandchild which, in his mind, was him.

Matias was crimson with rage as he swept the table contents onto the floor smashing the crockery and sending warm coffee and food in every direction.

Sabastian and Alfredo took cover in the adjoining room – they knew not to return until things had cooled off. They had spent the last five years experiencing his outbursts.

They had all grown up at boarding school together. The boarding school had really been another name for a wayward boy's home. In reality, it was where you sent your sons who had gotten out of hand or disgraced you in some way, or they were just surplus to the parents' needs, or perhaps the parents had moved on with new partners and they didn't fit in the new family. Some of the boys had been lucky and Christian charities had plucked them off the streets and placed them there for a better life. But it was the strong who survived; it was dog-eat-dog. Bullying and sexual abuse were rampant, and if you didn't have protection or money, you were at the bottom of the food chain. It paid to have friends like Matias, even if you didn't agree with many of his practices. Occasionally some of the boys got lucky and managed to escape overseas, like Hugo who went to Europe as soon as he left school. There were, of course, the less fortunate who mysteriously disappeared. They were disposed of, never to be seen again. All unexplained indiscretions were conveniently swept under the table.

Matias had been hated by every staff member at the facility, and except for his little gang of thugs, every other boy in the establishment would cringe when they saw him and avoid conversation or eye contact.

Even now, years later, secluded away in the hills in one of his father's mansions, the staff lived in fear of him. The whores had long since refused to visit and Matias took his sexual pleasures from women he had bought on the slave market, some often underage, sold by poor farmers, desperate, or scared of the consequences of saying no to Matias.

Matias had little contact with his father, so wasn't surprised that he wasn't on the wedding invitation list. It just made him more determined to think of a way to really piss him off. And as for that spoilt little bitch Sofia, he'd like nothing better than to torture her to death and watch her suffer and scream for her daddy, but no one would come.

Pirates

The definition of Zakar meant handsome in Somalian, but Zakar the pirate was anything but handsome, in fact, it was difficult to describe him and get the full sense of his putridness. He was a shade darker than black; a shiny blue-black – at least he would have been if he had ever washed. He smelt like a hyena, half-rotten flesh and part human excrement. His teeth, although white at first appearance, had rotted from gum disease. He could dry retch from his own breath. Zakar thought all white people were American, but what he thought he knew for sure was that all white people were rich.

He had been a failure at everything he did, he couldn't even carry water without incident successfully in his village. The allure of great riches generated from piracy was what had drawn him to be a pirate. He was sold on the dream. He understood that he'd have to work his way up the ranks – that was how it worked – but in his mind, it was worth it. All he wanted to do was return to his village swathed in gold jewellery with fine clothes for his mother and sisters. He would prove to everyone that he wasn't a failure.

Zakar had no sea experience at all, he had never seen the sea in his entire life until he went to the city of Mogadishu to live the dream. In his mind, Mogadishu held the key to his success. He had a lead on a man to contact who could induct him into this 'Amway' lifestyle of riches.

 MICHELLE THOMPSON

Kidnapped At Sea

Kane and Joseph were just leaving the port of Alexandra when they got the call from home that poor old Uncle Rod had passed away. They were both devastated by the news. The timing was bad, as one of them had to stay with the boat for the return journey to Iran as they had precious cargo on board. They played Rock, Paper, Scissors to decide who would stay with the boat and who would catch the next plane back to Australia.

Kane couldn't remember the last time he was separated from his twin; he wasn't sure if he was feeling separation anxiety or grief for Uncle Rod. Whatever it was, he felt a mix of nervousness and fear. As if Orhan read his mind he started giving orders to set sail, keeping them on track for their delivery commitment. Orhan also felt the fear, he had a keen sense of premonition probably honed from surviving the genocide of his people. He'd ask Smiler to keep extra alert.

They entered the Suez Canal without incident and as the days went by and they got closer to their destination the pressure in the air almost seemed to ring. Kane and Orhan both felt the hairs on their necks prickle. This trip just felt different.

As they rounded the coast of the Yemen Peninsular, they saw the three fast-moving skiffs heading towards them; there was no second-guessing that these skiffs meant danger. There was no way to outrun them, and they could hardly radio the authorities for help and risk the cargo.

Smiler looked like he had just won the lottery. He disappeared below deck for an instant and returned with a Dynamite Nobel AG rocket launcher and a fifty-calibre Barrett gun with enough ammo to resemble an Arnold Schwarzenegger movie. He spaced his feet apart to brace himself and took aim at the closest skiff.

The other bodyguard, Mohammad, appeared on deck with a military assault rifle; he, too, wore a necklace of ammunition. He yelled at Kane and Orhan to get below deck and hide, the steel hull would protect them from stray bullets.

Kane took the opportunity to hide Orhan under the seat that he had inhabited when they first found him. Orhan was still very little, stunted from growing through starvation in his migration from Syria. "You're not to come out unless I give the order myself," Kane told Orhan. "And no matter what you hear, please don't risk it. If this ends badly, it will be down to you to alert the authorities and get help, Orhan."

As he closed the lid and put the swabs back, they could hear heavy gunfire above. At that moment Kane felt helpless. There weren't many places to hide on a yacht. As he contemplated what to do, Mohammad's bloodied body tumbled through the hatch and landed at his feet – he was dead. The gunfire above deck went silent.

A short while later there was a lot of confused yelling on deck then Zakar came down the hatch carrying a huge machete in one hand and a rifle in the other. He gestured for Kane to kneel in front of him. Kane thought he was going to chop his head off, instead, Zakar used the butt of his rifle to knock Kane out.

When Kane came to, he was bound and gagged and bundled into the corner of the cabin and there was an overpowering smell of rot; he realised it was coming from one of his captors. He could tell the yacht was under tow from the jerky movements. There was no sign of Orhan; he dared not call out to him but only hoped he was still alive.

Zakar and his crew were drunk, and the cabin was littered with ripped bedding and vomit, and they had urinated on the floor. The cargo boxes were broken open, and for the first time, Kane could see what was inside them. They all contained electronic equipment except for two boxes that had radioactive signs on them. The pirates were disappointed with the haul – it was a complicated cargo for them to on-sell. They seemed more interested in the stores of food and alcohol they had found.

Kane pretended to still be unconscious. There was a pool of blood on the floor beneath him, and he could feel the dried blood crackle on his face; his head hurt. Through a porthole, he could see it was dark outside.

He was still alive for now, and he could end up being the most valuable commodity on the boat once the alcohol was gone.

Matias's Gang

Matias often bragged about his family's connections and his father's wealth, so when he finished his schooling and was given a huge villa in a remote part of Colombia to live in, his own little gang of friends from school thought it was all part of the plan. His family name and his now generous allowance made him more successful at being a fat bully. His friends had come from financially poor backgrounds, so Matias' money and his cruel demeanour made him a better ally than an enemy.

Sebastian's father had worked for Carlos but was killed in the line of duty. Carlos had paid for his education and supported his mother after his father's death.

Alfredo and Rodrigues were cousins who had been caught shoplifting and sent to the boys' home, sponsored by the Catholic Church. Alfredo was the dominant one of the two, Rodrigues was the sensitive one and was easily led by his peers. They had come from a small fishing village on the coast, where both parents struggled to earn a living.

Hugo had an attention disorder; his parents had separated after his father went to jail. His new daddy hated him, and his mother said he reminded her of his father, so he was shipped off to the boys' school so they wouldn't have to deal with him. He was the comedian of the group; he was also the best-looking and was handy when they were trying to attract members of the opposite sex.

The crew couldn't wait to leave school; it was going to be like a big summer holiday. They all shifted into the villa together with the prospect of parties and women being the only thing they could collectively concentrate on.

The first summer at the villa was every young man's dream, although they all agreed that they would need to think of a plan to make some money. It wasn't fair to keep using Matias' money, although he didn't seem to care.

Although Matias had very little communication with his father, occasionally his father would contact him and ask him to clean up a situation in the area. Matias' crew were ideal for this type of task, and they felt like they needed to contribute to justify all their spending, so they were always eager to get involved. Their first big break came when a truck transporting one hundred kilograms of cocaine had been involved in an accident and crashed over a bank. Carlos had asked them to rent a replacement truck, transfer the cargo, and then deliver it to its intended destination.

The transfer went smoothly, and it was Matias who decided to release a kilogram of cocaine each to themselves, and he would tell his father they had been damaged in the accident and could not be recovered. They took six kilograms, one each and one for the party house. To cover their tracks, Matias and Sebastian shot and killed the driver and the co-driver and buried their bodies in the jungle.

Matias didn't manage to entirely convince his father that the events happened as he said, and for a while, they all lived in fear that Carlos would send some of his older trusted associates to question them at length. This did not happen, and they soon relaxed and made bigger plans for the next call of duty.

It was all too much for Rod and Hugo to handle, so they approached Matias and asked if they could leave the group and go on an overseas holiday. They thought the idea of a holiday would sound better than they were just putting as much distance between them as they could to get away from Matias and his father.

Surprisingly Matias agreed without any conditions; he secretly thought they were both a couple of 'soft-cocks' and would be weak links if questioned so it was an easy out for everyone. He had fleetingly thought of just shooting them both in the head, but Rodrigues was Alfredo's cousin, and he liked Alfredo.

Hugo and Rod travelled together for a short while then they shook hands and parted company, both relieved to put some space between themselves and Matias. Hugo departed for Bogotá and Rod decided to visit his parents' fishing village in Buenaventura and buy a yacht.

Wedding of the Year

It was marked as the highlight of the social calendar, the who's who of South America were invited along with some favourable politicians whose influence would be of use later.

It had been Sofia's idea to invite Matias. Her father had warned her against it and said nothing good would come of it, but she felt enough time had passed and she wanted to do the right thing.

She rang Matias herself, and he was delighted with the invite to the wedding. They chatted for a while and even had a joke or two about the stress of organising a wedding with Carlos at the helm. He even asked her what gift she wanted, and he was even cheeky enough to ask if he could bring Sebastian, who he reminded her was a long-time family friend. She didn't want a gift and Sebastian was welcome. There were five hundred people coming, one more or less wouldn't matter.

The venue was in Cartagena, deemed the wedding capital of Colombia with its gorgeous Spanish-colonial architecture and colourful cobbled streets. It was decided that the event would be managed by a wedding planner, which settled the arguments between Carlos and Sofia, who clearly had a generation gap with regards to organising a society wedding.

The wedding day was a massive overkill; the stress nearly tipped the whole event into chaos with Gerald coping the only way he knew how by flying off to the remote jungle to collect frogs just days before the event. But now they had said their "I do's" and kissed in front of the now one thousand people, half of whom they had never met before, and the champagne was flowing freely.

Matias was an absolute gem and entertained everyone with hilarious stories and gave a speech at the reception about how blessed he was to have such a beautiful sister. Both he and Sebastian worked the crowd like pros. Carlos kept one eye on them. He wasn't sure what they were up to, but he knew not to trust them. Today was meant to be a happy day, so he let it slide.

Sofia and Gerald left the reception in a limo, with streamers and tin cans dragging behind the car and white paint on the rear window saying, 'Just Married'. They had planned a honeymoon in New Zealand for a month;

its beautiful scenery and clean green image appealed to Gerald. Sofia just loved it because no one would know who she was, and she could live freely without interruption and concentrate on her new husband. They both couldn't remember when they were more excited.

 MICHELLE THOMPSON

Anyone for a Car Boot Ride

Kane awoke to warm urine being excreted onto his face. Zakar was pissing on him; even his urine smelt like goat's piss. As he stirred Zakar kicked him forcibly in the ribs and knocked the air out of him. Zakar kept repeating "You American? You American?"

Kane tried to talk but his mouth was sore and dry, he could only scratch out a "No," but wanted to say Australian.

A rough hessian sack that smelt like fish was placed over his head, and he felt himself being half-carried and half-dragged by two people. Without any care, they hit his head on the roof of the cabin and awkwardly manhandled his body as they took him out of the yacht's cabin. Through the sack he got a burst of fresh air, he couldn't believe how much he had missed clean air. He thought he was being carried along a wooden pier by the sound, and then the footsteps were on concrete. In the distance, he could clearly hear the reverse beep of a forklift or truck. He knew by the coolness of the air that it was night. He didn't struggle; instead, he would try and save his energy to escape later if the opportunity came up. He guessed he was still at the port.

Kane wasn't a heavily built man, but his captors were out of breath and stopped a couple of times to have a breather. At one stage they stopped and had a conversation with a third party, but not in a language that Kane could understand. Then he heard a squeaky hinge, and he was rolled and pushed into the boot of a car, which he determined from the spare tyre he felt under him. The boot lid was slammed down, and all was silent except for the sound of striking matches and the smell of tobacco smoke.

The car door slammed only once, and once the engine started the car lurched off at speed with jagged movements. The vehicle had no shock absorbers, and the trip was painful and harrowing.

Just when Kane thought it couldn't get any worse, dust started to fill the boot, choking him, so that breathing through the sack was almost impossible. He lost count of the times he got thrown forcibly from the front to the back of the boot due to heavy braking or bounced to the top of the boot. He had bitten his tongue, and the metallic taste of blood was filling his mouth. How he wished he'd lost 'Rock, Paper, Scissors' now.

The vehicle stopped. The driver got out and slammed the door. There was a heated argument with another individual. Kane was drifting in and out of consciousness through dehydration and hunger.

The boot opened. "Are you American?" a voice said in English. Kane couldn't answer, his throat was dry with dust. He was punched in the head twice and asked again if he was American.

Both men dragged his body from the boot and carried him. The intense dry heat struck him instantly; it must be daylight. He was thrown down what seemed like a long flight of stairs, it was cool and dark. He drifted into unconsciousness.

When he woke, he was aware of someone trying to give him water and wash his face. His instinct was to fight, but he was too weak. There was the soothing voice of an American man in hushed tones. It was some time before Kane could work out that he was no longer tied up, the sack was removed from his head, and he was in the recovery position. He hurt all over and dared not move as it renewed the pain.

The American was helping him to drink water, little sips at a time. "My name's Daniel," he said.

"How long have you been here?" Kane croaked, his dry throat making speech difficult.

"Six months," Daniel replied despondently. He had been an innocent tourist, backpacking around third-world countries to save money and doing volunteer work. "They grabbed me in broad daylight in a public market in Mogadishu. No one came to my aid or tried to intervene."

He had been beaten, and his captives had starved him of food and water repeatedly.

"Now they're asking for a ten-million-dollar ransom for my release," continued Daniel. "My parents are pastors in Central America. They don't even own a house let alone have ten million dollars. There's no way they can raise that sort of money. I'm sure the US Government is trying to do something, although I've heard nothing, but I also know that the President has a no ransom money policy."

The only saving grace was they had started feeding him consistently as his wounds had become infected and they needed him alive to get the ten million.

"My best advice for you is to tell our captors that you came from a very wealthy family who will willingly pay the ransom. Then maybe you can get word to my family that I'm, still alive and, with a bit of luck, get us both out of here.

"But first, I will get our captors' attention and try and get some food."

For now, Daniel was just happy to have company; he had suffered miserably and thought he was going to die alone.

Days rolled into weeks. Kane had communicated his parents' identity and wealth to Mr Stinky. He had heard nothing back. He had suffered two more beatings since his capture. Drunken men with clubs had rushed in when they were asleep and bashed them as if it was some sort of a joke.

The food was always stale bread and occasionally a weak soup of unknown ingredients.

Kane had faith that his father would be on his way and this is what kept him going. He had not seen daylight the whole time he had been in the basement. It was silent except for the noise of the man who opened the door and left bread and water. It was a miserable existence, and he longed for home. He could only imagine what had happened to Orhan.

Sofia's Life Changes Forever

"Papa, I have not heard from Gerald today. I'm worried that something has happened to him."

Carlos assured her it was probably a technical problem and told Sofia not to worry, but he would ring the local constabulary and get them to check on him.

Sofia and Gerald had been married for six months now, and every day was still a fairy tale. Everyone joked to her the honeymoon would be over soon. They had been trying for a baby, but they had not been blessed yet.

She could count the hours on one hand for the number of times they went without talking to each other each day. Even if she or Gerald had to go away on business they always kept in touch, so her radar was on full alert now that she had not heard from him today; it was highly unusual.

Gerald was staying at Leticia in their summer house using it as a base while he was up there doing research. Leticia was termed the 'Gateway to the Amazon' and Gerald was a regular visitor to the area, fighting with local government over his precious frogs. He was convinced that increased tourism was harming their habitats. The Leticia villa only had servants when the family went to stay; beyond that, only a family who tended the grounds lived in a little cottage on the estate.

Sophia resisted an urge to jump on a plane and fly up there and rang his phone so many times she felt like an insecure wife and a bit like a stalker. Her appetite had completely gone, and she was running on pure adrenaline with worry.

As day turned into night, her intense stress was making her crazy. What if he had fallen and hit his head? What if he was lying in a hospital somewhere? She ran through every scenario in her head. It was killing her. Every time the phone rang it was like an electric shock on her jangled nerves.

Eventually, the local police rang her father back and said the house was all locked up and no one was there; no cars no people. On Sofia's request, and pleading, Carlos requested that the police start a search, and they all decided to start ringing around and see if he was at any of his known places, like the university or the wildlife centre.

     MICHELLE THOMPSON

Carlos did admit it was starting to worry him. This could go both ways, either Gerald would think they had all made too much fuss, and they would all laugh it off tomorrow, or he was half-munched by a crocodile or an anaconda. Either way, there was now a plan to wait for the police to ring back with news or fly there first thing in the morning if they hadn't heard from him. He hated seeing his daughter like this. His only advice was for her to try and get some rest and tell her she'd feel silly if he rang soon. Secretly he knew something was wrong, it just wasn't like him. Gerald was a nerd about communicating with her.

Rest was the last thing on Sophia's mind. She went outside to talk to Mr Biggles – he always was a comfort when she was feeling out of control or down. She found him waiting for her by the kitchen door, so she gave him some fresh salmon and took him upstairs to her and Gerald's bedroom. She lay back on the bed with one of Gerald's jumpers on her pillow so she could smell him while she waited restlessly.

At 3.15 am Sofia sat bolt upright; she must have fallen asleep. Mr Biggles needed to go out but that wasn't what had woken her. She had a sense of pure dread pass over her. She ran to her father's room and then to Camilla's room and woke them up. She was hysterical. "I think Gerald is dead."

They all got up and drank coffee while Carlos ordered the servants to get their belongings ready for travel. He ordered his private plane to be ready for take-off at dawn. In the following hours, while they waited for daylight, he made several phone calls to all his contacts in the area.

The wind on the airport runway was unusually cold and it bit into their skin as they climbed the steps to board the plane. Sofia's jangled nerves were making her angry with her father for taking so long. He was on the phone in the hangar. She just wanted him to hurry up so they could get going. She pleaded with Camilla to go and get him and tell him to hurry.

Through the window of the plane, Sophia saw her father collapse on the floor of the hangar, people rushing to his aid. As she got out of her seat to run to him, he was being sat up by his aides. He was ghostly pale and holding his chest. Someone had called for an ambulance, but he was telling them to stop. He said this was a family matter. The look in his eyes was that of deep sorrow and anguish.

"Sofia, come closer, please. Sit down next to me, I have bad news. The police have found a body in a local river, which they believe is Gerald. A homicide investigation is underway. He didn't slip and fall, it appears the body was dumped there. He's been decapitated ... his head is missing."

There was a ringing in her ears; she didn't blink or make a sound; she wasn't sure she even breathed. Everyone went silent; shock was setting in. Water seemed to gush from her eyes in a steady stream. No one knew what to do.

Sofia finally reacted. She stood up, helped her father up, and demanded that everyone board the plane immediately. She'd believe it when she saw the body. For the time being, she'd stay safe in the bubble she'd created in her head.

It seemed like the longest flight Sophia had ever been on. She'd sort everything out when she got there.

At her request, no one spoke to her during the flight, but she could hear her father and Camilla whispering. She wanted to tell them to shut up, but it was as if her jaw was wired shut. Her eyes were narrowed in thought; this just couldn't be true; was it even Gerald?

It was a sombre time at the mortuary – seemed silly that there was paperwork to sign. Presenting ID to prove she was Gerald's wife, Sofia had switched into her business mode, relying on one of her different personalities to take over the situation.

Both she and Carlos were ushered into an office and asked to take a seat. The police were advising her and Carlos against viewing the body. She threw them a vicious glance which was enough to make them recoil.

The Chief of Police explained that it would be an unpleasant viewing.

"Even after all my years in the police force, I have never seen anything as shocking," he explained. "I must warn you before you see him; his head is missing, and the body shows extreme signs of torture – Gerald must have endured the torture for many hours. So far there is no sign of alcohol or drugs in his system. And there is one more thing that is very disturbing; his tongue had been inserted into his anus and his testicles are also missing."

They all sat in stunned silence. Sofia felt like ash, ash with no body, no feeling, it was like she was floating. She wanted to vomit, then she wanted a drink of strong liquor, and then she wanted nothing again – she was just ash.

"Can I see the body now?" she requested in a cold, business-like, indisputable way.

The room was empty except for a table with the body on it and a simple

     MICHELLE THOMPSON

steel-framed chair beside it. As the mortician pulled back the white sheet and exposed the cold white and purple body, Sofia's legs buckled but she steadied herself on the table. It was Gerald; she didn't need a head to identify him. Some of his fingers were missing including his wedding ring; there were cuts and deep holes all over his body. The mortician told her he had the words 'Arse Licker' carved into his back.

She didn't know what she was going to tell his parents, was all she could think. The body could come back with them to Bogotá. She would have it cremated then fly to his parents and spread his ashes in his home country. She was already thinking ahead.

"Our forensics team are still at the summer house; that is where the murder took place," said the police chief.

Sophia asked for a chair so she could sit with the body for a while. She didn't know what else to do; she knew she didn't want to leave him just yet. She was numb; the ash in her mind seemed to be engulfing her. She just wanted to hold his hand.

Carlos left the room. He needed water and fresh air; he was going to be sick. His heart had taken a beating today, but he was trying to stay strong for his daughter.

Sofia asked the mortician if he knew the time of death. He predicted about 3 am. She finished the sentence for him; she already knew it was exactly 3.15 am.

The summer house was a crime scene, but Sofia and her father were permitted to suit up and enter the dwelling under police supervision. There was blood everywhere in the main lounge and kitchen. There had been a struggle; curtains were ripped, furniture moved. Gerald was strong; he would have put up a fight. His rucksack was sitting by the front door unopened. His wallet still had his cash in it, so it wasn't a robbery gone wrong.

The police had questioned the family who lived in the ground keeper's house. They hadn't heard or seen anything.

Carlos decided that, after the case was settled, the building would be burnt to the ground; he didn't want to think about it again. He certainly couldn't believe the extent that someone had gone to, to inflict so much harm on Gerald. He didn't have an enemy in the world. Frogs weren't enough reason to do this to him.

Sofia had had enough; she just wanted to get home now. She'd go back to the hospital and arrange for the body to come back with them. She'd get Carlos to contact the funeral service company that had looked after her mother. Camilla could get a doctor to have a look at her father; he was looking terrible. She had gone into full organisation mode. She wanted to get as far away from this place as possible.

She started packing everyone into cars and shouting orders. She was very, very angry now. No one dared get in her way.

As everyone drove off with their orders and assigned tasks, she noticed one of the groundkeepers' younger sons looking out from the bushes. She remembered she'd bought him a pushbike once for Christmas. He was a lovely boy. He had a strange name, so she always remembered it – Felix. He was a simple, gentle soul. She went over to reassure him that everything was going to be all right. He flew into her arms sobbing, it had been rough for everyone. The tears came. Sofia didn't stop crying for three days and three nights.

Carlos pulled as many strings as a man with his power and connections could pull, and they flew home in the early hours of the morning with Gerald's body. They had a funeral company ready to meet them at the airport when they arrived.

Sofia just stared into space crying. She had managed to ring Gerald's parents and give them the terrible news; it had been a long and sad phone call. The arrangements had already been made for her to travel with Gerald's ashes in the following week. They would meet her at the airport; she would travel alone. She now understood the term 'grief was heavy' – she felt she had a tremendous weight on her.

Sofia went to the back yard to look for Mr Biggles as soon as she got home. The staff said he was missing and had not eaten his breakfast or his dinner. She clamoured around in the dark with a torch and called him, rattling his biscuits.

After a while, he called back from under plants and seating. He was very frightened; it took her a while to calm him. He rubbed his face on hers, her tears wetting his head. She hugged him tight and kissed him. It would have been the absolute end for her if something had happened to him.

She carried him back to the house. He was so heavy that she couldn't aim the torch in the direction she was trying to negotiate on the path. She tripped and fell over a pot plant and went sprawling onto the path. Mr Biggles jumped to safety but was hissing aggressively at the item she had tripped on.

Sophia clambered for the torch cursing the gardener, skinned knee and all. Shining the torch on the offending obstruction she could see it wasn't a pot plant but a square box, wrapped in plastic.

She screamed for her father and security. She didn't need to be told what was in the box, she knew.

The face was bruised and bloodied. Eyelids blacked. With the grotesque expression captured on his face, it was hard to recognise it was Gerald. His balls were stuffed in his mouth. His wedding ring was punched into his eye socket. It was an image she would carry to her grave.

At the sight of the contents of the box, Carlos collapsed with a suspected heart attack and needed an ambulance. The day couldn't get any worse.

Sofia rang Matias to tell him the bad news. She'd need him to step up and support the family while she was away in Ireland. He said he was in town already at the airport waiting for Sebastian, who hadn't returned from a business trip in Australia, and he had lost contact with him. He'd come straight away. "Don't worry, sis, I'll be there for you."

Matias was a rock – she put aside the old reservations her father had. She was going to need his support while her head was swimming in 'ash'. He was a pleasant distraction from the horror she kept reliving. She hadn't slept in days and was running on pure adrenaline. He told her the full story about Sebastian's nccd to go to Australia. They both agreed not to tell Carlos – that would put him at a higher risk of dying if he found out where his cocaine had gone, and that Sebastian was missing.

Sofia couldn't help noticing that Matias had an infected wound on his hand. He said he'd been bitten by a dog, and it had taken out a chunk of flesh from his hand between his thumb and first finger. She wanted him to ask the doctor about the wound while they were at the hospital, but he wasn't interested in asking so she didn't push it.

Final arrangements were made for her trip to Ireland. She now had Gerald's ashes. Mr Biggles was in a cat home until her return. Carlos had been transferred to a private hospital and Matias promised to update her if anything changed regarding her father's medical status.

Sophia boarded the plane in a flood of tears. Everyone who had come to see her off was crying. She suddenly felt naked without her support crew around her, but she wanted to take this journey alone. She had received a copy of the autopsy report before she left and had not told anyone but kept it secret to read on the long flight – not quite the inflight entertainment she usually liked but she wanted to know Gerald's last hours in detail. The police had no suspects. Also, it was discovered that Gerald's phone was missing. She had managed to obtain his call and text records which she had not disclosed to any other party. She was going to solve this crime on her own.

Orhan's Hideout is Discovered

Orhan had listened for a while for sound; he was sure the pirates had all left the boat. He hadn't dared to move for hours least he made a noise. His bladder was screaming at him; his plastic bottles were full. He couldn't smell the stinky pirate, so that was a good sign. His joints were stiff and sore.

He lifted the seat top to see if the coast was clear – it looked safe; no one was on the boat.

He took his piss bottles out and made his way to the ladder of the cabin exit. He lifted the hatch; all clear.

He dropped over the side of the boat into the warm harbour water and immediately started to relieve himself. He set his bottles free in the tide. He'd look for some more bottles in the rubbish before he returned. He could move about reasonably freely in the dark where the boat was moored. There were plenty of low-life individuals creeping about. He'd skirt the area and hopefully stumble upon a food source or clean water.

One thing he had learnt from being a desperate refugee from Syria was survival. He always kept a knife on him. He was starving; he had been living on dry rolled oats and scavenging bread from the pirates occasionally. He'd gone days without food on and off for years; he'd adjusted again quickly.

He cautiously made his way back to the boat and checked his surroundings. Nothing seemed out of place although his instincts told him differently. No sign of any movement on the boat; the coast was clear. He crept aboard. No one was in the cabin; he was safe. He put the bottles down to open the lid of the seat. He smelt him before he saw him, his leering grin looking back up at him from his own hiding place.

Zakar was quick and surprisingly strong. He grabbed Orhan around the throat instantly restricting his breathing. Orhan was helpless against Zakar's strength and height. Orhan dropped the knife in his panic. Weeks without food had deprived him of any energy.

Zakar was cruel with his methods of inflicting pain. He started bashing Orhan's head against the exit of the cabin, standing on him in his attempt to drag him up the ladder.

Orhan was drifting in and out of consciousness. He was sure his leg was broken. But Zakar wasn't finished with him yet. He reached over the side and plunged Orhan into the water. He wanted to drown him. This stowaway had shamed him for not being vigilant, he was going to pay with his death. As Orhan struggled to draw air he also wanted to breathe in the water and end it as quickly as possible – he couldn't go on much longer.

Suddenly Zakar's grip was no more. Orhan gulped on a mouthful of seawater. He had a sensation of being lifted high up into the air as big hands held him and tucked him under an arm.

In an almost humorous Australian accent he heard, "He almost had you there, little fella."

Someone was running with him under one arm. Orhan was limp as the seawater left his lungs. He felt incredibly safe – he knew it was Doug.

Orhan managed a scratchy reply. "What took you so long?"

Doug had silently watched Orhan get off the boat as he was in the water sticking limpet mines along the hull of the yacht. It was too early to show himself.

While he was keeping one eye on the little guy, he saw one of the pirates return to the yacht. He had taken his eyes off Orhan for a split second, and he had disappeared into the darkness. He figured he'd catch up with him while he was wiring up the explosives around the warehouse where the pirates were storing the cargo they had stolen. Doug was always going to rescue Orhan, once he'd established he was alive. But suddenly Orhan popped up again and had slipped back into the cabin of the boat. That's when he heard the scuffle. He was set to enter the cabin until he saw the pirate emerge with Orhan firmly gripped around his tiny throat with a dirty brown hand. When he crept up behind them, he had already plunged Orhan under the water.

Doug smashed Zakar over the head with all his strength with the end of his steel torch. He heard bone crunch under the pressure and Zakar dropped to the deck unconscious, which was the result Doug wanted because he needed one pirate alive to find out where Kane was.

When he picked Orhan up he was as light as a feather. His shoulder was still sore from the bullet wound but not enough to stop him from running with the little bugger under his arm.

Joseph and a couple of elite Iranian fighters were waiting for his signal in the dark. It was an emotional moment when Joseph and Orhan were reunited. Doug fluffed the hair on his head and gave him a pat on his back. "It's ok, son, you're safe now." He meant it; he'd adopt the little bugger when they got home.

Doug had blocked all the exits to the warehouse except the main entrance. There had been four men playing cards around a table. They had all been consuming alcohol but weren't impaired enough to not put up a fight.

With the help of his new Iranian friends, they threw some tear gas canisters into the building. As the men exited the building coughing and spluttering, they ruthlessly cut their throats from ear to ear.

Doug and his men entered the building with gas masks and retrieved the cargo. He thought it was best that the Iranians packed their boat and left immediately. He'd have Joseph wait just out of sight for his signal. He was confident he could do the rest on his own.

Hell Breaks Loose in Mogadishu

CNN reported a massive explosion in the capital of Mogadishu with up to ten people confirmed dead in a storage warehouse at the port. A warehouse had been destroyed along with a yacht moored in the vicinity. No tourists or overseas nationals were reported injured in the blast. No one had claimed responsibility for the blast, although Islamic militants had been the main suspects due to localised civil unrest.

This was the distraction that Doug needed to keep the authorities preoccupied; it gave him a clear run to rescue his son. He still had Zakar gagged and bound in a plastic tarpaulin and tied down on the back of a land cruiser that he had borrowed from one of the dead pirates at the warehouse.

Zakar was a little bit the worse for wear, but he had given Doug all the information he needed. Doug had beaten Zakar until he got all the directions and the details of the people he would encounter, and the structure they were holding Kane in. Doug mused to himself that Zakar was better than a GPS. Doug could work on this one with some expertise. He hadn't finished with Zakar yet, smelly bastard.

Doug was dressed in traditional local attire so as not to draw too much attention to himself. His face was covered, although he was a lot taller than most of the locals he encountered.

He drove into the desert until he reached the outskirts of a small village; he'd wait here until nightfall before his final assault. Zakar had confirmed that Kane was still alive along with the American. Doug didn't care about the American, but if it was easy, he would rescue him as well.

Doug had left Orhan with Joseph. They were waiting offshore in an inflatable they had borrowed from the Iranian family who were not only their clients but were now good friends. The Iranians were happy as Doug had found and returned the radioactive nuclear parts that the pirates had stolen.

Just as night was falling Doug strapped Zakar to the bull bars on the front of his vehicle. It was a bit 'Mad Max', but he found the humour in that; after all, it was a great Australian classic. Zakar was still alive, a poke in his eyeball established that; a muffled cry came out a bit like deflating bagpipes.

He'd wait until the villagers had gone to sleep before he crept in to get his son.

The cluster of war-torn buildings where his son was being held captive were covered in bullet holes and holes from explosives from rebel fighting. Next to them were acres of Bantu huts made of sticks, straw, clay and bits of plastic sheeting. Rough pieces of corrugated iron were sometimes evident. They lived like refugees. There was raw sewage in the channels between the buildings, emaciated dogs scavenging what rubbish they could find and a sick crying baby in the distance.

The only difference with the building his son was in was that it had a crude basement carved out of the dirt from an old bomb crater. Zakar had told him it wasn't high enough to stand fully upright in places, so Doug would have to consider that Kane might not be able to walk or run. It had been covered with boards and dirt piled on top.

Zakar's partner in crime, Abshir, was meant to be guarding their potential road to riches but, just on dark, he had found a dusty bottle of King Lion Whisky, which was contraband, in the dirt where he was sleeping. As a Muslim, you weren't permitted to drink but that had never stopped him. He secreted it under his bedding, taking large gulps to quench his thirst. Fuck feeding his captives tonight, there wasn't any food anyway. Zakar hadn't returned from the city as scheduled and no ransom money had been delivered.

Doug needed a distraction, so he started a fire in the mountain of rubbish that was piled up on the edge of the vast expanse of tents and shelters. The fire caught on quickly, its putrid black smoke blowing towards the tents.

People started yelling and shouting, and rats were running away from the heat of the fire in their thousands. Potentially hundreds of people could have died from the fire, but Doug didn't care.

Doug skirted around the village following the directions Zakar had given him until he found Abshir propped up in his bed. Doug was still in heavy disguise, face wrapped and supporting himself with a crude walking stick. Doug waved a large stack of bills called 'shillings' at him, pointing to the lump under the pillow.

Abshir was instantly suspicious. How did he know what was under the pillow, and this man with the black eyes, why didn't he talk? The money was enticing; he had never seen that much money before. Abshir lured him closer so he could inspect the money. If this was a trap, and this frail old man turned out to be a Holy Man, he risked being ostracised and embarrassed. The police didn't get paid enough to care.

The old man handed Abshir the wad of money and held his hands together in a prayer or begging motion. Abshir turned his head to retrieve the bottle under his pillow with one hand, the other hand firmly clutching the cash.

Doug seized the moment and walloped Abshir across the head with the stick and kept whacking him with brutal force until he was sure he was dead. He kicked dirt on the small fire to extinguish the light. It was pitch-black now, everyone was still fighting the fire, and no one had seen or heard a thing.

There was a sack covering the entrance to the basement lightly covered in dirt. He dug away at it and flipped the crude door backwards, so the hole was exposed. The stench of human excrement spilt out of the hole making him gag.

He shone his torch down the hole and saw two pale, dirty faces peering back at him, frightened and gaunt with starvation. "Ready to go home, son?"

Doug stretched down and grabbed his son's hand and pulled him from the pit. Kane let out a slight blubber but bit his lip and hugged his dad; a single tear rolled down his face. "You must save 'Hank the Yank', Dad, he kept me alive."

Doug pulled Daniel from the filthy hole. Both boys confirmed they were able to walk.

Doug's aim was to get them safely to the outskirts of town where he had left the land cruiser and then get them back to the port where Joseph was waiting with the boat. He grabbed what was left of the whisky; he might need a drink after all of this.

The walk was long and hard, with the boys often stumbling and falling. People from the fire had started returning to their tents and huts. Often, they would have to lie down in the dark and hide till the danger had passed.

Eventually, they made it to the truck. Kane was about to ask what the blue tarpaulin was tied to the bull bar, but he recognised the smell and realised it was Zakar.

Doug gave Kane and Daniel some robes to wear and some headgear to cover their faces. They weren't safe yet; they still had to get back to the port and drop Daniel off outside the US embassy.

Both boys slept on the journey, only waking to drink some water.

     MICHELLE THOMPSON

It was still dark when they reached the road blockade two roads back from the embassy. Daniel promised to keep quiet about his rescuers until he had given them enough time to get safely back out into international waters. Doug had some more distraction plans to keep the authorities busy so he told Daniel to keep listening to the news to be sure he could gauge the timing.

Doug left the land cruiser in the middle of the main market and threw a hand grenade into the cab. He quickly tucked one into Zakar's plastic wrap for good measure.

He had left Kane a little further down the harbour hiding between some old oil drums, it was also a good vantage point for Joseph to come in and collect them. He made his way back to him carefully, weaving in and out of alleyways.

Doug could hear sirens and commotion from the market. He walked casually so as not to draw attention to himself. It was that sort of place; plenty of low-life, shady-looking motherfuckers skulking around and wafts of hashish smoke rising through the air. He'd have to tell his son soon that his mother was dead. What a fuckin mess.

Joseph glided in almost silently. There was another Iranian inflatable just out of sight, flanking them for safety. Together they idled out into open water back to the Gulf of Oman. Until they were back with their Iranian host, Doug wasn't going to rest. In the distance, it looked like the whole of Mogadishu was on fire. Doug had no remorse; the place was a shit hole.

Iranian Hospitality

Kane had taken the news of his mother's death badly. He was weak from starvation and infection; it would take him a while to come right. They were all very sad.

Doug kept Orhan close, on his knee most of the time. It was easy to get attached to the little guy; he helped to keep his mind off the death of Mellissa. If she'd been alive, she'd want to take him in like a stray dog and feed him up. She'd be happy that Doug was looking after him. Orhan also spoke Arabic, so he was handy for translation purposes.

Their hosts treated them like kings. They had their own accommodation and provided the best medical care for Kane and also Doug's shoulder which had opened again. Food was supplied in abundance and anything else if they required it.

Joseph was out with Little Mohammad most of the time while Kane was being fussed upon by Naz, short for Nazneen, who was Mohammad's sister, who had been their first passenger on their boat. Doug could see a little more than a nurse-patient relationship starting up there and Orhan confirmed his thoughts, insightful little lad.

Doug didn't want to outstay their welcome, but it seemed that wasn't possible. He was introduced to many of Dr Farhad's friends and family. Doug was driven around to events and functions in well-planned motorcades and treated like royalty. Dr Farhad, it turned out, was a Professor of Biochemistry and was worth about ten billion in oil and real estate, so he was a very interesting guy to talk to. Doug and Dr Farhad got on like old friends; it was a very natural relationship; very relaxed.

Dr Farhad turned to Doug. "So, my friend, what next?" he asked.

Doug's response was blunt. "I need to make my way to Colombia and murder the person responsible for my wife's death," he growled.

"I understand completely, my friend," Dr Farhad replied, unfazed and supportive of Doug's mission. "And I offer you my full support with logistics and advice, should you require it."

Doug needed to go by sea as he had a plan which, for the time being, he

     MICHELLE THOMPSON

was keeping to himself, but it had a time frame which he was committed to, so his next step was to buy a boat, one that was capable of crossing the Atlantic Ocean once they had followed the coast and reached Dakar. He was estimating about sixty days at sea with good weather. His hosts had several friendly officials at selective ports that could speed up any immigration issues, so they could quickly refuel and move on. Once they reached Panama, Doug had a New Zealand associate he would contact who could help them with their transition through the Panama Canal.

Kane was feeling much better, although a bit lovesick now, and the thought of moving on from the lovely Naz was causing him separation anxiety. He asked his father if he could marry her. Doug was a little taken aback. This was Mellissa's department, but now she was gone he found he had to wear multiple hats, so he advised him that the correct process was to ask her father. "They do things differently here, boy. If you don't get it right, I think it's not only your hands they chop off." So, Kane worked up the courage to ask Naz's father.

Dr Farhad, Naz's father, had a solution for everything; he confirmed it with Doug and they both agreed. First, he insisted that they take his superyacht to Colombia, then on to Australia, and when they were ready, they could return it which would mean that both Kane and Naz could be engaged in a long-distance relationship and the time that Kane would be absent would be more respectable to her culture and her status. If the relationship survived the separation, when they brought the yacht back the wedding could take place. Doug suggested the whole family could attend the wedding, complete with several more family members and an entourage of friends. They just needed some time to get organised.

Kane and Naz didn't really like the idea; it wasn't as instant as they wanted but they could see the sense in it and listened to both parents' sound advice. Anyway, if it took too long Kane could fly back and see her every now and then.

Doug needed Kane to skipper the boat, the next leg of the journey was a family affair, and he needed his boys with him.

Doug was completely humbled by the offer of the superyacht. He was grateful to his host for his hospitality, and it solved an immediate problem. They could leave as early as the next day.

Back at Sea

There were the usual goodbyes, with everyone shaking hands and hugging. Kane and Joseph were being given final pre-voyage instructions from the skipper. The boat was the doctor's very own superyacht: forty-three metres long, three double cabins and two twin cabins; it was the ultimate in luxury. It really needed a crew of eight to operate it, but Doug had faith in all their abilities to manage it.

Orhan was shown the galley and the cooking arrangements, and food and provisions were loaded onto the boat. Doug protested at the lavish quantity of supplies. He did explain that he had money to purchase such items himself, but his hosts wouldn't hear of it and continued loading the boat.

Dr Farhad had talked at length with Doug about taking some of his crew on the journey, but he understood the need for the family to venture on their own for many reasons, most of all grief.

Once the yacht was fuelled up, they untied the mooring and rather sedately proceeded to head towards the Suez Canal. They were given an escort until they got out into international waters. Those on the yacht were silent and sombre, each trying to process the events which had changed their lives forever.

Doug asked Kane and Joseph to set a course for the port of Alexandria on the coast of Egypt, after that he wanted to follow the coast stopping for fuel where possible: Tunis, Rabat, Dakar, then, fingers crossed, wait for a gap in the weather to cross the Atlantic Ocean and head for the closest point of South America at Paramaribo, then follow the coast again to Caracas then Panama. He said he would give further instructions once they hit Panama.

No one noticed, but Doug had a scarf around his neck that he often held up to his nose. It was Mellissa's and he just needed to breathe in her scent when he thought of her; it helped him keep going. He'd left instructions when he left home that no one was to enter their room, ever. He wanted it untouched, just as she had left it on that fateful day.

Doug continued to be very evasive about his plans after that, only offering to say that everything was underway and that there was a plan.

It was about this time that they saw him talking on a satellite phone – where he had got this phone from, how long had he had it, and who he was talking

       MICHELLE THOMPSON

to, were all a mystery. He'd often talk in muffled tones away from earshot, always brief. When they asked who he was talking to he said it was Stacey, but he didn't let the phone out of his sight, and he didn't let anyone else use the phone. They knew better than to push the subject.

Doug spent many hours of the journey sitting alone up the front of the yacht just staring out to space, day and night. He was struggling with the loss of Mellissa; he was torturing himself with the memories. He felt that she was still next to him in spirit, and he longed to find a psychic so he could talk to Mellissa again. He ran the shooting over and over again in his head. He just couldn't work out why this young man had just walked up and directly targeted her, it just didn't fit.

There was a tap on his shoulder; Orhan had bought him a sandwich. Doug hugged the boy and took the sandwich. It was as if the boy's soul connected with his, Orhan felt his grief. Doug said, "Thank you," to which Orhan replied, "De nada," which is Spanish for "Don't mention it." He was learning Spanish already; it brought a wry smile to Doug.

Orhan

It was reported by the Red Cross that civil war was declared in March 2011. Orhan had grown up in Aleppo. Protestors were demanding political reform and the release of political prisoners and then they tried to overthrow the President; before long all hell broke loose.

Orhan's father tried to protect him and his sister from the news and the reality of the situation, assuring them that everything was okay. But they would often hear his parents talking about the shooting of innocent civilians.

Orhan learnt the terminology, he knew the sounds of the mortars and sniper bullets versus the anti-aircraft guns. Jihadists bragged about the suffering they inflicted on their captives, often turning it into a game to outdo each other.

By July 2012 16,000 innocent people had been killed. The bombing of the city had increased, and it was time to get out. His parents were making plans to leave the country and head to Germany or Italy for safety and a better way of life. Orhan's sister had a medical problem with her heart that she was born with and required a specialist. They packed what they could carry, ready for a midnight departure.

Suddenly, without explanation, there was a dawn raid on their house and his father was accused of being a spy for a foreign organisation. He'd had a high-paying job working for local government for the water board and he was innocent of the accusations, but the frenzy of blame was rampant and now they were dragging him out into the street to publicly hang him for his crimes. Broadcasting in the street that he had sold information to the CIA. His mother had crawled into the street crying and begging for her husband to be saved from this madness. They shot her multiple times as she reached for her husband's feet as he swung from the makeshift gallows along with several of their neighbours' bodies.

Orhan watched from the window of their apartment as a pool of blood engulfed his mother's form in the dry dust. He ran and collected his sister, and they hid in a local field until darkness fell. He was only seven years old; his sister was three. He had heard his parents talk of the Syrian people walking to the coast and paying for boat passage to Italy. He decided this was what he must do to save himself and his sister.

As they started to walk, they joined more people walking; tens turned into hundreds, into thousands, everyone with a desperate story of grief and survival. They slept under a plastic sheet. It would have been bearable if it wasn't so cold. The only blessing was when it rained. The raindrops provided water which they saved in a saucer and an empty Coke bottle to drink.

His sister was getting sicker. They moved on every day. At night he didn't sleep for fear of their shoes or meagre possessions getting stolen, or dirty old men, offering him money to have sex with him or his three-year-old sister. Orhan always carried a sharpened screwdriver as protection in case he had to defend himself or his sister during the night.

After six months they made it to the Libyan coast, and under the cover of darkness, Orhan brokered a deal with a ruthless individual, using all the money his parents had prepared for the journey, for him and his sister to board a boat to Italy.

The vessel was unsafe and crammed full of people, many crying and moaning, some with open wounds. Most were desperate people with their plight etched into their faces from the grief and horror of witnessing the inhumanity. Orhan held his sister tight, they would be safe soon. They hoped that Italy would provide the aid and support and the medical attention she needed, that he had heard so many talks about, but realistically, no one had seen.

Orhan knew his sister was dead long before dawn broke. He pulled the blanket up over her body; she was still warm from the heat of his body. He kept it secret as long as he could, not wanting to face the reality of the situation. As people started to stir and reposition themselves, trying to move out of the urine and excrement from the bottom of the boat, the realisation that she was dead along with two others sent a murmur around the boat.

Other passengers helped Orhan wrap her body in their blanket; she became another floating ghost of the sea. Orhan sat silently, another face etched with grief.

There was the sound of a motorboat in the distance. Italian voices on loudspeakers sent passengers scrambling and upsetting the flimsy boat's buoyancy. Rescue was imminent. The Sicilian coast was in view. The passengers broke into song; many of them were from Cameroon.

Orhan was detained in a migrant camp. There was food and water and rough bedding. Sanitation was poor. Because he was single, he was housed in a gym with 130 others – a gym with a capacity for eighty. They were allowed outside the gym for three hours a day. It was like being in prison, although it was better than hearing the guns fire and bombs explode.

He decided to escape as soon as he could and head on foot for the German border. This was the destination that his father had sought for their safety.

Orhan picked up the Italian language quickly; he had always been good at languages. He already spoke French, English, and Arabic.

There were 4,000 people in the Sicilian camp when the authorities decided to shut it down and transfer the refugees to another camp. This was due to a murder in the village, which was blamed on the migrants.

They were rounded up like cattle and ushered onto buses, to be split into small groups and distributed all over Sicily. There was even talk of a humanitarian boat from Germany.

Orhan gave a gold watch that had been his father's to a guard, so he could disappear in the chaos of poor organisation. The guard smuggled him into the trunk of his car, where he stayed in the stifling heat all day. No one missed him. Later that afternoon the vehicle started moving; the guard wasn't worried about following the speed limit and the momentum of the cornering sent Orhan tumbling around in the trunk amongst fishing nets, rope and an anchor. The vehicle eventually stopped just on the verge of a small fishing village on the Sicilian coast. The guard released him at a rest area off the highway by the Salso River which led to the Port of Licata. He gave him a loaf of bread and a blanket, then disappeared at speed.

This was to be Orhan's home until he could find a way to get to Germany. He kept to himself and made a little bed amongst some Roman ruins. It wasn't comfortable, but it was dry.

Orhan loved Sicily, it was a beautiful island with many unique features. He was a good-looking boy, and American tourists were attracted to him. His light coffee-coloured skin gave him the appearance of a local. He quickly learnt that to survive he would need money, so he appointed himself as a tourist guide, touting himself at bus stations, train stations and the ports. He was quick with his words and his smile looked genuine as he offered to

     MICHELLE THOMPSON

carry bags to avoid the queues, explaining about all the archaeological sites, and the Americans paid him handsomely in tips.

It was while he was touting at the port that he first encountered the twins. He'd seen them arrive and approached them as they came ashore. They didn't want a tour they just wanted directions to the bars and nightclubs. They thanked him for the offer and gave him fifty euros. He followed them at a safe distance for the rest of that day and into the night. They obviously had no financial worries. That was when Orhan decided he'd try and board the yacht and at the very least get passage further up the coast of Italy so he could get to Germany.

Days turned into weeks on board the yacht. He was comfortable in the knowledge that the twins had a soft spot for stray animals and possibly small boys. He decided to test his luck and ask if he could stay on the boat.

Sofia Returns to Colombia

A cold, hard Sofia returned to Colombia. The kindness lines and the smile had been permanently removed from her face. It was all business now; she was possessed with a deep-seated hatred.

Carlos was gravely ill, and the doctors had advised them to prepare for the worst. He had suffered another catastrophic medical event in her absence. Details were sketchy, but when she questioned the staff all they could tell her was that Carlos and Matias had had a big argument and Carlos had collapsed, which led to his most recent illness. Normally she would care, but she was past caring now. Visions of Gerald's headless body haunted her every hour. Carlos had insisted that he be nursed at home with his family around him. His decline meant that he was on a morphine pump, so a private nurse stayed by his side if the family were unavailable.

Matias had been really helpful; he had been running the family businesses in Sofia's absence, and she couldn't fault his efforts. She asked him to continue, as she wasn't up to handling any more stress and he was happy to oblige. She informed him that she was going back to the villa to undertake its demolition, then clearing the site and selling the property. Matias had wanted to go with her, but she insisted that she needed to do this on her own. He could be more help looking after things while she was away.

She had decided to sell all her mines. This was a decision she didn't enter into discussion over with anyone else – it was her decision; they were her mines. She was in negotiation with an overseas buyer, so she travelled to the mine sites with him to introduce him to the mine managers and help him transition the takeover as smoothly as possible. He had been very understanding of her recent situation. He was very patient with the governing bodies and lawyers which slowed the deal down.

The buyer also supported her in the demolition of the villa. She had burnt the building to the ground, then she had heavy machinery come in and remove any trace of the building and outbuildings. Then Sofia had the property fenced and landscaped and turned into a free park and playground for the public to use. She knew Gerald would have approved of that.

In the process, she rehoused Felix's family who had lived on the grounds previously. She bought them a house on the edge of the park and made them custodians. The deal was to always keep it clean, and the lawns mowed and free of damage and litter. The new mine owner offered a moderate salary for the family to make sure the park could be maintained in accordance with Sofia's wishes. He also had a large fountain made as a focal point in the centre of the park and a plaque made as a memorial for Gerald. Sofia was taken aback by his generosity and his kindness; she knew she had sold the mines to the right person.

Sofia and the businessman had become quite close. He was a shrewd businessman acting on behalf of a multinational company. He had lived a full life. He was a great listener, and it was easy to spill her guts to him; often he'd help her drown her sorrows into the small hours of the morning. With her father's absence, she felt she could trust him and confide in him.

Sofia didn't want to go back to her father's house and watch him die, but it sounded like an inevitable outcome. She relieved the nurse so she could go back to her quarters for a break every night after dinner and insisted that Camilla, Matias and she keep a bedside vigil over Carlos as a united family.

Carlos's health was rapidly declining. There were long gaps between breaths and at times she was sure he wasn't going to take the next breath. They often sat in silence, with only the sound of the morphine pump to break it. It seemed a cruel way to watch him die and she often thought to herself that a pillow over his face would be the kindest thing. He had gone downhill drastically while she was away. He had lost all his weight and was a shadow of the man he once was. Lying in the bed he had developed bed sores, and his penis was infected from the catheter.

Sofia had insisted that the family sit around and talk and laugh and tell stories, while she made them all drink herbal teas to help them stay awake, which they hated but humoured her. If her father had any knowledge that they were present she wanted him to hear happy talk and stories and laughter and die in the knowledge that the family was united; this was her bedside wish for him, so they all complied. She hadn't been the easiest person to get on with since Gerald's death.

Time passed; days passed. Carlos was hanging in there – looking at him you wouldn't know that he was still alive, he looked dead already.

They sat quietly once again as the nightly ritual began. They all pleaded with Sofia to not make another horrible-tasting concoction of tea again, but she said she had a new recipe and insisted that they all partake. It had become a standard joke, with her straining the sticks and leaves, and taking such care, with the end results being almost unpalatable. But to everyone's surprise, tonight's brew wasn't that foul.

Matias' face began to get crimson and taut; his throat became constricted, and his eyes bulged as he tried to draw breath, clawing at his neck, trying desperately to get some help from his sister. He collapsed on the floor, blood and froth coming from his nose and mouth.

Sofia sat silently with a smug grin on her face as she signalled Camilla to stay seated with a silent finger. It would be over soon. She knew he was completely dead when his bowels gave way and a repulsive smell discharged from his body, wetting his pants in the process.

She held her father's hand as she spoke to him in his final breaths. "It's over, Daddy. Matias is dead. You can let go now. I'm safe." She recited the Lord's Prayer to him as he drew his final breaths; she had some gold coins waiting to place on his eyelids. She helped his passing with some extra morphine. He was gone.

She consoled Camilla as best as she could, but she had a mission to complete. She made a phone call to her businessman. It was brief as it was prearranged.

She handed a briefcase to Camilla with instructions, explaining that she would be leaving tonight and not coming back. There was a tearful goodbye. A car had pulled up and was waiting with the motor running.

In Colombian Waters

Kane and Joseph had taken turns skippering the boat. They had spent very little time ashore when they stopped for gas and fresh milk. There seemed an urgency in Doug's plan that wasn't discussed with them. Occasionally they would hear him speaking to Stacey on the satellite phone. Other than that, it was a solemn trip, each dealing with their own grief and loss of their mother and in Orhan's case, his whole family.

Doug sat up the front of the boat out on the deck. He sat for hours in any weather, deep in thought, staring into the distance. He hardly ever spoke to any of them. The boys knew to avoid him when he was like this. Orhan just knew when and how to feed him.

There was a little more activity when they picked up Doug's friend Mike from New Zealand at the beginning of the Panama Canal. He piloted the boat through all the locks, shook hands with the right people and he had a million stories. They sailed through without anyone questioning them.

Doug had given Kane GPS coordinates for a location in the Buenaventura Harbour off the Colombian coast. It took them two days to reach the exact position.

When they got there Doug told them to switch the boat off and wait; he gave no explanation. He opened a bag from a locker and produced several guns. He showed the boys how to load them and make them ready to fire but stressed that they weren't to panic and shoot him by accident, which they thought was funny.

He had a stern talk to Orhan and made him promise that if anything happened, he was to hide like before; no use trying to save anyone or be a hero.

The only thing that changed daily was Doug slept during the day and kept watch all night while the boys slept. This went on for three days and three nights.

On the third night, Doug shook the boys awake at 3 am and told them to be ready for action as a boat was approaching them in the dark. The motor of the approaching boat got louder and louder as it drew nearer – it was a reasonable size launch and very well maintained.

The boys lay strategically in different positions on the deck to get a clean shot if needed. Doug stood large as life on the port side; the dim lighting from the approaching boat mixed with sea fog illuminated his form, making him look bigger than normal. As the boat pulled up alongside, Doug nodded his head in acknowledgement and threw a rope to the skipper.

He turned to Kane and Joseph and said, "Hurry along boys, help Poppa Don tie the boat up, he's come all this way to meet us."

They almost didn't believe it was true, but there was Poppa Don with a big grin on his face. After the tension of recent months, their joy at seeing Poppa Don unleashed the tide of emotions they had been holding in for so long.

Doug picked up Orhan and said, "Here, boy, meet your new granddad."

Don handed over the first of the cargo and Doug lifted the heavy cage and looked inside. "Who have we got here?" he asked.

A female voice from inside the boat replied, "That's Mr Biggles."

Doug held his other arm out and caught her slender hand, effortlessly hauling her aboard. "Let's get you inside before anyone sees you, then we will unload the boat."

Doug started to bark orders. "Orhan, meet another refugee. Everyone, this is Sofia, she's going to stay with us for a while. Orhan, make a room up for her and make her comfortable. Boys, help us clean the boat out before we scuttle it."

They were all in shock but proceeded with the tasks at hand. They all quickly and silently went into action.

Sofia shook both the boys' hands and introduced herself, then crouched down and shook Orhan's hand and stooped to kiss him on his cheek but he pulled away – he sensed a danger in her. His reaction didn't go unnoticed by Doug, but he was busy and just banked it for later. Taking her handbag, he guided her into her cabin.

Doug brought Mr. Biggles down the stairs and placed him in her room. "Once we get moving, we can let him out of the cage and get his dirt box ready for him."

An hour later they were underway. Doug asked Kane to set a course for Galapagos for fuel only, then Papeete. Sofia would have to remain hidden when they got to the Galapagos because she would be easily recognised there.

Mr Biggles looked like he had been at sea all his life. He made himself at home and had many tricks to extort food from everyone. Orhan had never

     MICHELLE THOMPSON

been allowed to have a cat in the past, so it was special to him to play with Mr Biggles and feed him.

Sofia was lots of fun; she laughed till she cried at Don's stories. She liked a drink with the boys, and she fussed over Orhan like he was her child. He joked that he came second to Mr Biggles and that was probably true. She quickly learnt as much as she could about the boat and was already helping Orhan plan the meals. She was very supportive towards the boys over Mellissa's death and told them the gruesome story about the death of her husband. She was excited about Kane's wedding and was already offering all sorts of ideas for the day.

Sofia was adding much-needed life to the journey that they had not had for some time. When they stopped at the islands and atolls on the way, she insisted everyone get off and have some fun. She finally felt like she could relax. This was her new family; she was safe now. Doug made her feel as if nothing bad could happen to her again.

Sofia's Plan

When Sofia boarded the plane for Ireland, she already knew that Matias had murdered Gerald. In her hands, she had the evidence to link him for sure, along with the eyewitness story from Felix.

Felix had witnessed the whole thing. He'd been frightened to come forward through fear of retribution for him and his family. Sofia had assured him that she would keep him and his family safe, but he was not to tell anyone what he saw. Felix was deeply affected by what he had witnessed, a trauma so deep he would never recover.

She read and reread the autopsy report repeatedly on the long flight. The fear and agony Gerald would have suffered made medieval torture seem like child's play. Very little of the inflicted abuse happened after he was dead; Matias had expertly strung it out to get maximum results. At times the description made her vomit, and she would rush to the plane's bathroom.

Gerald would have been ambushed as he entered the villa at 7 pm – the time had been confirmed by the taxi company that had taken Gerald's fare. Matias possibly stunned him by hitting him across the head with the bloodied construction hammer that was found at the scene. Then Matias broke both his leg bones – tibia and fibula – with blunt force; this would have been to eliminate a chance of escape. Gerald then had all his fingers removed with a pair of heavy-grade secateurs, also present at the scene, but the fingers were never recovered. Gerald's jaw was broken and his tongue removed. The loss of blood would have eventually killed him. Both his eyes were gouged out – the coroner also thought this was antemortem, not post-mortem. His tongue was inserted in his anus post-mortem and traces of wood splinters from the handle of the construction hammer used were also identified. The words 'Ass Licker' were carved into his back later, as possibly an afterthought, with a steak knife from the kitchen. There was a bloodied chainsaw at the house and the neck wounds from the decapitation were consistent with the use of this instrument; it had sprayed large amounts of bone and tissue up the walls and on the ceiling. His body was found eight hours later. The time of actual death was perceived to be 3 am. An empty bottle of Johnny Walker whisky was found at the scene,

   MICHELLE THOMPSON

but no alcohol was found in Gerald's toxicology report.

The text messages between Matias and Gerald were brief but exposed a trap for when Gerald arrived at the villa. Then there was the bite on Matias's hand that he had explained to Sofia as a dog bite; Sofia had to use all her self-control to not shoot him dead on the spot.

She knew she should have stopped reading the report, but she was drawn to every detail, her heart breaking at the thought that Gerald would have been thinking of her during the attack.

When she finally got to Dublin Airport after stopping in transit at Miami then Heathrow, she was a physical mess. She hadn't eaten the entire trip. She had drunk a lot to help her drift into sleep between pages. The plane staff delivered her to Gerald's parents in a wheelchair, too weak to walk.

It was Gerald's mother who finally took the report off her and told her to live for the future, which would be what Gerald wanted. They burnt the report symbolically on the top of a hill overlooking the ocean and laughed that Gerald would say the smoke was pollution.

His parents and extended family were lovely; they toured all of Gerald's favourite places with her, visited relatives, and discussed her plans going forward. She thought she would never get over it, at least never get the image of his headless body out of her mind. And now her father was dying – double the hit. She had the offer to stay as long as she wanted, but she already had other plans, though she wasn't prepared to return to Colombia just yet.

Sofia touched down at Sydney Airport; it was a hot and clear day and Australia instantly warmed her soul. She hired a car and simply drove to Doug's house; she'd just searched online for it from the description that Sebastian had given Matias before he disappeared. The tomato farm was well documented on the web.

As she drove up the driveway towards the sign that said 'Office' and parked the car, a tall, well-built tower of a man appeared in the doorway, leaning on the door frame with one arm up, looking like he'd pull a gun and shoot you for fun, but he extended his hand instead. She was attracted to him sexually – a feeling she didn't think she would have again.

She greeted him in Spanish. "I am Sofia Hernandez, daughter of Carlos Hernandez."

He smiled and with a big grin said, "You come to get your cocaine back?" They both laughed.

"Not quite," she replied. They instantly connected.

Sofia was a looker; he could imagine her on the end of his penis if he wasn't married. He could look.

They sat in his office for hours while she told her story, even Doug was impressed with the details.

The intenseness was broken by the entrance of Mellissa – she seemed to float in and sat on his knee. Sofia was taken with her beauty. Doug grabbed her ass as she landed, he nuzzled into her hair and breathed in her perfume; they kissed briefly. He introduced her to Sofia as his beautiful wife who he loved with all his heart. The sentiment brought a tear to Sofia's eyes; she would have had that with Gerald.

"Honey, let me introduce you to the daughter of one of the biggest crime bosses in South America, Sofia Hernandez. She's come to us for help."

Mellissa saw Sofia with tears in her eyes and got up to hug her. "Come to the house and have dinner with the family. It's a madhouse but you're welcome. You can even stay in the empty nurse's quarters; it's all made up. We can hatch a plan together." Doug was already getting the suitcases out of the car.

At their insistence, Sofia stayed for a week. It was one of the best holidays she could remember. The house was full of laughter, and they all drank like fish. Mellissa's parents were away visiting the twin boys, so she didn't get to meet them, but Doug's dad was like her flatmate in their wing of the house, and he spoke a little Spanish. Although her English was good, it was good to have that buffer in translation. She met Stacey and Rod briefly; he was very ill.

Mellissa took her shopping for clothes and shoes and introduced her to Edith and Gay Kenny. But the highlight of the trip was when some of Doug's friends arrived, and they all went for a bike ride to show off the sights of Sydney. Her driver drove like a maniac, and she was so frightened and so exhilarated all at once.

When she left, she knew what she had to do – what Doug had suggested – when she got back home. She was genuinely saddened at leaving this family and the safety of Doug, and she and Mellissa shed sincere tears at the airport as she departed through the gates to her plane.

 MICHELLE THOMPSON

They Call Australia Home

Doug had one of his tourist boats meet them twelve miles out, just off the coast of Australia. They had cruised back in relatively good weather, but in the final part of the journey, a storm had kicked up and Sofia had taken ill with seasickness. Transferring her to the other boat wasn't so difficult but concealing her in a confined space was unpleasant for her, but they couldn't take any chances. Orhan was easier, he passed off as one of the crew's children. If the authorities had questions, the chances were they would overlook him.

Doug made sure it was only his family on their boat when they finally made the harbour entrance. He was sure the authorities would at least have been tracking them all the way from Panama. When they came in, customs met them as a regular precaution. They ran the dog through the boat, checked for any food source that caused a biological risk to Australia, checked passports, and let them carry on as if it was just another day.

Stacey was waiting with a vehicle and drove Doug and Orhan back to the farm. Don and Sofia took another vehicle while the boys secured the yacht and started to clean it and get it ready for the return journey. Doug suggested that the twins both fly back to Iran first and make sure the wedding arrangements were still on track; he knew Kane was missing his girlfriend.

Stacey set about updating Doug on anything he might have missed out on in his absence. They both joked that they were now widows. She was still coming to terms with her loss and so was Doug. They both agreed it was going to take some adjustment. Doug acknowledged that Orhan was in the same space. He'd make a point of making sure this little boy was well looked after.

It was decided that Sofia would set up in the room she stayed in on her previous visit and by the time Doug returned to the house Sofia was being well looked after. Mr Biggles had happily found a chair in the bar that he was now claiming. Everyone was exhausted but in good spirits. There was plenty of talk about the new mines they now owned, and to everyone's surprise, Sofia produced from her luggage a handbag full of emeralds and let Andrea and Stacey pick whatever they wanted from the bag.

The quiet adult conversation was broken by the noise of the rowdy twins' entrance followed by their sister, Edith, and Gay Kenny, all trying to out-talk each other. Edith and Kenny both dug into the emerald bag.

Doug suspected that he saw a change in Kenny's body language where Edith was concerned, and he wondered briefly if he had changed teams.

They drank, talked and ate well into the night, it was like a belated wake. Sofia and Mr Biggles went to bed early to give the family some personal time.

Doug's request before he left for Somalia was that his and Mellissa's room be locked up and no one was to enter. When he finally retired to his room in the small hours, he lay in the sheets and could smell her perfume; it was a cold comfort to him, but it was something he wanted to preserve as long as he could. He was still rocking like he was on a boat but eventually fell into a deep sleep.

—

Life had become very busy with activity and excitement. The wedding preparations were well underway, with Kane and Joseph spending most of their time in Iran. Stacey was organising flights and wedding suits; accommodation was being taken care of by the host. There were to be two weddings – one for Naz's religious requirements and one for the outside family. Orhan was going to fly to Iran under another identity with Doug and Stacey, as Doug hadn't worked out how to legally adopt him yet, but he had a lawyer working on it. Grandparents and many friends and family were taking up the rest of the plane seats. It was all abuzz as the biggest event of the year. Don and Brian were busy preparing speeches, designed to embarrass the groom.

Kane and his new bride would fly back to Australia after the wedding and they would sail back in her father's yacht with Joseph and Mohammad, Edith and Gay Kenny. But this time they wouldn't have to be the crew, just the honeymooning passengers and their escorting brothers and sister.

Sofia had suggested that as she couldn't travel, she stay behind and keep everything ticking over.

Sofia was more than comfortable. She felt for the first time in her life that she was free to relax. Other than keeping house and cooking she had a no-stress life, getting fatter by the day.

She wasn't pushing Doug for a relationship as she knew he still hadn't got over Mellissa and, likewise, her with Gerald. Occasionally he would slip into

    MICHELLE THOMPSON

her room at night, and they would have sex. It wasn't the most pleasant sexual experience; in fact, he was a bit rough. He would vacate the room before anyone woke up. It just seemed inappropriate at this point to be outwardly open about it. A part of her felt used, but at the same time, she was desperately trying to get pregnant. When he had asked, she had lied and told him she was on a contraceptive; she wanted his baby. Some might look at this as entrapment, she saw it as insurance. She was living in a foreign country with no identity; she had signed her companies over to Doug and she needed something to keep her hold on him.

The good news was, lately she had been experiencing a bit of nausea on and off. Once they had all departed for the wedding, she would go into town and buy a pregnancy kit from the chemist. If she was pregnant, she would wait until he returned from Iran before she broke the news. That way if there was talk of abortion, it would be too late.

Felix's Story

Felix was the youngest of eight children; his parents were good Catholics. He was different from the other children. The doctor told his parents he was born 'on the spectrum', which just meant he was a bit nuts, his father told him, but for Felix, it meant that everything had to be cleaned twice, doors shut twice, food couldn't touch on the plate, times had to be kept exact or his whole day went west. He could never seem to wash his hands enough and would pace backwards and forwards for hours if his hands got dirty.

They were more fortunate than most families in his village. His parents had accommodation and employment looking after the Hernando's villa and grounds at their summer house. Their home was a modest house but somehow all eight of them managed to fit in three bedrooms. Felix thought he must have been born there, as he couldn't remember living anywhere else before.

His early good memories were when Miss Sofia arrived every Christmas with delicious baskets of food and armfuls of presents for the family. He was only a teenager, but he loved her and dreamed of marrying her – she always looked clean. He didn't mind when she hugged him; she was clean, so he didn't have to wash.

On the night of Gerald's murder, Felix had been hiding in the house and had witnessed the whole thing. Felix would often let himself into the house without permission and sit in the chairs and sofas. This house was clean compared to his house and he didn't have to compete with others; he didn't feel the need to wash all the time. If his parents knew he was entering the house without their consent he would have been given a severe beating, so it was his guilty pleasure to take the key from his parents' room and spend hours sitting in the big house on his own, dreaming that he lived there with Sofia.

When he heard the front door to the main entrance being opened, he panicked. He ran around in circles for a few seconds; his brain couldn't compute the next step. Should he just apologise, should he try and climb out a window? First, he tried to crawl under a settee, but it hadn't been cleaned recently and was too dirty underneath. He only had seconds to decide on his next step as he could see a figure about to open the door from the main entrance and reception room to the front room which served as an open-plan kitchen and living area – very modern for traditional houses in this part of Colombia. He took a chance and hid under the drop sheet of the grand piano.

His worst fears became reality; it was Señior Matias who was entering the room. He was always mean, and Felix's family were very scared of him. Felix's father warned him and his brothers and sisters to stay well away from him and never look him in the eye.

Felix watched in interest as Matias dragged several strange items into the house: a chainsaw, some tools, a big saw, a large hammer and a portable blow torch. Matias disappeared back out the main entrance and returned with some bottles of whisky. He then sat in the same chair that Felix had been occupying. He was texting someone then laughing hysterically, swigging at the neck of the whisky bottle and texting again; it seemed a great joke.

When Felix heard a second car arrive, then heard it drive off, he decided that it must have been a taxi, and then, as if by magic, he noticed Matias had positioned himself behind the door from the reception into the front room. He had a stance like a woodchopper, feet slightly apart for stability, construction hammer in his hands.

As the white man entered the doorway, Matias made the first swing, stunning him with a blow to the head then snapping the first leg at the knee, dropping Gerald to the floor. The frenzied blows rained down on him, smashing his legs with every blow; Matias was like a man possessed. Why didn't anyone hear the screams?

Felix was petrified into position, staring out from under the bottom of the drop sheet, ignoring the dust in his face.

Gerald lost consciousness. Matias sat back in the chair, swigged on the whisky and waited while he caught his breath again; swinging the hammer was harder than he had thought it would be.

The well-choreographed attack seemed to go on for hours. At one stage Gerald came to and bit Matias on the hand. In the background, there was the continuous ringing of a phone which was strangely more annoying than the events in the room. A jet of blood reached the drop sheet as Gerald's tongue was being cut out. Felix fainted briefly but woke to the noise of the chainsaw and the smell of its fumes.

Long after Matias had left with the box containing Gerald's head Felix left the shelter of the piano, his legs were weak. He was careful to lock the back door with his mother's key then ran in the direction of his home. It was dark and he was guided by the light in the window. He stopped to vomit. When he got in the front door his mother scolded him for being late for dinner. She didn't question why he was late but just presumed that he had worked an extra shift at the supermarket where he had a job filling shelves.

He washed his hands then went back and washed them again and again.

His family was woken by the police the next morning. His parents were interviewed; they hadn't heard or seen anything. They were noticeably shocked by the news. No one asked Felix if he had seen anything. He was still more worried that he would get in trouble for taking the key.

When Miss Sofia arrived the next day, Felix was hiding in the bushes by the driveway. He knew that Gerald was her husband from the police conversation with his parents; she would be very sad. He waited for her to finish looking in the house then, as she left the house and looked around the garden, he caught her attention and ran into her arms. They both cried. She smelt so clean.

     MICHELLE THOMPSON

The Perfect Life

Sofia returned from Australia with new hope for her future. The only problem was she saw her future with Doug. She felt safe with Doug; no one could hurt her again if she was with him. She loved him – he was her soulmate.

It was sickening how nice Mellissa was, it was pretty hard to fault her. Anything she did, she did well, she even looked good in the morning. And it was that look that Doug gave her; the look that you knew deep down was such unconditional love that no writer had ever captured it properly to describe it in a book. She wanted that look! Fuck Mellissa.

It took her nearly a year upon her return to get all her ducks in a row. Following Doug's instructions, she signed over all her companies to him. She met Don and showed him all the elements connected with running the mines and set up all the other business affairs so they could be managed by Camilla once she left the country. And finally, the lead-up to and planning the death of Matias. Poisoning Matias as revenge for the death of Gerald was the easiest and most efficient way to dispatch him. It didn't give her the satisfaction of the pain she wanted to inflict on him, but it was final. The poisons she needed were bought on the black market by Don.

It was apparent to everyone that Carlos was not long for this world, his doctor had told him to go home and sort out his financial affairs some time ago. He had had several major heart attacks, was overweight and had congested lungs from years of smoking cigars. Deep down Sophia knew that Carlos knew it was Matias who had killed Gerald. Deep-seated revenge for the death of his mother all those years ago. In some respects, she blamed Carlos also.

She groomed Felix to kill Mellissa. He was a dim-witted individual, easily manipulated and he was infatuated with her which helped. She used her cunning and charm to lure him into thinking his perfect future and dreams were about to be fulfilled with her as his wife.

She secretly went with him and set him up in an apartment in Sydney, giving him plenty of money and plenty of sex. They followed Doug and Mellissa for a couple of weeks, and she convinced Felix that this woman was a part of the plan to murder Gerald. It was all too easy.

The plan was to get him extradited back to Colombia after the shooting once he handed himself in and claimed mental illness as his grounds for shooting her. Sofia could easily get him out of any prison in Colombia with the right number of contacts and money once he was extradited.

What she didn't count on was him turning the gun on himself. He had never recovered from witnessing the terrible death of Gerald; he was plagued by visions and nightmares. She had paid for some of the best therapists in Colombia to help him, but the lines got blurred with his autism. She never felt guilty for his death – it would be tidier this way; at least he was out of his misery now. Poor simple boy.

Now she had what she wanted. She was patient; she could wait till Doug grew comfortable with her. Time would lessen the hold Mellissa had on him. And now she was sure a baby was on the way.

    MICHELLE THOMPSON

Baby Doug is Born

The family had returned from the wedding and the house was back to noisy chaos again. Everyone had something to say at once.

Business took priority. Doug was complaining that they had lost too much money gallivanting around the world for too long. Both he and Stacey were back to cracking the whip making sure the work was completed.

Sofia knew for sure now that she was pregnant. Her excitement about the news was soon quelled when Doug's reaction was not that of joy and love, in fact, he asked her to have an abortion which she explained could not happen for two reasons: her religion and the age of the foetus. He retreated to the sanctuary of his room and became unapproachable for a few days. When he finally came back to communicating with the family he announced the news. It seemed that from the family's reaction, Sofia was the only one who was excited. There was no doubt over their show of support for her, although it didn't seem genuine.

Doug spared no expense. A nursery was decorated and equipped with everything the child would need till it was five and he insisted on a full-time nanny to care for the child. He came to all the scans and was delighted that the child was predicted to be a boy. He was going to call him Doug Junior or 'Baby Doug' as a nickname, which began to stick.

Sofia had a terrible pregnancy with continuous morning sickness for the whole nine months. The baby was growing at a rapid rate and was already measuring long and large on the scan. The child kicked and fought all the way. It was also going to be a breech birth. The best thing that the doctors could advise was to deliver the baby with a caesarean operation early as both the baby and mother were showing signs of stress.

Doug was delighted with the progress of the pregnancy. He bragged that 'Baby Doug' was going to be the spitting image of him, already fighting to get out. He told everyone "It's coming out the sun-roof early."

Baby Doug was born. He was thirteen pounds, had a long body and long, gangly legs, and already had hands on him like a four-year-old. He was also covered in a terrible skin rash. People couldn't control pulling a face when they saw him. Doug just loved him; thought he was the best-looking baby in the ward.

When Sofia returned to the house the baby was already on formula. He had savaged her nipples while she was in hospital, and she was no longer able to breastfeed. Doug couldn't have been happier.

The Brown Paper Bag

Doug was obsessed with the baby, though he'd hardly acknowledged Sofia for weeks. But today he was bright and full of vigour. He decided that Sofia hadn't had a break since the baby was born and told her to get ready; they were off for a day out and lunch at a vineyard.

He'd also bought a new off-road truck and thought it needed a test drive.

She was reluctant to leave the baby, but Edith and Gay Kenny had arrived and begged her to let them look after him for a few hours. They convinced her that they were baby whisperers, and he was normally a very quiet baby so all he demanded was constant feeding. Orhan backed up the support. He said he had had a lot of experience with babies and monkeys.

As they drove out of the city Doug gave Sophi a bit of a tourist guide narrative about kangaroos, snakes and other wonders of the Australian countryside.

She was enjoying herself, perhaps this was the turnaround she had been waiting for. He was chatty, engaging, and humorous.

They turned off the main road after what seemed hours and drove into the wilderness for what seemed like ages. Sophia wasn't sure where they were going but she didn't care, she was enjoying herself. This was the first time they had been alone together; she was all dressed up for the occasion. She hadn't quite got back her pre-pregnancy body, but that would come back with a little exercise.

They turned off the track for a way and when they reached a secluded cluster of rocks and scrub. Doug stopped the vehicle and, almost blushing, he asked her if she would be willing to have sex out here in the setting of nature.

At first, she refused, but he said it was something he and Mellissa did often, so she reluctantly said she would oblige. It had been almost three months since Baby Doug was born and they had not had sex since she announced she was pregnant, so it was nearly a year. She could understand his need.

"Why don't you take off your underwear and lean on the rock with your back to me," Doug suggested. He even produced a blanket to lie on. "This will keep your top clean."

Sophia was surprisingly turned on by the experience and her vagina wasn't sore as she had given birth by caesarean.

Doug came up behind her, stroked her naked backside a couple of times then used his foot to spread her legs slightly more apart. He looked her up and down – she really was a beautiful woman. He took the gun silently out of the back of his waistband and without remorse blew her brains out all over the blanket and the rock. She never knew or felt a thing. No life flashed before her eyes; she was just gone.

He dragged her body to the shallow grave he had prepared a month back, then used the truck's bull bars to move a large rock over the indent in the earth where he had just covered her body with dirt. He had no remorse. If anyone asked, she went back to Colombia with post-natal depression.

He would bring Baby Doug up on his own with the help of the nanny and the rest of the family. Baby Doug would want for nothing.

Doug drove home in silence. His heart hurt from missing Mellissa, but it was time to move on with life – he would make the bed for a start. And he wanted to give Orhan a good education. He'd expressed a desire to be a farmer and manage Doug's farms. There would be grandbabies soon from Kane and Naz. He predicted that Gay Kenny wasn't gay and would ask if he could marry Edith. Joseph would cruise the seas with Mohammad, and Don and Andrea and his dad would grow older disgracefully for a few more years yet. Stacey and Brian could run the glasshouses.

Three months earlier, Mr Biggles had drawn his attention to a brown paper bag down the side of his bed. Mr Biggles was tearing it apart. It took Doug a while to work out where the bag had come from until he read the tattered paper: 'Hospital property'. The contents of the bag contained Mellissa's blood-stained clothing and some personal items. He was rocked by the discovery. He must have dropped it there in his state of grief and forgotten about it; he hadn't made the bed for months.

All the memories of the day came flooding back. He shooed Mr Biggles away even though he knew if Mellissa had been watching from above, she would have thought Mr Biggles was funny ripping up the bag. Anything naughty the cats did she encouraged, but Mr Biggles had moved on from the bag and was obsessed with another item that had slipped under the edge of the bed.

Doug hung over the edge of the bed and felt around till his fingers touched

   MICHELLE THOMPSON

a cold object – it was another phone. Doug held up the phone and looked at it for a while before he processed his thoughts. It wasn't Mellissa's; hers had a cover with a family picture on it. The hospital somehow had given him another phone. He presumed it was flat as he couldn't get any life out of it. The charger from Mellissa's phone was still plugged in by the bed. It fitted: a standard Samsung charger. As the phone came to life the screen saver picture exploded into life – it was a photo of Sofia! Doug was caught up in space for a while, it was a close-up shot, almost a provocative and sexual pose. Doug's gut told him instantly that he had the killer's phone.

He knew for the time being that he had to keep the phone a secret. He needed a pin number to open it – his brain was racing. This was a job for Gay Kenny, he was a genius with this sort of thing, and he'd be able to find the messages or the call log.

Doug was sweating with rage, his heart felt like it was ripping. He caught a glimpse of himself in the mirror: his face was crimson, his jaw set. He'd have to act naturally and not alert Sofia to his change of demeanour. She was scheduled to give birth any day now. No use in her catching on and disappearing back to Colombia before the baby was born.

He told Orhan to get their helmets. He'd head into town and see Gay Kenny and take the boy with him. He'd been taking the boy everywhere with him since they got back, no one would expect anything different.

He went to the office to see Stacey and told her to track Gay Kenny down. His legs were shaking, and it was all clicking into place.

He got his bike out and told Orhan to hold on. It was a fast ride into town, weaving in and out of traffic. Orhan held on for his life, he knew that something was different about today's ride. He was such an intuitive lad and Doug liked that about him. Orhan had really bonded with Doug, and he knew not to talk, today was a listening day.

It didn't take Kenny long to open the phone – turned out it wasn't brain science; the PIN was 1, 2, 3, 4. As they read the messages of love, they saw the photos of Sofia and Felix together, the hundreds of photos of Mellissa and Doug taken from covert positions, mostly photos of Mellissa, photos of their favourite restaurant which was the site of the shooting, the messages of planning, the unanswered messages as Sofia was texting him to see if he had finished the job of killing Mellissa.

Doug screamed so loud that the whole building would have heard him. "MAD FUCKIN CUNT!" The different emotions tearing through him just played with his head.

Edith was crying. Doug hugged her. "It's going to be okay; we will sort this."

Doug pulled the situation together. He demanded that Edith, Gay Kenny and Orhan follow his instructions. Edith was to arrange a family meeting at Stacey's house tonight. They would know it was serious if he held it there.

Doug would wait till the baby was born and make sure it got the necessary nutrients it needed from its mother's milk. Then Sofia would leave them forever. If anyone asked, he'd tell them she went back to Colombia with post-natal depression and unresolved trauma from the death of her husband. The family would wipe her existence off the face of the earth.

 MICHELLE THOMPSON

PART THREE

Homecoming

As Doug waited in the prison car park, he cursed the time it was taking. He hated this place at the best of times. He drummed his fingers on the steering wheel, checking his watch frequently. So many scenarios were ticking over in his mind; each ended badly.

If he hadn't been picking up Baby Doug, he wouldn't have been here. Truth was, no one else wanted to pick him up, so he had to – after all, he was his son, as they all reminded him.

The family would put on a good show, have a homecoming party for him. Hopefully, he had changed for good this time. Doug really didn't know what to expect.

It had been eleven years since Baby Doug had gone to prison. He had served the full sentence due to his frequent spells in the pound or solitary for violent behaviour. Psychologists said he was a genius with an extremely high IQ, but it was hard to believe it given his offending history.

Finally! Baby Doug appeared in the doorway of the prison gates. He had no belongings, only an envelope with his release papers in it; no baskets he had made, no paintings. He was wearing the clothing that Edith had sent a few weeks earlier. He was swearing and cursing at the wardens upon his exit. Bet they were glad to see the back end of him; he had a nasty mouth on him. He strode towards the car, a big grin on his face.

It didn't look like he had any part of his body that wasn't tattooed, even his scalp was tattooed, exposed by a Mohawk haircut with a ponytail. It looked ridiculous to Doug, perhaps he was getting old. Personally, he thought this was just calling for attention, that sort of shit.

Baby Doug had obviously been working out; he walked like he had tennis balls under his armpits, almost like he was a bodybuilder on steroids. It was a lot to take in. He looked menacing. Doug had a gun in a secret opening in the side of the car seat just in case he had to use it.

"Hi, Dad, how's it been?"

Doug felt awkward and anxious. Before he could reply, Baby Doug was in full conversation, not bothering for a reply, just filling the trip with continuous talk about all the people inside that he either hated or really hated; it was tiring. He talked all the way home, thanked his dad for picking him up, and told him he loved him. It was like he was on speed; perhaps it was nerves.

Doug gave him a heads-up about the homecoming that was waiting for him. Just the immediate family; his brothers had flown over from the Middle East to see him. Edith and her husband Kenny had gone out of their way to make sure all his favourite food was served. Orhan had some best cuts of meat for the BBQ, and Aunty Stacey had knitted him a beanie. Doug was secretly happy about the beanie; hide that ridiculous hair. Fuck; that or dreadlocks. He didn't know what he hated more.

Doug thought he detected a tear in Baby Doug's eye. He hoped he was grateful; they really had made an effort. He was a loose cannon – it was a blessing when he was inside, and the stress was removed when he was absent from their lives.

As though he was reading Doug's mind, Baby Doug said, "It's different this time, Dad. I'm not going to fuck up anymore. I'm going to go straight this time. I've decided that I want to work on the farm with Orhan, that's if he will have me."

Doug didn't know how many times he had heard that, but it was a lot. Whether it was autism or mental illness, the proof was in his behaviour. High IQ my arse.

They pulled up in the driveway and parked outside the front entrance as per Edith's instructions. The three boys came out to meet the car. There were bear hugs all around, Baby Doug nearly breaking their ribs in the process. He picked little Orhan up and virtually threw him in the air but caught him and kissed his face twice. He loved this little guy; he looked like a little brown Gandhi.

The boys ushered him inside the door. He was met with balloons and pop streamers, and Gay Kenny was blowing a paper horn. Baby Doug shook his hand vigorously and then he ran to his sister; they both cried as they hugged. She had kept a constant flow of letters and visits during his incarceration – he owed her his sanity.

Aunty Stacey had a present for him. He unwrapped it, pretending he was surprised. He put the beanie on immediately and vowed to never take it off.

"Thank fuck," said Doug under his breath. He caught Orhan's eye – they were both thinking the same thing.

There was so much to tell him, eleven years of catch-up. The conversation and drinking went well into the night and the next day. He had missed out on some major milestones, like the death of his grandparents and Edith's wedding to Gay Kenny. Kane and Naz's children had grown up and now attended private schools, courtesy of Naz's father.

Baby Doug's Path to Destruction

The writing was always on the wall, even as a toddler there were signs. He was a quiet baby, a real thinker, but he was restless and just wanted to move all the time. Someone said once that it was like he had been dropped in a vat of coffee at birth. Nannies lasted all of five minutes then walked out. He was too heavy for them to lift, and he was constantly trying to bite them.

Eventually, it was Orhan who cracked it; he bought him a walker on wheels. It was well before they recommended the natural age an infant should walk, but it was an absolute blessing. The walker had a tiny tray in the front which Orhan kept constantly full of food.

Baby Doug took to it instantly and he was off. He would constantly run into your legs, almost crippling the victims he crashed into.

Then, rather sadistically, someone let him out into the yard and driveway. He narrowly avoided getting run over several times, but the vast distance he could travel kept him occupied and out of the house, to everyone's relief.

As he gained more and more strength, he learnt to pick the walker up and leverage it over small steps to gain access to areas normally out of his range.

Baby Doug became popular with the workers, who nicknamed him Spider. Firstly, because his arms and legs were working overtime, and secondly, it was less confusing with Big Doug around. The name stuck, and Spider soaked up the attention. He would resurface back at the house eventually and eat some more, have a little sleep and be back out again.

He eventually grew out of the walker and was given a little red bike with three wheels and a horn to scoot around on. This gave him access to paddocks close to the house. He was fascinated with animals and would spend hours just watching them eat.

What seemed like the next experiment was daycare. Spider seemed to like it at first then the trouble started; he would bite other children. If they told on him, he would get them in sleeper holds around their necks or leap on them from heights. If he had access to any water, he would try and hold their heads under. Kicks and punches were constantly aimed at any authority figures trying to discipline him. The daycare assistants would ring and ask for him to be removed.

 MICHELLE THOMPSON

On the way home Doug or Stacey or his grandparents would ask him if he knew that what he was doing was bad, to which he would always reply that he wouldn't do it again. But he always did.

Regular school was also a failure. He didn't have any skills in building relationships with other children so the school recommended correspondence schooling. He didn't study but he had the ability to just read something once and memorise it. He passed every exam with double A-levels.

The doctors said he was 'on the spectrum' with a high IQ, whatever that meant. He was fuckin' nuts, Doug would say, a very different individual.

Sport was his thing; he was a natural athlete. When he had any free time he ran, and he would run for miles. He joined every club he could and played Rugby, Cricket, Wrestling, and Horse Polo. It was a full-time job driving him to different clubs to attend training, let alone weekends taken up with tournaments and competitions. He was always winning player of the day or match champion. His aggressive approach made him an asset, but only if he was on your team.

If he spent any time at home, he would be out on the farm with Orhan, drenching animals, helping with general animal husbandry, caring for his horses, fixing fences. He was a great help, and he was incredibly strong, even as a toddler.

When he got older, he insisted that the panic room was his bedroom – Doug had installed this room when he built the house. They had never needed to use it, but Spider loved it, and the family loved it when he shut the door, and they couldn't hear him. He would spend hours watching everyone from the cameras in the room and he could play on the internet all night. He also had a police scanner, and he would listen for hours to the action on the emergency channel. It was the ideal set-up for him and everyone else. He'd come out, grab food and retreat back into the room.

Orhan would occasionally brave the room to collect clothing for washing which was always neatly folded because of Spider's OCD obsession for tidiness.

Baby Doug the Hero

Spider set his mind on becoming a fireman; he became obsessed with the idea. He started as a junior volunteer for the NSW Rural Fire Service. The starting process was easy; he simply had to apply and fill out a form. They interviewed him and he passed all the acceptance criteria to join. He then had to complete a six-month probation period with training, after that, he was accepted as a full member. He made himself available for every call-out and he was well respected within his unit.

He then applied to join NSW Fire and Rescue. He applied as a retained employee rather than full-time as the full-time employees had to live at the station whereas the retained employees were on call from their own residence. He became a valued employee not only because of his strength but for his commitment to any call-out, any task, no matter how difficult or how many hours he was needed.

He struggled at times with the effect of fires on the wildlife. It gave him sleepless nights, and he'd always be rescuing koala bears, putting his own safety in danger in the process.

A ferocious fire started in the southwest of Sydney. By the time it was over a total of 2500 hectares were burnt. Houses in the path of the fire stood no chance, people died, and it made international news. The fire had been fuelled by extremely high temperatures and wind. There was an investigation underway because it seemed that this fire was deliberately lit. Baby Doug could never understand that. Not when he had a baby koala inside his jacket with burnt hands and feet.

His shift had finished when he heard a call over the radio that another random fire had started at Sandy Point. It was too obvious that this one was deliberately lit – it was miles away from the last fire. His crew was the closest to the area, so they diverted back towards the scene. Several houses were too close for comfort to the amber sparks that were being driven by 60 mph winds. The houses were being evacuated, and the crew, although buggered from a fifteen-hour shift, immediately went into full firefighting mode to save the properties.

       MICHELLE THOMPSON

Spider heard the frantic screams of the mother of a young girl, who had run back into the fire to save her cat. A policeman who was first on the scene had already gone into the burning building through the window. Spider scaled the ladder to gain access through the same bedroom window the policeman had gone in.

As he threw himself through the window to gain entrance to the room a huge explosion from a gas line sent the policeman sprawling against the wall, knocking him unconscious. He was ill-equipped to be in this position and his clothing was on fire. Spider was so strong he picked him up, threw him over his shoulder and bundled him out the window to one of his colleagues who was now yelling at him to get out as the fire had gained hold and the whole room was an inferno.

Spider went low and crawled on the floor towards the bed in the corner of the room. The heat was intense, but he could see the little girl lying in the foetal position under the bed with her cat securely in her arms. He roughly grabbed at her arm and pulled the fur and skin on the back of the cat's neck and forced it inside his jacket, then he pulled the little girl towards him. Before she could resist, he stood up, using the whole bed as a cover while he carried it on his back, and charged towards the window.

As they broke free from the window, he handed the little girl to his colleague waiting on the ladder. He almost tumbled down himself, making sure the cat couldn't move out of his grip.

Unaware of the burns on his face and neck, Spider waited until the little girl was in the care of the paramedics in the ambulance before he handed her the cat. He caught his breath as he saw the cat for the first time; he'd had a similar cat as a child, Mr Biggles. He was glad he had made the effort.

His rescue made the 6 pm news, and his burnt face was plastered all over the *Sydney Herald*. It was the first time his family had any knowledge of what he had done, he just considered it to be a job, not anything special. That night he had simply come home, had a shower, and gone to bed. He had never mentioned it.

The newspaper journalist requested, through his superior, for him to reunite with the girl and the cat so they could do an article on him and give him an award from the local mayor. He was more embarrassed than anything. In his mind, it was a team effort. The police also wanted to acknowledge him for the rescue of one of their own. In their eyes, he had saved lives and was a hero.

Spider reluctantly agreed but ended up being disappointed that they made more of a story about his family history in the article, pointing out that there was one good family member in a criminal cartel, with old pictures of his father in his gang colours rather than him. He was deeply hurt by the article and felt sorry for his dad. The lady who did the interview had been so nice, but she had been tricking him to get a more sensational story; he hated her. Although he had to admit, Doug wasn't at all fazed, he even laughed.

There was a bright side; he got to see the cat again.

Arron the Fire Starter

Arron didn't know what he liked about fire, but he knew he was addicted to watching the orange glow and the smell of the smoke.

A common belief is that the arsonist lights a fire to conceal another crime. Was he mentally ill? He had googled the description of an arsonist. He didn't think he was ill, and he wasn't concealing anything. He just loved the excitement and the adrenaline it gave him; sometimes he even got an erection in the build-up.

His first real fire was a simple pile of rubbish bags waiting by the side of the road. It soon caught fire to the surrounding scrub, and although he tried to stomp it out the recent high temperatures and the wind set it racing across the surrounding paddocks. He panicked and jumped in his car and drove to a public phone booth and called it in anonymously.

Then came the excitement of the fire trucks and the sirens, and the firemen, with stern looks on their faces.

He drove around till he found a good vantage point and watched with fascinated interest; he was addicted.

He googled again and saw himself more as a pyromaniac. Pyromaniacs start fires to induce euphoria and often fixate on institutions of fire control like firehouses and firemen. Pyromania is a type of impulse control disorder; yes, he self-confirmed, that was his description. He set about starting many fires, randomly driving around and setting fire to scrub.

Hunt for the Arsonist

Spider put a giant map on his wall, and he used red stickers to mark where each fire had started in the last three years. He discovered a pattern, apart from a couple of random places which might have started by a natural cause like lightning. He narrowed down what he considered were the next couple of possible sites for another fire to start. He couldn't work out why no one else had thought of this. He fleetingly thought he might tell his supervisor about his findings but didn't want to make a fool of himself.

Night after night he would park his car at public parks and he would run for miles and miles in the quiet and the darkness of the night, scoping out any evidence of a possible arsonist doing reconnaissance on future sites. After a month of running sometimes ten kilometres at a time, he met a young man called Arron. Arron had a heavy smell of petrol about him.

He frightened Arron as he crept up behind him in the dark. Dressed in black from head to toe in a running suit with only a circle open for his face, it was an almost futuristic look.

Arron kept his composure at Spider's sudden appearance. "Mate, you started me. How did you get way out here?" he asked nervously. "It's miles from anywhere."

Spider didn't speak.

Spider walked right up to this skinny, pleasant-looking young white man and started sniffing him. Spider guessed his age to be between twenty-one and twenty-four.

Arron started to sweat more; he instinctively became very scared. Spider sniffed his whole body and then focused on sniffing the trunk of the car, still not speaking a word.

The prickly feeling on his skin intensified and the hairs on his neck rose. Arron tried to jump back into his car but couldn't reach the door handle before Spider grabbed him and wrestled him to the ground. Then, with incredible strength, he picked Arron up and grappled with him back to the trunk of the car. He opened the trunk and forcibly pushed Arron into the dark space, then closed the trunk lid.

Arron felt safer in the small trunk, so pushed his way as far back as he could among the fuel cans so he could get away from this obvious madman in the black ninja suit. He listened hard. He could hear Spider searching through the car; perhaps he was going to steal the car, or was this strange man looking for money?

Then there was silence. Arron listened again with all his attention.

The silence was broken when the trunk lid reopened, and a fiery mass of papers was thrown into the trunk then the lid was immediately slammed shut again.

Death for Arron was almost instant as the petrol containers exploded, the intense heat buckling the car as more explosions sent it bucking in the dark.

Spider casually started jogging back the ten kilometres in the dark to where he had parked his car. He felt strangely happy with the outcome.

Bridgette Sumner

Bridgette didn't care who she stood on to make a name for herself. She was a ladder climber. Her early days at reporting stemmed from a brief stint in local radio but that wasn't challenging enough, and the path to glory didn't have enough men she could sleep with to rise to the top.

She had a pleasant face, shoulder-length brown hair, and a small waist, but very short skirts weren't as flattering as she thought; she never seemed to see her fat arse and dimply thighs in the mirror. But she had a vagina and that worked very well.

Bridgette had gone back to school and studied journalism. Her first job after graduating was a small column in a local newspaper where she reported on the protection of local bird colonies. Her big break came when she exposed a local business that was polluting an endangered bird habitat, and her career took off from there. She milked it for all it was worth; in her mind, she had become famous.

She started having an affair with the editor and not surprisingly she got handed the weekly celebrity gossip column. Overnight her social life became a constant string of events and parties, all hosted and attended by would-be actors and socialites, all false people.

She loved every minute of it. She would look for any opportunity to add a bit of spice to an article, make a bit of fake news to grab the reader's attention – her column grew in popularity. Her victims varied from those who got exposed to those who wanted to be exposed. It paid to have Bridgette in your court rather than try and avoid her and expose yourself to her vicious writings.

Three failed marriages later, often her articles were about herself. She would lay the ugly bones of her divorces out for all the public to read. Of course, she was never to blame.

She had always made a point of marrying well, gaining from the proceeds of the settlement. She lived a comfortable life.

She had manipulated a chance meeting with the notorious Doug Henderson many years ago outside court. Dressed in a low-cut top and a denim mini-skirt, she had thought she was a sex magnet. He was about to jump on his bike and roar off when she literally threw herself at him asking for an exclusive interview. He simply looked at her and said, "Fuck off bush pig," revved his bike so loud it hurt her ears, and then he was gone.

Now, years later, she was interviewing one of his sons. She deliberately planned her revenge.

No More Bad News

Spider watched the woman night after night when his shifts allowed the time. He would park his car miles away and run the streets and parks for miles in his black running suit until he reached his destination. He memorised the path during the full moon and where streetlights permitted.

Bridgette lived alone – tired old bag. She thought she was really something with her flash words. Naked she had saggy tits and cellulite. Spider hated her. She had embarrassed him with her news article about his family.

He was worried about her cat. She was such a bitch she would leave it outside some nights when she'd had too much to drink and couldn't be fucked calling it in. Didn't she care that it might get run over or attacked by a predator? Selfish cow.

One night she had one too many drinks with the girls from work and left her back door unlocked. He thought of entering the house but thought against it, he didn't want to risk accidentally leaving his DNA anywhere. Instead, he turned the outside hose on and placed it inside the door to the kitchen and flooded the house, then removed it hours later. He laughed all the way home, thinking she would get up for a piss and find the carpet all wet, then she would have the expense of hiring a plumber to find the leak, then the insurance claim. It was too much; he nearly tripped over laughing.

He started to feed the cat when the opportunity arose; better make it his friend and he liked cats.

He put dog shit in her mailbox, right at the back, so when she felt around it would get under her nails; he searched for hours in the parks for a sticky, ginger shit.

A couple of weeks later there was a huge rubbish skip outside the house full of stinky wet carpet. When he looked in the windows, he could see the disarrayed furniture and the chaos inside. Must have been so inconvenient for her. "Poor Bridgette," he mocked.

This gave him a good idea. He purchased several sex toys, mainly huge rubber dildos. This time he waited till she had been asleep for some time, her breathing settled in a regular pattern, and he broke into the house.

          MICHELLE THOMPSON

Spider took great care to leave the dildos and sex toys in different locations all around the house, then he made his way to the kitchen and loosened the gas pipe. With all the carpet pulled up and the furniture moved it was quite feasible that the gas fitting in the kitchen could have been disturbed; he saw this all the time at work call-outs. The explosion would be huge, but in the evidence, they would find masses of melted rubber; that would go in the fire investigation report – he would make sure of that.

He'd also make sure an anonymous letter made its way to a rival paper about the orgy group she was a member of.

The house exploded into matchsticks. Bridgette died almost instantly.

Doug and Orhan

Together these two had a special bond; it was almost like they knew what the other was thinking.

Doug mused at the new cat they seemed to have inherited from God knows where overnight. He looked across the room at Orhan. They both had a good idea where it came from and nodded in agreement.

Orhan silently placed the morning paper in front of Doug at the breakfast table and pointed to the article about the death of the reporter; gas explosion, house destroyed.

They both looked in the direction of the panic room. Spider was at work, but they didn't enter, you never knew if he had anything booby-trapped.

They decided to go for a walk together so they could talk freely, still paranoid that the house could be bugged.

There was no doubt that it was Spider who had done this, and they were certain that he was also responsible for the 'arsonist boy'. Orhan had watched Spider sneak in and out of the house in his black running gear at all hours of the night. When he had gone into the panic room to clear out his dirty washing, he had noticed the map on the wall, which had since gone missing. There were also the cat biscuits that had gone missing leading up to the appearance of the new cat. When he asked Spider its name, he didn't know but casually said he would find out.

They both agreed that Spider was a difficult rooster to negotiate with. He was never wrong and would argue his case no matter what evidence you presented to suggest otherwise.

They decided the best thing they could do was tell him that they knew he was responsible for the reporter's death and ask him what repercussions they could expect if the police worked out it was him.

It was also decided that they would tell Stacey, secretly, and if Spider decided to murder them in their sleep, she would have enough to go on to end his life.

They would wait till he came off shift tonight and have that conversation. Meanwhile, they decided to drive to Stacey's house and brighten her morning with the news.

When Spider returned in the afternoon, he said he was going for a run, but he was headed off at the pass by Orhan. "Dad and I need to have a private conversation with you, outside."

He knew what that meant, he was in trouble.

When they presented him with their summary of the facts, he simply agreed and said it was him.

"That kid, the arsonist, was harming the public, and the newspaper reporter was just a mean bitch and shouldn't have said those things about the family." Spider replied. In his mind, their crimes justified his actions. He went into detail about the lengths he had taken to cover his tracks. "The tracksuit contained any of my hairs that could be used in DNA evidence, and in both cases, the fire destroyed any trail leading back to me."

"What about the cat? Doug asked.

"It was suddenly left homeless as its owner had died in a fire. I rescued it." Spider made it seem like the most natural occurrence.

He promised not to do it again. He was famous for promising never to do it again … until the next time.

As if to have the last word, he announced that he also had some important news. "I've been accepted into paramedic school. I applied a few months ago. First, though, I'm going to go on a bit of a holiday driving around Australia, just to have a break from killing," he joked "before the semester starts."

He was very excited, and they all agreed it would be a nice change from killing.

Orhan

Orhan had never grown very much in size. Starvation as a child had hindered his growth. He looked more like Gandhi, the Indian, with lovely light brown skin – he even had the glasses. What he lacked in size he made up for in humour, sharpness of mind and love for his new family. Doug had adopted him almost immediately and Orhan would often say to people that he felt more loved now than he had by his own parents. Mostly it had been more of a cultural thing with his real parents, but here his new family treated him like their equals, and they weren't poor. They even went as far as calling him Dad's favourite, and Edith didn't care one bit. She loved Orhan like a brother who stole her spot, she would joke.

Doug supported him in his request to farm the land, and he went off to agricultural school three days a week until he got his diploma and then he became a homebody, taking care of the property and the many farms that Doug owned. He had a permanent staff of ten people.

Orhan wasn't overly interested in women. He wasn't gay, he just hadn't got around to it. He told Doug he wanted to make sure she was the right woman, not a practice one. He had plenty of female friends, but he kept his private life just that, very private.

He was too small to ride a motorbike, so Doug had taught him to drive and had given him a big automatic four-by-four so he could use it on the farm or go to town in it. He didn't drink or smoke so more often than not he was Doug's sober driver. He would spend hours at the motorcycle clubrooms playing pool and darts and listening to bands, then he would drive Doug home in the wee small hours of the morning – some of the best times in his life. They would laugh all the way home and stop for breakfast on the way at Stacey's and tell her stories of the night before. He certainly had no regrets; he told people he had landed in a good paddock.

The one thing that Orhan, Doug, and Stacey all shared was their scepticism about Spider. He had been an unusual baby, an unusual child and now was an unusual adult. They blamed it on the mad Colombian blood running through his veins.

Spider Travels

"I've been accepted into the NSW Ambulance Trainee Paramedic course for the next intake. So, I've decided that I'm going to take a year off and I'm going to travel around Australia and see the sights." This news from Spider explained his usual, self-imposed recent silence. He looked uneasy about telling everyone and shuffled nervously.

For a moment the family was silent, they didn't know how he would cope leaving the shelter of his panic room. To anyone's knowledge, he didn't have any friends. Yes, he had work colleagues, but he was a real homebody. They were suddenly flooding him with a million questions: where would he sleep, what would he take with him, what car would he take, what would he eat? Would he email and keep everyone posted?

He didn't seem to have the answers. "I haven't really thought it through fully, I just thought I'd see how it unfolds as I go along," he replied.

Doug assured him that money wasn't going to be an issue. He would provide him with a company credit card. He would ring Edith and arrange for Spider to pick up a spare card on the way.

The family sat in awkward silence. There was a part of them that would miss him and his odd behaviour, but there was also a part of them that would welcome the absence.

Spider wasn't mucking around. "I'll be leaving tomorrow morning. I want to get on the road early before the heat of the day makes the drive unbearable." With that, he retreated to his room.

Early the next morning he was up at 5 am and literally jumped into his car and left. No sad goodbyes, he just drove off.

Orhan and Doug were awake. They always rose early and started the day with a cup of tea and a read of the morning papers. They watched Spider with interest as he packed the car and fluffed around with the car seat and the seatbelt. They both felt that he was hiding something. He had recently received several parcels from online shopping. When Orhan questioned him about one larger parcel Spider explained it was a life jacket, which given they had a boating company seemed odd, but he was an odd boy anyway, so Orhan just dismissed it.

He had become very quiet recently, quieter than usual. They knew he was up to something but couldn't put their finger on it. Short of having him followed, they decided to let Edith question him when he went to pick up the credit card, he'd often confide in her. But one thing was for sure, they both felt uneasy.

Colombia Calling

Camilla had tracked Spider down through Facebook. It had taken a while, but she had finally made contact with him and opened the door to communication. He had been reluctant at first but had come around after his curiosity had been sparked by the complexity of the ever-growing story.

So now here he was sitting on a plane in business class flying to Colombia via Argentina from Sydney. All the flights and the travel arrangements had been made by Camilla. He was flying under a false identity and passport in the name of Douglas Carlos Hernandez. All the finer details were also taken care of by Camilla, who he now knew as his Colombian grandmother and the stepmother of his birth mother, Sofia.

He had so many questions. He realised now that his birth mother was missing, presumed dead. He had never asked about her and she was never spoken about. As a young lad, he was told she had been ill with post-natal depression and had left to go back to her family in Colombia. He hadn't felt a need to ask about her. Between his grandparents, his dad and brothers and sister and Orhan, he had all the love he needed. But had it all been a lie? As the growing story emerged, his feelings of guilt about lying to his father about what he was doing were counteracted by the things he was learning.

He had set up a post office box to collect his mail from Camilla on her instructions. He had ordered a bulletproof vest online and had it sent to the house. Orhan was on to it immediately, nothing got past him, so he lied to Orhan and told him it was a lifesaving vest for the boat. He figured that Orhan was in on the 'great deception' also. In fact, he wondered who wasn't. Aunty Stacey? The list went on.

His plane touched down in Argentina where he was suddenly surrounded by people fussing over him. He was met by several officials who treated him like royalty and insisted on carrying his bags to a buggy that resembled a golf cart. He was then escorted swiftly through transit, then driven by bus to a smaller runway on the edge of the airfield where he boarded a private jet. The officials never left his side until he was seated on the plane.

It was exciting and frightening all at once. He just wanted to yell stop and go to duty-free and buy some more presents for his new grandmother. At the same time, he didn't want to make it seem like he was new to all this fuss. His instincts told him he was opening a Pandora's box to something big. Even his dad didn't have a private jet.

The staff on the plane offered him champagne, food, a massage, in fact, anything he wanted. He declined it all, he just wanted to sleep and reduce the anxiety he was spinning into. They stood back nervously so he told them he didn't require any more help and just looked out the window. He didn't see them again until they were about to land in Bogotá.

It was night when they finally landed in Bogotá, and the plane taxied on the runway to a hanger entrance. He could not see anyone from his window. The tension on the plane was thick, and the cabin crew shuffled nervously.

Spider was suddenly pissed off with the whole situation. His ears were ringing, he was homesick, and wished he hadn't come, and just wanted it all to be over.

Camilla made her way energetically up the plane steps; she didn't look as old as he had pictured her in real life. She had a hell of a firm grip when she grabbed his hand. He thought she was going in for a handshake, but she pulled him forward and went for the full hug. She had tears of joy running down her cheeks as she kissed him many times on the cheek and the forehead. She kept stepping back to get a better look at him, patting his arm then going for the hug again. He wasn't used to the affection, but he didn't resist. He suddenly felt calm.

Camilla snapped orders in Spanish for all the crew and staff to wait outside and give them some privacy. She signalled Spider to sit and sat opposite him, not like a lady, more like a bloke on a mission, legs slightly apart, hands clasped between her knees, until she used them to talk and emphasise more intense parts of the conversation. For one whole hour, she briefed him on what to expect next.

They emerged from the plane together. He was no longer Spider. He was now Señor Douglas Carlos Hernandez.

The Hacienda

As they entered the gates of the property, a guard who opened the huge metal gates checked the driver's details and looked into the car. As they passed Douglas could just see a pistol in a holster under his arm.

The driveway was in a full circle with an ornate water feature as the central focal point. It was beautiful, all lit up with beautiful, coloured lights which, he was told, his mother had installed.

The house was a mansion of Spanish architecture. It had three distinct wings with two stories of large windows and the main entrance in the centre.

The car pulled up and a manservant stepped down from the landing and opened the car door, offering his support as Spider's grandmother stepped out of the vehicle; not that she needed any help, it was more of a duty than an aid.

Other staff removed Douglas's meagre luggage from the trunk. Douglas slid across the seat and exited the vehicle on his grandmother's side. He was happy to be on solid ground and stood tall to stretch his legs and body. He caught a few startled glances from the staff that were in, what he called, the 'arrival party'. He was happy about that; he planned to keep them all on their toes.

The main reception was a vast marble and gold spectacle: he likened it to Caesars Palace in Las Vegas. On both sides of the main reception were elaborate staircases, each winding up to the second floor with a balcony connecting the two, then you had a choice to go either left or right to the different wings. But more imposing were the two magnificent portraits in the centre of the twin staircases. Douglas stared in awe at the lifelike detail of a man he presumed to be his grandfather on the left and then what was the first photo he had ever seen of his beautiful mother, Sofia, on the right; he was overcome with emotion. She was literally in his face, she was captivating, and her eyes followed you around the room. He would spend many hours looking at that face in the days to come.

As with tradition, all the staff were lined up for the official introduction. He made no effort to remember any names. He knew one thing for sure; he was filthy rich.

As if she read his mind, Camilla ushered him into the right wing, where they entered a formal, quiet sitting room where he was offered coffee or an aperitif, he chose neither. He was tired so he told her he just wanted to go to sleep.

Camila informed him that the staff were getting his room ready, and he would be able to retire soon. "We have some big days ahead of us," she said, "so we will wait until you are over your jetlag and feel up to the task. There is a lot for you to learn, and I want you well-rested before we begin."

The one thing they both agreed not to disclose to anyone was that he spoke fluent Spanish. For now, they didn't need to play all their cards. She was convinced that they had a spy in the works, and they would use this tactic to sniff her or him out.

After a short while, Douglas's personal manservant directed him to a room off the second floor of the left wing. He was shown to a huge room with a four-poster bed. The room was decorated in such opulence that it looked like it came out of *Vogue Magazine,* with room for its own en suite, and a walk-in closet already full of clothing for him. A pair of silk pyjamas with his initials embroidered on them were laid out on the bed. His manservant, Henry, advised that it was house protocol that he wore the pyjamas to avoid embarrassment to himself if the house staff were to accidentally catch him unprepared for company. For now, Douglas agreed to conform but only because he was tired.

He didn't remember going to sleep, he thought this must have happened before his head hit the pillow. Someone tucked him in, and he went into a deep, long, restful sleep.

When he awoke, in what seemed like days later, he had no regrets.

Settling In

Camilla and Douglas spent many days and hours in the office going over the books, stopping only to eat and go for little walks around the gardens at the back of the estate so they could talk secretly. They were always accompanied by armed security, which he hated, so his grandmother gave him a gun so they could be alone when they wanted to be; he never used it, in fact, he kept putting it down and forgetting where it was.

Douglas had no complaints about the food or the service. On the rare occasion, he would explore the other parts of the house and sit in his mother's room, which had been untouched since she left. He didn't touch anything; he wanted to keep it as a shrine. He was in the process of sealing off her wing of the house for himself only. He met with little resistance from Camilla, so he instructed Henry to make the necessary arrangements to change his room to the one next to Sofia's old room. And he had another request. He wanted an office in his wing, completely fitted out with the latest surveillance equipment, just like his panic room back home. Here, just like home, he would spend hours watching the staff, any visitors, and his crusty old nana, whom he loved surprisingly deeply for someone he had just met.

A directive was given to all the staff not to enter past the door of his wing, and cleaning staff were to always be accompanied by Henry but only if their services were requested. Douglas had one other non-negotiable – no pyjamas! He loved the freedom of running around completely naked in his wing like a man possessed, often screaming and yelling or laughing hysterically to himself.

Occasionally he would cut and paste a photo of scenery from around Australia on his computer and post it on his Facebook, just to give the illusion that he was still travelling in Australia. He was careful to make sure the picture depicted reasonable travel times between each location. He didn't want to send a photo of Perth was he was meant to be in Alice Springs.

—

It was clear to Douglas that although the cartel made lots of money there was a leak in the tank somewhere. It was haemorrhaging moderate sums of money, not enough to be obvious but enough to make a tidy nest egg for someone. After reviewing all the facts both he and Camilla had a very sure idea who and where it was leaking. Proving it was complicated and risky, and it would take both their cunning and intellect to outfox the culprit.

In the meantime, his presence in the country was still meant to be a secret. Camilla wanted him to have a firm knowledge of every business interest and every business partner before she introduced him to the wider family.

They planned a huge welcome event, a grand party to announce him as the son of Sophia, Carlos's long-lost grandson, to the rest of the Cartel. Camilla and Douglas would have to be ready, and it would have to be well choreographed.

Meanwhile, Douglas adjusted to his new position in the household, soaking up the riches, spying on the staff, and sending pictures back home.

When he got the urge, he would wait till the wee small hours of the night and creep out through a secret entrance to the estate at the back of the garden that his grandmother had shown him. From there he would run the streets of Bogotá in his black running suit, memorising every street, every camera, every barking dog in the neighbourhood. The only difference now, he wore his Kevlar vest over his running suit.

He'd spy on the prostitutes at work, the bums and the street urchins, the drug dealers, and the junkies. Occasionally, just for the sheer hell of fulfilling a need, he'd hide, and surprise-attack a small-time drug dealer. Within the cover of his black suit and using his brute strength, he'd snap their necks or seriously injure them enough to hospitalise them, then take the drugs and any money, only to drop the drugs at the feet of a junkie or prostitute some blocks away, laughing as he went at the double carnage, as they greedily consumed the contents of the little bags. The money he'd always tuck in the mailbox opening of the animal shelter.

He was careful not to frequent the same areas often, as suspicion would have the pimps and the dealers on edge; they were all armed and would be lying in wait for a ghost.

Occasionally he'd take his phone and snap pictures of the prostitutes at work giving blowjobs in the front seats of cars or just hitching up their skirts behind a dumpster. He'd spend hours reviewing the photos back in his room, beating himself with a leather strap until he gained an erection.

In the morning, he would have breakfast with his nana and butter wouldn't melt in his mouth as if he was the perfect grandson.

Paulo Hernandez

Paulo sat chewing and sucking on his Cuban cigar, deep in thought. He mused over that scary old fossil, Camilla.

What was that sneaky old lady up to now? Who was this mystery grandson, bastard son of Sofia? According to rumour, he was ugly! Surely, he couldn't be Sofia's offspring? And he's a bloody Aussie. *Que mierda*? WTF?

Paulo was the great-nephew of Carlos. He had a reputation for being unpredictable and often irrational – he'd shoot first and ask questions later. He'd dress in a flamboyant manner and strut around like a colourful peacock in his silk suits and his alligator boots, all handmade and of the finest workmanship. Paulo's father had taken over running the cartel after Carlos died. They felt cheated from the start; the only legitimate money was in the emerald mines, and they had been sold off to some foreign offshore company before Carlos died.

The cocaine trade was getting complicated. They had had to shift to Buenaventura so they could control the port, buying up all the land around the port under different companies with false trustees to keep the FBI and the CIA and every other bastard guessing, and paying off the FARQ, a gorilla group who you were never sure were run by the police or the crooked government officials.

The government had also been running a campaign to encourage farmers to grow heavily subsidised alternative crops like cocoa, but it was slow and unproductive, whereas a cocaine crop could reap a return every three months. Farmers tended to go with what they knew best, which was generations of cocaine farming.

Paulo's biggest trade was to the USA, and this was where the complication came in. Paying off the right officials. Paying off the big guy, paying off the little guy; it seemed everyone had a handout.

He maintained the upper hand from his rivals with the fear factor. His unpredictable nature gave him the reputation of being an arsehole who lived like he'd watched too many movies. Making sure that enough violence was distributed to give everyone the message, that there were always consequences, kept him busy.

His father had even invented a 'chop-house' – more fact than rumour and so highly effective in controlling the feral. In the centre of an old warehouse on the port, they had a pully system over a hole in the floor where they could string people up over the hole and chainsaw off bits and pieces to make a point or extract information. The bodies would be dropped into the sea for the sharks and the fishes.

Staff were cheap. Most came from poverty-stricken districts, happy for a roof over their heads and a hot meal. Some were purchased slaves, mostly dispensable females, daughters sold by poor farmers from here and from overseas, even as far away as India. These girls were used for the end process of packaging and quality control. If necessary, you could send an employee on a one-way journey to the 'chop-house' if you wanted to send a clear message to everyone if you caught them dipping into the profits.

On the other hand, you had to maintain a respectable public image; nice little high-class wife from a good political family – the trophy wife, handsome young son to carry on the dynasty and prove you had enough sperm in your balls to produce a son. The mansion, the celebrity parties, the whores.

Yes, the cocaine business was complicated, but it was fast, exhilarating, it was a lifestyle Paulo didn't want to give up any day soon. And he certainly didn't want that old goat Camilla sticking her nose in and fucking it all up. He sniffed the handwritten invitation with its embossed gold lettering, no expense spared; she was sending a message.

     MICHELLE THOMPSON

The Grand Party

Camilla insisted on putting across the right image, which included a whole new wardrobe for Douglas. The family tailor arrived, a family firm that had clothed his grandfather and his mother over the years. Douglas hated being all trussed up, but he had to admit he did look sharp. Camilla let him wear Nike's with his suit, which was their private compromise.

They hired the Marriott for the function. It had the capacity for three hundred people and the chef had a reputation for delivering one of the best catered functions in Bogotá. Camilla gave the chef free rein. There was valet parking and guests from overseas could stay if they wished, courtesy of Camilla and Douglas.

Special family guests like Paulo and his lovely wife Maria and their son Dennis were invited to stay at the family home in the guest wing.

They arrived two days before the reception and Paulo took to Douglas instantly. He thought Douglas was a bit basic, a bit naive, but overall, he didn't mind taking him under his wing, he liked him. He drove him around Bogotá, showed him a few clubs and bars. He was surprised that Douglas didn't drink or smoke and insisted he would have to teach him if he was going to stay for any length of time.

After the party, he announced that he was going to take Douglas on a road trip, just the boys, around a few tourist destinations; Paulo was looking forward to it.

Douglas's head was in the game as he was led around the party by Paulo and introduced to many people who he would not remember two seconds later. Paulo said he didn't remember half of them either, just arse-lickers or wannabe's he called them.

Paulo had a sense of humour and would make a joke about some guests before they were introduced but was always professional in his delivery. As Paulo said to Douglas, "This is a PR exercise, and it is about time I had a family member I can trust to work alongside me; take some of the workload."

The function was a huge success and the following day there was a picture on the front page of *The Bogotá Post* of Douglas and Paulo comically posing with a couple of belly dancers. The word was out and now they had invitations streaming in from all over Colombia.

On two occasions during Paulo's short stay at his grandmother's hacienda, while Douglas was spying on his visitors, he witnessed some tense domestic issues between Paulo and Maria. It seemed that the wife's name turned into the word 'Cunt' once Paulo had one too many drinks.

Douglas confided in Camilla, and it seemed that Paulo's short fuse was well known. Douglas was careful not to react so early in the arrangement, but he was embarrassed by it and didn't think it was fair to poor Maria.

Paulo's wife Maria was extremely beautiful and held polite, intelligent conversation when prompted. She almost looked like fine china that could break at any moment.

Dennis, the precious son, was a quiet child who didn't want to leave his mother's side but was encouraged by his father to show off his football skills in the back garden with Douglas. Douglas loved it but pretended to pull an old ankle injury so as not to give away any indication that he was extremely fit.

Camilla packed Douglas off with his clothes for his road trip with Paolo like a small child going away to camp. She was surprised by Paulo's openness and his acceptance of Douglas. She wasn't sure how long it would last, but she knew Douglas had everything in order. Paulo made fun of her fussing and ribbed Douglas about being treated like a baby. Paulo was quite the comedian.

Orhan Has Rustlers

A neighbour came up the driveway very early in the morning. Orhan and Doug were at the breakfast table with their morning cup of tea and the newspapers. They knew it was serious for two reasons; the timing of the visit and the fact that the neighbours feared Doug and would much rather poke pins in their eyes than talk to him up close.

The neighbour had been on his way to work and noticed an injured beast along the fence by the main road. He said there was a terrible amount of blood. He thought it might have been hit by a car.

Orhan and Doug raced to the scene and were met by a grisly discovery. A large beast had been slaughtered by the fence and cut up, leaving skin and carcass in no order; it looked rushed and amateurish. The tragedy was that another beast had been shot in the belly but not killed and had crawled to the corner of a fence adjoining the yards and was bleeding to death and in pain. Doug swiftly put the animal out of its misery with a bullet in the centre of its forehead.

Orhan was too distraught to talk. He had raised these beasts from small calves, he knew their parents, their lineage, their weights – they ate out of his hands. He loved his stock, and he often joked that they had landed in a good paddock, like him. It was the first time Doug could remember the little guy being that upset, as Orhan sat next to the dead beast and stroked its neck.

They had no option but to call the police and report the crime.

Doug left Orhan at the scene and drove back to get the tractor so he could collect the remains and take it to his abattoir; they could use it for dog food.

The police had no leads. There had been no other incidents locally, so it was established that someone had targeted Orhan directly. They took photos for any future prosecution, but the police really didn't look like they had taken it seriously. They hated Doug, so they thought he probably deserved it.

Orhan took photos also, and posted them on Facebook, offering a substantial reward for any information. He called an urgent staff meeting and showed them the photos and offered a bonus if they heard anything themselves. The local paper did an article on it; people were generally disgusted at the actions of the rustlers.

Doug spared no expense and arranged to have cameras installed on the sheds and barns around the property, he was determined to catch them just for Orhan's sake. They both knew one thing for sure, it certainly couldn't be anyone who knew Doug or the family history, they would have to be an idiot.

A month later another similar situation occurred, but this time it was on another property owned by Doug. This property was some distance away from the main farm. The thieves drove in at night and simply herded fifteen sheep onto a truck and disappeared. No one saw or heard a thing. Now it was personal.

Six months passed without incident then there was another butchery of a beast, but to cover their tracks the perpetrators burnt down the barn so the camera's served no purpose. This time they had herded the beast into the yards and cut its throat – not an effective way to kill it instantly. They were clearly amateurs.

The police sent a forensic team this time and they found a tyre iron in the grass, which was taken away and fingerprinted, but no leads came from it.

Short of the expense of hiring security, it was going to be difficult to catch them.

Paulo and Douglas

Douglas wasn't used to being close or a buddy to anyone, he'd always been a loner. It was taking all his might to continue this charade of 'family' with Paulo. The hugging and the kissing with every new person they met were literally turning his stomach. But the boys' trip was on, and they were constantly on the road, going from city to city and stopping at villages on the way to meet business partners and extended family members. A couple of times they went to prisons where the family's reputation was legendary. They were met like they were the royal family. Paulo handed out American $100 bills like candy.

Paulo was having a really good time; he liked the new cousin. Yes, he was a big overgrown ape and a bit green behind the ears, but it was an endearing quality in him. He was pleased that Douglas was slowly picking up a bit of the Spanish language. Paulo had forced him to drink a Baileys Irish Cream on ice once and laughed for hours as Douglas instantly got drunk and vomited.

For Douglas, there was a baptism by fire as they visited an actual cocaine farm, and Douglas saw the entire process of turning coca leaves into cocaine; he was surprised how complicated it was. Then Paulo took him to a warehouse where thirty naked women at one time worked shifts around the clock, sitting at tables under lights grading and packaging bags of cocaine. Douglas asked why they were naked, to which Paulo laughed and said, "They can't steal if they don't have pockets, although occasionally they find a way. So, I have a reward system, and they get a cash bonus if they report someone stealing."

Of course, you'd get the bitch mob once a month when they were menstruating, and they'd sometimes accuse an innocent party. She would be dragged kicking and screaming to the 'chop-house' declaring her innocence.

But other than that, they were well looked after, they had good accommodation in one of his apartment blocks, and they had a full-time cook who ran the communal cafeteria.

In most cases, the girls sent all their money home to support their families. Paulo had the belief that they were better off now, rather than living in a leaky hut eating dirt.

Douglas was shocked by the vulgarity Paulo showed towards women. He had a beautiful wife at home, yet he insisted on liaising with cheap whores at every opportunity. He would brag about his sexual exploits. Perhaps it was reputation or money, but women would throw themselves at Paulo, even going so far as to perform oral sex on him under restaurant tables with no heed to others around the same table.

Paulo showed no honour towards his friends and associates and would fuck their wives and girlfriends when they were at work or away on business. Back home in Aussie, they would have called him a creep. Douglas was careful not to show any emotion in these situations. If he could, he would wait in the car until Paulo was finished.

When Paulo found out Douglas was a virgin it became his full-time obsession to 'fix' the matter. He would cry laughing as Douglas visibly blushed or turned bright red during discussions about women's labia.

The worst experience for Douglas was when Paulo told his wife at the dinner table with Dennis present, then literally fell off the chair laughing. Maria didn't laugh; she looked embarrassed for Douglas. For the first time, Douglas witnessed emotion from Dennis, as he flashed a dirty look at his father. It was brief, but Douglas saw it. He knew then that this perfect family hated Paulo.

Douglas was conscious of outstaying his welcome, but Paulo assured him that he was still welcome. He had set Douglas up in the guest house on the property, so he had his own space.

Douglas had listened in on a couple of Paulo's conversations with his Spanish speaking associates and he had never heard Paulo badmouthing him. In fact, he had reassured his associates. "The Gringo is with me. He's alright, he's family."

Douglas spent many nights just watching the big house in the darkness, luring the guard dogs with treats, creeping around in his suit watching and monitoring the security guards, always conscious of the cameras. He didn't know when he would make his move, but it would be soon.

One night he was surprised in the darkness by a visit from Dennis. The small, frail child simply entered the guest house as quiet as a mouse. Dennis handed Douglas a bag of dog treats.

"Here, they like these ones better."

He confessed that he had been watching Douglas every night since he arrived.

"Are you here to kill my papa?" he bluntly asked.

"Maybe," said Douglas. "Would that bother you?"

"Not in the slightest," replied Dennis.

With that, he disappeared into the dark again and vanished. Douglas was impressed.

Time to head back to Bogotá and update Camilla.

Tammy

Douglas had been spying in the dark in an alley frequented by desperate prostitutes. At times, if he got to his spot early enough, he could hide behind the dumpsters and be practically within touching distance from the prostitute's arse. He'd breathe in the smell of their vaginas deeply, often mixed with the smell of cheap perfume, not always a clean smell. The sex was often quick and at times brutal; money would change hands, and they would be back on the street looking for another trick.

The clients came from a wide range of personalities: fathers, sons, businessmen, football players; all secreted away down dirty alleys fucking cheap prostitutes. Sometimes it was just a blowjob, or they wanted fingers up their anus's. The ladies of the night weren't fussy, they needed money for drugs and to feed families.

On one occasion, while the prostitute was giving a blowjob to a very drunk man, Douglas slipped his hand behind her and lifted her skirt so he could stare at her vagina which was exposed due to her not wearing panties – she didn't seem to notice. It was an ugly hairy looking thing with bits of toilet paper stuck to it. He put the skirt down again.

On one of his spying nights, he was in position behind the dumpster eager for the night's entertainment when a fresh-faced young girl led a fat middle-aged man down the alley. He was already breathing heavily, his shirt swelling at the buttons. The walk down the alley nearly killed him, so Douglas wasn't sure how he was going to fuck the prostitute and survive.

The fat man ordered the girl to bend over and not face him; she held the side of the dumpster to brace herself. She pulled her skirt up and moved her G-string aside; he was really puffing now. Her face was practically inches away from Douglas's face and he could smell the cigarette on her breath.

The fat man was masturbating himself, taking his time, then for no apparent reason, he viciously punched her in the back of the head, her face smashing into the steel dumpster. She slumped to the ground. He ejaculated all over her head then he put his cock away and turned to leave but, to Douglas's amazement, he swung his leg back and proceeded to kick her and stomp on

 MICHELLE THOMPSON

her head, preaching the whole time that sinners go to hell and ranting verses from the bible.

At first, Douglas was in shock. For a split second, he fought an internal battle about what choice to make, his instinct for protection versus not blowing his cover. Then his instinct for protection kicked in and he leapt from behind the dumpster and lunged at the fat man. The fat man went white with shock and fear. He started swinging his fists at Douglas, but he was unfit and was soon out of breath and lifting his big fat arms became impossible.

He had two choices: fight or flight. The choice was obvious but as he turned to run away, he tripped and landed with a loud groan, his big arse protruding unnaturally into the air due to his fat belly.

Douglas stepped up behind him and kicked him as hard as he could in the balls and kept kicking until the fat man vomited, then he stomped on his face until he was sure all his teeth were broken. He searched his pockets and took his wallet, he might need to visit this fucker later, teach him a lesson.

Tammy was moaning and trying to stand. Her face was all bloodied and her hair was matted with sperm. She was disorientated, her eyes wide.

Douglas held his hands up and told her she didn't have to be afraid. He quickly told her he was a good Samaritan who had witnessed the attack and came to her aid.

She felt around in the dark for her purse. She was shaking, trying to get a cigarette out to light it. Douglas suggested that they get out of there before someone found fatty and called the police. She was reluctant at first but needed support to walk. When they got into the light, she looked him up and down in his black running suit.

"You some sort of weirdo?"

"Yes," said Douglas.

They both laughed, the blood streaming down her face.

"Best you help me get home. Come with me to my flat so I can get cleaned up. No one will want to fuck me looking like this. Tammy is my name, by the way. What's yours?"

"Douglas, but at home, they call me Spider." They shook hands.

Tammy had had a hard life; she'd been an orphan from the age of eight. Both her parents had gone to jail; there was no state care. She had lived on what she could steal or scrounge out of dumpsters. At times she had got food and clothing from charities. She soon fell in with other children like her, living rough, abandoned by the authorities. Nothing surprised her anymore – this wasn't the first time she had been beaten by a trick.

Girls like her quickly learnt if you had no support or money, and were living under a bridge, that if you wanted a better life, you start selling your vagina. If you looked at it from a business point of view, you were sitting on a fortune. With no formal education, it was all that was on offer to make lots of money. Plenty of men wanted sex with an underage girl. She kept her body slim and shaved her pussy so she could hold on to that underage scene for as long as she could, that was where the big money was. She didn't take drugs – she had seen what that eventually did to all her friends – but she liked a drink or two, or three.

She had a surprisingly nice flat in an apartment building, it almost looked like a hotel suite. "I rent it out to tourists through an online hotel agency – make reasonable money in the peak season," she explained to Douglas.

She put the jug on and went into the bathroom to clean up. "Make us a coffee, aye? I won't be long."

When Tammy re-entered the room, Douglas looked her up and down, she wasn't a bad looking girl. She had lots of bruising and a cut on her face and lip. She was wearing tights and a T-shirt which made her legs look long.

Now it was her turn. She looked him up and down, noticed that he had an accent. "You normally get around like that? You're a strange looking fucker."

She looked at his face up close as if she was trying to read something in his eyes. He noticed that she had pockmarked skin on her cheeks, probably acne scars. He could smell tobacco on her breath mixed with peppermint.

"You're a loner." It was more a statement from Tammy, rather than a question.

She sat down next to him on the settee. "You want sex now for rescuing me?"

Douglas assured her that was not why he'd helped her. He even gave her the money from the wallet, and he added a couple of hundred of his own. She probably couldn't work for a couple of days until her face got better. She didn't argue and took the money. "What do you want?"

He thought about it for a while then Douglas told her he just wanted a friend.

"Ok, friend, but don't start hanging around too often and get on my nerves.

     MICHELLE THOMPSON

Come back tomorrow at eleven thirty am and we can do lunch together. And for Christ's sake wear something fuckin' better than that fuckin' shit." They both laughed.

He turned up the next day in a chauffeur-driven car and a flash suit. She laughed. Here she was thinking they would grab a burger and a Coke, and Mr Flash pants pulls up dripping of money. They got on well and Douglas shared stories of life in Australia, told her about his mother and the reason he came to Colombia. She told him stories about her experiences and her idea to save enough money so she could travel the world.

Their relationship grew. Every time he was back in Bogotá they would hook up and go on adventures together, go to fun parks, restaurants or just go for a drive. He would always pay and generously leave her plenty of money; she never said no. She knew this would run out eventually so she would take it while she could.

Tammy was blunt and honest with him, he liked that.

Douglas continued to sneak around in his black running suit at night and spy on her and other prostitutes; he got such excitement from watching. It was not just the sex, but the chance of getting caught made it more of a challenge.

One night he was standing in the shadows and Tammy brought a client into the alley. It was a simple transaction, quick: money changed hands, the client was off. As Tammy was straightening her skirt, she called Douglas out of the shadows. "I know you're there. I can smell your aftershave."

He crept out like a naughty child caught stealing apples from the neighbour's tree.

"You're going to have to stop this shit, it's fuckin' creepy. You're coming home with me right now. I got a present for you."

She had bought him a big coat from the charity shop.

"When you leave in the morning you can wear this."

Douglas was confused, he didn't understand why he had to leave in the morning.

"Do I have to spell it out to you? Take your clothes off, I want to fuck you."

He was stunned, he didn't know what to do.

Tammy started to undress; her skinny naked body was white. He could see traces of bruising around her thighs and hips where clients had held on to her roughly, and she had a couple of scars from historical stab wounds. Douglas traced these with his finger while she started to undress him. They fell over laughing trying to get the running suit off him, it was clinging like a wetsuit.

: Embarrassed, Douglas awkwardly confessed, "This is my first time. I don't know what I'm meant to do."

"Lucky I've had a bit of experience, isn't it, Douglas?"

With that, they rolled around on the bed, her tiny body comfortable in his big frame. Tammy was extremely fit and energetic She felt like a small child in his arms; it only heightened his arousal. She was an expert, she explained everything as she went, taught him all the tricks and spots to make it pleasant for the woman; he was a good pupil.

He stayed all night, and he thought in the morning that they had practised every position in the book *The Joy of Sex*. He laughed as he told her his cock was sore; he was sure he had a blister.

He rang Camilla to order a car to come and pick him up. He left a roll of bills. He felt like the happiest man in the world.

—

Tammy was daydreaming. It had been nearly a month since she had seen Douglas, she actually missed him. It wasn't her modus operandi to get attached to anyone, but the big dumb ox had a way about him. He wasn't thick, but he was odd. He disappeared enough times to not get under her skin. She didn't have to pretend to be anyone else around him.

Tammy crammed her way into a busy bar. Lots of punters in this bar, any one of them could be potential clients. It had been a busy night as a major football tournament was on in Bogotá. She wasn't in to socialise; she just needed a double shot of whisky to take the taste of semen out of her mouth. The bar was about six-deep in rejoicing drunks; their team had obviously won.

She put her hand up and waved, signalling to the barman that she had pesos to buy coffee. A middle-aged white woman brushed past her and apologised for bumping into her, at the same time she felt a small sting in her back around her kidney area. The crowd was so thick around her she stayed upright for a few minutes, the crowd moved, and she slumped to the ground.

The coroner said that someone had injected deadly snake venom into her. That was what killed her.

  MICHELLE THOMPSON

Spider to the Rescue

Douglas was on the next plane home once he saw the Facebook photos that Orhan had posted. He had barely scratched the surface with Camilla, but she understood his need to return after she read the shocking story herself, and he needed to keep up his charade. It would be natural if he was still in Australia, to return home for this matter. Douglas reassured her that he would return as soon as he could. He was armed with his own credit card now, so he could book flights on his own under his fake name.

He left with one request for Camilla to complete. "Find me an abandoned building with a basement, buy the building outright if you must. The building must be soundproof. In the basement, we need to build a jail-like containment area. Make sure it has a working toilet and perhaps a hand basin for running water and a basic bed inside the bars of the jail. Have a TV installed on the outside, so it can be seen from the cage. Google some prison cell ideas if you have to and hire tradesmen from out of town. And I'm going to need a vehicle with a large trunk compartment, capable of an eleven-hour drive."

With that, he kissed her cheek and departed through customs.

When he touched down at Sydney Airport, Spider felt strangely homesick. He retrieved his vehicle from the long-term car park and headed home. He couldn't wait to see Orhan.

He wasn't sure about just who was in on the lie about his mother but now was not the time to expose that he knew anything.

Spider was on the case as soon as he walked in the door. He was persistent, asking for any information about the animal rustlings that Doug or Orhan could provide.

He drove to every scene and read all the police reports. The amateur slaughters had stopped since the barn burnt down, now cattle and sheep just disappeared. The consensus was that it had to be someone with inside knowledge, a current or past employee. Given the family history, they would have to be very brave or very stupid.

After a couple of days, Spider was exhausted. Jetlag set in, and he retreated to his panic room. He could be totally cut off in this room – the silence was golden. His bed felt like bliss. He went into a deep sleep.

He awoke just before midnight and went to the kitchen to eat whatever he could find in the fridge. To his surprise, his father was still up, having a drink at the bar. There was a distance between them now. Spider tried to hide it by stuffing a sandwich in his mouth. His father looked sad.

Doug still missed Mellissa and found it worse at night with no distractions to take his mind off her. Instead, he would drink until sleep overtook him. There were days Doug wished he had died as well so they could still be together, but the kids needed him and that kept him going.

Spider finished his sandwich and went back to his room to put on his black running suit. As he was walking out the door his father called out.

"You go find them, boy, make sure they pay for what they did to Orhan."

"I will, Dad."

It took him several nights of visiting the farmworkers that Orhan had on his payroll before Spider was certain he had the right person or persons.

Pat, who was Orhan's lead farm supervisor, and Bev his partner, had been hiding a secret – they were both heroin junkies. Disgusting, dirty, skinny junkies with bruised and infected arms from injecting into worn-out veins. No longer able to support their habit on Pat's farm wages, they had decided to supplement their income selling meat on the black market. Spider would look in the windows at night and see them passed out on the couch, TV still blaring. The house was a shambles; dirty needles everywhere, ashtrays filled to the brim with used butts. They were an advert for a youth prevention programme.

The kitchen was too dirty to see if there was any evidence of a recently butchered animal or bagged animal meat, and for some strange reason, they had a horse float but no horse. He would have to wait the long game to see if they were using this float to collect the animals and take them to another location to slaughter them.

Spider reflected on how betrayed Orhan would be; he did a lot for his employees, trusted them. Pat and Bev had the added perk of a free farmhouse that came with the position. The ironic thing was they were also given a beast for free twice a year as part of their employment package.

Spider was about to head out for one of his midnight-surveillance runs when he approached Doug at the bar.

"Hey, Dad, you wouldn't happen to know a guy, who knows a guy, who might know where I can get some heroin from would you?"

"I might know that guy," replied Doug. "How much do you need?"

"Just enough for two people to have a really good hit, pure would be preferable. A couple of point bags should do it."

Spider watched Pat and Bev with interest night after night. He never saw them have sex; they just drank a lot of coffee and argued a lot about petty shit. Both as sneaky as each other when it came to heroin, or rather, who got the most. They didn't discuss meat or the taking of meat. But Spider had made a perfect match of the horse float tyres to the tracks at the yards where the sheep had been stolen. He felt that was all the proof he needed for now.

Spider made a mental list of the items he would need before the heroin arrived. He would have to move quickly; his father wouldn't muck around with his request.

Body in the Park

A member of the public phoned it in on the 000-emergency service number.

"There's a dead cow in the middle of the park with a human head poking out its rear end."

Within minutes it had gone viral with the photos posted on Facebook and Twitter. Thousands of people shared it before the police had a chance to pull the shots and restrict public access. Channel 9 was at the scene filming and interviewing the witnesses. It was a bizarre and gruesome scene yet strangely amusing.

The scene was immediately cordoned off. Forensics were doing a detailed search of the area, but it was on the edge of the car park to a popular running track that circled the park, and many people and their dogs had walked extensively around the scene contaminating any evidence.

It certainly was a strange sight to see. At one end was the head of an unidentified breed of cattle beast, and at the other end, poking out its rectum, was a human head. Pale in complexion, eyes and mouth wide open, at first glance appearing alive. The body had been stuffed inside and the carcass sewn up along the belly. It was almost like the animal was giving birth. The end of the tail, grotesquely poked inside the victim's mouth, was covered in shit. Big cat-gut stitches ran along the belly between the animal's legs.

Autopsy results later indicated that the victim, Patrick Clarke, had died of a heroin overdose, and as a result, the contents of his own stomach were also blocking his airways. Just how he got sewn in the animal carcass was the mystery.

When police finally identified him, they tracked him to his residence where they found his partner, Beverly Archibald, in a weakened state evidently suffering withdrawal symptoms. She was less than cooperative, having imagined in her head that Pat's disappearance was due to a relationship split. In her mind, he had run off with another junkie and abandoned her. She was hysterical and unkempt, and smelled putrid. They didn't want her stinking out the police station, so they called mental health to admit her. They would question her some more once they cleaned her up a little.

She had no recollection or knowledge of Pat's whereabouts when questioned; she didn't believe them when they told her he was dead.

She told police that two or three evenings ago they had had a fight because Pat had found some heroin and wasn't going to share it. He greedily took the lion's share and left her a small taste, so they had traded blows until he gave her some more which he administered. That was the last she could remember of the night. She didn't know where he'd got it from, and she'd accused him of having an affair, her only explanation for the source of the heroin.

It was one hundred per cent pure and their bodies couldn't handle the strength. They had been surviving on cheap, homemade, cut heroin, possibly made up more from drain cleaner than heroin.

During her absence from the property while she was in hospital there was a mysterious fire which investigators later said had started in one of the beds, possibly from a smouldering cigarette. The house was burnt to the ground; nothing was saved, including the vehicle and the horse float. Beverly had no accommodation to return to.

Police could see that there was a direct link to the Henderson's farm as they had been recent victims of unresolved animal rustling and Pat just so happened to be an employee. But there was no direct tangible evidence to connect them.

The police strongly suspected the Henderson's personal involvement but, of course, they all had solid alibis. The detectives who were involved in the original investigation were secretly happy for two reasons. One, they didn't want to keep the file open and have a reason to talk to Doug and two, they thought a bit of bush justice went a long way. Although they would never admit that publicly.

Back to Colombia

Douglas was met at the airport by Camilla, who was as spritely as ever. He felt comfortable around her now, even missed her. She said Paulo had been asking about him, excited for his return. Douglas hated staying at Paulo's house, but it was necessary for the meantime. He still had a lot more to learn about running the business, so he thought of it as an educational process. He made a deal with Camilla for her to visit more often so he wasn't there alone all the time.

She had acquired the items he had requested so they made plans to look at them the following day. He'd take it easy for a couple of days before he flew to Paulo's.

Both he and Camilla wondered if Paulo's wife and child were the keys to finding out if Paulo had any hidden safes or bank accounts but the risk of involving them too early might be detrimental to their plans.

—

Days later, Paulo, in a heavy disguise, met Douglas at the airport and instead of taking him home they boarded another plane and flew to a region called Vaupes, where, like a well-informed tour guide, Paulo informed Douglas that this region was reportedly where sixty-two per cent of Colombia's cocaine came from.

They arrived at Fabio Alberto Airport just before sunset, with none of the usual fan-fair or armed security to greet them. Paulo asked Douglas to hire a vehicle in his own name in case anyone recognised him. Paulo waited outside until the arrangements had been made, chewing on a fat cigar, hugging his duty-free alcohol and his briefcase, and sticking out like dogs-balls.

As Douglas drove them out of the airport car park Paulo pulled his briefcase forward from the back seat. He unclipped it and pulled out two Glock pistols. He checked that they were loaded. He gave driving directions to Douglas, and when they got to a less traffic-condensed road, he asked Douglas to pull over.

"Have you ever killed anyone Grasshopper?" asked Paulo, making fun of an old American television series *Kung Fu.*

"Never," replied Douglas.

 MICHELLE THOMPSON

"Have you ever shot a pistol?"

"Never," said Douglas again, and this time he wasn't lying. There were plenty of guns around the house at home and the one Camilla had given him, which he lost, but he was never interested in them.

Paulo almost looked happy at the revelation. They were going to have to hire a hotel room for the night, so he could at least show Douglas where the safety was on the pistol.

First, they drove around the streets in what seemed like no order. Then Paulo, peering into the dark, burst to life with excitement as if he'd just won a prize. He put their location into a handheld GPS that had also come out of his briefcase from the back seat.

They drove a little way across town and found a shabby two-star backpackers' accommodation. Douglas went to the office and booked the unit and paid in cash. He was more worried that the owner would think it was for some gay sexual liaison, sneaking his boyfriend in in the dark, than he was about why they were there. They bought some simple sandwiches from a local café close by and went back to the room.

Paulo told Douglas the plan for coming to Vaupes. "One of my main adversaries, and our family's direct competition, has a very lucrative operation working out of this district. I plan to kill him and stage a direct takeover of his business. There is no bad blood between this man and the Hernandez family, so no one will suspect that I am here to kill him."

Paulo just planned to walk up to the house and shoot him in the face; he was talking all crazy. It was a side of Paulo that Douglas didn't much care for.

Paulo babbled on, "I promise you, Douglas, that this new acquisition will become yours, and together we will take over all the other cartels, one by one."

He paraded around the room swinging his arms about to show how big the takeover was going to be.

Douglas thought it sounded ambitious and full of holes with no real plan, but when he put this to Paulo, Paulo said this was the genius of his idea; no one would see it coming.

Douglas could just see a disaster waiting to happen. He'd have to think quickly and come up with a better way before they both got killed.

For now, Paulo would have to make sure 'Grasshopper' didn't shoot him by accident in the hotel room. It didn't help that Paulo commenced drinking a bottle of gin from his duty-free stash and found everything Douglas did wrong with the pistol hysterically funny. Douglas kept topping up his drink.

Douglas waited until he was sure Paulo was asleep; the gin had put him into an alcoholic coma, and his snoring was consistent. Peace at last. At least the burbling 'Swahili' had stopped!

Douglas put his black running suit on and headed back in the direction of the property they had staked out earlier. He felt like a run.

Douglas woke Paulo very early the next morning with the smell of freshly brewed coffee. The plan was to go out for breakfast at the café they had bought the sandwiches from the night before and, at Douglas's suggestion, continue to find a better way to dispatch their intended victim.

They sat silently, waiting for their cooked meal. Paulo, still in disguise, picked up the local morning paper. As he was reading the front page with its bold headline and dramatic photo, his mouth dropped open. He started stabbing at the front-page picture, trying to get Douglas's attention without talking out loud.

"You won't fuckin' believe it, the puta is dead! He died in a house fire last night. His whole family has gone!"

Paulo didn't want to wait for his breakfast. He raced back to the hotel unit and took off his disguise. He would now say he flew in to support the cartel and pay his respects. He saw it as a gift from God. All those donations to the Catholic Church were finally paying off.

—

Paulo offered a collaborative solution and put it to the other members of the Vaupes Cartel, and he could guarantee export without problems from officials. Some of his processes were quite advanced, and through trial and error he had learnt with his own operations, so they could adopt some of his practices. In the meantime, he would leave Douglas in Vaupes to oversee his investment in the business.

Douglas was in his element. If he had a problem with anyone who resisted the takeover, they would suddenly have an unforeseen accident. They would fall from the top of skyscrapers, leaving suicide notes. Brakes would fail on their cars, and they would roll into a lake or river and drown. They would be strangled from the back seat of their cars, then a hand grenade would somehow be taped to their faces, and they would be blown up. The sudden increase in violence put everyone on edge, but it was effective in getting everyone to conform.

Once things settled down, Paulo and Douglas had Vaupes under control.

My Last Case

Detective Richard Gomez, whose work associates called DIC, Dick for short, was due for retirement. Unhappily for him, he'd been sidelined to a desk job in the mailroom. He wasn't well-liked by any of his so-called workmates, and he had never bothered to socialise with them after hours. He was too old and serious. He had also been born in the USA, so he was never considered a local. He was an outsider, the American Gringo.

Gomez was consumed by personal failure. His last case was meant to be his swansong; he'd pictured a promotion and thought he would end his career with his head held high. But it had crashed and burned when the evidence had mysteriously been destroyed. He had let the case consume his every waking hour, resulting in a failed marriage with his wife and kids packing up and going back to the States, disowning him. Now his brain was racked with internal madness. He thought he was the laughingstock of the whole precinct.

His superiors told him to take it easy, retire peacefully; here's a nice little desk job, you can't get shot in the line of duty in the mailroom. He felt confined and suicidal. He wanted to be out on the street sniffing for clues, listening to the street talk, which was where the action was.

His failed assignment had been to bring down Paulo Hernandez, but he was a slippery fish who seldom made mistakes that could be directly linked to him.

It was Richard who discovered and exposed cocaine being smuggled in the catering trolleys of the diplomatic planes; he had an informant who worked at the airport who gave him the tip. Richard had spent hours and hours on unsanctioned stakeouts watching the catering company, watching Paulo's thugs, and watching the foreign diplomat.

When he finally made his move, the FBI got involved, the diplomat got a smack on the hand, the cocaine went missing, and Paulo went free and shifted to Buenaventura. And Richard ended up in the mailroom. Colombia was so corrupt, he was surprised he didn't get murdered at his desk. But the mailroom had its bonuses: internet and newspapers, and no timecards to monitor the hours you were in the office. No one cared about him anymore.

    MICHELLE THOMPSON

Suddenly, Richard had discovered that there was a new man on the scene, some big half-wit from Australia, the bastard son of one of the Hernandez Clan. Richard had one chance to redeem himself; he wasn't going to let this one slip through his hands. And he wasn't going to tell anyone that he was investigating until he had the cat in the bag.

—

Richard was surprised to see old Camilla had dusted off her glad rags. She had been dormant for a while, but here she was, fluffing over this young man.

Richard managed to infiltrate the big introduction party at the Marriott. He'd bribed his way into a job as a drinks waiter where he could mingle in the crowd.

The big half-wit was called Douglas; he was the son of Sofia, who had disappeared years ago. Richard had searched the birth records but couldn't match Douglas's details with the name on the passport he flew into the country on, so it would take a while to find his real name.

As he shuffled in the crowd, he came within a couple of inches of Paulo, who was jumping around like a jack-in-the-box, showing off. Richard made sure not to make direct eye contact. Paulo was the sort of guy who would just pull out a gun and shoot you. But he did get close enough to offer Douglas a drink, but Douglas asked him for a glass of soda water – he didn't drink alcohol.

Richard took annual leave and followed Paulo and Douglas to Vaupes. He slept in his car in the backpackers' car park, so he was able to follow Douglas to the house fire. It was dark, but he got some grainy photos of the running man and the explosions caused by the fire. He also got photos of Douglas standing and watching as the fire brigade tried in vain to put the fire out.

When Richard went back to work, he watched the internet with interest, reading the list of sudden, unexplained deaths and suicides that were reported in Vaupes – all cartel members. He collated them in chronological order. He was building a case.

Richard noted that Douglas spent time between all three locations: Vaupes, Buenaventura, and Bogotá. Nothing out of the usual, just a visit to a funeral home and Douglas had a girlfriend in the city, some cheap two-bit whore.

Then Camilla and Douglas purchased the warehouse in a run-down part of town. He couldn't put that piece together yet. It was abandoned and pretty run-down. It had been vacant for years; he would plan to stake it out next time Douglas was in town.

Richard got an alert that Douglas had used his credit card to book a flight. He would follow him to the airport and see which flight he checked in for. Might be a clue to his real identity.

Export Solutions

It started as a normal day, well, normal for the daily running of a drug cartel. That's when Douglas came up with an idea that solved a lot of problems and cemented his value to the family business.

"It's all very well producing vast amounts of cocaine, but it's no use to the planet if we can't get it out of Colombia!" Paulo was ranting again, pacing the floor of the guest house where Douglas was residing. He didn't wait for Douglas to answer but carried on.

"We did have a fool-proof system once, flying it directly into the US in the catering carts on diplomatic flights. But those bloody arseholes in the FBI fucked it up by arresting one of our favourite politicians. I still think we had a rat!"

"Grasshopper! If you're going to have a future in this business, you better start thinking outside the square."

Douglas said that he had been thinking about an idea. "It's a bit left-field. Why don't we fly it in inside dead bodies? Not in the coffins, that's been done before. I mean, stitch it inside the corpse. I'm talking full scale. It will mean we will have to buy or start a funeral business. Then the objective will be, go big or go home – all or nothing. Even start a franchise chain between here and the USA, incorporating the whole of South America. Offer cut-price body transfers for tourists, repatriation of bodies for temporary residents. The motto could be *'Get Your Loved Ones Home'*.

"All the bodies must go via the US. When the bodies get to our US connection, they cut them open and remove the bags. Hell, surely you could get at least a kilo in a brain cavity. It's like taxidermy in a way; the organ cavity is replaced with our bags of cocaine."

The idea was so bizarre that Paulo loved it. Even if it didn't work, it would go down in history. Paulo loved that sort of shit. He started googling embalming processes on his phone.

"Fuck me, Grasshopper, I think that will work."

Once they got started, it grew into a can of worms. They would have to hire a full-time CEO to run the company. Someone with a knowledge of the industry and an iron-clad public image, obviously, someone who liked money or had a secret they didn't want anyone to know. The website would have to be very professional, spending good money on advertising and lots of it, both here and overseas. The call centre could be outsourced from India for a reasonable price, which also removed a direct link to the company managers. They would need upmarket premises. Clients would have to think they were spending good money on a travel insurance package, and clients' families would have to visually think they were getting value for money when the finished product was returned home.

The staff were the key. They needed to be the right front people, and they had to be experts in their field because when the bodies reached the US, they had to be unstuffed and refilled again to maintain the high standards that the company claimed. When the crying relatives viewed the body, it had to be passable.

It turned out that sometimes they got lucky. A busload of tourists would fly off a cliff in Peru, and by the time the bodies were dragged up the cliff by donkeys, they were all rotten and stinky, so those relatives seldom, if ever, wanted to look in the aluminium bag.

The normal cost of sending a body home could be anywhere between fifteen hundred and fifteen thousand American dollars, depending on the weight and the distance and could take up to three months.

Paulo's company could guarantee a flat rate of eight hundred American dollars, and he did a deal with a travel insurance company and advertised in all their brochures and websites and offered a high commission for selling. A reputable airline took up the offer. The bodies were put in the unheated cargo hold of the plane, and they guaranteed that each body would get to Paulo' American base within seven days.

'Funerals with Love' took off in a bigger way than they could ever have imagined. Business was so good, they had to buy a crematorium in the US. That was for those family members who didn't want the maggot-ridden body of the cheap-arse backpacker who had been on their intrepid overseas journey and who'd thought it was a good idea to ride on the top of the train for free, where they got murdered for their wallets or they just fell off. You could get them back in a box as ashes at no extra cost. Sometimes, all it took was to provide the family with a photo of the dearly departed once they had been expertly dressed for dispatch.

                MICHELLE THOMPSON

Paulo and Douglas often joked that if the cocaine business ever became unpopular, they would go into the dead body business and go global.

Crazy.

Camilla Delivers the Car

Paulo couldn't believe the old tart drove the car all the way from Bogotá. He didn't know if she was mad or if he admired her spirit. It was a gift for Douglas, a beautiful two-door Mercedes, black with dark-tinted windows. It certainly looked the part.

Paulo was a little put out. If he had known Douglas wanted a car, he would have wanted to buy one for him. But it was apparent from the surprised look on Douglas's face that he didn't know she had bought him a car, so Paulo let it go. He insisted that they immediately go for a drive. In fact, he wanted a car now. He suggested that they should drive to the local dealer and order him a matching one.

Camilla insisted on sleeping in the guest house with Douglas. Maria tried to persuade her to stay in the main house but gave up. Camilla was a determined woman, and when she made up her mind about something, you wouldn't win. Anyway, Douglas was looking forward to hearing some midnight stories about his mother.

Later, after the dinner, Camila, Paulo, and Douglas retired to the office, where they talked about the growing success of the funeral business. The profits were being laundered through the vacant apartments that they claimed were tenanted along the foreshore of the harbour. But still, the books just weren't adding up. Camilla had gone over and over the accounts, and there was money going missing somewhere. Paulo had noticed it as well, but he had no answer for the shortfall. Yes, they were making millions, but that just made it easier to lose track of money. They felt comfortable in the knowledge that their vast number of employees were not taking the money; it wasn't really possible. Short of hiring an outsider or a private investigator, they couldn't put their finger on the haemorrhage.

Camilla and Douglas retired to the guest house after the meeting, where she had a surprise for Douglas. It was a scrapbook that his mother had made, which she had started at a very early age.

Douglas was delighted, and the timeline narrative that Camilla gave just gave it more relevance. As they neared the end of the book, there was an old newspaper clipping of the official ribbon-cutting for the fountain donated by the new owner of the emerald mines. The park and the fountain had been dedicated to Gerald, the murdered husband of Sofia. The picture, unfortunately, was yellowed with time and was of very poor quality. Douglas just couldn't help but think that the businessman cutting the ribbon with Sofia looked strangely familiar. He couldn't put his finger on it, but it would come to him.

The next day, they were up early. They called it general housekeeping; checking in on the caretakers of the high-rise apartments, making sure the authorities weren't asking too many questions. They had wired all the lighting to one main switch so that the building appeared to be occupied at night. The caretaker confirmed that no one had been asking questions: it was business as usual.

They visited the factory, and, for Camilla's sake, the naked workers were on a break. They finished the day by taking the local government officials out for a very long lunch and making sure they all received a generous gift in the process.

Later that evening, Paulo made a toast at dinner to his newly found relative and credited him with the exceptional luck they were having. It was a great night of celebration.

Camilla flew home the following day.

Fast-Forward the Plan

Douglas was in a deep sleep for a change. It had been a long week of socialising, and he was dreaming that he was dancing with his mother, and someone was calling his name. He was comfortable in the dream, and he was happy, then reality stirred him, and the small, frail figure of Dennis was patting him awake on his arm.

"Come quickly, please, Uncle Douglas. There's been an accident and Papa is dead." The boy looked like a ghost in the darkness, but he was quick to warn Douglas not to turn on the light, so the security and the CCTV didn't see them.

Douglas was trying to think quickly, but his head was swimming. He pulled on his sweatpants and a hoodie and let Dennis lead him through the gardens to the back entrance.

It was a bizarre and blood-splattered scene. Paulo was sprawled out on the marble floor of the kitchen, his unfinished dinner on a plate on the table. Blood had seeped from a serious wound to his head and what looked like another wound to his neck. A heavy brass plant stand was lying on its side next to him.

Maria was slumped on the floor a little distance from him, supporting herself with her back to the cooking island. She was out of breath, and she had been crying. She also had a black eye.

"What happened here?" he asked Maria.

"We were arguing," Maria replied raggedly, "and Paulo slapped me across the face. Dennis tried to protect me, but Paulo, he was so drunk. He picked Dennis up and threw him onto the ground. I tried to protect us both, tried to fight him off, but Paulo was too strong. He overpowered me and hit me in the eye. I was so frightened for Dennis. I grabbed the nearest thing to protect us both, that plant stand, and swung it at Paulo. I hit him on his head. When he fell, I couldn't stop; I kept hitting and hitting him." She was sobbing now, pleading with Douglas for help. She said it was battered woman's syndrome, which made her go ballistic.

Douglas's fire and emergency training kicked in. He put Paulo in the recovery position and felt for a pulse in his neck; there was a faint one. He looked Maria in the eye. "He's dead, Maria, you killed him."

Douglas started barking orders. "Dennis, get some blankets so I can wrap the body up, and an old carpet. I will dispose of the body. Maria, start cleaning up the blood and rearranging the furniture. I'll back the car around into the garage. Everyone, move! We haven't got much time!"

Douglas made a phone call as he drove back to Bogotá to let his nana know he was coming earlier than expected for the visit they had planned. He stopped just off the highway and made sure that Paulo's mouth, hands and feet were bound with tape. If he did regain consciousness any time soon, he didn't need him screaming and shouting from the trunk. Not that Douglas planned to stop for the eleven-hour trip; he'd get the petrol topped up now, just in case.

He had left Maria in a state, but he had to leave quickly in case Paulo woke up. Letting her think he was dead was the better option for what he needed to do. He promised to be back in a couple of days, and then they could discuss a plan going forward. In the meantime, if anyone asked, which wasn't likely, she was to say Paulo had gone on a business trip and she didn't know when he would return.

Douglas thought it was wise also that she remained behind closed doors, no use letting people see that black eye. She seemed to respond to orders well. Dennis had wiped the CCTV footage and was already back playing video games on the television. Dennis looked very relaxed, possibly in shock.

They didn't ask where Douglas was taking the body.

The trip back to Bogotá went without incident, and Paulo didn't wake up. As Camilla and Douglas stood looking at him lying on the single bed they had bolted to the floor in the cage, with a blanket over him, they discussed what would happen if he did die. The best idea was to lock the building up and make it look like an accidental fire had broken out.

In the meantime, if he did regain consciousness while they were away, they left him with ample drinking water, Tramadol, and the television remote. It was their first kidnap/hostage situation, and they joked that they were still learning what to do.

They turned the light off, leaving only the glow of the exit light to illuminate the room. After all, if he had a massive headache, he wouldn't want to be under bright lights.

Two days later, Douglas flew back to Buenaventura and had Maria pick him up from the airport. She was calm and collected; makeup had expertly disguised the bruised eye. They both decided whatever their next move was, Dennis needed to be included in the conversation.

Douglas and Maria sat around the table with Dennis, to work out a plan going forward. They would wait a week and report Paulo missing, then make a media presentation for the newspaper and the television. Douglas and Camilla would continue to manage the business and see that Maria's needs were met. Maria was concerned that Douglas would want some sexual favours from her in return as a form of blackmail, but he assured her that was furthest from his mind. But, in time, what he did want were photos that might suggest that the grieving widow had found love again with her new protector, the cousin of Paulo; she agreed. Douglas offered to formalise the arrangement with marriage after a respectable period of time, but only if she wished. Also, he could adopt Dennis. Maria agreed. She was agreeing to everything. She was making this surprisingly easy. Douglas would commute between this house and Bogotá. In the meantime, it was business as usual.

Maria and Dennis never enquired after the location of the body. There was obviously no love lost. They proceeded to go about their everyday lives as if nothing had changed. The only difference that Douglas did detect was the laughter at the dining table. They would all laugh and talk and tell stories. Dennis had really come out of his shell. Douglas deduced that they must have been living a nightmare for so long.

Paulo Wakes Up

His mouth was dry; he moved his jaw, trying to make saliva. Paulo attempted to sit up, but the pain was too much; his head ached, and it hurt to move his eyes.

He looked around without moving his head. He could only see bars above him. There was no noise at all; he was surrounded by complete silence. He was confused. He drifted back to sleep with a massive headache.

Paulo woke again. He didn't know if one day or two had passed since he was last awake. He turned his head to the side and saw a steel table and a chair. He hung his arm over the side of his bed and felt the floor and a bottle. He had no strength to lift it, but he knew he needed to try hard. There was something that felt like paper next to it; it was a sheet of pills. How thoughtful, he thought. He managed to lift the water, took four of the pills and washed them down with it.

He couldn't remember what had happened to him. Had he had a car accident? Where was his family? It looked like a strange hospital. Perhaps they don't know who he is; that would explain it. It almost looked like a prison cell; he couldn't remember committing a crime. He went back to sleep.

He thought he heard a noise. He opened his eyes; a door closed. He tried to shout, but his head hurt. He felt around for the pills again. Someone had placed water on the steel table. He could see more things on the table, but from the bed, he couldn't make out what they were.

He needed a piss. If he couldn't get up, he would have to piss in the empty water bottle. He lifted himself up onto his side; his head was swimming with pain. Better wait for the pills to take effect before he planned a move. He steadied himself and looked around.

It was a bare concrete room, no windows, with a steel cage in one corner, which he was in. The wall opposite, outside the cage, had a huge television attached to it. There was a primitive, stainless toilet in the corner and a basin, the table, and the chair. On the table were a black item, what he presumed was the remote for the TV, more water, and some packaged crisps.

He couldn't make sense of it. He lay back on the pillow, felt around in his hair and discovered his head was wrapped in a bandage. He felt his ribs as they were tender, and one of his knees was also smashed and swollen. Had he been in a fight? He realised then that he was naked.

He lost track of time. There was only artificial light in the room from the exit sign. No noises came from outside, no traffic or horns. No building noises. Today, he would make it to the table if it killed him. He'd turn that TV on; that would be a start.

He dragged himself across the floor. His right leg wasn't working properly, his ribs ached, and he felt like his head was going to explode. He reached up from the floor and felt around on the table. More pills, more water and a plastic bottle of juice, the crisps, some chocolate, which he noted was his favourite. The TV control, yes! A small victory.

He turned the television on, grabbed the juice and crawled back to his bed. He had no strength to make it to the toilet, so he pissed in an empty water bottle. Tomorrow, he would set a goal for the toilet.

As he scrolled through the channels looking for a time and a date, the news popped onto the screen. There was his face: they were looking for him. His wife and Douglas, and Dennis, all looking sombre and concerned. Dennis gave an emotional come home Daddy speech; the reporter was reduced to tears. Douglas was offering a substantial reward for any information.

Paulo broke down and wept into his pillow. He had been kidnapped; that's why he was in this awful place. He cried himself to sleep.

Paulo Meets His Captors

The door to the room creaked open, and Douglas walked in; he had a box in his arms. Paulo was up and managing to get around the cell slowly. "Thank God, you've found me, Grasshopper. Oh my God. I knew you would come and rescue me; I prayed for it every day. I am in pain, my head hurts. Have you murdered the bastards that have kidnapped me?"

Paulo's elation quickly turned to confused despair. Douglas made no move towards the lock. Instead, he went to the side of the cage where the table was and started placing items on the table through the bars, verbally itemising them as he went in Spanish. "Chicken sandwich, salad with a plastic fork, more juice, fresh bread, toilet paper, a bag of lollies, two bottles of wine that I decanted into plastic bottles, a bar of soap. Oh, and I have hung a bag for rubbish on this side of the bars – we will replace it every couple of days."

Paulo's demeanour suddenly turned nasty; his eyes narrowed. "You speak Spanish, Grasshopper? What more surprises do you have up your sleeve? What is the purpose of keeping me prisoner here?"

"Yes, I speak fluent Spanish, actually," replied Douglas.

"Surprises? A few. One, Camilla and I planned this a while ago to find out who was taking the money from the company. Two, I'm fucking your wife. Three, you better get used to it, as I don't really have a plan to let you go anytime soon.

"Maria will collect your life insurance money soon when they find some of your clothing washed up in the harbour. Then we will get married, and I will adopt Dennis." It was a cruel sermon.

"And don't get any funny ideas and try to escape, or I'll hire someone to fuck Dennis up the arse. Some despicable, low-life degenerate who preys on young boys. I might even sell him to the sex trade.

"I'll come back in a couple of days when you're more civilised."

With that, Douglas left.

Paulo slumped to the ground after Douglas had gone. He was weak with injury and pain, devastated by the cruel betrayal of Douglas. It was like a bad nightmare that he couldn't wake up from; nothing made sense.

Two days went by, and Paulo heard the creak of the door again, this time it was that sour-faced old prune, Camilla. She didn't talk, just went to the table and placed some food items on it and left, face on her like a slapped arse.

Days later, Paulo watched the television as the Commissioner of Police held up the blood-stained items of clothing that his detectives had fished from the harbour. It was a foregone conclusion in the eyes of the authorities that Paulo had met foul play. And there, at the press conference, was Maria with Douglas comforting her, and young Dennis holding Douglas's hand; it sickened Paulo to watch it.

How quickly she had gone to another man's bed and opened her legs. It had been the basis of all their domestics – his jealousy. Now his beliefs were confirmed, she was a slut with her big hairy beaver hanging out. He rationalised his beliefs with more wine. It was all right for him to go off drinking with his mates, socialising; that's how business got done; that's how he made the money that she freely spent. They always argued that he never took her anywhere. Truth was that he hated taking her anywhere; men were always dribbling over her. And she was so polite and friendly, it made his blood boil. Now he thought it was gross that that big overgrown ape was hanging out of her vagina.

Paulo would have to play it smart if he was ever to get out of this cage.

Two days later, Douglas returned. He put some oil on the door, changed the rubbish bag, and asked if Paulo had any requests. This time he had brought a box of food, some gin and tonic, a jigsaw, and a pack of cards. Paulo didn't speak. Douglas left again.

This was the routine. Every two days, Douglas or Camilla would come and refresh things.

Once Paulo asked for a prime steak meal and some clothes, and a simple throw-away razor to shave his head. Douglas returned a couple of hours later with a hot steak but no steak knife, just plastic cutlery, and a bright pink towelling jumpsuit, which was an old one Camilla didn't wear any more.

Paulo didn't complain. At least it was better than being naked with his junk hanging out. It looked ridiculous on, and Paulo thought he looked like a gay porn star, with his pink suit and his gold chains and rings. Thank God, they always left him with lots of alcohol; it helped him sleep.

A month later, there was a public announcement that Douglas and Maria were to be married. There was big publicity on TV.

Strangely enough, on Douglas's next visit, Paulo didn't comment. He was no longer agitated. He had become very calm.

Who The Fuck Are You?

Paulo woke. For a moment, he wished that when he opened his eyes, it would all be a dream and he'd wake up in his big, comfortable bed. He didn't know if it was the cheap wine or the head injury, but he thought he heard someone, yet it wasn't one of the rostered days.

His focus was blurry; he could just make out the frame of the big ape. This time, he was checking the lock and tugging on the bars. It wasn't Douglas, but this man was strangely familiar.

"Who the fuck are you?" asked Paulo in Spanish, then again in English. He was strangely afraid. Perhaps this was it; they had sent someone to kill him.

"I'm your ticket out of here, mate." The big man extended his arm and held his big hand out to shake.

Paulo was hesitant; this guy looked strong. He could easily pull him towards him and stab or shoot him. Paulo would be no match for his strength.

"I'm Doug Henderson. The man who has locked you up is my son. He doesn't know I'm here or that I'm even in the country. I need you to trust me and listen carefully to everything I tell you, or I'm afraid you'll never get out of here alive."

Paulo took a gamble and extended his hand. They shook hard.

It was several hours before Doug left. He squeezed Paulo's hand hard through the bars. He left as silently as he arrived.

Paulo didn't know whether it was relief or loneliness, but he wept like a baby after Doug left. One thing he knew for sure, he'd have to trust this guy. He sort of liked him. He'd promised he would follow Doug's instructions to the letter. It had been a lot to take in, and remember, but at least he had nothing else to do. It was almost exciting now.

Finally, he would get his revenge on Douglas and Maria. "Cunts," he muttered under his breath.

—

Doug and Stacey were back to Colombia after seeing an internet news article said that Paulo was missing. Doug put two and two together and worked out why they had the jail cell in the basement of the warehouse. He wasn't sure where Spider and Camilla were going with their plan, but he thought he might like to fuck it up for them.

Doug and Stacey took turns watching the house and the warehouse. The two-day routine was to take food and supplies, and they seemed to be consistent.

Doug would have to think of an exceptionally good reason for Spider to jump on a plane and head back to Aussie.

Wedding of the Year

It was deemed to be the wedding of the year. Douglas made sure of that. Inviting as many media as he could to guarantee Paulo didn't miss any of it on TV. Paulo was a stubborn bastard. He hadn't divulged anything about the missing money. He told Douglas that he had been having headaches, and memories of the night he got his head injury were coming back to him.

Douglas and Maria lived in Bogotá now. It had been Maria's idea to shift to Bogotá – her parents lived in the city, and Camilla was getting older, and she felt she could support her more. It saved Douglas from travelling so much.

Douglas said she could keep the proceeds from the sale of the Buenaventura house. The Bogotá house was huge, so they did not need to buy another.

Douglas had kept to his word and never asked her for any sexual favours. Although they did have a rather hilarious photoshoot once for a celebrity magazine with Maria in a compromising position.

Dennis was a different child now, free to express himself; they did things together as a family. They looked like the model family.

Camilla loved having the house full, and there was always laughter, and she found no reason to object to the new arrangement.

The good news was, the money haemorrhage had stopped, so it proved their case that Paulo was the common denominator.

Both Douglas and Camilla agreed that after the wedding, they would have no choice but to kill Paulo. Douglas wanted to keep him alive a little bit longer; he liked the aspect of the mental torture he was inflicting.

The morning of the wedding, Douglas called in on Paulo to show him his suit. Maria had picked it out. Grey with a pink tie. He looked sharp. He told Paulo all the details: who was coming, what the food was going to be like. He had opted for a family honeymoon at Florida's Disneyland for Dennis's sake.

Before he departed, he told Paulo, "Since you've been gone, the business isn't losing money anymore, which can only mean one thing. So, unless you want to come clean, you're not going to get out. In fact, you could die here in this cage."

     MICHELLE THOMPSON

Paulo did surprise Douglas with an announcement as he looked at Douglas with a strange smirk.

"You are a fool to marry Maria. I have worked it out. The night of my injury, I was eating my dinner, that's all I remember. I think she tried to kill me, and you have fallen into her trap. You do know that her father was a chartered accountant when I met her? She comes from an accounting background. That is where the money is going. You have caged up the wrong person, Grasshopper. Good luck with your fake marriage."

Douglas tried not to falter on hearing Paulo's statement, tried not to let any expression show on his face. It was something to consider. He would have to tell Camilla as soon as he got a chance, maybe in the car on the way to the wedding when they were alone. Paulo seemed different today, confident.

The day turned into night. It was hectic, and at times, Douglas was overcome with requests and protocol. He felt awkward when the marriage celebrant said, "You can kiss the bride," but Maria gave him a polite peck on the lips, and it was all over.

It was midnight before they arrived home. Dennis was already asleep in the back of the car. Douglas carried him upstairs, and Maria put him to bed.

Douglas retired to his wing of the house and turned his phone on to check his Facebook and messages. Now he wished he hadn't. There was terrible news from home; Orhan was in intensive care and possibly not going to make it. He had been in a motorcar accident, and they wanted Douglas to come home immediately. He knew it was late, but he woke Camilla up and she organised a plane for first thing in the morning. He couldn't sleep; the thought of something happening to little Orhan really worried him.

What a fuckin' mess! He'd had to get Camilla to tend to Paulo until he could return, and he wouldn't be able to tell her when he could return until he got back to Australia and assessed the situation. He would have to wake Maria up now and tell her, as he'd be gone before she woke up in the morning, and she and Dennis would have to go to Disneyland without him.

It wasn't until he was sitting on the plane somewhere across the Atlantic that he remembered he had forgotten to tell Camilla what Paulo had told him about Maria's father being an accountant. It didn't really matter; the money wasn't going missing now that Paulo was locked up. Just Paulo playing with his head, jealous over the wedding.

Innocent Until Proven Guilty

Spider collected his car from the long-term car park at the airport. He went to throw his bag in the boot, but the lock was stuck. He was tired and stressed, and he hadn't been able to contact anyone, so no one from the family had been able to give him an update on Orhan's status. He didn't even know which hospital to go to. He threw his bag in the back seat; he'd head for home first.

He left the car park. It felt funny to be home again, but he sure did like it; so much simpler. He was almost home when he saw a roadside breath testing unit up ahead. He hadn't drunk on the plane, and he didn't take drugs, so he wasn't too concerned. It was a big unit, lots of police cars.

He was waved over to the side of the road. There was a high armed police presence, which seemed strange; perhaps they were looking for an escaped prisoner. They asked him for the keys and asked him to step out of the car, which he complied with. Then they asked him to open the trunk.

"The lock's stuck, mate. I couldn't even put my bag in there. See, my bag's on the back seat."

Suddenly, they were putting him in handcuffs and reading him his rights.

The car was surrounded by men in full black protective clothing. They were the Armed Offenders Squad; all their faces were covered with balaclavas.

Spider looked baffled as they used a crowbar to lever open the boot, snapping multitudes of photos as they proceeded.

In the boot was a badly beaten woman, all bound up and gagged. She was barely conscious. Suddenly, Spider became aware that an ambulance and paramedics were present as they cut her ropes and tape and started applying oxygen and administering CPR.

As they manhandled him to the police wagon and read him his rights again, he was frantically trying to protest his innocence. No one cared. He'd need his dad to get him out of this one, he didn't know what the fuck was going on.

Hours later, after they had questioned him repeatedly, he was permitted to make his one phone call. He couldn't get hold of his father, so he rang Edith.

It was all going to get extremely complicated. He'd flown back into the country under his false name, and he could hardly tell the police that he was the head of a Colombian drug cartel. Edith had sent some shit lawyer, not their usual guy. His head was spinning; he didn't have a sound enough alibi.

Then, to complicate the matter further, the victim turned out to be the girlfriend of Pat the junkie who he had sewn into the beast's body. He was going to be held on remand without bail until his first court hearing in one month.

It was two weeks before he got his first visitor – his father wasn't permitted to visit as he was an ex-convict. Edith had sent phone cards, underpants and socks. She was his first visitor. She agreed that it was a set-up, but she didn't know why or who was responsible.

Spider proceeded to tell her the full story, which, she said, she was trying hard to believe, let alone absorb. She told Spider that she was locked in a conflict-of-interest battle, as she would have to tell their father, and he would be so pissed off. Spider begged her to keep it a secret. She promised Spider she would not tell Doug.

She was about to leave when Spider asked how Orhan was. "He's fine, why? Just the same old skinny Orhan playing on the farm."

Spider used the phone cards to bribe another inmate for the use of his phone – one he had smuggled into the prison – to Facebook Camilla, then Maria, then Dennis; no one was online.

The newspaper headlines read *Girl in the Boot*. She was on life support, but it was likely she would recover.

The authorities wanted to throw the book at him. They could try and pin the body in the beast on him, kidnapping and grievous bodily harm. He was easily looking at eleven years behind bars.

Edith kept sending him phone cards, which he relentlessly chewed through, trying to get hold of Camilla. Paulo would be dead now for sure if something had happened to Camilla. He had planned to shoot Paulo eventually, make it quick, but starving him to death wasn't what he intended.

He finally got hold of his father on the house phone. The whole family couldn't wait to talk to him: grandparents, Aunty Stacey, Orhan. His dad kept a stiff upper lip. They agreed it had been a set-up also, but a good one, and it would be hard to dispute his innocence.

Maria Makes Her Move

When Douglas woke her just after midnight and apologised for his sudden departure, Maria promised to still take Dennis to Disneyland. She lay back in her bed and smiled. It was all going to plan.

She would have to find a way to kill Camilla while Douglas was gone, get that meddling old bat out of the way. She wasn't sure what plan she had for Douglas yet – big ape, with half a brain. But she would need to convince him that she could handle the finances from now on.

For years, it had been a good set-up, her father helping her expertly skim off money. Then Camilla started looking too closely. She had secretly listened in on their conversations with Paulo about the missing money, and she knew she had to act quickly and make it look like it was Paulo after all.

She had drugged Paulo's wine with her sleeping pills. It hadn't worked, but it made his senses slower. He took so much cocaine normally that it took a lot to slow him down.

She made sure the first swing with the plant stand was a good one, and she kept swinging until she was sure he was dead. Then Dennis helped with the aid of a tight fist and gave her a whack on the face for the black eye. It wasn't completely successful, but a bit of makeup made it look worse. Then he ran and woke up Douglas as planned. Dennis hated Paulo; he was sick of pretending he was his real father.

Maria had had a secret lover for years, a childhood sweetheart – Ricardo, her soul mate. She was setting them up financially so she and Dennis could escape with Ricardo to Miami or somewhere like that, but she hadn't counted on Douglas arriving on the scene. She had heard about Sofia but didn't know she had a son in Australia.

When Maria was sixteen years old, she had fallen pregnant and was going to disgrace her strict Catholic family, so her father, a prominent businessman, had made arrangements with Paulo's late father and married her off to a more respectable husband, one with money. Dennis was born late, so the timing worked out within reason.

Paulo had always known that Dennis wasn't his, but he had brought him

      MICHELLE THOMPSON

up as if he were, and the child never wanted for anything. He suspected that Maria was not faithful, but he could never prove it.

The nights when he would demand his pleasures made her almost vomit. She would become dry and frigid, and sex was always painful. Paulo would refer to her vagina as the Sahara Desert. She was convenient to have on his arm at official functions, but that was about it.

Maria planned to arrange for Camilla to be accidentally, and conveniently, caught in the crossfire of a neighbourhood drive-by shooting; Ricardo would see to that. Camilla left the house alone every two days like clockwork, and she always went on her own. Maria would have her followed and shot in the street like so many others here in Bogotá. Given her reputation, the authorities would think it was just another gangland war.

Freedom

"I promised you I would be back, mate." Doug's big grin lit up the room. "Now let's get ready to get you out of here." He assured Paulo that he had thoughtfully brought some new clothes for him to change into later.

Doug looked closely at the cage door again. There might not be too much to it that a good crescent wrench and a cordless drill couldn't solve to remove the whole door from the cage.

Paulo hugged Doug through the cage with all his strength. He tried to kiss Doug on both cheeks. Doug held him back. "I'm not a fuckin' homo."

They both laughed. It was just good to have some other human contact.

Doug updated Paulo on the current situation regarding Spider. Paulo seemed to accept that this was step one, and he had to trust Doug and leave it in Doug's hands for now. After all, Doug had kept his word up until this point. Paulo had massive trust issues; he had trusted his son and look where that got him.

The next step was to wait for Camilla to come and restock the food and water before they could make their next move. They needed a body to put in the pink jumpsuit, and they would have to shave her head. Paulo wasn't quite sure why they had to put a body in the jumpsuit, but this Doug guy seemed to know all the tricks. Perhaps he might learn something from him. He sure was enjoying seeing it unfold.

The story that would unfold was that Maria would be murdered after Paulo's kidnappers had made a botched attempt for his ransom money. Letters addressed to Maria would be found in the house with the ransom demands. Paulo would be found bound and gagged after being released by his kidnappers. Camilla would be missing, presumed to now be in the hands of the kidnappers. Paulo would eventually make a dramatic reappearance on public television. He looked the part: pale and weak from starvation and lack of exercise, head shaved. He would vow publicly to do everything in his power to find his dear old Aunty Camilla.

—

 MICHELLE THOMPSON

Camilla made her way to restock supplies for Paulo. It wasn't ideal that Douglas had gone back to Australia at such short notice. If she had her way, she would have just shot Paulo and left him to rot in the cage. That was what she was going to suggest when Douglas returned in a couple of days.

As she entered the basement of the building where the cage was, she could hear the noise as she made her way down the stairs. She was pissed off. Fuckin' Paulo had that bloody television blaring at maximum volume. If he carried on like that, she would turn the TV off at the wall, and he would have no TV. It was so loud it was hurting her ears. For fuck's sake!

She could see Paulo lying face down on the floor of the cage, and there was a pool of blood near his head. It dawned on her to just leave now and let him die, save her or Douglas having to shoot him. The TV was starting to annoy her.

She crouched down outside the bars as close to the body as she could; he didn't appear to be breathing. She looked around for a stick or something to poke him. She plucked a water bottle from her bag of supplies and threw it forcefully at his head; he didn't flinch.

Paulo had one chance, and he didn't want to blow it. He played dead, even absorbing the blow from the bottle bouncing off his head. Then, with all his strength, he leapt up towards Camilla and shot her in the chest at close range with the gun Doug had given him.

The force of the bullet threw her body back across the room. There was a look of surprise and a crooked smile on her face all at the same time before she hit the ground. There was no twitching. Paulo was sure she was dead; there was a big hole in her chest.

He turned the sound on the TV down. He'd wait for Doug to return now.

Doug waited in the alley next to the building. He never heard the shot, but he was calculating the time it should take. He checked no one was watching and entered the building again. As he crept down the stairs, he could no longer hear the television, so he knew Paulo had it under control.

He had thought of every scenario and had given Paulo a bulletproof vest to wear under that hideous pink jumpsuit, just in case the wise old cow got a round off herself. He had taken precautions to wear one also, after all, Paulo might try and shoot him. He was crazy and had been driven crazier after being locked up for nearly a year. He had thought of only putting one bullet in the gun, but decided not to, so he could build some trust with this crazy Colombian bastard.

He'd come prepared if that had happened; he hadn't come alone. He'd brought a wingman, someone he trusted to finish the job if he couldn't, and if he didn't exit the building before Paulo, their instructions were to shoot Paulo on sight.

Doug went to work on the cage door. A portable drill and a crescent wrench made short work of the hinge.

Together, Doug and Paulo dragged Camilla into the cage and dressed her in the pink jumpsuit. They lay her on her side in the foetal position on the floor, then shaved her head. As much as Paulo didn't want to part with his gold chains, they placed them and his rings on her body; at first glance, it had to look like Paulo. Doug promised to buy him some new ones. Then they reattached the cage door and cleaned up the blood and the hair.

Paulo still didn't see the sense in doing that, but Doug reassured him it was part of a bigger, elaborate plan. He would eventually see why Doug did this.

—

Paulo strode into the hacienda before sunrise as if he had just left yesterday. Henry, the manservant, formally greeted him. Henry was no fool; he knew who paid the bills around here. Paulo handed him a roll of American $100 bills. "Best you round up all the staff and tell them to have a holiday for a couple of days."

Henry and the other staff couldn't wait to leave the building. They knew the ramifications of crossing a man like Paulo. They didn't want to be responsible for answering questions from the authorities.

Maria was sitting up in bed watching TV when Paulo entered the room without knocking. He marched towards her quickly, stood next to the bed and stared down at her.

She was white with fear; her throat was dry.

He grabbed her hair and pulled her head back, aggressively put the gun in her mouth, smashing a tooth in the process, and shot her. The back of her skull blew out all over the pillows. He raised his hands into the air as if he had just scored a mighty goal.

He then marched down the hall to find that little fuck Dennis. He had no remorse, as far as he was concerned, they were all in on it. He'd raised that bastard child, spent hundreds of thousands on the little puke.

Dennis had heard the gunshot and was hiding under the bed. Paulo lured him out. "Come to Papa, son, quickly. I have to take you somewhere safe.

There are bad men in the house. If they catch us, they will kill us. Come, I'll take you to Mama so you will both be safe."

Dennis scrambled out from under the bed and put his arms around Paulo. "I missed you, Daddy."

Paulo almost laughed. What a fuckin' little actor. His mother had certainly trained him well.

As he pushed Dennis towards the door in front of him, he shot him in the back of the head. His little, frail body slumped to the ground like a toy with the air taken out of it. The bullet entered the back of his skull and blew his face off.

A call to the authorities by an unknown source led the police to discover Paulo's bound and gagged body on the floor of Maria's room. He was bald, emaciated, but alive. His kidnappers had let him go after a year of failed attempts to get a ransom from his family. The kidnappers had been writing to Maria for the last year, but she had ignored their requests. As a result, they had killed her and her son. Paulo suspected that they had then kidnapped his Aunty Camilla, hoping that now he was released, he would pay the ransom.

Paulo was smart enough to blame the FARQ, a right-wing gorilla paramilitary group operating in Colombia, often financed by corrupt government officials. No one cared, it was in the too-hard basket, the police could see a drug war escalating over this.

They agreed to discreetly step away to let Paulo handle this his way. A generous donation to the police retirement fund helped with their decision.

Doug loved the level of corruption in Colombia. Both he and Stacey were treated like special guests, and he had a couple of good drinking sessions with Paulo before he left.

Paulo drove Doug and his 'wingman', Stacey, to the airport personally. He insisted that they go home in his private jet. They agreed that it was vital that they stay in touch and when he could, Doug would update him on Spider's trial.

The Court Case

Spider had two options: option one was to tell the truth, confirm all his travel arrangements in Colombia. But then Camilla and Maria would be jeopardised. Investigations might uncover Paulo and his cage, another kidnapping. Then there was the cocaine in the bodies going to America. All his spending. The new Mercedes in his false name. It didn't look good. His lawyer was keeping client confidentiality privilege, but that wasn't going to last long if the truth came out.

Now the police were trying to pin Pat's body sewn into the beast on him. And how did that skinny junkie bitch end up in his boot? What the fuck? He also couldn't prove he was travelling around Australia as there was no spending trail, no accommodation trail, or cell phone locations.

Option two, his lawyer's only solution, was for him to plead guilty to the kidnapping and the GBH but deny the body in the beast as they had no DNA evidence. Hope for a lighter sentence for an early guilty plea. That was the best the lawyer could come up with.

If only he could get hold of Camilla. Somehow, he had to let her know what had happened to him.

And who had posted on Facebook that Orhan was in hospital?

—

Beverly Archibald gave the jury a harrowing and dramatic version of events of the night she was kidnapped. She looked frail and was shaking in the stand. Her rotten teeth painted a picture of long-term intravenous drug use.

She revealed that she and her boyfriend, the now-deceased Pat, had rustled stock from the Hendersons' farm to support their heroin habit. After Pat's death, she had fallen into depression, which had accelerated her heroin habit, so she had turned to prostitution to support her needs. All she could remember was standing on a street corner on Kings Cross, on the edge of a darkened alley, and a tall, heavily built man had offered her money for sexual favours. They had gone into the alley, and that was the last she could remember. Her lawyer asked her if she could identify the man who offered her money, and if she could point him out in the courtroom? She looked directly at Spider, pointed and said, "That's him," then burst into hysterical tears, and the court had to be adjourned while she was consoled by Victim Support.

The hospital painted a picture of a sustained vicious attack: she had broken cheekbones, a fractured skull, and multiple contusions with the possibility of long-term emotional damage. In their opinion, she had been left for dead. They had kept her in an induced coma in the ICU for seven days until they could stabilise her.

The prosecution then described how she was found bound, gagged and hogtied when the police found her in the trunk of Mr Douglas Henderson Junior's vehicle after an anonymous tip-off. They were suggesting that the charge be escalated to attempted murder as well as kidnapping.

Spider's defence team had no real comeback. They were unable to obtain CCTV footage of the car park where the car had been parked, as the day before the discovery of the victim in his car boot, there had been maintenance on the car park camera system. They argued that it wasn't attempted murder as, due to her state of health at the time, she had fewer reserves to bounce back on than most people. They also pointed out that Douglas Henderson Jr had made an early guilty plea, and the family were prepared to pay for ongoing rehabilitation and long-term health care, aiming to help Ms Archibald get off heroin once and for all.

The jury's decision was unanimous: guilty of kidnapping, guilty of grievous bodily harm. The judge set a sentencing date, and until that time, Spider would be held in a secure facility.

Spider's only family member in the courtroom was Edith, who showed no emotion. Beverly's family clapped and rejoiced. Spider hung his head and was led away by an officer of the court.

Since he had been back in the country, he had not seen anyone other than Edith. None of his extended family had visited him, and apart from the phone calls, he felt very alone and very angry.

He pleaded with Edith to keep trying to contact Camilla, but she was never able to make contact. Somehow, Camilla's Facebook account had been closed, and her phone numbers no longer existed. Local authorities in Bogotá told Edith that the Hernandez property had been on-sold to a private owner, and Camilla was missing, presumed dead.

He briefly thought of Paulo. If Camilla couldn't feed him, he would starve to death in his cell before anyone would work out the ownership of the building.

On his sentencing date, Spider received an eleven-year sentence in a maximum-security prison. He didn't appeal.

Orhan the Detective

Orhan had noticed a change in behaviour with Spider; he had become secretive and quieter than usual. Then the parcel arrived, and when Orhan questioned Spider, he said it was a life vest. He waited for Spider to go to work and searched his room for a packing slip or a product guarantee; his instincts told him it wasn't going to be a life vest. He found nothing.

He knew Doug had sensed it as well, so they arranged with Edith to meet at the office in town, and they watched as Gay Kenny hacked Spider's computer remotely and looked at his online shopping history.

It all started to unravel from there: the bulletproof vest, the Facebook and email contact with Camilla, the confirmation of flights, the questions about his mother. Then, the sudden announcement to his family that he was going to travel around Australia on his own. He never picked up the credit card from Edith the morning of his departure, and he wasn't touching his own bank account.

Doug was furious; this could open a can of worms. By now, both Spider and Camilla would know that Sofia was dead. Before long, Spider would work out it was Doug who had bought the emerald mines, fronted by Popa Don, who negotiated all the logistics. He was crazy enough to follow orders from Camilla, and the likelihood of him getting revenge for his mother's death was possible, he was a nutter.

Gay Kenny had since tracked his car to the long-term car park at the airport.

The cattle rustling post on Facebook had allowed them to track his return to Australia. They were able to get a passenger list for the incoming flights departing from South America – the name he was travelling under meant that he must have a false passport. From there, they could trace his new credit card details.

Doug felt he had no choice but to travel to Colombia himself and keep an eye on the boy. It was more a sense of self-preservation rather than love.

He'd been happy when Spider was born, but he was born as the result of entrapment by his mad mother, so Doug's love turned sour. Then Spider turned into a fuckin' weirdo as he grew older.

Mellissa had been a great mother. All the other kids had turned out all right, but this little fuck was so unpredictable.

When he announced that he wanted to live in the panic room, no one challenged the move. He was lucky he had Orhan, who had taken the time to look after him when he was little.

Doug and Stacey touched down in Bogotá ahead of Spider after the cattle rustling incident. They hired an SUV, then waited for Spider's flight to arrive. Doug planned to follow him when he left the airport. He'd set them up in local hotels once he established Spider's movements. With Kenny's help, they had GPS tracking on his phone, so if he went to another part of the country, they could track him down.

It turned out you could just google the Hernandez family and could even get a Google Map view of their houses, so it wasn't going to be too hard to follow Spider if he lost him in traffic.

As a second precaution, Doug had acquired a wig and a trench coat, and with the aid of some thick-rimmed reading glasses, he looked surprisingly different.

He watched the flight arrivals board and could see that the plane had landed and was being processed.

What he didn't expect was the sharply dressed man who emerged into the arrivals' hall. He had obviously changed on the plane. He had a bag from duty-free, and by the look of his body language, it was a gift for the older woman who embraced him.

This was the first time Doug had set eyes on Camilla. He shuffled into a seat and put his head down behind a newspaper. He had noticed her earlier. She had stood out as she was scanning the people waiting; there were no flies on that smart old fox.

She made a phone call, and they left the hall, and as they emerged outside, a vehicle was just pulling up. Doug was going to miss the opportunity to follow them as they would have too much of a head start on him.

He was about to get up from his chair when he noticed a man hurriedly trying to follow Camilla and Spider; this wasn't in the plan.

Doug followed him to the public car park while he rang Stacey to bring their car closer to his location. They followed this man all the way to the hacienda, where he parked up for a while, took photos, then drove off. Then they followed him to the police station, where he entered through a side entrance; he was a plainclothes copper.

Doug made several drive-bys of the property. The grounds nearly took up the whole block in a very upmarket neighbourhood. Still, consistent with the area, there were bars on all the windows of the houses in the street, due to long-term civil unrest and gang violence. But it certainly was a better part of town. The property had big entrance gates that were closed.

On the second day, Doug and Stacey followed Spider and Camilla to an older part of town. Here, there was a vacant concrete building, about four stories high, huge concrete surrounding walls and big iron gates. From the outside, it looked to be unoccupied, abandoned. Spider and Camilla had a key to the gate and drove into the complex. They stayed inside the building for about an hour, then left, locking the gate again behind them.

The man from the airport was waiting for them too; he was parked up the road a way. They could see the flash of his camera from the front seat of his car.

It took a couple of days, but Spider was on the move again. This time, he went back to the domestic part of the airport and boarded a private jet on his own. Camilla stayed behind. He left for what Doug could only presume was another business arrangement or family connection. Doug would have to wait till Gay Kenny rang them with a location update before they could follow. Meanwhile, he was intrigued by the vacant building that Spider and Camilla had visited. While they were waiting, he would check it out. It might be important later.

Doug and Stacey were on a flight two days later to another part of Colombia, Vaupes. The ironic thing was that the only accommodation they could find was the backpackers and the unit next door to Spider and his travelling companion, whom he had now deduced was Paulo Hernandez, a cousin of Sofia's and the head of a well-known drug cartel. His picture was even on America's Most Wanted list, but he seemed to be walking around Colombia like he didn't have a care in the world – that's what Doug loved about South America, the corruption!

As the night wore on, they could hear the drunken antics of Paulo through the wall, always followed by laughter. Paulo seemed to be quite the comedian when he wasn't murdering people.

After a while, it went quiet in the adjoining unit; too quiet. There was the faint noise of a door closing, and in the dark, Doug could see the silhouette of a man running in the all too familiar running suit.

It was too late to start after him. Instead, they would wait for him to return, time his absence, then try and judge the distance he could have travelled.

A car pulled out of the car park with its lights off. This could be a fly in the ointment if the copper was still following Douglas. Doug could hear Paulo snoring through the wall.

The next morning, Doug didn't hear them get up, but he heard them leave in a hurry. After reading the paper, he later drove past the burnt remains of the head of a rival cartel's private residence. The newspaper verified that all the occupants had died in the fire. This was the work of Spider for sure.

A couple of days later, Doug and Stacey flew out from Buenaventura on the start of their journey home, back to Australia. Doug had seen enough for the time being. Next time, he'd bring Stacey again so they could take turns covering different locations. She had always been reliable, and she spoke fluent Spanish. He could rely on her to finish the job if he couldn't.

Prison Life

Spider paced the floor of his cell. He had some understanding now of what Paulo was experiencing. Only Paulo wasn't permitted to leave his cell for a few hours a day to exercise. He was still angry over the injustice of the charges and the sentencing. He thought he must have written close to a hundred letters to Camilla and Maria. None were replied to. Then one day he got a parcel with all his letters stamped 'Return to Sender'. They had somehow been posted from Australia. There was a note inside that read *'Stop fuckin' sending letters!'* so that was clear.

The prison system played with his head on multiple levels. He liked the food, only he knew all the sex offenders worked in the kitchens, so you never knew if you were eating someone's sperm or faeces in your meal. If you pissed anyone off, you certainly did.

Your time started in remand, waiting for your sentence to be handed down by the judge. This was a very aggressive time; fights broke out constantly and stand over tactics were used for your shoes or anything else that someone thought was of value. Spider could never work out why the prisoners just didn't unite, after all, they were all criminals. You either had to join a side, whether it be a gang or an ethnic group, or you had to have enough money to bargain your way out of danger. He used his strength to stand alone; he was ruthless in his attacks.

If you went into segregation after sentencing, you faced other barriers. Most of the segregated prisoners were sex offenders, gay, or just plain scared. And you suffered the jibes of the mainstream prisoners, who would try and give you the bash or stab you as you went past; actions often overlooked by the prison guards. But segregation often meant better jobs, including kitchen work or the library. It wasn't honourable to go into segregation, so Spider did it the hard way.

And then there was mainstream, where you were in big dorm blocks with other prisoners. Here, you truly lived in a dog-eat-dog world. People would get stabbed or beaten. Some would die at the hands of others or mysteriously be found hanging in their cells. The exercise yard was a hotbed for trading, favours, and violence.

Most of the time was spent in a strict routine, which could be broken by behavioural and self-discovery courses, sessions with your case manager, meals, and exercise. Visiting days could be a highlight if you were lucky enough to have visitors. You were cable-tied into a full one-piece jumpsuit to reduce the successful transferring of smuggled contraband.

Spider went straight into mainstream. He had the legacy of his father's reputation behind him, and he was considered a special case by the guards and the other inmates. There were even members of his father's gang in the same part of the prison as him. But that didn't stop the pecking order attempts, or the need to establish his place in the order. Through an unwritten rule, if his father's club members got into any conflict, Spider was obligated to support them, which he did, as it was a good way to release the anger inside him.

It became quickly apparent to the prison staff that Spider was never going to conform to the rules of the system. His first cellmate was found black and beaten the next morning, so Spider was placed in isolation, which he liked. But when he was reintegrated back into the mainstream, he was placed in another sharing situation. The outcome was predictable, and this continued until he was transferred to a single cell in the most serious block in the prison for the most violent prisoners. It reminded him of the panic room; he loved it. He attacked anyone who came into his bubble without remorse. Then he would be placed in solitary again, and again. He really got satisfaction from the mayhem it caused. His visits were cancelled, and any letters or money he received were held back until he could agree to stop fighting, so he had to weigh that option up.

He eventually agreed to disagree, and if he stopped fighting, he could have his letters and visits from his sister.

His psychiatrist, who saw him once a week, arranged for him to learn to paint. He wasn't permitted to have any privileged prison jobs as he was deemed too dangerous to get access to tools or other weapons. But he had to agree to settle down and not stab anyone with the sharpened end of an artist's brush.

It took a year for him to settle down, and by that time, the other prisoners on his wing communicated briefly with him from time to time. But he never shared his meals with anyone and preferred to be on his own.

His sister made sure he always had money in his prison account, and he was very generous with his money, particularly if his fellow inmates didn't have families or outside support.

The other inmates had a nickname for him, 'Horrendous-son', which they coined together from connecting his surname, Henderson, with Horrendous. He didn't mind, in fact, he liked having a prison nickname. He also liked it that everyone else was afraid of him, even the screws. They just called him Horrendous.

To keep up his image and reputation, he would shave his head and carve primitive tattoos on himself; he took pleasure from the pain. He would melt the soles of his footwear to make the black ink. His art classes didn't help with any of the design features; they were crude, ugly tattoos.

Edith always had news from home: motorcycle events his father went to, his brothers' overseas travels, nieces and nephews being born, how the company was coping during economic downturns. She would always send photos of the animals and share farming news about Orhan. Unfortunately, as time went by, she had to share the passing of all his grandparents. She was still affected by it as they had been a big part of their lives growing up. She broke down crying when she told him the news. Spider was not able to attend the services; he was deemed too high risk.

Spider had one focus; he would sit it out and do his time. Once he was released, he'd catch a plane back to Colombia and find out what happened to Camilla and Paulo. He'd played it over and over in his mind; was Maria behind the missing money? Was Paulo right? Had Camilla met foul play, or had she had some catastrophic event that had ended her life? What had happened to Maria and little Dennis? Dennis had always been on Facebook; it was his age-group thing. Why had he gone off the grid? Who had set him up and put that useless junkie in his boot? He would get so worked up over these matters that he would lash out and end up in solitary confinement again.

It was during one of these times in isolation that he thought about the picture he had found in his mother's scrapbook – the newspaper clipping. It suddenly just clicked why the person with his mother looked so familiar; the white businessman was his Popa Don when he was younger. Did his father own the emerald mines now? This was a question he would ask Edith next visit. He would look her in the eye and see if she was going to lie to him like everyone else.

He wasn't permitted to use the gymnasium; the guards didn't want him getting any stronger than he was now. So, for hours on end at night in the darkness of his cell, he'd exercise; push-ups, one-armed push-ups, squats; he wanted to be all sinew and muscles. With the hair and the tattoos, he looked awful.

All he had left was counting down the days and the weeks and the years. He was never eligible for early parole, as he was always angry and always in solitary. He would have to serve his full sentence.

On Edith's next visit, he was different. They talked about the usual things: the farm, the animals – she sensed a question coming. He broached it awkwardly, and then he just told her about the newspaper clipping he had seen with Popa Don and that he was told Sofia had sold the mines to an overseas buyer. He locked eyes with her, looking for any sign. She didn't flinch. She had no knowledge of this transaction, and she handled the books, so she would know. She couldn't explain how Popa Don got into the photo – if it was Popa Don at all – and as he had now passed away, they couldn't ask him.

He looked at her again closely, looking for signs of perspiration, twitching of her lip or eyelid, anything to give away the lie; she remained unchanged. He was prepared to gouge her eyes out if she was in on it, sister or not; he was sick of the world lying to him.

It wasn't till Edith was in the car park after the visit, sitting in her car, that she started to shake. That was intense. Luckily, her father had prepared her for that very scenario. They had even role-played it, which she thought was a bit dramatic at the time, but now she could see her father's reasoning. It was the first time she had experienced just how unpredictable Spider could be. He was going to be a danger when he got out. She hoped her father had a plan.

Three Funerals and a Wedding

Popa Don had woken up at the same time every morning for his whole life. He hadn't needed an alarm clock; he just naturally woke at that time. It was his ritual to sit up in bed and turn the telly on and watch a bit of news until Andrea woke up. Then Orhan would bring them a cup of tea, and they would plan their day.

It was the same every day but today was different – Andrea was cold to the touch. He instinctively knew she was dead. He lay quietly beside her and kissed her forehead, tears rolling down his face. The love of his life was dead. He was thankful for small mercies. At least she had gone in her sleep, without pain and suffering. After losing Mellissa, he didn't think his heart could be more broken; he carried on crying. She looked so beautiful to Don. he kissed her forehead again.

He didn't want to leave her side. He groped around in the low light and grabbed his phone from the bedside cabinet and rang Doug to come to the room.

It was a slow morning. The doctor arrived with the local funeral director and Edith and Kenny arrived. Edith started the process of informing everyone who needed to know and making the service arrangements with the funeral director.

Don just sat in an armchair staring blankly at the empty bed, tears still rolling down his face. Rob, Doug's father, came in with a cup of tea for Don, he had been crying also. It was a rotten day.

"Well," said Don, "it's just you and me now buddy. No one to boss us around and plan our outings."

Doug remembered the days when Andrea would meet him and Mellissa from the school bus, take him in and bandage his cuts and ruffle his hair. Everyone was going to miss her; she was kind-hearted and always had a smile on her face.

The doctor said it was her heart and that she had simply got too old, and it had stopped ticking.

Don and Rob sat around for weeks after the funeral with no motivation to do anything, the humour had gone out of them both.

Doug decided to send them both to Colombia, to prepare the mine managers for a potential sale and work out what a good price would be. They were both reluctant to go at first, but after they got their itinerary and saw that Edith had booked business class seats and a guided tour of South America, they decided to go and make the most of it. They took a little jar of Andrea's ashes with them.

While they were away, Doug would have their wing remodelled and updated so Edith and Kenny could start the transition to relocate to the farm to live. Doug had seen their body language change, and he had a sneaky feeling Kenny wasn't gay anymore.

He was right. Before Don and Rob flew out, Edith and Kenny announced that they were thinking of getting married, but Kenny hadn't worked up the courage to ask Doug yet. The two old comedians gave him some pointers and role-played hilarious renditions of Doug's lame attempts to ask if he could marry Mellissa. It made for a good farewell party and broke the state of mourning that the family had spiralled into.

Only Rob returned from South America; Don had developed a virus near the end of their tour and had died in a private hospital in Rio. Don had been adamant that he didn't want to fly home for medical attention, he said Rob could bring his ashes home in a box with Andrea's ashes. He felt that he had lost the will to live and just wanted to go to heaven and be with his wife and daughter. He was Rob's only surviving friend, and Rob held his hand till his last breath and placed two coins on his eyelids after he passed on.

Rob continued on to Colombia and carried out the assessment of the mines, then returned home.

Doug had hired a live-in nurse to care for his father; he didn't want his father to go into a rest home. Rob lived for another five years with mild dementia without incident, until he wandered off one day and they couldn't find him. Search and rescue eventually found him face down, drowned in a pond which was miles away from the property. They found his slippers at different locations along the way and tracked him to the pond. He had walked for eight miles across country and had taken his clothes off at the edge of the pond. No one knew if he drowned as a result of his illness or if he committed suicide, but it had been a difficult situation to grasp, and they all blamed themselves for not keeping enough eyes on him. The nurse hadn't detected any drastic change in his mannerisms or behaviour, so she hadn't felt the need to have him admitted to a rest home facility. No one had seen it coming. He had helped Doug put some shelves up the day before he disappeared.

"Let's have a big wedding," suggested Doug. "God knows we need to lift the mood around here."

Edith wasn't really a flowery, flamboyant personality, but Kenny was. This was Doug's only daughter, and he wanted no expense spared.

Doug and Kenny's dad were still getting over the shock of the marriage announcement, but they had it on good advice from Orhan that Kenny had never been gay, he just liked pretty things.

Kenny had worked in close contact with Edith for nearly twenty years, and they were always comfortable around each other. He'd never made any moves in a romantic direction, he had never wanted to scare her off too early, and the timing was never right. They travelled together overseas like a couple frequently and never seemed to fight or get on each other's nerves. They both had the same select group of outside friends. They often laughed that they certainly couldn't share their work stories with other people.

One day Edith caught him looking at her breasts and rather than look away or apologise, he simply said he'd love to bury his head in them, and Edith let him, and it all started from there.

They found their relationship very natural. They never had to explain anything to each other; they were a perfect fit. They had both kept it a secret from their parents for a while because they didn't want the pressure of all the questions. They knew they also didn't want the complication of children. Let everyone else breed, was their moto.

Now that a marriage ceremony was being planned Doug suggested that, after the marriage, they shift into the farmhouse permanently and run the business from there to save on travel. Most things could be done remotely now, and Kenny was a computer genius.

So, while Kenny planned an extravagant wedding, Edith hired an architect to renovate their half of the house.

Kenny chose Edith's wedding outfit for her. He said if it was left up to her, she'd turn up in a flour sack. To be different, Kenny wore a bright red suit, and Edith wore a white pants suit. It was all about the food for Edith, and for Kenny, it was all about the flowers and the decoration.

The day was a mix of happiness and sadness as they remembered Mellissa and their grandparents, who they would have loved to have had there to share the moment with them.

Going to See a Man About a Mine

Paulo collected Doug and Stacey from the airport in Buenaventura. It was like a reunion, with a bit of banter and laughter.

Paulo updated them on the progress he'd made since they had last seen him. He had sold the hacienda in Bogotá; the place gave him the creeps, he said. The only staff he'd kept was Henry, the manservant. He'd proven to be very loyal and a good set of eyes and ears for Paulo. He ran a tight house, so nothing got past him.

Maria's parents were found dead; bound and gagged in their home. Someone had poured petrol over them and set them alight. Maria's so-called secret lover had died also. He was found on a remote road with his cock chopped off; he had bled to death. "I carried out the executions personally," Paulo told Doug and Stacey. "Tying up loose ends, as they say."

"Speaking of loose ends, there might be a problem," said Doug.

He told Paulo about the policeman who had been tailing Douglas. He wasn't sure how much he knew or had discovered, but it might be important. Stacey had taken his car registration.

Paulo called Henry in and gave him the registration. "Find out who owns this car for me, please."

Henry was back within minutes. Paulo was familiar with this guy; he had unsuccessfully headed a case against Paulo in the past. He would need to be taken care of immediately; he could cause a real problem for all of them. Paulo was more annoyed that he had been promised that this guy would see out his days in the mailroom and now he was back on the beat. It didn't make sense. He would sort it out once and for all.

On Doug's instructions, he had kept the building with the cell in it. He had never been back, as instructed by Doug, but Paulo could confirm that it had never been breached. He never asked why Doug wanted it kept, but he liked Doug's style so he would wait. It was in a shit part of the city; he could wait.

Since selling hacienda in Bogotá, Paulo had purchased a flash new modern mansion on the waterfront in Buenaventura which had harbour views and views of the marina. He was proud to show it off for his Aussie friends.

He insisted that they relax for a couple of days to get over their jetlag, and then they would start visiting the mines. If Paulo was going to buy them back, he wanted to pay a good price.

Paulo was keen to show off his other investments and business interests and had a full itinerary planned for their visit, including showing them the cut-price funeral business that had grown so big they were franchising branches across the world. This meant they could be selective with the bodies they chose so they didn't clutter up their specialised funeral homes with empty bodies. Also, if someone leaked to the authorities, they would not find any cocaine in the bodies they searched; at least that was the plan.

Doug was fascinated with the funeral business. He gave Paulo credit for pulling it off. He didn't take up the offer to see the process from beginning to end, though.

Doug updated Paulo on the growing obsession that Spider had developed over the mines true owners, therefore making it an easy decision to sell. It wouldn't take him long to get someone on the outside to google the mines' owners and then he would discover his father had owned them the whole time. They also suspected that he would try and come back to Colombia after his release from prison to find out what had happened to Camilla and Maria.

Paulo had changed his trading name to Julius Caesar – he thought it was funny. Doug saw the similarities as Paulo strutted around like a cross between Mick Jagger and a Roman emperor in his brightly coloured dupioni silk suits. Paulo thought the new name might make tracing his business interests a bit trickier should Spider start looking.

Doug introduced Paulo to the mine managers for each mine. They all operated legitimate books and had proven to be honest reliable employees. Doug wanted to make sure that they would be personally looked after when the business changed hands, which would be reflected in the price.

The bonus was that some mines weren't doing so well, so it would be an opportunity for Paulo to launder money through these mines without any undue attention.

It was also decided to put a new public face as the CEO of the mines so that Paulo's interests remained silent, very much the same as the way the funeral homes operated. The transaction took place, with mutual agreement on the price. Doug practically gave them away; he didn't want them.

         MICHELLE THOMPSON

Paulo had found the scrapbook that had been in Sofia's room containing the cutting of Don, which they ceremoniously burnt in the fire pit after a few drinks.

Doug helped Paulo interview the new CEO candidates for the mine, all of whom were family relations. They settled on a chap who looked very much like Don in build and colouring.

On one of his planned excursions, Paulo took them way up into the hills and introduced them to the cocaine farmers and Doug got to see first-hand the whole process. It looked way more difficult than it was worth, but everyone liked cocaine, so they kept buying it.

Doug and Stacey never lost sight of the fact that Paulo was crazy. A couple of times during their visit they witnessed him go off his tree and shoot a man in the street for no apparent reason, and a factory worker on one of their outings, but it turned out he shot the wrong person, so he had to shoot another person to make up for his mistake.

Paulo was interested in the relationship between Doug and Stacey; they had separate rooms, but they finished each other's sentences. Doug explained that they had been neighbours for years and that Stacey ran his commercial produce operation. He also said that if anyone had the balls to follow through and have Doug's back, hands down it would be Stacey. He knew he could trust her and vice versa. And no, they had never thought of having sex, it wasn't their thing. They were genuine friends.

It made Paulo look at her in a different light. He could see the killer instinct in her; he liked her.

Spider Takes Flight

Booking a flight wasn't easy without money. The credit card that Camilla had given him had long since expired. He was also faced with having to explain why he was leaving again so soon after he had just been released from prison. This was made easier by his father's sudden departure. Both he and Stacey had a business engagement they couldn't change and had booked to fly back to Iran with the twins and their families.

Spider only had one avenue, and that was to ask Edith for some money. His passport had also expired, and he would have to get that fast-tracked before he could fly, all of which Edith would have to lend him the money for and keep it a secret.

Edith was already on to it; she had started the online application once he was released. It took a full week before his new passport arrived.

Edith was surprisingly accommodating. She didn't ask many questions and agreed to help him with his transition from prison to normal life. She gave him a credit card with an unlimited credit balance.

He decided to tell her everything he was going to do once he touched down in Colombia. After all, she had kept her word all this time and hadn't told their father, and she had supported him in prison. She even offered to drop him off at the airport.

The first thing he would do would be to visit the house and see if he could find any news about Camilla. Perhaps he could find Maria and Dennis. And then there would be the matter of finding the body of Paulo if there was one; he'd cross that bridge when he came to it.

He had to take two flights, first directly from Sydney to Argentina, then from Argentina to Colombia. Due to his criminal record, he could no longer go via LAX or Miami.

When his flight touched down in Bogotá, he hired a car and drove straight to the hacienda. The gates were open and there were no guards. The grounds looked well maintained, the fountain still bubbling away.

He was met at the door by a British woman in her late fifties. She told him she was the wife of the British Consulate for Colombia. They had been

     MICHELLE THOMPSON

stationed here for the last three years. She had no idea who owned the property, as she and her husband were just tenants. They took the premises over from the previous British delegates. She seemed guarded and didn't offer to invite him in.

From the doorway, he could see into the vast foyer. Replacing the picture of his mother was a smaller picture of the Queen of England.

"I suggested that you inquire with the local government authorities, they might know who owns the building," the British woman suggested.

She was trying to close the door, and she looked frightened, so he hurriedly told her he used to live there. She sceptically looked him up and down and he realised he must appear intimidating to her, with his Mohawk and his tattoos. He thought better of it and decided to leave the property before she called the police.

He was suddenly tired; jetlag had hit him. He'd thought for a moment that he would have another go in the morning, then he would go to Maria's parents' house, but changed his mind; he hadn't come all this way after eleven years to wait another day.

Spider went to Maria's parents' house; this also had new owners. He was about to leave when he saw an elderly lady in the next driveway. He asked if she knew where the family had gone. She looked him up and down, then retreated back behind her iron gates and disappeared.

He found a street sweeper. Spider asked him if he remembered the previous owners of the house. The street sweeper looked him up and down and continued on with his work. Spider wondered briefly if he was deaf. He could resort to beating him to a pulp, but instead, he pulled out a US $100 bill and scrunched it into his palm.

"They died years ago, shot or something, botched home invasion. Nice couple. Police said the father was tied up in laundering drug money." With that the street sweeper looked around nervously and quickly returned to his cart of brooms; he was deaf again.

Spider's next move had to be made sooner than later; his body was reacting to being overtired. Best he got it over and done with, and head to the warehouse where he and Camilla held Paulo captive.

He still had the key to the lock, which he had on him when he was arrested. It had been sitting in a prison envelope all this time with his clothing, and although the lock was tight and rusty, with a couple of turns it sprung open.

The best solution to not raise suspicion from anyone in the street was to park in behind the wall and lock the gate after him.

As he entered the building, he was strangely nervous. He didn't know what he was going to find. The building was completely quiet. Apart from the cobwebs, he could only detect a slight chemical smell, a bit like petrol. There was no odour of rotting flesh. Judging by the cobwebs no one had been here for some time, probably eleven years.

He proceeded down the stairs to the basement. When he opened the door, he tried the light; it no longer worked. He waited for his eyes to adjust to the only lighting, which came from the exit sign. He vaguely noticed the TV on the wall; it was dark, no standby light.

He could make out the figure on the floor of the cage curled in the foetal position in the pink jumpsuit; it looked like a dummy from a sideshow ghost house. A bony skeleton hand poked out of the sleeve with gold rings on it. The dry, almost petrified skin had dried tight over the skull. The protruding teeth looked false, and the stubble of hair on the skull was missing in parts; just a bit of gold chain poked out from the neckline.

He crouched down and looked closer. What were the brown things everywhere? They looked like raisins or liquorice. Then it dawned on him while he inspected them; it was rat shit.

He was fascinated with the way the body had dried. The eyes were missing – perhaps the rats ate Paulo's eyes? His lack of sleep was making this seem like a movie – a 3D movie – and he was enjoying what he was seeing. He bent forward to smell the body.

He heard a click behind him a split second before a bullet hit the back of his skull. His head was blown off his neck in several large pieces.

   MICHELLE THOMPSON

Paulo Gets His Wish

The courier arrived at Paulo's house. Normally the staff took care of any incoming mail, but this courier said he had strict instructions that the parcel was signed for. Paulo was semi-annoyed by his persistence. The parcel had no return address on it. He felt it all over, and although it was heavy it didn't feel like a bomb. He signed for it but made Henry open it, just in case. They all stood back, partly because it might blow Henry's arm off and partly because Paulo was using them as a shield, laughing.

Two gold chains and some gold rings fell onto the table – Paulo recognised them instantly. He felt a little emotional, and physically felt like his heart was lighter. He smirked, then noticed everyone was looking at him oddly.

Henry asked, "You ok, boss?"

Paulo replied. "Couldn't be better, my man, couldn't be better."

It had been a busy month for Paulo. An old warehouse his company owned in Bogotá had burnt to the ground. The fire had been so fierce that some of the floors had collapsed in on themselves. The authorities said it was probably a gas leak – old building, old pipes. There was no saving it, so Paulo took some business advice from his new mate Doug and hired a demolition company to bulldoze the sight. He built a new apartment block with the insurance money. It was traditionally a poorer part of town but, sticking with the plan, he bought up the whole street and turned it into affordable housing apartments, offering loans and home ownership to people trying to get on the property ladder. It was not only profitable, but it was a great way to launder money.

He created a gated estate and marketed it as a safe place to live – his sales slogan was that it was 'safer than a jail'. The idea was to keep criminals out, and he named it Freedom Estate. The centre of the estate was a shopping centre, so technically residents could work locally and shop locally if they were so inclined. Once again, he kept his name out of the paperwork. Had the residents known they were funding a drug laundering operation they might not have been so keen to take up the cheap loan offers.

He loved some of Doug's ideas and was currently looking into a dolphin explorer tourist venture to operate out of the harbour in Buenaventura. He considered Doug a good friend now, to whom his door would always be open.

Body in the Coffin

Edith was surprised by the call from the funeral company which had come out of the blue. They had handled all their family deaths: her mother's arrangements, then her grandparents, Uncle Rod. They had always done a good job and shown that they really cared. Of course, they liked to charge well, and Doug always paid on time, often in cash so they didn't have to declare the money.

They had rung to say that they had received the body of Doug's son. It had been sent from South America. They didn't know he had died and hadn't expected it, and they were not sure what to do with it.

Edith was as shocked as they were. She quickly explained that her brother had gone on an overseas holiday, and she also didn't know he had died, so it would be a shock to the whole family. She would ring her father immediately and they would come directly there; she confirmed a time.

Doug was as shocked as Edith was at the news; this just couldn't be right. He gathered up Stacey and Orhan and they arranged to meet Edith at the funeral home.

When they arrived, they were ushered into a viewing room. It was all very professional, and they were not sure what to expect. The owner of the funeral home, who dealt with the family directly rather than one of his staff, had arranged for them to view the body privately and then they could decide what they wanted for the service.

They all stood around the coffin, not sure what to expect as the funeral director removed the lid. He commented as he was removing it, that whoever had embalmed the body had done a really good job; he had personally been extremely impressed at the workmanship.

They all gasped in shock as the body was exposed.

The funeral director left them to take it all in and grieve as he slipped quietly from the room and closed the door behind him.

There was shocked silence for a long minute. Doug was the first to speak as he stood over the body, peering intently into the coffin.

"Who the fuck is that?"

They all looked down at the fat bastard in the box in stunned silence. The body was in a well-made suit, around its neck were two gold chains, and the hands clasped together on its chest sported two big gold rings.

Doug said he looked vaguely familiar, then it clicked. "It's that fuckin' copper that was following Spider in Colombia."

They all burst out laughing.

When the funeral director returned to the room it was Orhan who broke the awkward silence. He asked if they could have the body at home for a couple of days for friends and relatives to view, then have it collected for a private cremation. They all talked in unison agreeing that this would be a good idea and help them get over the shock that Baby Doug had unexpectantly died. Arrangements were made to have the body delivered later that afternoon. Doug liked Orhan's quick thinking and patted him on the back.

"We will have to draw straws on who's going to open the fucker up," said Doug. They suspected from the gold chains that the body was going to be full of cocaine and looking at the fat bastard he wasn't travelling light. Orhan handed Doug the knife.

They opened the suit and the shirt and exposed stitches to an opening down by the pelvis. Doug carefully plucked at the stitching with a hunting knife, making sure he didn't pierce the aluminium bags inside.

One by one they removed the bags, and Stacey wiped them down in the kitchen sink before they decided where to store them. It was a macabre scene.

Once they established that they had all the cocaine, Doug removed the chains and the rings – he would mail them back with a thank you note. He wondered how many more relatives were going to die in South America.

It looked a fuckin' mess when they had finished with it, so they used gaffer tape to hold it primitively together and did the shirt and the suit up. It still looked a mess, so Doug got the drill and some big wood screws and made sure the coffin wasn't going to open.

When the funeral home came to collect the body, Doug travelled in the hearse with the coffin. The other family members followed in a car. It was a short and simple service, with a video link to his brothers overseas. The extra cash payment Doug made ensured the coffin went into the flames immediately, so they could guarantee all the evidence was destroyed.

The funeral director told Doug that he was happy to do business with the South American company again if the opportunity ever came up. He put the cash inside his suit pocket.

PART FOUR

Pandora's Box

It was Tuesday, Doug liked Tuesdays. Tuesday 10 am, not a minute before, not a minute after. Tuesday, 10 am was the day and time the refrigerated truck arrived to pick up the supplies for his high-end clients. It was never late; Doug did not know if it parked up the road to be on time, it just was. This specially handpicked produce was distributed to some of the top restaurants in the heart of Sydney. Tuesday was not of interest to Doug because his reputation for growing good produce was on the line; it was the truck driver who held his interest.

Jane drove the truck, helped load it, and gave his boys a bit of stick. She was a good-looking blonde woman of a more mature age, Doug's age. Her arrival brought the distribution boys racing to greet her. Her laughter could be heard all over the loading bay, lifting the mood, which stayed with the team for hours later. She was unforgiving if they were lazy and cracked the whip, called them 'moles', gave them all nicknames, and joked about their mothers in a less-than-ladylike way. Her loud New Zealand accent and her comic mimicking of the Australian accent made for a humorous half hour every Tuesday starting at 10 am.

Doug was strangely shy of her. He would often watch her on the cameras in the office or from the back of the food racks in the storeroom. Some days, he would have to quietly walk away so no one could hear his laughter. She was really funny. He had become so obsessed with seeing her that he changed his schedule to be present every Tuesday at 10 am.

He ran scenarios through his head about approaching her for a date. It had been years since he'd had a real date, one that he enjoyed for reasons other than sex. He still missed Mellissa; it always felt like a betrayal to look at another woman, even though he knew Mellissa would be telling him to move on. And he didn't think he would end up wanting to murder this one; Jane struck him as capable of murdering him, she had that street-smart look about her, which just intrigued him more. He wanted to know more about her. Orhan and Stacey would have all the answers; they were like little detectives. He would bring it up at breakfast tomorrow with Orhan.

The boys waved to Jane as her truck pulled out of the loading bay, and as Jane put the truck into third gear, her arm came out the window and she gave them all the 'bird'. Doug could see her laughing in the wing mirror. His day brightened.

—

Orhan knew nearly everything about her; Orhan and Stacey had bumped into Jane and her sister one weekend in the shopping mall. Orhan knew enough to pique Doug's interest and give Cupid's arrow a nudge in the right direction.

She was a widow, aged in her late fifties and had shifted to Australia to be closer to her sister, who had lived here for several years with her Australian husband. Their parents had died naturally of old age.

Orhan agreed that she was a comedian; he had not picked up any bad vibes from her. Jane and Stacey got on well, 'widows-in-common' Jane had nicknamed them. In fact, Orhan had decided to suggest that Doug ask her out; he'd just been waiting for the right time to suggest it.

Doug instantly dismissed the idea, "Too awkward," he responded. Doug went back to reading the morning newspapers, pretending not to be interested in the subject anymore.

Next Tuesday came around, and Doug watched from the office cameras: the truck rolling in at 10 am on the dot. It backed up to the loading dock. Jane jumped out of the cab and climbed up on the loading bay; she was fit, she did this with ease. No one was there to greet her, just some unmanned pallets.

Jane opened the refrigerated doors of the truck and started loading the goods marked with her packing slips attached to them: she did not seem at all fazed.

Doug was furious. Where the hell was everyone? They had all fucked off; he could not even find Stacey.

He suddenly felt big and awkward as he stumbled out to the loading dock. His throat was dry, and he struggled for words, or at least words that didn't sound stupid or pathetic. Under his breath he was swearing he'd punch the cunts in the head when he caught them, he knew they had set him up.

Jane looked him up and down as if to say, "You'll do," ordered him to get in the truck and stack the boxes as she passed them to him and told him, quite sternly, to be careful not to bruise or damage the stock. He was glad he was in

     MICHELLE THOMPSON

the dark of the truck so Jane could not see how crimson his flushed face had become.

They worked silently for a while; she was pushing the pace; Doug was keeping up. Jane could see the veins in his arms protruding as the blood pumped through them. His T-shirt sleeves ended halfway down his firmly muscled biceps. His arms were completely covered in a tattoo sleeve; they looked good.

As his shirt had risen up slightly from his leather belt and Harley-Davidson buckle, she caught a glimpse of his firm abs and some light body hair just peeping out from the belt. He certainly was a hot unit for an older guy.

They were nearly finished when Jane suddenly asked him a question. "How come you drew the short straw to help me today?"

Doug felt like saying that the cunts had set him up and he had no option but instead said, "I own the company. I was the only available straw."

Doug bounced back with his own question, "How come you drive the truck every Tuesday?"

Jane looked him in the eye and smiled from one side of her mouth, "I own the company. I'm the only available straw Tuesdays."

With that, she secured the doors shut, shook his hand with a firm grip, jumped off the loading dock and climbed up into her truck. As the truck pulled away, he caught her looking back at him in the wing mirror with a knowing grin on her face; their eyes locked for a moment. She gave the horn a little nudge and was off down the drive, without the 'bird' in third gear this time.

Doug turned around to an audience of staff, with Orhan and Stacey hiding behind the pack of wide-eyed employees. They were all laughing and met his stare with a round of applause.

"You've opened Pandora's box, you cunts!!!" announced Doug over the rabble of giggles, before ordering Orhan and Stacey to the office and everyone else back to work.

Jane

Jane felt a smug satisfaction all the way back to base as she made her deliveries. She could not help but find it funny that the staff had tried to set them up. And then she had to pretend that she did not know who he was and that he owned the company. She saw the twinge of shock on his carefully guarded face when she announced that she owned the trucking company. She had googled Doug. She was in no doubt about who he was or his history, or about the tragedy of losing his wife – she knew that feeling. All those weeks of him skulking behind the produce stands, Orhan and the widow Stacey's hints at the mall; she'd noticed it all.

If she were in the market, he would be her type, with well-defined arms, biceps just big enough to strain the short sleeves of his T-shirt. The T-shirt wasn't tight, but it wasn't loose; you could just make out his six-pack through the cloth, and the Harley-Davidson logo on the shirt under his high-vis vest. A pair of snug-fitting Levi jeans hugged his legs. He had the look, and he was rich, a perfect combo. But she had not come to Australia to date a bipolar gang member. She had come to Australia to track down and kill the man who had murdered her husband.

Jane and her husband Jim had lived a good life, a lucky life. They had met as teenagers at an outdoor discovery group. It was really a Christian-based tough love course for dysfunctional teenagers, which was recommended by the courts and social services. They had both come from middle-class families, both their parents had married young with few parenting skills – they were virtually babies themselves. It was drummed into their parents to work all day, every day, to get ahead, while their children ran wild.

Jane fell in with the wrong crowd, likewise Jim.

At 'Camp Run Amuck', they instantly bonded, it was like they knew each other from a previous life, soulmates, perhaps you would call it. They both had one mission in life, and that was to be rich.

Their first profitable financial venture evolved from the very camp they were sent to, to be reformed. They often, later in life, told the story of how they had each smuggled a litre bottle of spirits that they had stolen from home into the camp, and sold nips or shots and made a tidy profit, stating that great minds think alike. They would have made more money, but they both shared a love for alcohol and drank a fair bit themselves, which eventually became their undoing, as they were both sent home in disgrace. Jim promised to search the ends of the earth to find her, and that was exactly what he did.

A month later, they were on the run and had escaped up to the top of the North Island of New Zealand, where Jim's tribe had some Māori land. They camped out in the bush near a public camping ground at a place called Spirits Bay. They often reflected that it was the best summer of their lives. They would sneak into the camp at night and have showers and take advantage of the careless campers who left behind all manner of things like shampoo, towels, and blankets.

They targeted campers who had a habit of drinking too much and would wait till they flaked out drunk and then sneak in and take their alcohol, often replacing it with empty bottles. The campers would wake up in the morning, either thinking they'd had a better night than they imagined, or they couldn't be bothered alerting the authorities that there was a thief in the camp.

Jim was a skilled fisherman and hunter-gatherer, so there was always an abundance of food.

Eventually, Jim's family caught up with them and returned the pair of them to Jane's parents. Jim was now of age, so his parents did not force the issue when he insisted on staying with her. Jane's parents welcomed Jim into their home, and they remained together for the next thirty-six years.

Let's Have a Party

Orhan waited till Doug had his first morning cup of tea and was comfortably picking through the morning newspaper, looking for the business section. Orhan placed an open laptop in front of Doug, pointing at the screen, prompting him to read the article from two years ago that he had found while researching Jane and her company.

The title read 'Home invasion kills local identity'. It was a ghastly story which outlined how Jane's innocent husband had been gunned down in their own home. One of the criminals had also been shot dead during what the police said was more than likely a confrontation between Jim and the criminals. A second criminal had managed to get away before the police arrived and had never been brought to justice. The story went on to say that the police could not establish a motive and suggested that it might be a case of mistaken identity:

The retired couple, Jim and Jane Henare, had a strong connection to the local church and often volunteered on community projects. They were well known in the district and highly regarded for their generosity. The event affected the whole community, said the local police sergeant. The article went on: During the home invasion, the family pets had also been poisoned and subsequently died as a result. Mrs Henare was making plans to shift to Australia to be near her only living relative, her sister, for support. A family spokesperson had requested privacy and suggested that Mrs Henare was taking the death of her husband incredibly badly.

There were photos of the property from the air, probably taken from a drone with X's marking the spots where the two bodies lay, and a photo of the funeral, which had been held at the local football grounds, the only venue big enough to support the huge crowd that attended. Doug looked closely at all the motorbikes in the photograph; none were Japanese. He knew there was more to the home invasion story than anyone was letting on.

The article instantly saddened him; the death of Mellissa flooded back to him. He closed the laptop; it was too painful. He knew how Jane felt; she was a broken soul, like him. He did not much care for his breakfast after he'd read the article. Orhan poured him another cup of tea.

They sat in silence for a while. "Why don't you ask her out?" suggested Orhan.

Doug flatly refused. "Not likely! It'd be too awkward. I'd feel like a bloody teenager again, wouldn't know what to do."

At the club there were always sluts and skanky bitches wanting to suck his cock in return for cocaine, no emotion involved, he could be brutal and uncaring.

Orhan wisely had another suggestion as a backup. "What if the company holds a huge staff party and invites some of our suppliers? Hire a band, put some food on, lessen the awkwardness."

Doug was sceptical; it was all getting a bit too much, too forced. "Let me think about it."

A day later, Doug decided he would let Orhan and Stacey organise the whole thing. Orhan could tell Edith what he needed, and Doug would just go along with it.

"Just make sure you invite plenty of my friends in case it gets too boring, or she turns out to be a nutcase and I need an escape plan."

They both laughed, but secretly, Orhan knew Jane was the one; it was only a matter of time.

The Cannabis Years

Jim and Jane had saved up from casual cleaning jobs and bought a second-, more likely third-hand Ford station wagon off a mate. It used more oil than it did petrol, but it was big enough to put all their camping gear in, along with some bags of seed raising mix, fertiliser, bottles of tomato plant growing food, spades, water bottles, and fishing rods. Jim had secured some marijuana seeds, which he had germinated in the hot water cupboard leading up to their departure. They made camp again in their old spot; this way, they could avoid the camping ground fees.

They were certainly amateurs at the growing business. You could have all the advice from so-called experts you liked, but no one really knew the conditions and the physical endurance required to make this venture succeed. So, in the beginning, there were many failed attempts with extraordinarily little return and plenty of superficial injuries.

Finding the right spot to dig your holes for your plants was the first step. Close enough to fresh water so you did not have to carry it too far in the incredible heat of the summer sun, yet the right distance from the stream so recreational hikers would not stumble across the plots of marijuana, or worse still, professional scalpers who camped in the north every year with the sole purpose of finding other people's weed and ripping it off.

The ground and the native scrub were harsh and unforgiving, with no tracks to follow except the occasional wild pig trails. On the flip side, you did not want to leave a trail, or you may as well put signposts up for the scalpers. Then you had to carry your fertiliser in, often in twenty-litre bags, and your plants and your water, stopping often to catch your breath or administer first aid to a twisted ankle or puncture wound from a sharp stick.

Jim's idea was to have several plots in different 'test' locations. He would experiment with each plot, like putting fish guts or seaweed in the bottom of the holes for fertiliser. Horse shit was always good, as was store-bought liquid fertiliser. Mind you, that was after the gruelling effort of digging the holes in soil that had never been dug in the history of the continent being formed, cutting through root mass and rocks, only to ask yourself was it all worth it, did everyone find it this hard or was it their lack of experience and knowledge?

If the plants actually made it to maturity, which was a miracle on its own – that is not plucked from the sky by the police helicopters on their annual swoop, or the plants stripped to stalks by the scalpers – then you had the problem of drying pounds of cannabis and manicuring it into different sales categories: the good heads, the cheaper heads, the cabbage for the oil manufacturers and the hash off your fingers rolled into balls. Everything had to have a market. The first year was a total failure; all they got were suntans. The second year, they just broke even.

The third year, Jim and Jane hit the jackpot. They just tin-arsed the right weather, a little mechanical intervention to the scalper's vehicles, the right location of tried and tested plots, and the Labour Party was in government, so they didn't spend any money on helicopters like the Opposition did. They were away laughing.

But did they grow good weed? The crash test dummy on whether or not they grew a good product boiled down to Jim's younger brother, Wiremu. Neither Jim nor Jane smoked so they would get Wiremu to smoke a cone from the different batches and see how shit-faced he got; this was their only indication of the potency. So, the third year, when everything came together and Wiremu spun out on the first joint, they knew the stars had lined up, and their operation started making a reasonable amount of money from that year onwards. They weren't rich, but they were comfortable.

Jim and Jane shifted north to live full-time and built a basic tin shed on a remote part of Jim's family's land. They lived rough for the first year; you needed a four-wheel-drive vehicle to get to and from the shed from the only connecting district road, and even that was covered in potholes, which meant you didn't have many, if any, visitors, which suited Jim and Jane for privacy and security reasons. You couldn't trust anyone in the weed business. The shed had a couple of uses; one, it kept them dry if it rained, and two, it was great for drying lots of weed.

The next year, Jim bartered a flash caravan for a couple of pounds of weed and, as bartering was the flavour of the way business was done up north before long, they had a solar unit and could pretty much survive without any human contact for long periods of time.

Wiremu was their dealer. There was never a link between the client and Jim and Jane; it was always done through Wiremu. He had his regular supply and demand chain and would go out to the property once a month on his own with their shopping order and share of the cash from the weed sales, then take back what he needed for his next month's orders. They kept it tidy like that purely because they knew the risk of getting caught; 'loose lips sink ships' was their motto. No conversations were held over phones, and extraordinarily little money made it to a bank account unless it could be substantiated from the sale of a car or livestock. Jim paid cash for everything, even his first digger, which he taught himself to drive so he could dig a big hole to hide his first container underground to store all manner of things in, including their marijuana.

For the few months of the year when Jane and Jim were not growing pot, they were fishing in the local harbour of Houhora, or on holiday, flying business class around the world, visiting as many exotic places as they could. They worked hard; they deserved it.

     MICHELLE THOMPSON

The Life of the Party

Orhan thought he had choreographed the party well. He had two bands lined up. A Bluegrass band was booked for the earlier part of the night, mainly for the suppliers and their families, so the noise would not be overbearing for casual conversation. If there was one thing Orhan hated, it was music so loud you had to yell to hear the person next to you, and they yelled back with a combination of spittle and bad breath. And half the time, you just pretended that you could hear what they were saying. He'd picked a more classic rock band for the partygoers that hung in till the bitter end and got completely pissed and did not care if their breath smelt or had lost all sense of smell by that time.

For entertainment, he had booked a mobile pet farm and a magician who came with a children's face painter and the inevitable bouncy castle for the children, then he had a comedian booked for the adults between the bands.

Orhan had hired their regular caterers, who were simply going to put on a buffet with 'the works' as Orhan put it. The guests would be seated for the meal while the comedian was on stage and the second band was setting up their gear, and, somehow, he would engineer that Doug ended up sitting next to Jane. Stacey and Edith might help with that, as they were all secretly in on the Cupid thing.

Since Orhan had permission to go ahead and stage the party, he had not mentioned it to Doug once. Forcing the issue was just going to put Doug off, and he was unlikely to attend his own party to avoid the pressure.

Jane had accepted the invitation with two questions; she asked if she could bring her sister and what wine was being served, as she had a particular taste in wine and insisted that she bring her own. Jane and Orhan had a humorous debate over New Zealand versus Australian wines, but settled on a selection of both.

Gay Kenny insisted on being the photographer for the night and even suggested a video.

If the weather turned to shit, they had a storeroom that could be converted quite quickly if needed. The area for the band had been purpose-built many years before Orhan came on the scene, and it had a covered stage for the band, which overlooked an area of grass and the man-made lake. It was always a great place for a party.

The day of the party, the tension in the air was palpable due to Doug's stress affecting the family. He didn't look happy.

The guests started to arrive with the crunching of gravel as the cars jockeyed for position in the car park. Orhan had a parking attendant working to keep it all in order. The sounds of shrieking children and peals of giggles could be heard as they saw the little ponies in the petting enclosure.

The bar staff and the waiters were run off their feet as the guests were hungrily knocking back the free drinks and nibbles. Occasionally, you could hear Kenny saying "Smile," as he got groups of people to pose for photos.

Doug was constantly surrounded by clients, excited to be invited, in awe of his stature and reputation, and all wanting to have their photo taken with him, which he hated.

Orhan could see Doug was getting pissed off with the whole event. Stacey kept him sane by telling him they should have done this years ago; they had already increased their sales pipeline by forty per cent, and it was only one hour into the event.

Hours had passed, and Jane had still not arrived. Doug had that sinking feeling in his guts, and he felt hurt and foolish for even trying. He caught Orhan's eye across the bar. He knew he was also worried; it seemed everyone was, even Edith was looking forward to Jane coming. Doug thought she must have got a better offer.

Doug perked up when he heard the rumble of Harley-Davidsons as some bikes from Doug's club came down the drive at full throttle. The crowd's excitement heightened at the sound of the big Harley's. *Just in time*, thought Doug, as he was on the verge of blowing a fuse; take his mind off the prospect of this bullshit relationship shit and get into some serious drinking.

As the bikes got closer, he spotted Jane on the back of Brian's bike wearing Brian's helmet. Doug made his way down to greet them, his mood instantly altered. There had been a major accident on the motorway, and Jane and her sister had been stuck in traffic. As the boys came past, she had literally stepped out and stopped them. Brian recognised Jane from the deliveries and brought her the rest of the way on the back of his bike. Her sister had stayed with the car and would follow shortly.

   MICHELLE THOMPSON

Doug took her hand as she threw her leg over the back of the seat to stand up. Doug caught a whiff of alcohol on her; she had already been drinking; he steadied her. She stood up tall and let out an almighty "Fuck." She had thoroughly enjoyed the high-speed ride.

She thanked Brian and apologised to Doug for being late. Her next words were, "Where's the piss?" She followed the boys to the bar.

In normal circumstances, Doug would have been pissed off if his missus was on another man's bike, but she wasn't his missus yet, although he already had a twinge of jealousy. He seriously had to thank his best mate for saving the day. His mood change was evident to everyone. Doug was happy. The whole party took on a different vibe, and the family relaxed. Brian had had a secret word with Stacey. He knew Doug would be 'out the gate', so he had arrived with the goods, just in time. They both knew him too well.

All Doug's worries instantly evaporated. Jane was everything he imagined she would be. She kept intelligent conversation; she joked at the right times. She laughed and networked with clients for her own business. She drank like a fish; Doug was surprised at just how much she was putting away; it was bottle after bottle.

Her sister finally arrived, dropped off by a scruffy-looking Māori. Jane said he was her brother-in-law, and he would be back later to give them a lift home. She returned from the car with another box of wine, much to Orhan's protests.

Doug lost sight of her as Jane disappeared into the crowd. Instantly, his anxiety rose again until he heard her voice coming from the microphone on stage, as she thanked the boys for the lift, explaining to everyone why she was late. Then she and her sister produced guitars they had borrowed from the Bluegrass band, and they sang a couple of comedic country folk songs to a roaring ovation from the warehouse boys. There was no end to her skills, Doug thought to himself. He was well and truly hooked.

Dinner was announced ready to be served, and Orhan's worry about seating was out the door as there was no juggling of seats needed. Jane simply told everyone where they were going to sit, which left her next to Doug.

If Doug thought her drinking was extreme, then her eating surpassed it, with Jane going back for seconds, then dessert. As if she knew what he was thinking, Jane, through her laughter, told him that she was putting a lining on her stomach so she could drink more later and soak up some of the alcohol she'd already drunk. Her blunt honesty was refreshing.

The next band was setting up behind the comedian, while guests with children were planning to leave the party. Doug, as host, was seeing them off, which gave Jane some time to talk to Orhan, who she noticed had been watching her every move. She had a message for him to pass on later to Doug if, and only if, he felt it was necessary.

"Don't hold your breath," Jane said quietly in Orhan's ear. "It is possible that something could happen, but I have something I need to get past first, and until that is off my agenda, I can't move on. I am not going to drop my knickers in the meantime, but it doesn't mean that I don't want to know Doug and go on occasional outings, so don't worry, all your efforts have not gone unnoticed."

With that, she hugged the little guy, and he felt the sadness in her heart. As she stepped back, the tear in her eye mirrored the one in Orhan's. They laughed it off and blamed the Australian wine, not the New Zealand wine.

It was about 3 am when the scruffy Māori reappeared, and Jane and her sister said their goodbyes to everyone. Doug was surprised that they were still walking; they had given him and the boys a good run for their money. Jane didn't seem to even be slurring her words. Her sister had danced with everyone while Jane held up the bar.

Doug had stood next to her throughout the night, close enough to feel the heat from her body and close enough to smell her perfume. There were moments when he almost reached out and touched her; it just felt natural and familiar.

Orhan had long since vanished. He didn't drink, but he had spent hours watching Jane and Doug together, and he went to bed happy in the knowledge that his dad could finally be happy again.

Edith and Kenny had gone to bed, so Stacey took the opportunity to ask Jane for a lift home. Doug, Brian and Wiremu helped all three ladies to the car. As they drove off with much laughter and cheers, Doug took a deep breath and, with a part of him already missing her, another part of him was exhausted from the gamut of emotions he had gone through in the last twelve hours.

His thoughts were broken by Brian's departing comment, "She's the one, mate, she's the one."

A Sweet Deal

Wiremu arrived for his usual monthly rendezvous. Jim could tell from the nervous look on his brother's face that he had a worrying question he wanted to ask. It could not be finances. It might be stress from his studies, as he was at university. Jim was paying for his tuition to be a lawyer. Wiremu was planning to be a Māori Land lawyer, a subject he was passionate about.

He stepped out of the car, reaching into the back seat for the bags of KFC, a special treat when you did not go to suburbia often. They all went inside the caravan to have lunch. They had a secret signal if there was a topic that had to be discussed outside of the caravan, far enough away from electronic devices. Wiremu tipped the egg timer upside down; that was the signal. The three of them quietly looked at each other, part excitement, part fear.

They left the caravan after lunch and walked down to the beach. Wiremu did all the talking.

"I've been approached confidentially by a syndicate; they are looking for the right person to do a cash deal for one hundred pounds of top-quality dried marijuana heads; too paranoid to shift it themselves. They want a hundred K for the lot, and they'll arrange delivery almost all the way. Currently, the average market is paying three K a pound. That's a two K profit on each pound."

Wiremu went on. "There are ten people in the syndicate, which you would think increases the risk of big mouths blabbing, but here's the catch: all ten people have too much to lose; they are all prison officers from Ngawha prison.

"The weed is currently on Great Barrier Island; they can get it to the mainland. I'm only dealing with the one guy, he's their spokesperson, he's doing part-time study with me at university. The other nine don't want to meet you or me; it's all down to just him and me doing the deal. They are only interested in the folding cash, no electronic transactions.

"Their idea is that if this is a successful operation, then they are prepared to do the same deal every year or even twice a year. They say they can guarantee a seamless transaction, no interest from the police or coastguard, apparently, they have that all under control, confidential inside information between government departments regarding their movements.

"Our only problem is getting it here once they get it to the mainland, which is going to be to either Auckland or Whangarei ports.

"Oh! One other thing, they want an answer by next week – tides and weather conditions are good, and they have annual leave."

"Fuck," said Jim, "that doesn't give us much time. I like the idea, beats the hell out of dragging our arses through the scrub every year. Let me think about it overnight, but tell them yes in the meantime, let's not lose the deal due to us fucking around."

Jim started talking fast like he did when he was executing orders and plans. "I will start on digging another hole with the digger; we're going to need to bury another container. I'll put it away from the house, start a new area. We can put a signpost above ground pointing in the direction of Barrier. Christ, we'll start an underground town at this rate.

"Jane, you go visit old man Bell down the road. Sweet talk him and his missus, I think her name is Helen. And ask if we can borrow their Winnebago. Tell them we're going on a holiday for a couple of days.

"Another question, why you, Wiremu? What made him ask you? Are you sure it's not a set-up, some undercover bust?"

"He knows us from school, big local family. If it turns pear-shaped, he'll bring a lot of shame on his old man. He's got as much to lose as we have. Said it started off just a couple of pounds a year, amateurs playing around, then they all went into a syndicate and bought a deceased estate of forty acres on the island. Turned out it had a huge greenhouse on it, good water supply, the rest just fell into place."

"If he goes for it, you can lend him Bell's Winnebago," said Jim. "It'll be safer if they don't unload at this end. Load it up over there, bring the vehicle back on the car ferry.

"Wiremu, you drive it straight from the port to here. We will give it a good clean, top the gas up. I'll give Bell half a beast as thanks for lending it to us and all that bullshit; everyone's happy.

"Hear that, Jane? You can hang up your camouflage gear. Might even be able to buy you a house now."

They all laughed and celebrated well into the night with some of Jim's homemade moonshine.

   MICHELLE THOMPSON

The End of the Hunt

Jane and Wiremu had temporarily relocated to Australia for one reason only. They had tracked the man who murdered Jim to Sydney. It was only a matter of time before he slipped up and stuck his head above ground and they would find him.

Since their arrival in Sydney, Wiremu had grown his hair long and dressed like a homeless person. He'd bought a thousand-dollar car that was barely roadworthy and set himself the undercover task of visiting all the lower-society hangouts frequented by drug addicts, alcoholics, and unregistered sex workers. He lurked around alleys and Centrelink locations waiting for a break. Back home in New Zealand, he had someone checking Alan Peters' mother's mailbox daily for any clues, with no results. Today, his own surveillance paid off.

It had been a chance sighting; he'd caught a glimpse of a pale, balding, ginger-haired man in grey oversized sweatpants with a bag of groceries, waiting to catch a bus in Redfern as he was driving past. Call it a sixth sense or his brother Jim guiding him from another dimension, but his gut told him this was Peters!

By the time Wiremu managed to turn around, the bus had picked the fat bastard up. He took a gamble and followed the bus. It hadn't travelled far when it stopped at the train station. Wiremu's heart sank. He couldn't get a park, and he couldn't stop in traffic; this place was chaos. If Peters was catching a connecting train, it could take Wiremu weeks to identify him for sure.

Wiremu slowed to a crawl. Horns were tooting at him, people swearing. Another lucky break: he caught the man he had been trying to follow leave the station and head around the corner, down Little Everleigh Street.

Seeing a gap in the traffic. Wiremu made a right turn. He motored past Peters and parked a little way down the street. Peters was still walking his way. The groceries looked heavy, Peters' face was red and shiny with sweat, his underarms drenched, forming a ring on his T-shirt. Wiremu hung his head down as Peters came closer, pretending to look at his phone.

Peters stopped right beside Wiremu's parked car. Wiremu was shaking with adrenaline. Had he been spotted?

Peters was paranoid, looking up and down the street. He wore a lanyard around his neck that he pulled out from his sweaty top and fitted the key on the end into the door of an industrial building, took another look up and down the street, then entered the building.

Wiremu took a moment to regain his composure. Tears running down his face, he looked to the sky. "Brother, I've found him."

Two years of looking had finally paid off. He took a photo of the doorway before heading back to tell Jane. His relief and grief were overwhelming; he blubbered like a baby all the way back to Jane's house.

Jane knew the second she saw his face – the time had come.

They planned to do a drive-by past Peters' place when it got dark to case out the street – surveillance cameras, neighbours, night activity – then take turns watching the place during the day. At night, they would watch together; it was a bad neighbourhood. They would do a property search, find the blueprints to the building, so they knew the layout. Might even be an idea to rent another industrial building on the street. If she had to, she would buy the neighbouring fucking building.

They were going to be busy from now on, so Jane would give up the Tuesday run driving the truck.

Jane and Wiremu hadn't discussed the details of how they were going to kill Peters, but they both wanted him to suffer before he died.

When they left New Zealand, Jane had hidden a pistol in their shipping container, breaking it down into pieces and spreading them amongst their belongings. The gun was untraceable and would disappear into the sea after its use. Through Wiremu's contact, they also had a taser, something to subdue Alan Peters first before they took their wrath out on him.

Waiting for darkness to fall had never felt so long.

—

They parked across the road from where Wiremu had positioned himself earlier in the day, but facing the opposite direction. The street was deadly quiet and devoid of people until about 1 am. Until then, the silence was only broken by the noise of trains and cars, with the more than occasional sound of police sirens.

Jane and Wiremu watched for weeks on end. All they saw were just your average citizens coming and going about their business; the days dragged.

     MICHELLE THOMPSON

The people of the night were silent and crept about, always looking over their shoulders, occasionally stopping to exchange small bags of drugs. Drunks would scavenge in the street looking for butts.

Peters had a straightforward routine. Each week, he would emerge on the same day, at the same time; this was more than likely his unemployment benefit day. He would catch the bus to the shopping centre close to where Wiremu originally discovered him. He would return later with a bag of groceries, always sweating like a pig. His only other daytime outing was to Regent House Methadone Clinic, which was within walking distance from his building.

The blueprints of the building suggested that it was a simple industrial garage set-up with a narrow set of stairs leading up to what would have originally been an office, a toilet, and a staff room.

Once a month, he received mail from New Zealand. Jane and Wiremu discovered this by scraping a piece of wire through the gap under his door and retrieving the envelope. In the envelope was another brown envelope containing his bank statement forwarded by his mother. The statement summary suggested that he was receiving money from his mother weekly. That and his benefit payment from the Australian Government probably made it just sustainable to continue to live here.

One night, about three months into watching him, an associate knocked on his door. From the body stance and build, they presumed it was a male, always in a long, hooded trench coat and heavy work boots. The man and Peters had a brief discussion, and the associate left. Peters met this same person two more times that month. The next time Jane and Wiremu saw the associate, both he and Peters met at Regent House for their methadone. After that, their meetings were more frequent, always brief.

Peters' behaviour changed, he started having more visitors, they were in and out, quick transactions. The associate would drop off a parcel, Peters would have a quick succession of visitors, a repeat cycle.

Peters started going out more. Then the associate brought a car to the unit, and they parked it in the garage. It was Jane and Wiremu's first view inside. It looked like the garage had been empty up until that time. The car was a tidy-looking 2005 Holden Commodore Sedan. When Jane had the plates traced, they came back as not stolen, but she couldn't work out the Aussie system. The car had been registered to someone outside the state of NSW for some time.

As days turned into weeks and then months, Jane and Wiremu had to ask, was Peters going to get away on them? This new friend, and the probability Peters was earning an income from his frequent visitors, could mean he was likely to move on, and they might lose track of him again.

Their options were either to break in when he wasn't home and wait for him, or simply knock on the door like the other drug buyers and overpower him from there with the taser.

Another decision also had to be made soon: to start the process to leave Australia for good. Once they had killed him, the plan was to board a flight back to NZ that same night. So, all their business affairs had to be tidied up by then, sell the business, the house, the vehicles. Cut ties with anyone they had made acquaintances with.

—

Jane felt bad when she announced to Doug and Stacey that she was giving up the driving on the Tuesday run as she was in the process of selling the company and would be too busy to do both, which technically wasn't a lie. She felt bad because she liked them, and they had pretty much been her only friends the whole time she'd been in Australia.

There was a long, awkward silence after her announcement. Stacey spoke first. "What are your plans once the business is sold?"

"We're going back to NZ. I've got a farm to run, top of the North Island and Wiremu's got a law degree he needs to finish."

Doug just stood there, no words. He looked at Jane sceptically, nodded a few times, then just said, "I'll pick you up for lunch tomorrow and we will talk about it, 11 am sharp." Then he just walked away.

Confused, Jane looked at Stacey for an answer. Stacey just shrugged her shoulders and said, "That's Doug."

"But I haven't told him where I live."

"Oh, he knows, don't worry about that. Eleven o'clock sharp. I'd wear your bike gear if I were you."

With that, Stacey gave her a big hug and retreated to her office, leaving Jane standing on the warehouse platform.

     MICHELLE THOMPSON

The Exchange

Wiremu stood on the street outside the SeaLink Ferry building entrance and watched the ferry slowly idle its way to the loading and unloading ramp for vehicles. He'd had a nervous four-and-a-half-hour wait for the ferry once he had news that it had departed Great Barrier. He had been able to walk from the city bus station to this point, although he was still sure he was being watched by someone else, other than his brother and sister-in-law. He didn't look around; he didn't want to appear nervous, although that is exactly what he felt.

The deal was the Winnebago would leave the terminal and park, the driver and his mate would jump out, a brief exchange of handshakes and exchange of identical backpacks and then Wiremu would jump in and drive straight to Cape Reinga. They had prearranged to leave a full jerrycan of diesel in the vehicle, so Wiremu didn't need to stop for gas on the five hours, twenty-one-minute journey. If he needed a bathroom, he could stop and use the one in the Winnebago.

Wiremu could see the vehicle unloading from the ferry. It glided smoothly towards him and parked up.

His mate jumped out, let out a huge breath and a massive fart. "Fuck that was intense bro; nearly shit myself a couple of times."

He gave Wiremu a big hug, fumbled around with the backpack he dragged through the door of the vehicle and swapped it with the backpack that Wiremu had positioned between his feet.

"It's all yours, bro, see you at Uni next week." They both started laughing; it was the nerves.

Wiremu got in the driver's seat, remembering all the things his older brother Jim had told him to do over and over again; familiarised himself again with the vehicle's tricks, lights, indicators, window wipers, tested the brakes. Like Jim said, no use drawing the attention of the police by doing something silly, like trying to activate wipers or indicators on the opposite side of the steering wheel from what he was used to in his own car.

As Wiremu drove, he followed the directions they had gone over previously, looking for Jane's car up ahead as she pulled out to lead the way back onto the motorway heading north, knowing that Jim would pull out soon and follow behind at a safe distance. Jim was making sure of two things, one that they weren't followed, and two that if Wiremu did have to ditch the vehicle and run that Jim would be in a position to pick him up if needed. His nerves started to settle once he saw Jane up ahead.

They had agreed to complete phone silence until they got back to Kaitaia. Unless it was an emergency, all phones were turned off on the way to Auckland the day before. Right now, Wiremu wished he could talk to Jane. She had a way of calming everything down, but seeing her up ahead was enough for now.

—

Jim had dropped Wiremu off at the bus station earlier that morning. He'd then made his way to the SeaLink terminal on Hamer Street in Auckland. He parked his car about a hundred metres up the road and walked back towards the terminal. He walked right past, careful to take a mental note of the cars parked along the way. His disguise was simple: dark glasses and an All Blacks' cap. He was taking a risk if they were being watched that he would be recognised, but it was a risk he was willing to take if it meant calling the deal off to save Wiremu.

It was a busy place, and it reminded him of the reasons why they didn't live in a city, the noise, the pollution, and the wankers. Everyone seemed in a hurry or on drugs. It certainly made him thankful for what he had at home.

Due to the timing of the ferry, it was easy to see the pattern in the parking change throughout the day. The nine-to-five workers had come and gone, the dog walkers and the runners had arrived. Jim managed to find a perfect vantage point to park and monitor the cars as the car park filled and emptied to coincide with the arrival and departure of the ferry. So far, nothing was causing him alarm.

He watched Jane's car pull up a little further down the road and find a parking space. She didn't acknowledge him as she passed him; she was too smart for that. He couldn't help but think how much he loved that woman as she drove past and parked. Nothing on this earth would make him want to spend a day away from her, and it was the same for Jane; he felt confident about that fact. He always smiled when he saw her. She just had that effect on everyone.

The ferry was due in any minute now. Wiremu had walked from the bus station and was standing in his spot outside the ferry building, backpack in his possession.

Then he saw it, a slow-moving car, just creeping along looking for a park. The number plate surround had a Whangarei car dealership logo on it, so he knew it was from up north. There was only one person in the car. Jim knew this was going to be the Winnebago driver's transport. Jim didn't get a burning feeling in his nerve endings; he didn't sense danger. The driver was ringing someone, probably the Winnebago driver, letting him know the location of the park.

The Winnebago's nose was just pulling out of the ferry terminal entrance.

It parked, and the driver got out. Jim recognised him instantly. He was a local boy; his father was high up in local politics. Yes, he did have a lot to lose.

Wiremu and the driver exchanged hugs, a bit of 'bromance', then it was over. They swapped backpacks. Made it look like it was an easy exchange. Wiremu jumped in the driver's seat and pulled away. Jane pulled out in front of him. She had practised the route several times, there would be no fuck-ups.

Jim watched till the Winnebago was out of sight. He'd catch it up easily.

The driver looked up and down the street, then he walked directly to the waiting car and got in the front seat. Both men inspected the contents of the backpack. They high-fived each other, their body language suggesting they were very happy. As they pulled away, they turned around and drove back past Jim. They didn't recognise him; they were too obsessed with the contents of the backpack.

Jim pulled out slowly and proceeded to catch up to the Winnebago. He finally let out a long breath.

A Date With Destiny

Jane heard the bike before she saw it, noisy bloody thing. Doug was obviously making an entrance. As he pulled up, she felt a slight flutter in her heart. Doug was grinning from ear to ear. He certainly looked happy with himself. He also looked exceptionally cool.

It was 11 am sharp. Jane was dressed in a black leather jacket that looked like it was tailored to fit her, straight-legged jeans over her boots, her hair tied back. She put her helmet on, then her dark glasses. Neither of them spoke. It was intense.

She threw her leg over the bike and settled herself into him. He reached around and patted her thigh, giving it a hint of a squeeze. She knew what to expect. He would roar off at high speed, making as much noise as possible. Jim would have done the same.

Jane held on tight for the first few gear changes. She felt safe; he obviously had a lot of experience riding the bloody thing.

As they headed towards the coast, she knew one thing for sure, she'd have a sore arse tomorrow, it had been a while since she had been on a bike. She had kept Jim's bike – it had been parked up in the garage since his death. The memories of their trips brought a lump to her throat.

Eventually, around two hours later, they arrived at Port Stephens. Doug pulled up at a casual little restaurant called Poyer's. He had already booked a table.

It was a hot day, so Jane peeled off her jacket, revealing a V-neck T-shirt. Doug held her helmet while she squeezed life back into her bum. As she bent over, he could see down her cleavage; he liked what he saw. Her tits were firm and full, not like old spaniel ears – flat empty sacks.

He spoke for the first time, "You're the only woman I've ever let on the back of my bike, other than Mellissa."

"Does that mean I have to sleep with you now?" retorted Jane.

They both laughed, but he quickly said, "Yes."

Doug took her hand and led her towards the restaurant door. The owners knew him and made a fuss of him, giving him the best table. They were interested in his new friend; it was the only time he had been there with a different woman since his wife had died. They were very excited and offered them a special menu.

Jane's first priority was the bathroom and a drink, in that order. Doug ordered a large beer for Jane and a juice for himself, as he was often targeted by the police, and they would test him for alcohol whenever they saw him.

While Jane was in the bathroom, she could overhear the staff out the back having a little gossip about Doug, someone even called her a 'lucky bitch'. Jane smirked to herself. She had to admit she was really enjoying his company. The ride was great, but she wasn't sure about the sleeping with him bit; that wasn't on her agenda. One thing was for sure: she was hungry and thirsty; she was going to make the most of her day. She would ring and check on Wiremu later, see how the surveillance was going and update him on her day. Wiremu had been supportive of her going for a ride with Doug; he didn't mind him, and it was only a matter of days before they left the country.

Doug got straight to the point. He wanted to know what her departure plans were. He asked a few questions in quick succession: What date were they leaving? What if the business hadn't sold? Would that delay things? Did she want him to buy the business? Was money a problem?

She didn't want to lie to him, but she didn't want to involve him in her shit either. She told him the departure date. He was shocked that it was so soon, two days' time. Money wasn't an issue. In fact, she was selling the company below market value, so he could buy it if he wanted.

For the rest of the afternoon, Doug shared stories about Mellissa, his children, and the farm, and he gave an edited version about Orhan, saying how he had bonded with him as if he were his own son. He had a lot to say; his lifestyle and reputation meant there were few people he could share these things with.

"Stacey's my wingman," said Doug. "Maybe, when we get to know each other a bit better, I'll explain things in more detail. For now, it's best I don't say too much."

Before she realised it, hours had passed, and Doug was suggesting they head back to the city before it got dark.

Jane made a phone call to Wiremu, they talked in code, 'everything was quiet on the western front'.

As Doug listened in, he knew that it was a secret language, some Māori words to throw him off track. But he did laugh when she held the phone up and said, "No, I'm not going to sleep with him tonight," and told Wiremu off, "he can hear you!"

Doug talked back to the phone, "I'm trying, mate." He looked Jane directly in the eyes. She could see he was serious. She felt her face flush bright red.

They collected their belongings and prepared for the ride home. Doug pushed some cash into the restaurant owner's hands and refused to take no for an answer. The owners hugged Jane and hoped they would see her again.

Doug helped Jane with her helmet strap. She was a little drunk, and her coordination was a little off. She certainly was a bundle of humour.

She held on tight; he was going to try and make it home in half the time.

When they arrived at Jane's house, Wiremu was waiting in the drive. He apologised to Doug. "Sorry mate. Normally, I'd invite you in for a drink, but something's come up and I need Jane to come with me."

Doug seemed to understand and thanked Jane for the outing, kissed her on the cheek and left.

Jane felt a sense of loss when he left. Was it the alcohol?

Wiremu wanted to do one last practice run. Time the trip to Peters' house and time the trip to the airport. He didn't want anything unforeseen to happen in two days' time.

Reminiscing

The trip with Doug on the bike had brought back memories, making sleep impossible for Jane. It had taken years for her to become safe in her own skin. Sleeping pills helped, and although the pill bottle said not to be taken with alcohol, she found no other way to escape her grief.

Jim had never been able to sleep on a stormy night, and the night of his death was no different. "Good night for thieves," he would say, every time there was a storm.

There had been a random pair of visitors earlier in the week, couple of guys with a bullshit story about looking for a lost pig dog. Jim didn't wear it at all, told them to fuck off. He recognised one of the men, a skinny, local no-hoper who he knew had drifted in and out of jail for years. The other was a fat ginger guy. Jim didn't know who he was but felt the hairs on his neck stand up when he saw his crimson face with a matching neck of blubber.

Jim remained agitated after their departure and set about hiding anything of value in different parts of the property.

Two days later, the wind had blown in hard from the east, a direct hit on the property. Gusts of dirt and sand periodically blasted the windows, the trees shaking loose any unwanted leaves and branches. As night fell, Jim lay awake next to Jane, eyes wide in the darkness.

Jane awoke to Jim, with his hand over her mouth, his weight upon her. He spoke slowly and quietly. "Shh. I heard a noise at the back door, someone's trying to prise it open."

Jim got up quietly and looked out the windows. In the shadows, he saw the darkened form of a person, using the moonlight between cloud cover to move around the property. As they headed towards the house, Jim caught the outline of the second man, carrying something long and thin. Jim's guess was either a crowbar or a gun.

Jim whispered in Jane's ear, "Quickly, take the blanket and hide in the closet. Now! I'll shut it after you. Do not come out of the closet until I give the word that it's safe. Remember, the code word is blue. If you don't hear from me or hear the code word blue, and you have no choice, dial 111 for the police. I love you."

Once she was in the closet, she could hear him moving a set of drawers up against the door.

There was silence for a long time, then the first gunshot. Fear raced through her body like electricity. Another long silence followed. Every part of her wanted to call out for Jim, to hear if he was alive or not.

The second shot rang out, shattering the night. This shot sounded different, closer. A different gun. Jane listened for a long time; the confusing sounds mixed with the battering wind.

A third shot boomed out, same sound and distance as the last one.

Another long silence, then Jane thought she could hear a car drive off, spinning stones on their gravel driveway in the distance.

Jane's heart broke. A light inside her was dying. She knew Jim was dead.

Jane found her phone and dialled Wiremu's number, her fingers shaking so much she had difficulty pressing the buttons. Wiremu's phone went to voicemail; it was 3 am. Her next call was emergency services.

—

Jim had crawled along the floor, standing only to look out the windows, trying to catch a glimpse of the intruders. As the fast-moving clouds parted and the moonlight lit up the grounds, he could see a man aiming a gun in his direction. Jim stood upright to take the shot. As he fired, he saw the man go down. Just then, from behind him came another gunshot at close range. There was someone in the house who was now in the same room as Jim.

Jim lay on the ground. He knew the gunshot wasn't going to be fatal; he felt no pain for some reason, perhaps it was the adrenaline. The shot had taken his legs out, and he'd lost the grip on his rifle when he went down. Out of the darkness, the man with the shotgun appeared, standing over him. Jim recognised him.

Peters stepped out into the moonlight as it lit up the room, laughing. The next shot was at close range; the shotgun pressed to Jim's chest.

Peters dragged Jim's body out into the moonlight and turned him over to check that Jim was dead. He contemplated going back inside to find the wife but changed his mind, the bitch would have heard the shots and called the pigs by now. He ran for his car and drove off.

     MICHELLE THOMPSON

Jim didn't want to die; he didn't want to leave his Jane. Darkness fell over his eyes.

—

Hours had passed since Jane made the call to emergency services. She heard a helicopter in the distance. It was just going on 6 am: the remoteness of the property had made the rescue difficult. She could tell from her hiding place in the closet that daylight was just breaking from the east. Then she heard the voices of men yelling in the back yard. "Two dead!"

"Have you found the wife?"

A loudhailer boomed through the air, first letting out a shrill, high-pitched scream as it tuned, "Mrs Henare, it's the police. You're safe now. I have your brother-in-law here, Wiremu. He said the code word is blue."

The 111 operators had stayed on the line the whole time, trying to comfort Jane and keeping her abreast of the time frame and the movements of the emergency services. The call operator directed the officers to the closet.

Retribution

The car was packed with their hand luggage for the plane. Everything else was being shipped by a professional moving team, which included the contents of the house that were being donated to charity. The business was under contract with a private buyer, Jane suspected it was Doug. She and Wiremu would dump the car at the airport.

Jane and Wiremu sat in the car across the street from Peters' house, just waiting for the quiet that darkness would bring.

Activity had been unusually quiet at Alan Peters' residence for the last couple of days. They hadn't seen Peters or his drug-dealing associate for a couple of days, but they could see the light was on upstairs. No one had come knocking on the door looking for drugs. Wiremu hadn't seen Peters leave, so they hoped he hadn't moved on and they had missed it. It was an anxious wait. Jane had a bag which contained rope, the gun, nails, and a hammer. Wiremu had the taser, which he placed in the bag.

To complicate the issue, tonight there was a planned road closure and road workers at both ends of the street. Jane and Wiremu were let through without any questions.

If there was an investigation, Jane was sure they would be out of the country and back in New Zealand by the time security cameras picked up the car in the airport car park, but they would wear disguises, just in case, when they parked the car and reported it stolen.

Suddenly, the cloaked, hooded figure of Peters' drug-dealing friend appeared in the doorway of the house. He stood there briefly, just out of the light, then abruptly he bolted and started to run in their direction. In the darkness, he appeared to float in his cloak as he ran from the front door, directly across the road and swiftly made his way right up to their car window.

Wiremu and Jane hadn't factored in this scenario. Wiremu was frantically clutching around in the bag for the taser when a familiar voice said, "Quickly, lock your car up and come inside." He turned and raced back to the unit. The voice was muffled by the hooded cloak, but there was no mistaking who it

     MICHELLE THOMPSON

was. This was a twist they weren't expecting, although Jane wasn't surprised now that it was happening.

They both left the vehicle and hurried across the road and entered the building.

The hooded man beckoned them inside, shut the door behind them and, pulling back the hood, revealed his face; it was Doug. Wiremu just stared at him like a stunned mullet. Jane shook her head in disbelief and laughed.

Doug started giving orders, "I'll explain later. The fat ginger cunt is upstairs already tied up. Jane, do with him what you want.

"Wiremu, follow me. I've rigged the place up with enough explosives to blow it to China when we've finished.

"Jane, in case you don't get time to ask him, he told me it was a home invasion gone wrong. They were looking for drugs and money and the plan was to rape you and make Jim watch till he gave up where the dope and the cash were hidden. They had been casing the joint for weeks."

Jane walked up the stairs, her knees were weak, as though the energy had been sucked out of her. She had to snap out of it; this whole thing was surreal. She had to do this now and do it properly if she was ever going to have any peace of mind in the future. She straightened up, sucked in a deep breath, and made her way up the stairs.

Peters was a pitiful sight; he had been severely beaten. He lay on the floor, naked and hogtied, a stick of dynamite with a long fuse poking out of his bleeding anus. The colour of the bruising suggested that he had been like this for a couple of hours, maybe even a day. His teeth were all smashed out but were missing from the room.

His eyes met hers, and he started hissing blood and weeping like a baby. Jane had no sympathy. She walked around his pathetic body. She thought he was trying to say sorry, but as she got closer, she realised he was asking for help.

She laughed, "Help you! You killed my husband! Did you think you would get away with it forever?"

A wave of rage came over her. She was burning with a new sense of strength, a blind rage. Adrenaline kicked in.

Jane looked around; Doug had thought of everything. There was a pair of long-handled garden shears on the table, all bloodied and lying amongst some severed fingers. Jane picked the shears up and showed them to Peters.

She wanted to make sure Peters acknowledged that more pain was coming.

His tiny, limp, blue penis was barely visible below his fat guts. "And you were going to try and rape me with that? You fat, ginger, disgusting pig!" Jane dug the shears into his belly, catching the tip of his penis as she snapped the handles shut. Peters passed out from the pain.

Jane realised she still had the bag over her shoulder. She got the taser and shocked him back to consciousness. Fuck him, the least he could do was stay awake for the torture. She was just lining up his ball sacks when Doug and Wiremu appeared in the doorway.

"I'm nearly ready to blow this joint up, Jane. When I yell out, light the fuse, then get down the stairs and out of here as fast as you can."

Jane snapped the handles shut again, severing the left ball sack. Peters passed out again, blood pumping out the end of his severed penis. Doug handed her a lighter; he couldn't be prouder of her at that moment.

Wiremu tasered him again. There was blood everywhere. Wiremu lost traction on the slippery floor, falling heavily on Peters' naked body. He heard the air expel from Peters' lungs.

Wiremu went into a chant, like a Māori warrior about to go to war. From deep inside him, the passion, the grief, and the intent consumed his whole body, as though his ancestors were talking through him; it was dramatic and spine-chilling.

He got up, then slumped to the floor at the top of the steps, spent emotionally. He had dedicated every waking hour for two years to finding this murderous prick and avenging the death of his brother.

Doug yelled from the bottom of the stairs, "Light the fuse, Jane."

     MICHELLE THOMPSON

The Barrier Gang

Marijuana is always worth more around Christmas time in New Zealand. Jim's business plan was to wait and sell it for top dollar during this time of the year. But it's not easy to sell one hundred pounds of dope without attracting the attention of the police.

The plan was that any potential clients would have to buy in bulk. Cash up front wasn't always an option, so a taxed rate for 'on tick' was developed for the right clients, or they could pay by barter system.

Jim never sold to people he hadn't developed a long history and association with. They had to be either people he had been to school with, people he and Jane knew from their younger days or had some sort of verified connection with. Never extended family, they were always 'ratshit' at paying.

When Jim and Jane had been at the camp for misfit adolescents many years ago, Jim had come to the aid of a skinny white boy they had nicknamed 'Whitey', who was getting the shite kicked out of him by a couple of youths. Jim stepped in and swiftly evened up the score and fought the boys off, resulting in him and the skinny white boy becoming friends for life.

The skinny white boy grew into a tall, well-built man, thanks to the boxing lessons his parents had decided would be a good idea to stop him coming home with blackened eyes. He showed skill in the ring, even winning some amateur fights, then trialling for the Olympics. Years later, he was the owner of a boxing gym. Still the bad boy at heart, he loved motorcycles and joined a well-known motorcycle club, eventually becoming the president. His friendship with Jim and Jane had always been close, and with all his connections, he was a natural choice to become Jim's main middleman.

Through Whitey, Jim made key contacts within the gang network and secured a system to swap large quantities of cannabis for cash or assets.

Jim always met Whitey on back roads or, in some cases, delivered by courier, as they discovered that when cannabis was transported in oven bags there was no smell.

The men that Jim dealt with had good reputations, and he shared a mutual trust with them built over years of association. They didn't want to go to jail either, so paranoia made everyone careful. You always had to take precautions. The police weren't stupid and had the technology, the narks, and the undercovers; it could be a tricky path to negotiate.

But the police were the least of his problems. Thieves were everywhere, jealous bastards who just weren't happy to see you making money were worse than the thieves.

Jim bought and sold carefully and increased his net worth through shrewd dealings.

The Barrier Gang, Jim's nickname for the corrections officers, had increased production to twice a year. Everyone was kept busy.

Where Am I?

Jane could see a bright light. As her vision cleared, she could make out a completely white room, its brightness hurt her eyes. She tried to focus. She could see Jim. He was packing a strange, old, brown cardboard school travel bag on the bed. She tried to move her legs from under the bag, but her legs didn't work. Jim was looking at her, smiling. She tried to talk to him, but no sound came out of her mouth. She struggled harder, trying to move her legs as she tried to speak. Tears fell from the corners of her eyes and burned as they ran back towards her ears.

Jim finished packing the bag and clicked shut the shiny chrome catches. He finally spoke, "I'm leaving now, Jane, you're in safe hands." He bent forward and kissed her forehead. "I'm happy to leave you now." With that, he seemed to float out the door.

She was desperate to talk to him, but no words would come out. A flood of tears fell from her eyes, making her neck and pillow wet. *Where am I?* She felt foolish. Why couldn't she speak? Why couldn't she tell Jim how much she loved him and missed him?

Jane woke again, this time, there was no Jim. Was it hours, was it weeks? She had no concept of time, only the white room. She could barely make out a dark form in a chair close to her. She tried to focus on the shape, but her eyes hurt; everything hurt. She gave up trying and let sleep take over, just as she felt the reassuring warmth of a hand on hers – it was comforting and annoying all at once. She still couldn't move or speak.

Jane woke more often, each time managing to keep her eyes open a little longer than the last. The room was so white it was blinding, confusing. Now she could hear a faint constant beep; she must be in a hospital. The dark form in the chair was always there; she knew it was Doug; she could smell his cologne.

—

Jane had been awake for a while. Doug was still in the chair, asleep – he looked older, unshaven, stressed.

The door opened; it was Orhan. He smiled at her and placed a blanket around his father. Orhan moistened her lips with a wet cotton swab, then dabbed her face with a wet cloth. She lost consciousness again.

The next time she woke, she had an audience, lots of faces looking at her, all of them smiling and waving. Doug, who was now clean-shaven, ordered everyone to get out. He swabbed her mouth with the wet cotton, then tried to work the remote on the bed to sit her up a little. She noticed his hands were bandaged.

He looked down at her, "The doctor will be here shortly to check on you," he said. "You might not be able to talk for a while, so don't force it."

Jane wanted to ask what happened, but as if he could read her mind, Doug said, "Before you ask, I accidentally blew you up."

Was he grinning, or was that a nervous smile?

When she awoke next, the doctor was checking her oxygen, the drip, and her limbs; she could see her arms and legs were all bandaged. Any movement was extremely painful. The doctor wiped her eyes, and she could see blood on the cloth.

"Don't be alarmed," he said. "After an explosion like the one you were in, it's not uncommon to bleed blood tears, but I can assure you it's nothing to worry about. It will come right."

He left Jane's line of sight, and Doug reappeared. The doctor looked at Doug's hands and removed the bandages; they were more cut and bleeding than burned. He applied lotion and bandaged them again.

Jane had started to find her voice, and she had a lot of questions. She discovered she wasn't in hospital after all; she was in the room at Doug's house that he had converted into a medical room for his father when he was alive. And the doctor wasn't a real doctor, but Doug's funeral director. He'd studied to be a doctor once but got struck off for some reason that no one wanted to go into.

Doug's family took turns sitting with Jane. When it was Orhan's watch had told her that Doug had barely left her side except to shower and change when Orhan forced him. She had been there for three weeks.

Over the next few days, she had plenty of visitors: Edith and Gay Kenny came in for an hour every day, Stacey brought magazines and read to her, and

Doug's twin sons, Joseph and Kane, who had come home to live permanently along with Kane's wife Nazneen with their two children.

Doug's friends normally visited at night, all of them sporting bandages on their hands to some extent after they had helped dig her out of the rubble.

Naz took over Jane's medical and personal care, as she had trained as a nurse before she decided to have a family.

On one of the many family gatherings around the bed, Doug announced that he was going to retire from the day-to-day running of the companies and all his children would run them like a trust. He admitted that it would be difficult to let go, but he wanted to spend some time travelling and doing nothing. All the children thought that the doing nothing part was a joke, calling him a major control freak.

The grandchildren entertained Jane with their antics when they managed to get past Grandad and run riot in the medical room.

The best and the saddest surprise for Jane was a visit from Wiremu. This time he was clean-shaven, had had a haircut and was wearing a suit. He looked sharp. He was sporting a scar on his forehead from the explosion, but other than that, he had no major injuries. He was about to catch a plane back home to New Zealand to finish his studies and check on the farm. Wiremu confirmed Jane's burning question. Alan Peters was one hundred per cent dead.

Jane had taken the full blast of the explosion, as she had been closest to the dynamite and had less time to get out of the room, whereas Wiremu and Doug had been blown into the street.

During her days of recovery, Doug spent every day by her bedside, issuing orders to everyone from his chair.

Jane and Doug grew closer, sharing stories about their lives. Doug's stories were a bit wilder than Jane's, but she wasn't fazed; he liked that about her, in fact, she laughed at the most gruesome details.

Jane told him how Jim had visited her in her dreams and how it gave her comfort that she had seen him. She felt she could lay him to rest now that she had eliminated his killer.

Undercover

Doug had spent hours following Jane; he had someone else following Wiremu. It didn't take long to piece the puzzle together; they were looking for Jim's killer. His men had a breakthrough the day Wiremu nearly caused a major accident by doing a U-turn on a busy highway outside the train station. They followed him to a street just around the corner from the station, and eventually to Alan Peters' place.

It could have been considered a bit creepy, Doug watching Jane, but it dispelled his paranoia knowing that she wasn't meeting with other men. It attracted him to her even more. His jealousy made him snap very easily, so knowing that she had no other male interest made him less manic.

—

It was relatively easy for Doug to befriend Alan Peters; he was a drug addict, and Doug had his medicine. Doug hated him immediately. He was a fat, useless fuck, unclean, always smelt of bad underarm odour, and to top it off he was a fuckin 'know-all'. Doug nicknamed him the Oracle; he was a bloody expert on everything, so many times, Doug wanted to punch him in the face!

Doug gained his confidence quickly as Peters was a greedy drug-taker who wanted more all the time. He worked out a deal with Peters to pay him rent to store a car in his garage, securing a key to the building so he could come and go when he wanted. Doug planned to fill the car with explosives to make sure the evidence of his killing would be covered up with a huge explosion.

Doug was concerned that his cover would be blown on numerous occasions. There were times that he passed Wiremu on the street outside the addiction clinic, but the hood on his cloak looked more like a monk's habit, so he could hunker down inside his disguise. He even stopped wearing aftershave on these occasions so he could smell more like Peters.

When Jane announced that she was going back to New Zealand he knew he would have to step up the plan and keep a closer eye on her, that's when he decided to take her out for the day to nail down the date and time of her departure flight, which he figured would be her escape plan.

As they got closer to the moment of Peters' premeditated murder, Doug planned the fake road closure due to an alleged gas leak in the street. Men in high-visibility vests and hard hats with stop and go signs never seemed to get questioned.

Doug went to the house a couple of days before and took the car out. When he returned, the trunk was full of explosives. He told Peters the car was running rough, and he needed to do some work on it.

Doug had decided to stage the fake roadblocks at either end of the road just in case he needed a quick escape route. Timing was everything. If there was going to be an explosion, it had to be timed to coincide with the arrival or departure of a train which ran on the tracks behind the industrial units where Peters lived; this would help to mask the noise.

On the morning of the attack, Peters was playing his part as the Oracle, telling Doug how to fix the timing on the car, while greedily sucking up Doug's free cocaine through a straw on the kitchen table upstairs, with his back to Doug. Peters sickened Doug; he was the ultimate lazy slob.

In one swift movement, Doug bludgeoned Peters on the head with a large crescent spanner, stupefying him briefly, then knocking him unconscious as the blows rained down on him.

Peters had been so sure of himself, he didn't see it coming. Doug hogtied him with cable ties and continued to beat him and humiliate him. The torture lasted for several hours until Doug got the information from him that he needed. Information that he would later relate back to Jane in detail.

—

It was time, he received the call from one of his team, using their burner phone, that Jane and Wiremu had just entered the roadblock. Doug went downstairs and bolted across the road under the cover of darkness to the shocked Wiremu and Jane as he hurriedly beckoned them to come into the unit.

Doug derived some satisfaction watching Jane and Wiremu take out their grief on Peters. In a way, he found it therapeutic for the death of Mellissa, and he liked a good murder.

Everything had been going to plan, but it all went horribly wrong when he yelled out to Jane to light the fuse of the dynamite stick protruding out of Peters' rectum. Doug had let a little too much LPG go, and Jane igniting the fuse caused a chain reaction with the gas and the dynamite in the boot of the car.

In hindsight, it was a miracle they all didn't die. Their saving grace was the age of the building and the tired brickwork. The building crumbled in the massive explosion, and they all got blown onto the street with the rubble. Doug's men, who had been stationed at both ends of the street, had to suddenly abandon their stations and rescue their mate. They all dug frantically, first uncovering Doug, then Wiremu, and together they all got stuck in to find Jane.

At first, Doug thought he had killed her; she was limp and blue. He started CPR in the car while Brian drove, and they rushed her to Doug's funeral director's private residence. The others took care of Wiremu and the scene, including disposing of his old car in the process.

By the time the firemen and ambulance arrived, who had initially been delayed by receiving the wrong directions, everyone had drifted off into the night. The human remains would have to be sent away for DNA identification.

The Long Road to Recovery

It was accepted without saying that Jane was going to stay for a while at Doug's house. Doug had not asked her outright, but talked with her as if she were a permanent fixture, involving her in household decisions.

His two grandchildren called her Nana. They all had Arabic names that she could never remember, so she just collectively called them 'Minions'. She discovered they were great at fetching things for her and eager to do little tasks, anything to get out of homeschooling.

Doug had bought her a walking frame, and together with the help of the whole family, she could get around the house and was covering more and more distance every day.

Doug had moved her hospital bed into his room next to his bed, and like a couple of school children, they would laugh and giggle all night, telling stories, until Orhan, who lived in their wing of the house, would come in and tell them off.

Jane was recovering well. She had received burns to her hands and arms, but the rest of her body had sustained the impact of the explosion, and the crushing weight of the bricks on her ribs had collapsed her right lung. She had also suffered blunt force trauma to her pelvis and legs.

Doug's hands were now out of bandages and had almost healed.

Jane, Doug and Orhan lived like a married couple with a son. They continued the tradition of Doug and Orhan's morning ritual of having breakfast together. They would all put on their reading glasses and read the newspapers, drink tea and engage in adult banter. Jane just fitted in; it was never awkward.

It was during one of these morning rituals that it dawned on Jane that the whole time she had been unconscious, she had been naked. When she asked Doug if he had looked under the sheets, he laughed, "Yes, all the time."

Orhan's face went bright red, which was difficult for his already tanned skin.

Jane whacked Doug playfully with her paper, to which he replied, "I thought I should inspect the goods before I bought them." And without looking up from his paper announced, "You agreed to marry me when you woke up from your coma."

There was an awkward silence for a minute before Jane asked, "Where's the ring?"

Doug laughed, pounced to his feet and scrambled around in the butler's pantry, leaving Orhan with his mouth hanging open, unable to speak. Jane wore the same expression as she watched Doug's movements with a surprised look.

Doug returned from the pantry. "Close your eyes and put out your hand." He got down on one knee and produced a Cheezels ring. "You can open your eyes now. Will you marry me?"

Jane let out a whoop, "The answer is yes, but I'll be wanting a better ring," she grinned.

With that, Doug picked her up and kissed her, forgetting that she was still in pain from the explosion, and laughed that he'd nearly broken her ribs again.

Jane hugged Orhan next. He was so excited and was already planning the party.

Doug set off to wake up the rest of the family and ask them all to meet at the bar in Edith and Kenny's part of the house. All he told them was that he was going to make an announcement.

He returned to Jane and Orhan and asked them to meet him at Edith's part of the house, where the bar was, while he gathered everyone up, and he told Jane to make sure she was still wearing the Cheezels ring.

—

The whole family waited impatiently, trying to guess what the impromptu meeting was about. Imaginations running wild, Naz and Kane had unknowingly already guessed right. Gay Kenny thought it was a baby. Everyone was happy and laughing, the noise level loud for an early morning gathering.

Jane, with the help of Orhan, was shuffling along with her Zimmer frame. Doug was clapping his hands in agitated excitement, trying to get everyone to shut up.

As Jane got closer, Doug asked her to show everyone her hand with the Cheezels ring, which she did with a royal wave, and laughingly assured them all she would refrain from eating the ring on dark days. This was met with cheers and congratulations, but before anyone could hug her, Doug silenced them again by raising both his hands. He positioned himself between his family and Jane, saying, "I have one more surprise." They all fell silent.

"Is it a baby?" yelled Kenny.

Doug took the Cheezels ring from Jane's finger and threw it to Orhan. He dug around in his pocket and pulled out a beautiful diamond and emerald ring. They all gasped at its beauty and brilliance. All Jane could say was, "Wow."

"Officially," said Doug, "will you do me the honour of being my wife and life partner?"

"Yes," said Jane, "and hurry up and put the bloody ring on my finger. I need a drink."

Someone popped a champagne cork, and the family showered them with a flood of congratulations.

Doug turned to Edith and Kenny. "One of you get on the phone and invite Stacey and all our close friends to come and help celebrate."

Doug tapped his glass. "I'd like to make a toast." He turned to Jane and raised his glass. "Jane, welcome to the family."

The room erupted with cheers, everyone talking at once. Edith was crying with joy at the announcement and said she couldn't think of a better new mother. Kenny was already wanting to go shopping with Jane for the wedding dress, Joseph wanted to teach Jane to sail, and Naz and Kane said they already knew she was their kids' new nana.

When Stacey arrived and suggested that Doug didn't knock this one off as he might be outnumbered this time, they all laughed raucously and agreed. More people arrived, and the festivities continued. Everyone said they had been expecting it.

When no one was listening, Doug whispered in her ear, "Speaking of knocking something off, can I sleep with you now?"

Jane laughed. "You could have ages ago, but you didn't ask!"

Headline News

Orhan was frantically tapping the front page of the morning paper. He brought the article to Doug's attention.

The CIA had arrested the head of a notorious drug cartel – Paulo Hernandez. There was a picture of Paulo smiling for the camera, with his arms pinned behind his back, escorted by an army of armed CIA officers in full assault gear, all their faces covered with balaclavas to avoid recognition. Paulo was dressed in a bright red silk suit, forever the show pony.

The story went on to inform the unknowing of his wealth and connections, and his history of criminal activities. It was almost complimentary; they were making a hero of him, thought Doug. Following Paulo's arrest, there had been mayhem and protests in the streets and riots in the prisons. Paulo was portrayed as a charismatic individual who was well-respected and loved by the people for his generosity and care for the poor. The date of the trial was not published to avoid possible attempts to disrupt the process. And the location of his incarceration was also being kept secret from the public.

Doug blew air out of his cheeks. He smelled a rat. If it was true, he felt sorry for the little bastard. He was a rotten little shite, but he liked him.

Jane remembered the story Doug had told her of his first encounter with Paulo in the cell, and, by all accounts, on some level, Paulo sounded like a likeable character.

Something about the article made Doug uncomfortable; he had a premonition that something was about to happen. He would try to put it out of his mind for now. He would talk about it later with Jane, get her spin on it.

—

Things around the farm returned to relative normality for Doug's world.

Every day, Jane got stronger and fitter. She couldn't be in one place for too long; cabin fever made her determined to get out and about. She loved Doug, but fuck he was intense! He was by her side every minute, so getting out gave her a much-needed break for her sanity.

There were a variety of activities to keep her active, horse riding and farm work with Orhan, learning to sail with Joseph in Stacey's yacht, which she had gifted to the twins after Rod's death, and shopping with Gay Kenny.

She still had to tread gently at times, the pain was still present, but she didn't want to rely on painkillers, although she often preached there was a pill for everything.

There was so much going on: a wedding to plan, which Edith and Orhan seemed to be taking care of, Naz was home schooling the grandchildren who took any opportunity to escape and follow Nana everywhere, until Doug made a rule that they didn't come into their part of the house after 5.pm, and Edith had architects in, building on an extension for Kane and Naz and the children.

Meanwhile, Joseph came and went as he pleased, a roaming bachelor who still had no plans to settle down. Jane would spend hours on the ocean with Joseph. He was the quiet one, but possibly the most like his father in many ways. He shared his thoughts freely with Jane – nothing shocked her – how he always felt that he was born into something he couldn't get out of, but at the same time, he loved the notoriety. He loved sailing and he used Jane as an excuse to get out of work on the greenhouses. Kane didn't care; he thought he was running them better than his father and didn't need Joseph's help.

Jane loved the freedom of the ocean and the wind, and the yacht had been meticulously looked after and restored.

Then there were the bike rides with Doug. For these, she needed the painkillers for bumps in the road. Sometimes both boys came on their bikes, but more often it was just Joseph and Doug's friends. Often Jane would pinch herself; it didn't seem real that she could actually feel this happy. She discussed this with Doug often, and he said he felt happy too, for the first time in a long time.

Stacey

Doug was woken very early by a phone call from Stacey's daughter. When Doug answered the call, he said straight away, "I know what you're going to tell me."

She was letting Doug know first; Stacey had died in her sleep. They spoke briefly, he asked the usual questions, wanting to know the details, then hung up. A suspected heart attack, sudden, unexpected, yet peaceful. It was fortunate that Stacey's daughter and her husband and children had driven up from Melbourne, where they lived and worked, a couple of days ago. The visit had been a surprise for the school holidays, so the family had spent a few great days with Stacey before she passed. No one had suspected she had any health conditions. Doug had never heard Stacey complain about her health, ever. This was a sad day for them all.

Doug and Stacey had been close; they had spent their lives covering for each other in all sorts of situations. Doug would often refer to Stacey as his 'wingman' – 'today he had lost his wingman' would be part of his eulogy at her funeral.

Doug went into autopilot. He got out of bed, leant over and kissed Jane and said he would be gone a while – he needed to do the rounds knocking on doors to deliver the bad news. Then he quietly got in the car and went to Stacey's house alone.

He stayed with Stacey, holding her hand until the doctor and police formally pronounced her dead and the funeral director took the body away. Stacey's daughter and Doug decided that the best place to bring her home to rest was Doug's place, where she'd worked, and where the people she'd spent most of her life with were. She would have liked that. Stacey had been a mother to hundreds of young people over the years and a trusted mate of Doug's friends. It seemed fitting to give her the last send-off from there.

The days that followed seemed to have the joy taken out of them; even the grandchildren were quiet for a change. The place was abuzz with visitors and catering staff, all sombre. The sky even seemed to be in mourning, a dull, overcast grey, with no wind.

—

  MICHELLE THOMPSON

The funeral was a huge event. It took both Doug and Jane back to their own lost partners. It was exhausting and left them both tired and drained. Doug made Jane promise she would never leave him. On that day, they made a pact: not even death would separate them. When they left this earth, it would be together.

Never one to miss an opportunity, Doug made Stacey's daughter a generous cash offer to buy Stacey's house, which she accepted immediately. She never wanted to return to the property. She understood the significance of Doug and her mother's friendship, and she wasn't stupid; without Doug's support, they would have had a much different life. It was handy knowing that if she ever needed help, Doug would be the best person to ring, but she wasn't about to explain anything about him to her husband, who had led a sheltered life.

Doug gave all his kids the option to move into Stacey's place, but they decided that Joseph could live there. Maybe he'd be able to find a woman to put up with him. The jokes and the ribbing that took place at Joseph's expense lightened the mood.

Joseph suggested that Orhan move in with him, but Doug protested. "He's not leaving me, who will look after Jane and me when we get old and incontinent?"

This last comment was met with a chorus of voices, "Eeewww," followed by laughter.

Doug made a toast to Stacey. "To the best wingman a bloke ever had." They raised their glasses and drank into the night in Stacey's honour.

The next morning, a courier arrived with a parcel that could only be signed for by Doug. He was a little frustrated by the time they found him. Doug signed and took possession of the parcel.

The family stood around with guarded excitement, wondering what this little parcel was going to contain. It was a small, square, bubble-wrapped parcel, which was surprisingly heavy. There was no return address for the country of origin, but it was post-stamped from Colombia. When he cut the parcel open and emptied the contents, two gold rings and a solid gold chain tumbled onto the table. A note followed, which simply read: *Fake news. I need your help, come find me.*

Fancy a Trip to Colombia?

Doug, Jane, Joseph and Orhan stepped off the plane into the air-conditioning of the Bogotá Airport. They collected their luggage and headed for the arrivals hall. Waiting for them was the chauffeur from the tour company, holding a travel card with their name on, 'Henderson Family: Exotica Travel Tours'.

It was Jane's idea to pose as a honeymoon couple on a seven-day tour. Doug had wanted to go alone originally, but he didn't want to leave Jane for any length of time. Then Joseph decided that Doug wasn't as young as he used to be and might need a backup. After all, this was Colombia. Then Orhan had a premonition that something was going to happen to Doug and wanted to go to Colombia as well.

Doug threw his toys out of the cot with frustration at one stage and said no one was going. Finally, Jane put her foot down and made the decision, they would all go, experience the tour, and both she and Orhan would come home via New Zealand. Joseph and Doug would stay on if it became necessary.

Jane was bored shitless and wanted to travel or do something away from the house and the farm life. They booked a couple of suites at the Marriott. Doug agreed it would be a good excuse for a honeymoon.

Doug and Jane had got married before the trip. Wiremu had come over for the wedding. His visit made Jane homesick for New Zealand. He had graduated from law school, but was finding there wasn't a lot of work in his field, not if he wanted to stay close to home and manage the family land at the same time.

As Jane and Orhan entered the hotel foyer to check in at the reservations desk, Doug and Joseph collected the luggage. They had deliberately travelled light with one piece of luggage each, but as the driver handed the bellhop the luggage from the trunk, Doug noticed an extra bag. He was about to tell the driver that this bag was not theirs when the driver took his hand firmly and placed the handle in Doug's grip.

He moved close to Doug to be heard over the noise of the traffic around him. "It's my understanding that you will be needing this extra luggage, sir."

With that, and without making eye contact, he closed the trunk and returned to the driver's seat and drove away.

The family regrouped at reception; the staff were treating them like VIPs, with free cocktails on offer any time in the bar, and a banquet dinner with a private chef for the honeymoon couple and family. They decided to meet later at a set time for drinks. In the meantime, the boys were free to go their own way, while Doug and Jane retired to their room.

As Doug and Jane made their way up to their floor in the elevator, Jane noticed the new suitcase gripped firmly in Doug's hand. He looked down at the bag and jokingly said, "I don't think it's a bomb."

When they got to their room, Doug placed the bag on the end of the bed to examine the contents. On opening it, he discovered the items inside were a thoughtfully provided Colombian necessity. They included two Glock pistols, ammunition, and two small-sized Kevlar vests, which he presumed were for Jane and Orhan. There was a simple note: *See you in seven days. Enjoy the tour.* There was no point wondering how Paulo knew that Jane and the boys had come with him. Paulo would have been tracking them as they boarded the first plane in Chile en route to Bogotá, possibly even from their departure from Australia.

The one good thing about the next seven days for Doug was the joy they brought Orhan and Jane; with umpteen silly photos, nice food, lots of laughter, and everywhere they went, they were treated like royalty. Not surprisingly, they were the only people on the tour, so the tour company had swapped the normal bus service for an SUV, which was much more comfortable and, Doug now discovered, the vehicle was armoured, courtesy of Paulo, he presumed.

Joseph pretended not to notice Doug's wariness and the tension in the air because of it, but he knew they all felt it. From the outset, they knew that someone was watching their every move. It was even possible that Paulo was secretly in the wings somewhere, also enjoying the tour.

As the trip neared the end of the seventh day, while they were heading back to Bogotá to leave for home, they all felt the heaviness of leaving each other and the stress of what was to come. So far, the holiday had been event-free. Doug was still regretting that he had buckled to pressure and agreed for the family to come along.

The SUV was just heading into the city outskirts when they were forced to detour through a lower-class area with tall, dilapidated housing slums on either side of the street. Then there was a traffic stop for road repairs. Doug knew instantly it was going to be an ambush. He pushed Jane and Orhan onto the floor of the vehicle, searched around in the back pocket of the driver's seat and passed Joseph a pistol. "Only use it if it's to save your own life. We don't know if they're on our side or not.

"Jane, Orhan, if I have to shoot, you play dead. And tell me you are wearing your vests today."

Jane and Orhan assured him they were.

The road workers pulled masks over their faces. One of them approached the driver's window and signalled the driver to get out of the car. When the driver refused, he shot at him, aiming for the driver's head. Luckily, the bulletproof glass did its job, and the bullet ricocheted off the glass, nearly injuring the shooter. Others in masks waved the passing cars on, the drivers didn't stick around to question the masked men, a common occurrence in Colombia.

A masked road worker signalled for the family to open the door of the vehicle, demanding that they step out of the vehicle and kneel, facing the SUV with their hands on top of their heads. Doug couldn't help noticing how calm his family was: no one moved, no one was panicking, just going through the motions.

There was some heated discussion between the masked men. The one in charge was yelling at the others; they didn't sound Colombian. Doug guessed they were Mexicans.

The man with the gun identified himself as the man in charge through the closed window.

He spoke in Spanish to the gangsters, not knowing that three of the tourists in the SUV spoke fluent Spanish. He was confused and thought he had the wrong vehicle.

"These people," he was saying, "don't look like the foreign special forces that I thought they would be. They look like a white tourist family. I think we have been tricked, these gringo's look like pussies."

The gangsters started arguing amongst themselves, questioning their own planning, perhaps they had swapped vehicles. There seemed to be a verbal battle of blame taking place.

Doug counted eight men; the odds were against them if they managed to get them out of the car.

The one in charge tried to identify himself to Doug through the closed window, saying he was a friend of Paulo Hernandez.

Doug told the driver to move over so he could get behind the wheel, he'd run these fuckers over if he had to.

The driver assured Doug they would be fine. "I have special training in hijacking, señior." With that statement, the driver produced an assault rifle from under the front seat and a pistol from the driver's centre console.

Outside the man in charge was ordering his men to line up and shoot the same spot on the window to try and gain access, but before Doug could order the driver to throw the SUV into gear and run him over, from out of nowhere a bullet went straight through the forehead of the man in charge, shattering his skull. A rain of bullets from the surrounding buildings killed the remaining masked road workers. The driver then proceeded to drive backwards and forwards over the fallen bodies in a circular motion until he was sure everyone was dead.

Doug counted thirty or forty heavily armed men who now presented themselves from surrounding windows, doors and rooftops. A drone flew around the SUV.

He told Jane and Orhan they could sit up now.

Once again, they calmly looked out the windows as if it were natural to see such carnage. There were bodies and blood everywhere, with armed men dragging the bodies into the opening of one of the buildings and stacking them out of sight.

A glossy black limo appeared from around the corner and glided quietly up beside the SUV. As the chauffeur opened the back passenger's door, Doug could see a white, handmade snakeskin shoe make its way out of the vehicle, followed by a garish burnt orange coloured, dupion silk trouser leg.

Paulo made his grand entrance, smiling from ear to ear. "Amigo. Welcome to Colombia."

As soon as Doug was out of the vehicle, Paulo hugged him. He looked tiny, latched onto Doug's long body. He was excited and gestured that the rest of the family present themselves so he could introduce himself. He fussed over Jane, telling Doug what a catch she was, patting Orhan on the head and calling him Gandhi.

He shook Joseph's hand firmly and looked him up and down, "He's better-looking than the last one. Now, what would a Colombian holiday be without a bungled attempt at a hostage situation?" Paulo laughed at his own joke.

"I'm sorry to break up the honeymoon, but I'm afraid I must take my friend Douglas away; my limo will take Jane and the boys to the airport."

As an afterthought, Paulo asked Joseph if he wanted to stay. It would mean he would have to follow with his men, not with Doug and him.

Joseph looked at Doug for approval. Doug was reluctant to say yes, but he could see it in Joseph's eyes; he was itching for a purpose and some adventure, and he didn't know if he would need Joseph later. After all, he could sail a boat; he might be handy for Doug's escape if he needed one; he knew Paulo would see him right.

Paulo ordered his men to strap Joseph into a vest and give him some weapons, then ordered him onto the back of an open jeep with men who looked like commandos from the jungle. Joseph didn't hesitate; he was already following orders and saying, "Yes, sir," to Paulo.

From nowhere, a helicopter appeared over a tall building, coming in to land next to them, dust and dirt churned up by its blades; the dirt and debris stung Jane's face. Orhan was standing beside her, covering his face from the small stones.

Paulo hurriedly ordered them to get in the limo. Jane only had time for a brief kiss, and suddenly Doug was gone, whisked away in the helicopter.

As Doug looked back at the scene, he could see blood from the dead bodies everywhere. There was no way of seeing the limo through the dust and dirt. As they got higher, Paulo signalled the pilot to follow the limo and make sure it made it to the airport. Doug could see no sign of the open jeep with his son, weighted down by heavy artillery strapped to his body. Part of him had missed the excitement, another, older part was dreading what was about to come next.

—

Jane and Orhan were met at the airport by a man called Henry, who introduced himself as Paulo's personal assistant.

"You are booked on a private jet, which is ready to leave almost immediately," Henry said. "There is some urgency, as I regret, I cannot guarantee your safety if you remain in the country."

     MICHELLE THOMPSON

Henry was very frank when he spoke to Jane and Orhan. "Unfortunately, you have been caught up in a gang war between the Hernandez Cartel and a Mexican cartel, which are trying to stop the flow of cocaine out of Colombia. They are unhappy that it is affecting the profits from their own methamphetamine trade." Henry smiled, "Happily, all those who were killed were Mexican citizens. None of our own men have died."

He confirmed that a team of men had been following them since their arrival in Bogotá. "We were prepared for an attack, but I assure you that at all times you were safe."

Jane and Orhan boarded the private jet for San Francisco, from where they would change to an Air New Zealand flight, direct to Auckland. There was no time to ask about Doug and Joseph as they were rushed onto a waiting plane. Jane would make some calls, once they were safely in the US, to Edith and Wiremu.

It wasn't till they were seated on the jet and about to take off that she realised that Orhan had gone into shock. The crew had to fit a portable oxygen device to his face to calm him, and they produced a small white pill and told him to wash it down with water. He was asleep shortly after.

Jane welcomed the champagne she was offered; she really needed a drink today. It was definitely a honeymoon to remember.

Joseph Makes Friends

All at once, Joseph's life had changed forever; no Kane to boss him around, tell him what to do as the alpha twin. Yet suddenly he was missing him.

He wasn't sure where his dad was or when he would see him again, but what he was sure of was the thrill of the power he felt with all the guns and SWAT gear he was now wearing, the wind rushing past his ears as they sped through the back streets, destination unknown. With his sunglasses on, he knew he looked cool. He knew the people of the street had a love-hate relationship with them, much like the way things worked with the bike club back home.

He was welcomed into his unit like an old friend. His reluctance to sit inside the vehicle brought him respect, as did the fact that he spoke Spanish.

The crew was followed by another two jeeps; in all, Joseph calculated thirty men. They stopped every hour or so at different locations for food and drink. Each jeep had a leader who reported to the squad *capitan* in the first jeep, Joseph's jeep. The leader paid for everything and decided where and when they stopped.

At the second stop, his jeep captain received a phone call; he called Joseph over and let him know his mother and brother had safely landed in the USA. Joseph thanked him for the update but resisted asking about his father, he didn't want to be looked upon as a sissy or getting favours.

Different men shuffled around the different jeeps at each stop until Joseph felt like he had met them all. They all hugged and kissed him, which Joseph thought was very European.

As darkness fell, they were going further and further out of the city, heading towards the coast on good, well-signposted roads towards Buenaventura. Eleven hours later, they arrived at a huge, gated estate overlooking the harbour. Armed men let their convoy through the gates, and the three jeeps drove to the rear of the estate to the crew barracks. Joseph could see a helicopter parked on the back lawn, so he presumed his father was already here. Joseph's backside was numb; he was glad they had reached their destination. The only saving grace of the entire journey was that the local temperature meant he hadn't frozen to death on the back of the jeep.

A stately looking gentleman was waiting for them at the entrance to the barracks. He introduced himself as Henry. Henry offered Joseph a room in the big house. Joseph politely declined, embarrassed in case the others heard.

The *capitan* interjected. "He's one of us now," he mimicked Henry's posh voice, "*he doesn't want your canapés.*" He slapped Joseph's back in a manly fashion and led him away to the rooms the other men shared.

The barrack-like rooms were of a high standard. Joseph was shocked by the level of comfort. He was shown a bed with a fresh supply of clean clothing on it. Each bed had a curtain you could pull around for privacy and had its own small fridge and power points, and the beds could be operated by remote if you wanted to sit up or lie down.

The *capitan* introduced himself as Angelo and continued the tour, the kitchen and dining room greeted him with a mouth-watering smell. There was a bar that served drinks like any club, a TV room, a recreational room, and even a picture theatre, an Olympic-size swimming pool, and some hot tubs. Joseph felt like he had booked into a resort. The bathrooms were equipped with towels, soaps, shampoos, and other luxury toiletries.

Angelo told Joseph to settle in. "We will be leaving here early tomorrow, so get a good night's sleep. If you need a sleeping pill, let me know, you've had a big day. Other than that, join the boys for a drink and dinner, they really want to get to know you, after all, your father is a bit of a hero around here." Angelo went on to say, "Paulo credits him for saving his life. The story is legendary now, in the whole of Colombia."

At 0600 hours the next morning, a crew of thirty, including Joseph, was being hurried onto a plane headed to Bolivar, on the border of Peru.

On the way to the airport, Angelo had given him the brief and explained the history of the feud. The Mexicans were trying to stop the transport of Paulo's cocaine to the US. They were either stealing it outright or destroying it in the process. Their own market for methamphetamine was so profitable that they found cocaine a threat to their profit margin. Seemed ridiculous, but in Angelo's opinion, Mexicans were too stupid to work out a deal without being greedy.

"They have made many assassination attempts on Paulo, which thankfully have failed, so Paulo created the news article that he was arrested and was now in US custody. This has tricked the Mexicans up until now and bought us some time. They are blaming the deaths of their men in Bogotá yesterday on your father and, due to the legend of his rescue of Paulo all those years ago. They find him the same, if not an equal threat, as Paulo. They think he has returned to Colombia this time to rescue Paulo's empire.

"We have men and intel on the ground the whole time, and today we are getting ready to protect a shipment of three hundred kilos of cocaine across the border of Peru towards the coast. Mexicans are lazy and disorganised, so we will have a day's jump on them."

Joseph noticed that today, Angelo was wearing a body camera. Angelo and many of his men were ex-special forces, originally hired by the Colombian Government to tackle the Colombian drug trade. But years of low pay and poor working conditions meant that now they worked for the highest bidder. Paulo not only paid well for loyalty, but he let captains like Angelo make high-level decisions, which gave him more authority and respect from his crew.

Angelo didn't sugarcoat what today and tomorrow could bring. He looked steadily at Joseph. "Today, men could die or get injured. In fact, even you, Joseph, could die."

"I'll do my best to avoid that, if possible. And thank you for your honesty, Angelo." Joseph boarded the plane and sat alongside the wall with the other soldiers.

Complications

Doug watched the jeeps arrive just after dark from one of the windows of Paulo's mansion. The crew boss, who Paulo said was called Angelo, was staring up at the house. Doug felt a cold sweat wash over his body. He listened to his body often: it saved him a lot of trouble.

He caught a glimpse of Joseph on the back of the first jeep as it pulled up outside the soldiers' barracks. He saw Henry talking to Joseph and could tell from their body language that Joseph had declined the offer to come up to the house. He wasn't sure he was happy with that, but he also wasn't sure he was happy Joseph was even still in Colombia.

Paulo handed Doug a drink, "Just give me the word and I'll have him sent home."

"He'd probably refuse," replied Doug, "he's never found his own feet, that boy, always in the shadow of his brother."

Paulo made small talk to distract Doug from his thoughts. He gave him the good news that both Jane and Gandhi had made the flight to New Zealand. "They're probably lying back in business class by now, not worrying about you."

"Orhan will, but I'm sure Jane will be drinking her way to NZ by now." It brought a smile to his face when he thought of her.

He told Paulo the story about blowing her up, which made Paulo laugh until he nearly choked. Over the next few hours, they caught up like old friends. Paulo was saddened by the passing of Stacey, he'd liked her.

Doug gave Paulo a bit of stick about his evening attire. Always the peacock, he was in emerald-green silk pyjamas, with handmade black velvet slippers. When Doug started to rib him, Paulo surprised him with a set he'd had made for Doug which Doug refused to wear, announcing that he slept naked, but as he was a visitor in a strange house full of servants, he'd put them on after his shower to humour Paulo so they would look like odd-matching twins from an old movie.

They laughed for hours at the ridiculousness of the outfits and had Henry take a funny photo with Paulo tucked under Doug's armpit.

"Okay, let me have it, what have you got me into?" interrupted Doug.

Paulo explained the current war between him and the Mexicans. "Originally, we were all friends, had been for years, doing deals, going to parties together. Everything was going smoothly until I had sex with Hector Garcia's wife.

"First, someone started blowing up my planes, then the US Government was being tipped off anonymously about shipments, and one by one, my underground storage bunkers were discovered. The final blow came when a shipment bound for the US got blown up, twelve tons – gone, white powder filled the air for days."

Paulo continued, "I hired Angelo and his men to go into the jungle to sniff out the culprits and kill them. That's when Angelo uncovered the plot to run me out of business. Turns out they had such a roaring trade going from their shitty crack that they didn't want a healthier alternative like cocaine on the market in the USA.

"I had Angelo track every single person connected to the Mexicans in Colombia and sent a message back to Mexico to teach every single one of them a lesson. Angelo's men would send them home in pieces, send videos back to their families of their men screaming and weeping while they were cut up with chainsaws or machetes.

"If any of them managed to escape capture, the others that weren't so lucky would give up their cover before long. Angelo's men would kidnap their families and film the torture of their wives and children and play the videos back to them when they finally caught up with them.

"This has been going on now for a year. The dumb bastards just keep coming, and I keep killing them.

"Then I started getting ill, and I thought it was stress. Turns out, old friend, I've got cancer and I'm going to die. My whole body is riddled. Doctors say I've got six months to a year.

"So, I staged my arrest, thinking if they thought I was out of the picture, they wouldn't see my next plan coming.

"Meanwhile, I've been living in Cuba, visiting the Castros and having experimental treatment on my cancer. It worked for a while and slowed down the illness, but I'm still going to die. The only person here who knows that I am ill is Henry."

Doug was taken aback by the news; he had to stay seated. It saddened him;

he liked Paulo. It was not often he was shocked, but this news caught him off guard.

"That's where you come in my friend, if anyone can think of a plan to fuck them up for good it would be you. I will make it worth your trouble, but I need you to promise me you will take care of Henry after I'm gone and put a bullet in my head if the suffering gets too bad.

"I'm leaving you my entire estate in my will."

Homeward Bound

Jane touched down in New Zealand, and she couldn't be happier. She even thought she might kiss the ground once she got out of the airport.

Her to-do list was running through her head long before she landed. She would have to go shopping for clothes for herself and Orhan at the very least. Everything they owned was still in Australia and would have to be sent over. Jane didn't feel like going back to collect anything. She'd had enough of Aussie for the time being.

Orhan was still in shock. He was also very emotional and tearful. The events in Colombia had brought home his tragic childhood experiences, and he was back with the black dog of depression gripping his throat. He was convinced something was going to happen to his father. Jane felt a sense of duty to keep him with her, and she liked the little guy. Once he saw the farm and the animals, Jane was sure he would come right, and if and when Doug resurfaced, he could have the best of both worlds.

Wiremu was waiting in the arrivals hall, holding up a sign that said *Welcome Home Sis & Bro*. When Jane and Orhan saw him, there were tears all around. Wiremu hugged Orhan, lifting him off the ground in the process.

"We gotta fatten you up, boy."

Jane updated Wiremu on the way home; it made for a story out of a movie.

Orhan had the front seat at Jane's insistence so he could get a good look at the countryside, it was his first time in New Zealand. Wiremu was like a tour guide, pointing out all the sights on the way. It was a long drive, so it would be dark by the time they got home, not that Orhan noticed; he had fallen asleep about an hour into the trip.

Wiremu updated Jane on the farm, the local gossip, the state of the nation, and his job prospects.

The next day, Wiremu kept Orhan busy with a local tour, taking him to the famous Ninety Mile Beach, where they pulled up their trousers and used their toes to find pipis. He told him about the cultural significance of Spirits Bay, at the very top of the North Island. Orhan just loved New Zealand; the air was so fresh. He was pleased he was here.

Jetlag was still catching up with Orhan, so on the way home, they stopped at a small, local, family-owned supermarket for an ice cream to give him a sugar burst. Orhan seemed fascinated with the little shop. He marvelled at the number of goods crammed onto every shelf and spent longer in the shop than Wiremu thought was necessary.

On the way home, he announced to Wiremu that he wanted to buy the shop. He would tell Jane when he got back to the house, and regardless of whether it was for sale or not, he would make an offer they couldn't refuse. He wanted a change in his life, and this was going to be it. He perked up immediately, and the life came back into him.

The next day, Jane set about approaching the shop owners about a potential sale. They had not considered it before now and were reluctant. They had made friends in the community and had no reason to sell.

Jane phoned Edith for ideas. Edith's solution was to just throw money at it. Grant the current owners whatever they wished for.

They drove a hard bargain, and although it was a foolish investment as far as Edith was concerned, she purchased a tourist operation in the South Island on behalf of the current shop owners at more than twice the value of their supermarket business. In exchange, they offered to stay and support Orhan with the transition and teach him all the things he would need to know to continue to run the shop efficiently.

As it turned out, Orhan was a natural and took to shopkeeping very quickly, hiring some locals to help in the shop, quickly becoming a valued addition to the local community. He was lucky he had the financial backing of his family, as the shop never made any money in the year to follow, as his insistence on sponsoring every cause that was presented to him resulted in Edith making several stern phone calls to New Zealand.

Jane kept right out of it, Orhan was happy, and he was so busy that it gave him little time to dwell on his father's fate.

Jane tried not to think about Doug. Part of the time, she was angry that his ego made him go in the first place, but she was also to blame, wanting a bit of adventure herself and suggesting a honeymoon tour. The rest of the time, she thought of the terrible situations that he would run into, not to mention Joseph. He was a dark horse, who knew whether he would survive or not, or if he would really turn to the dark side. She didn't feel that he was going to die, which gave her peace at night.

There was no way to communicate with Doug, and it would have been unwise to discuss him at all with anyone over the phone. Wiremu knew what had gone down, but they had decided it would also be unwise to talk about it, so it was never mentioned again. In fact, very few people knew Jane had remarried. Those who did know thought Doug was away on business; it wasn't really a lie.

 MICHELLE THOMPSON

In the Heat of Battle

There was a seven-hundred-and-fifty-mile border between Colombia and Peru, and Angelo and his men were unofficially relied upon to make sure the enemy didn't cross it.

On the journey, Joseph discovered that there was also an ongoing tussle for the cocaine that was grown in Bolivia and Peru to be brought across the border to Colombia for processing and exporting.

Paulo had an extensive worldwide distribution network servicing Europe and Asia. The problem was, the Mexicans wanted this market also.

Local farmers supported the cartel; without the money they got from people like Paulo for their cocaine their families would starve.

The government had tried unsuccessfully to supply incentives for other agricultural schemes, but very few, if any, had been successful. Growing cocaine was all many of the farmers knew, and they knew it well, a skill handed down by generations. They were emotionally attached to the coca plant and its spiritual connection.

The Mexican syndicates had tried buying what they could or considered was their territory to claim. If that didn't work, they turned to just aggressively taking as much of the cocaine as they saw fit. All in another attempt to push Paulo out of the market.

To counteract this, Paulo paid more to the peasant farmers than the Mexican syndicates did, if they paid at all.

Paulo had international obligations and needed to guarantee the overseas demand. When the Mexicans couldn't get their own way, they would slaughter the peasant farmers and their families to put fear into the other farmers in the area.

—

Suddenly the air became electric, there was a change of plan, Angelo had received a call on the radio. He gave out orders, men started running for their jeeps and trucks. The convoy of trucks and jeeps that had left the airport earlier now had a new, unexpected mission, they veered left off the highway at high speed.

At Angelo's order half of the convoy stopped and set up a roadblock on the secondary highway, while the other half pulled off this road and sped along a dirt road through dense tropical jungle for what seemed like miles. Ahead of them, Joseph was informed, a small farming village was under attack.

From a vantage point at the top of a hill, Joseph could see smoke from chimneys and a few basic houses in the valley. Here they left the vehicles discreetly hidden in the jungle and set off the rest of the way on foot. They waited in the dark, stationed around the village, none of the village residents had any knowledge that they were there. Angelo stayed by Joseph's side. There was no conversation between him or any of his men. They took turns on watch.

Just on dawn, Joseph was awoken by the noise of a heavy truck. As it got closer, he realised it was the sound of a helicopter engine. It got louder and louder until it came into view and landed in the middle of the village, dust and leaves blowing everywhere.

Six heavily armed men exited from the sliding doors on each side. From Joseph's observation, it looked like an ex-military chopper reminded him of *MASH*, a TV programme he had seen as a child. A soldier dressed all in black got out of the passenger seat of the cockpit. He shot a round of bullets in the air from a long-barrelled rifle, then strode into the nearest dwelling, kicking in the door. He returned with a frightened, frail older man, half-dragging him by the hair, the elderly man barely able to walk to keep pace.

Now standing next to the helicopter, the soldier in black started yelling to the other villagers to come out and bring their cocaine with them. He threatened that the consequence of not doing this immediately would result in the pistol in his hand blowing a hole in the elderly man's head. In the distance, Joseph could hear a baby crying and someone trying to hush it. The soldier cocked the pistol, finger on the trigger, he started counting backwards: ten, nine, eight. Instantaneously there was a shot which, due to the speed of sound, came slightly after the hole that appeared in the forehead of the man in black clothing.

A barrage of gunfire erupted from all around him. Joseph found himself instinctively shooting at the men around the helicopter. Bullets whizzing past his ears, he took careful aim, his bullets meeting their targets. Not wanting to waste his ammunition, Joseph let his breath out slowly and aimed for the head and flying helmet of the helicopter pilot; the six men around the helicopter

   MICHELLE THOMPSON

were down. Joseph squeezed the trigger, the helicopter pilot slumped in the seat, the bullet fragmenting as it went through the Perspex bubble of the helicopter windscreen, spraying blood all over the cockpit. Angelo gave the order to cease-fire.

The sudden silence left a ringing in Joseph's ears. Joseph was instantly addicted to the chaos of the battle, he didn't even notice that his arm was bleeding, a minor surface wound from a glancing bullet. Joseph was surprised at how natural it felt doing this. Was it a family legacy, or just family mental illness? Whatever it was he wanted more.

Angelo called for his men to start dismantling the helicopter, he wanted it in enough pieces that they could take it away on the back of trucks. "Make sure you get the black box or GPS; we will need to divert the trail. We will dump it in the nearest lake or river."

Angelo strode over to Joseph and patted him on the back. "You did well amigo. I give you the honour." As he said this, he handed Joseph a large machete. He saw the bewilderment in Joseph's eyes, "Chop his head off, we will post it back to his family as a message not to fuck with us."

Joseph, adrenaline racing through him, walked over to the body of the man in black, he held his head back by the hair as he swung at the Adam's apple. When the blade connected with the neck the voice box made barking noises until the head was completely severed. He wanted to vomit, yet he was strangely enjoying the process.

Joseph thought it was over, but Angelo said, "Now grab the man's balls and cut them off with a knife and stuff them into that gapping mouth."

Joseph hesitated; he'd never held another man's balls before. As if Angelo read his mind, he came over and slit the trousers of the dead man, grabbed a handful of scrotum, and with one swift movement he separated them from the body. He laughed as he forced the bloody handful into the dead man's gapping mouth, it was just another day at the office for him. Angelo ordered one of his men to put the head in a sack.

As the villagers came out of hiding, Angelo handed out bundles of cash and the locals helped load their cocaine on the trucks that had now arrived from the junction up the road.

Under the cover of darkness, the crew made their way back to base; there was much celebration for the successful mission. Joseph was given many accolades from the men for having the foresight to shoot the helicopter pilot, and his clean shots had not gone unnoticed either.

As the night wore on and the alcohol flowed, a group of girls arrived from their shift at one of Paulo's cocaine production sites. They came by private bus to mingle and drink with the men. Angelo brought one of the girls over to Joseph and introduced him as his new Aussie friend.

Joseph was lost for words. She was beautiful, tall, and slim with golden skin and long flowing dark hair. Her name was Audrey, and she was every bit as beautiful as Audrey Hepburn.

Joseph fell instantly in love; they connected on every level. His first instinct was to wrap her in cotton wool, his next instinct was to wish to see her naked. He had forgotten about the fact that about six hours ago he had chopped a man's head off. And Audrey forgot for a moment that she had been sold into slavery, and up until now had been miserable and had wished she was dead.

Let's Make a Deal

Henry was serving a lavish breakfast of fine meats and eggs and pancakes for Paulo, who wasn't hungry due to his medication but picked occasionally. Doug was sipping tea; he had no appetite. He'd had very little sleep. The news of Paulo's illness had floored him, he was missing Jane, worrying about Joseph, and had spent all night thinking of a way to sort this shit out and get back home as soon as possible.

Paulo read his mind and smirked, "Joseph got lucky last night, and as a favour to you my friend, I will let you view the live camera footage of yesterday's actions recorded on Angelo's vest."

Doug declined. "Why was it filmed? It could be used as evidence; how can you guarantee that it won't get into the hands of the law?" Doug ordered that the original footage and the digital copy be brought up to the house immediately.

It was an odd relationship Doug and Paulo had when he thought about it. People in their professions didn't have friends they could share such complex situations with. He liked Paulo, and he knew Paulo liked him. Paulo was a crazy little bastard, and he was incredibly funny. Doug felt guilty and responsible for the time Paulo had spent in the cage at the hands of Baby Doug.

Doug changed the subject. "How do you currently get the bulk of your drugs across to the other side of the world?"

"Simple," said Paulo, "I keep acquiring abandoned ghost ships. I hire modern-day pirates, mostly Indian or Pakistani nationals, and pay them exorbitant amounts of money to bring the ships back here to the port. I dry-dock them and paint them up to mimic other international shipping companies, get them reasonably seaworthy, load them up with shit and sail them around the world.

"I'm not concerned if they sink once they have delivered their load, but it's a bonus if they don't. Sometimes the skipper must abandon the ship at sea to avoid arrest, but not as often as you would think. Depends where they are heading, and the deals I have with the people running those countries. You won't be surprised how high up some of my clients are on the world stage, that's how I get past customs and drug detection. I have more trouble if the authorities find prohibited food items in the galleys; biosecurity is a nightmare," laughed Paulo.

Doug thought about it for a moment, "What if we did a deal with the Mexicans, offer to deliver their methamphetamine to countries you're not really bothered with? Drop it offshore into their own waiting boats out past the twelve-mile mark in international waters, then continue your way. They take the risk of collecting it at the destination, we take no responsibility. We don't charge them for delivery in exchange for a truce, and obviously, the profit they will make is their business and has nothing to do with us. We can start with a test first, see if we can pull it off."

Paulo stared ponderingly into his coffee, "I can see one big problem, the Mexicans are dumb, they will fuck it up."

"Yes," said Doug, "but once it's left our ship, we have held up our end of the deal, we will make that clear. We won't be responsible for their failures if there are any. If they make a success of it, they can start their own trade."

Paulo instructed Henry to take Doug down to the dry dock after breakfast to see the ships. Doug asked Paulo if Henry could also fetch Joseph to come with him.

When Doug was ready to leave the entire crew, led by Angelo, was waiting in the convoy. Paulo reminded Doug of the risk of getting shot, as now the Mexicans would have spies out to see what this legend from Australia looked like, now he was running the show for Paulo. There was a high risk of Doug getting shot and killed. "You will need a full escort everywhere you go in Colombia now."

Doug travelled to the dry dock with Henry in the back of a shiny black bulletproof Lincoln. Henry told Doug that Paulo had bought the car from President Nixon; it was his favourite car. Henry instructed him to stay in the vehicle until the men were in position.

Doug asked Henry to find Joseph for him and bring him to the car.

Moments later the back passenger door of the Lincoln opened, and Joseph stepped inside. To Doug, he looked suddenly older. He was heavily armed.

"This is some far-out shit, Dad. I can't begin to tell you what I've seen and done in the last week—"

Doug didn't want to continue with the subject and cut him off mid-speech, "Do you want to get out of here, fly home?"

Joseph flatly refused.

Doug asked about the girl, which made Joseph blush, but he quickly composed himself.

"Remember," said Doug, "getting involved with one of Paulo's women will come at a cost, no matter what friendship I might retain with him. His women are his business, and his business makes lots of money. If she stops being useful, he will kill her. If you want to keep her, it will be costly. But if she pisses him off in the meantime, she will be made an example of, and you will not be able to help her. So, if she's what you want, you tell her to keep her head down! Do you understand me?"

Joseph nodded but was so consumed with emotion at the thought of something happening to Audrey that he didn't trust himself to speak.

Doug lent over and whispered in Joseph's ear, "Stay close, boy, I need you to watch for my hidden messages. We're going to sail this bastard home."

They got the signal from Henry to exit the vehicle. Doug couldn't help but notice Angelo's eyes on him again, his sixth sense made the hairs on the back of his neck stand up for the second time; Doug had learnt to trust his instincts.

The ship was covered in scaffolding and there were men welding, with sparks flying in places, accompanied by the sound of swinging hammers. A whistle sounded from somewhere and all the workers downed tools and stood with their heads bowed, not making eye contact with Doug. They were all covered in oil and grease.

It was one hell of a big ship. Doug couldn't guess the nationalities of the ship workers; they were all brown-skinned. Doug gave the order through the project manager for them to all continue working. The whistle went again, and the workers returned to work, like trained robots.

It took a full hour to walk through the ship, a 2400-ton 250 MV cargo carrier.

Followed by Henry, who was now wearing the body camera so he could be Paulo's eyes and ears, Doug and Joseph went over the ship with a fine-tooth comb. Of particular interest to Doug was the steering bridge of the ship. Would Joseph be capable of captaining the ship if push came to shove? As he worked his way through the ship, he tapped everything twice that he wanted Joseph to take particular notice of.

Doug's next point of interest wasn't docking at Paulo's arranged ports, but how practical was it to load cargo onto another boat while at sea, and what were their options here? They might need to install some sort of Hiab system. A ship this size normally needed twenty to twenty-five crew; this wasn't an option. So realistically, how many crew could they reduce it by, and who do you choose to be on the ship, given the fact that any one of them could get greedy and try and murder you in your sleep?

The crew accommodation was basic but comfortable. Doug needed to make sure his accommodation, which he planned to share with Joseph so they could take turns watching each shift, had a secret space to hide in and escape from if necessary. If the ship became compromised and they were trapped in their cabin for any reason, there had to be an exit plan. He chose the captain's quarters; one, because it was big enough and already had two entry points, and two, no one would suspect that there was a third exit, which he would need to fashion himself to avoid detection. Which would mean coming back when all the repairs were finished just before they set sail and completing the job himself. This wasn't a country where you could trust anyone.

As if by instinct, Joseph worked out what Doug was checking for; escape routes, and alternatives for transferring cargo. Joseph was pretty sure once they were out at sea that he wouldn't have any trouble steering the ship, after all, they would be using shipping channels and GPS most of the way.

They would need to have a few secret stashes of weapons and explosives. Including, possibly, scuba equipment hidden in a sea chest below the waterline. Joseph was also considering where he could hide Audrey, as he fully intended not to leave this country without her. He knew the risks, but if anyone could make it happen, he knew he could rely on his dad.

Doug asked the project manager how long until the ship would be ready to sail. As there were only cosmetic and minor mechanical issues, the only real problem had been the hundreds of rats that were living on the ship when they found it, had eaten all the wiring. And the colour. He asked Doug what colour he wanted it painted. All up, he predicted a month till finished if they worked around the clock.

Doug was about to leave and get back into the Lincoln, when, as an afterthought, he asked, "Henry, how many ships has Paulo got ready to go, or almost ready to go immediately?"

Henry replied, "This one is the most advanced. Two more are seaworthy and two need lots of work, so not close."

Before he got back in the car to return to Paulo, Doug asked Joseph if he was still on Facebook with his brother. "Send him this message: *Get ready to go to New Zealand and visit your stepmother, don't take your wife but take her passport, and don't take the grandchildren."* Joseph grinned from ear to ear; he knew the passport was for Audrey; Naz and her looked similar.

"Also, tell Edith to order me a Chinese takeaway, she will know what that means." Doug patted him on the back. "Tell no one!"

That night, after Doug helped Henry put pillows all around Paulo in his bed so he could sit up, Doug went over the video that Henry had taken at the shipyard. He told Paulo about his plans for the second ship and the escape exit. "I need to take care of this work myself. Joseph can help with welding gear."

He also told Paulo his master plan, which was going to require Paulo to come out of hiding and make his grand entrance before he got too ill to leave the house. Paulo seemed to be declining in health more rapidly now that he had handed over the reins. Doug spent as much time as he could by Paulo's side.

For the icing on the cake, he told Paulo what colour and branding he wanted the boat painted. They laughed for hours over the boat's name and made jokes into the wee small hours of the morning.

Jane Receives a Gift

It wasn't often Jane's phone rang. In fact, she only knew a handful of people who knew the number.

It wasn't a number that she recognised and answered it reluctantly. She felt a sickness inside her, like it was going to be bad news. Just like getting a phone call at three in the morning.

At first, she thought it was a fake caller, some marketing organisation, talking about a boat. The man was talking fast, excited.

"Good morning, Mrs Henderson, my name is Boris Botha, from Marine Brokers International. We have the boat you ordered; it's just been delivered by ship from Europe."

"Okay … where is it now?"

"It's at the Auckland Viaduct Harbour."

"Can you deliver it to Opua Harbour?"

"Yes, Mrs Henderson, we can. Our thoughts had also been Opua, given the size of the super yacht. We have already completed the temporary rental of your berth up there, with the option for a permanent mooring if you choose to."

"I will also give you my brother-in-law's details," Jane replied, "his name is Wiremu. If you contact him directly, you can give him the details and arrange a date and time for us to connect with you at the Opua wharf."

"Thank you, Mrs Henderson. We appreciate your business. I look forward to meeting you."

—

A month later, Jane, Wiremu, and Orhan were standing in the galley of a huge forty-one-and-a-half metre luxury yacht. They stood in awe, in complete silence, taking it all in. It was virtually a house on the water. It even had a spa pool. It was so nice Jane didn't want to dirty it by walking around, she made everyone take their shoes off.

Orhan said that he and his dad had travelled to Colombia once on a similar yacht when he first became a member of the family.

It had a large kitchen, a separate bar, and outside and inside dining areas. Jane lost count of how many bedrooms, was it five or six?

The salesman was eager to show Wiremu how to operate it. Wiremu's head was spinning. Orhan was frantically reading the manual.

Jane held her hands up in the air and, in a controlling tone said, "Everyone, stop what you're doing and sit down." She took charge.

Jane thanked the salesman and the crew he had brought with him and confirmed they had a flight back to Auckland from Kerikeri Airport and transport back to the airport, before taking the yacht keys from Boris. Shaking his hand, she told him it was okay to leave, they would work it out from here. Yes, she had his phone number if they ran into any problems.

Boris couldn't wait to get away as fast as he could, he knew this was a suspicious deal, he had been extremely overpaid for his services, but it meant he no longer had any debt and could start his own business. For that reason, he loved Jane, but for every other reason, he never wanted to see her again or tell anyone anything relating to the purchase and sale agreement for the yacht.

Boris had even considered a name change and leaving the country, but if he just kept his mouth shut the man with the money might think him useful later. Right now, he wanted to run for his life.

Once the crew were gone Jane made it clear to Wiremu and Orhan that no conversation about the boat's source or purpose would be discussed on the boat or anywhere that the authorities could be listening into.

This boat was certainly a surprise and would be attracting a lot of interest, just by looks alone. Meanwhile, they would find a trustworthy local to show them how to drive the bloody thing.

Jane turned to her brother-in-law, "Wiremu, can you see if the boat can be moored closer to home, say Mangonui Harbour, or Houhora Harbour, somewhere closer so we don't have to drive for bloody miles to get on it.

"Right, now," announced Jane, "let's have dinner at the Opua Cruising Club, get some alcohol and spend a night on the boat. Let's dirty the sheets."

A Grand Entrance

The front pages of the El Tiempo, El Espectador and the Diario Amanecer in Mexico, just for good measure, showed a full-page photo of Paulo riding in a Pope-mobile vehicle through the streets of Bogotá, standing up and waving to the crowds.

Thousands of people had come out to join the ticker-tape parade. The streets were joyful chaos. The authorities had little control, but none was needed; the spectators rejoicing in the return of their beloved hero.

Paulo, of course, was dressed in a diamante-encrusted purple outfit. Doug had earlier told him he looked like a character from the movie *Priscilla, Queen of the Desert*, which just made Paulo happier.

The headline read 'The Yanks Can't Crack the Cartel'.

Hector Garcia, head of the Los Rosa Cartel in Mexico, smirked and then blew air through his nose as he gripped the Diario Amanecer, which had been hand-delivered to his residence. "Cheeky prick," he muttered.

But today, Paulo Hernandez was not going to dampen his mood with his antics. Today was a celebration, one he had been waiting months for. Today, his eldest son, Rafael, was being released from an American detention centre after being caught crossing the border illegally three months ago.

Luckily for all concerned, Rafael had crossed the border with a false identity, so the authorities in America didn't know the significance of their prisoner, or his real intentions for trying to enter the USA. The complication of not being able to prove his identity had meant a longer-than-normal stay in the purpose-built facility at the US border. The conditions had been horrid with frequent deaths; some from suicide, others from illness, or injury, and not always at the hands of the Americans. Even within the confines of the detention centre, the internal feuding of their own people continued, turning on one another for personal gain.

Rafael was lucky; his secret status meant he had power, unlike his friends and fellow gang members. Rafael was what he called a 'Clean Skin'; he didn't have any identifying tattoos, no permanent ink for the authorities to photograph and catalogue in their books of illegal immigrants or their America's Most Wanted database.

Rafael received privileges from other detainees, although the food was disgusting and often consisted of reheated burritos and frozen sandwiches with traces of some sort of meat, he always received a double helping. Rafael didn't complain, just kept his head down, did his time, put up with the process so he could get back home to his father, his nice cars, his wild woman and his drugs. He was going to take over from his father any day now; he couldn't wait. He had been groomed for it his whole life.

—

The duty officer comes to the cell door with a clipboard; he calls out the names of the detainees who are going to be transported back to Mexico today. One by one, the men whose names are called present their hands behind them, through the bars. Another officer handcuffs each man and places an identification band on their right-hand wrist.

Rafael waits for his fake name to be called. He backs up to the bars, avoiding eye contact with the officers, feels the handcuffs go on and the identification tag, George Lopez; it had been the only name he could think of in a hurry, and it was a very popular name in Mexico.

In single file the detainees, ten of them in total, were directed down the corridor towards another door. Officers on radios talk to other unknown officers over the airwaves. The process takes a long time, Rafael is patient. The door opens and the men are directed in single file into another corridor, only to wait at another door while radio conversations go backwards and forward again for a long time.

The door opens. This time they are split into groups of five. The first five are led towards an open door where an armoured truck is waiting. One by one, they are placed in the truck and handcuffed to their allocated seats on each side of the truck. The door closes, and they are gone.

More radio banter between the guards. Rafael is separated from the other four men. They go out the same door as the first men and are loaded into another truck. The door closes, and they are gone.

Rafael is reluctant to ask questions; he knows he is getting special treatment, his father would have organised something far more comfortable for him.

The door opens. This time there is a much smaller van waiting. Rafael is ushered into the back and handcuffed inside a metal cubicle. He doesn't ask any questions. He thinks to himself that they probably must wait till they are on the other side of the American border. He has been patient for three months now; he can wait another hour or so.

There is the sound of a hand slapping the side of the van, it starts to move.

The metal cubicle is dark, hot and uncomfortable. The change in the sound of the traffic lets him know that they are travelling at speed now and no longer in the congested city. He bashes the side of the cubicle, "Come on, guys, let me out. I'm getting cramp in here."

He is answered by an Australian voice in English, then in Spanish, on an intercom system. He is told that if he feels around, he will find a bottle of cold water in the cubicle.

His skin prickles as cold reality strikes him, the icy sensation creeps over his face and down his body; he's not going home, he's being kidnapped.

Rafael loses track of time, might be an hour, might be longer. He is overcome with heat and thirst; he gropes around in the corners of the metal cubicle and finds a semi-cold bottle of liquid. It's refreshing, more like an energy drink. There is no noise from the cab of the van.

The van slows to a stop, Rafael can hear the passenger getting out; he sounds like he's opening a gate. The heat and the cramped conditions are taking their toll. Incredibly, Rafael feels like sleeping; could the drink be spiked?

The van slowly moves on; there is the sound of engines.

The van's outer door opens, then the cubicle is opened; a burst of fresh air is immediately cut off by two men in balaclavas placing a hood over Rafael's head. Rafael is led out of the cubicle still in handcuffs; his joints have seized from the confined space.

He is supported for a short distance, then pushed down into a long box; it feels like a coffin. There is a slight prick in his neck. Then, as if he were as light as a feather, he is launched up in the air and slammed down on a metal platform. He can hear his abductors strapping his coffin down. They could have killed him by now, so they must have another use for him. He is incredibly sleepy, but while he is awake, he will listen for clues and try to stay alive. His abductors don't talk; there are no clues for him to listen to.

The sound of engines increases; they are the engines of a plane. The motion suggests that they are taking off, it's all very quick, the runway is very bumpy, suggesting it might be a paddock somewhere. They are in the air, must be a smaller plane as there is turbulence.

Sleep overcomes Rafael.

     MICHELLE THOMPSON

Audrey

From an early age, Audrey knew she was different. Her mother had brought shame upon her family by getting pregnant to a white tourist in their home village, just outside New Delhi. Her mother's parents had sold Audrey to a man forty years her senior from another village, as his wife, so they could hide the shame brought upon their family. Audrey was brought up by one of this man's many wives. She never knew her birth mother or her true family.

As she matured into a woman, with her lovely light brown skin, her long, shapely legs and her beautiful face, she became a threat to the other, much older wives, and they constantly beat her with sticks and refused to feed her.

From the age of twelve, she was forced to perform sexual acts on her now fifty-two-year-old husband, and often his wives, for his amusement. If she refused or complained in any way, she was beaten and chained up outside in all weathers with the dogs until she learnt to obey. Audrey was always resisting and was constantly being taught a lesson; the dogs became her only friends.

One day, Audrey was spotted outside, chained up with the dogs, by a man called Harrold who had a travelling wagon and claimed to be a circus owner. He made her fifty-two-year-old husband a very generous offer to buy her. Audrey was now fifteen years old.

At first, this man treated her well. He had Audrey cleaned up, bought her nice clothes, fed her well, had her hair cleaned and braided. He didn't make any sexual advances, but her instinct told her to be wary.

In the wagon were other men and women, all unique in their own way. One woman's entire body was covered in brown hair; she looked like a monkey, and one had a strange, extra, half-grown leg protruding from her stomach. Another woman had a massive growth on the side of her face which she covered with a hood at all times unless on stage, where adults and children laughed at her or exclaimed in horror at the sight of her. There was even a limbless man who was known as the Human Caterpillar; people paid a lot to see him. There was one man with a giant penis; he was always naked and covered in white ash, with long fingernails and long matted hair.

Audrey wasn't quite sure where she fitted in with this group of travelling performers until one day, Harrold told her she was going to be in a special show. It was very late at night when Audrey was taken into the centre of a darkened room and asked to remove her clothing. She stood naked in the middle of the room while a spotlight shone directly on her, exposing her. She was aware that sitting in the dark around her were people she could not see – she could hear the creaking of their chairs and could smell cigars, or was it hash?

Harrold disappeared into the dark, then reappeared and put a collar and chain around her neck and demanded that she present herself on all fours on the ground in the middle of the spotlight. Audrey obeyed, as if it were a normal thing to do. Then, to Audrey's horror, another man appeared with an angry muzzled dog. The dog was excited and aggressive, coming towards her with froth dripping from its muzzle.

Audrey tried to scramble away, but Harrold held her tightly with the collar. What she had failed to notice in the beginning was the electric cattle prodder in his other hand. He shocked her to subdue her resistance, and at that point, the dog mounted her and started penetrating her vagina with its penis, the dog's claws scaring her back in the process. Audrey heard clapping from the darkened viewers and some laughter. The creaking of chairs intensified.

This was Audrey's new life. Seeing her tied outside with the dogs had given Harrold the idea. It was a real money generator, catering to the rich and perverse. He could see his riches mounting. Audrey was a good investment. Harrold had many ideas for private peep shows for the men behind the scenes who were willing to pay. Barring Audrey's actual death on stage, money could buy you anything you desired.

Audrey continued as a member of this travelling circus for another five years. The lifeless souls of the other performers matched her own soul.

The hairy woman taught Audrey to read and write, and wherever possible, Audrey helped the Caterpillar Man with his basic needs, like eating and going to the bathroom. It was fair to say that Audrey had won the hearts of the rest of the troupe.

The annual event of the year for the travelling circus of freaks was the Pushkar Fair in Rajasthan, the pilgrimage site for Hindus and Sikhs. The fair attracts nearly two hundred thousand people, both domestic and international, over the seven days. Harrold based his entire year's profit on this event.

It was the same this year as any other year that Audrey had been, the same dirty old men requesting the more bizarre every year.

Audrey returned late from her show, and surprisingly, the rest of her castmates were still up. They were excited by gossip from the fair. They had heard there was a western gentleman at the fair who was offering a life overseas, passage by sea, accommodation, guaranteed income. All you had to do was work in a warehouse packaging sugar for a wealthy sugar cane grower. He had put the word out that he was paying good money for healthy young females.

The Caterpillar Man encouraged Audrey to seek this gentleman out the following morning. The prospect of getting away from this madness was exciting yet terrifying to Audrey, but nothing could be worse than her current arrangement.

The following morning, Audrey was up before Harrold, dressed in her best outfit. The others stuffed her bedding with pillows to make it look like she was still asleep under the covers.

The woman with the growth on her face, Hilda, led Audrey to the rumoured meeting place of the western gentleman. Hilda and Audrey moved swiftly through the back alleys of Pushkar, wrapped in their cloaks and hoods.

When they arrived at the meeting place, there was a large crowd gathering, all desperate people trying to find a better life with the promise of riches. Audrey's heart sank. It was impossible to get near the man, let alone ask him questions.

Audrey's travelling companion had an idea. She instructed Audrey to remove the hooded garment, and legged Audrey up onto a mud and plaster wall to elevate her above the crowd. Then Hilda, with her grizzly, deformed face, removed her hood and made a direct path towards the man.

The crowd gasped and scattered immediately, frightened that whatever was on her face might be contagious.

Hilda started to screech like an injured bird, causing her face to become more inflamed and burning red, provoking the gentleman buyer to look her way. His eyes quickly averted from her ugly face, only to fall on the tall, slender young lady perched on the wall, high above the hideous sight of Hilda.

"You!" he yelled and pointed directly at Audrey. "Come here." He beckoned Audrey towards him.

When Audrey got close, she could smell his sweet aftershave. She recognised the fine cut of the material of his suit. He wore shiny, pointy crocodile boots that looked expensive and a huge gold belt buckle. He wasn't ugly, like most of the men who had abused her. Everything about this man screamed rescue. She didn't care at that point what he was selling; she wanted in.

—

Pedro thought he had found a diamond in the rough. She was a pleasant-looking girl. He inspected her hands to make sure she had all her fingers. He checked her hair for nits, opened her mouth and checked her teeth. He could feel her trembling as he held her hand.

"Can you read and write?"

Audrey strained to get the words out, her mouth suddenly dry, she couldn't speak.

Her sideshow companion stepped up to the man. "Please take my daughter, we are poor, and I can't afford to feed her," she begged, tears running down her face with a genuine feeling of loss for her beautiful little friend, as she could see from his body language, he was already committed to taking Audrey. Hilda knew that any other life would be better than the horrors Audrey was subjected to now.

Pedro didn't waste the opportunity. He discreetly handed the lady with the grotesque face a pile of Indian rupees and shook her other hand. "We have a deal," he said in English, with his Spanish accent.

Hilda nodded in agreement. She hugged Audrey goodbye, both women overcome with emotion, then placed the money in her underclothes, pulled the hood back over her head and disappeared back into the merging crowd.

A Strange Kidnapping

Raphael woke to the smell of onions cooking. He had been dreaming of them for a short instant, then realised he was not where his dream placed him. He had enough instincts to lie still and listen for a while.

Upon checking his surroundings, he found he was in a very upmarket room. His bed had fine linen; the carpet was a luxurious shagpile. Except for the bars on the window and the Perspex door to his room, he could have easily been in a private suite in a hotel; he even had an ensuite.

There were cameras in literally every corner of the room, following his every move. Then, as if whoever was watching him could read his mind, a gentleman came to the door with a trolley of food. Raphael took the dishes from the waiter through a carefully constructed flap in the Perspex door. Whoever was feeding him had thought of everything. He had even been supplied with a very nice Chianti. The meal was a blessing after his incarceration at the US border. He ate in silence. What sort of strange kidnapping was this?

Once he was finished, the waiter returned, and Raphael thanked him for the meal, returning the plates through the flap.

After taking the empty plates from Raphael, Henry introduced himself and suggested that Raphael take the opportunity to get cleaned up, as he had an important meeting coming up. The penny dropped; Raphael knew that Paulo's manservant was called Henry.

There was no point in being difficult yet, so he did as Henry suggested; he had a long shower. He dressed in the comfortable clothing he found in his size in the drawers, then went back into the lounge to wait.

Raphael vaguely thought of arming himself with some sort of weapon, but decided against it. His time would come. Meanwhile, he would play this silly game while he was still this side of death.

Henry returned and asked if Raphael required anything else, and told him to be prepared for a guest. "It would be best if you pull up a seat by the door so you can hear clearly."

Doug quietly appeared before him. He was a tall, well-built man, not unpleasant looking, but with some facial scars. He wasn't young. Raphael knew exactly who he was; this was the Australian man they talked about who had saved Paulo's life. Strangely enough, Raphael felt quite honoured.

Doug picked up a chair with one hand and effortlessly moved it closer to the door. They talked long into the night as Doug laid out his plan.

It was complicated with a surprising twist; Raphael wasn't free to return to his family anytime soon, but meanwhile, he would be made very comfortable, and if Doug was true to his word, he would be very rich at the end of it.

Doug had prepared a carefully worded letter for Raphael's father, and that, complete with a photo of Raphael with today's newspaper as proof he was alive, would be couriered to his father's private residence.

Raphael had other parts to play, but for now, he could only proceed as far as Doug needed him to advance. The difficulty would be convincing his father that this was a good idea. He needed to prove to his father that he was capable of running the business. Raphael was a gambling man; he was willing to take this chance.

One of the conditions in the letter was to cease all fighting between the two cartels to get to the next stage, which was to bring two-and-a-half-thousand pounds of methamphetamine across the border from Mexico to Panama, ready to place on the ship for the Pacific. There was some urgency as the shipping was planned for less than a month from now. Raphael would also need his passport and would be given limited access to a burner phone to communicate with his father when it was necessary.

Doug assured Raphael that he wasn't going to be killed, and that Doug would be on board the ship so he could confirm the delivery of the shipment. After the shipment was delivered to Raphael's business connection in the Pacific, Raphael would be free to fly home.

He understood that Doug couldn't afford to trust him at this stage, but was giving him a huge opportunity, which seemed strange. What Raphael couldn't work out was what was in it for Doug, or Paulo, for that matter?

Doug appointed Angelo to be Raphael's full-time guard. Joseph would be his relief, so he could have a break. Angelo would also be on the ship with Raphael on the journey, as Doug and Joseph had intentions of flying home once they knew the ship was safely on its way.

　　　MICHELLE THOMPSON

Doug told Angelo that he would build a purpose-built holding cell in the hull of the ship to contain Raphael till they got into international waters.

More importantly, Doug needed to know if Raphael could keep a secret, or whether he wouldn't be able to help himself and would tell Angelo the plan.

Audrey Arrives in Colombia

There were eight women in the shipping container, and it was hellishly hot. They'd had very little food or water for the last five days. All the women had been using a single bucket in the corner as a lavatory. There were some mattresses at the other end, which they all shared.

The other seven women were mostly of Pakistani descent, with the exception of a little Arab dressed in expensive silks who had sobbed virtually every day.

Audrey did her best to be a support for the other women, who all looked scared. Audrey wasn't scared; she was looking at this as an opportunity. For the last month no one had wanted to fuck her, so that was a good start.

—

After the man in Pushkar paid for Audrey, he hurried her into a white taxi. They drove to another village close by in silence. The taxi pulled up outside a modern private residence, where Audrey was asked to leave the taxi and follow the man to the rear of the building.

Here, Audrey was surrounded by several fat, sweating businessmen. Her heart dropped. Had she fallen into a trap? These men could be worse than Harrold's travelling freak show. Instead, they offered her tea or a bottle of Coca-Cola.

She was ushered into a room where she saw a sea of female faces peering back at her. She heard the door lock behind her. The room was bare of furniture, with only a pile of mattresses in the corner. There were basic toilet facilities in an adjoining room.

Audrey counted fifteen girls ranging in age from twelve to about twenty-five. No one spoke for some time, then the door unlocked, and some trays of food were presented. All the girls seemed like they were starving and ate the food as quickly as it appeared.

They were much more talkative with full stomachs, and Audrey discovered that some had been in the room for over a week. They had all been sold into slavery, and their destination was yet unknown.

When they were moved, they travelled at night. They would be stuffed into a Toyota van and driven to their next destination. Tonight, they would move again. None of the women had suffered any violence or sexual assault, but they were all concerned that it would be a risk in the near future.

That night, as the women predicted, they were all ushered into a white van; the windows were painted black, the seats had been removed and replaced with the mattresses from the room. The journey took two days, with a stop the next day at another small, hot room: destination unknown. The girls were fed and were able to wash with minimal facilities until the next night, when the journey continued again.

On the second night, the driver told them they had entered the city of Mumbai. When the girls climbed from the van, after a long wait in silence in the pitch-black, they realised they were in the dockyard of a busy port.

Seven of the girls, including Audrey, were hurried into a shipping container. The mattresses were piled in with them, along with a bucket, which they were told they could use as a toilet. The driver and another man shut the heavy doors. Suddenly, the container was hoisted into the air, which sent the girls flying about inside. When it was set down, Audrey took stock of the situation.

It was pitch-black, so she felt around for the bedding and instructed the girls to help her make a place at one end for sleeping. It was in this corner she discovered a large sack, tied with a tight knot. Audrey could feel a human form through the sacking. She bit at the knot until she released it. Inside was a small, frightened girl, who, she later discovered, was dressed in exquisite silks.

The ship spent fifty days at sea. Once they were in international waters, the women were allowed to leave the container for several hours a day. They had a small area where they ate and could sit in the sun, always with an armed guard watching over them. The ship was, in Audrey's opinion, very old and tired; it was even possibly not seaworthy. Meals were brought to them by a Chinese cook; they were basic but adequate.

As they got closer to their destination, the girls were placed back inside the container and only permitted to go outside for food or to empty the bucket. They had been in there for five days.

Audrey could tell the ship had slowed. She could hear the sounds of horns and birds in the distance. She expected that they would be docking at a port soon.

With the ship motionless now for over an hour and the shouts of the men who were tying up the boat long since gone, everything had gone quiet. The women were startled by a huge, metallic clunk on the roof of the container. As it was lifted into the air, the bucket tipped over, the stench of faeces and urine was overpowering.

With a heavy clunk, the container was placed on the back of a truck. As the truck changed gears, the container was jolted again and again. Whoever was driving it was speeding, so with every corner, the urine swished across the floor, soaking into the mattresses. Audrey didn't know how she managed to sleep, but when she woke, the truck had come to a stop.

The man who swung open the container doors dry retched, recoiling back from the smell. He ran and got the firehose from the wall and beckoned the women to stand outside the container, then turned the hose on them. Audrey took the initiative and removed her urine-drenched clothing. The Pakistani women did the same. The timid Arab girl just huddled in a ball, unable to commit to being naked. Audrey helped her up, washed her hair and got her as clean as possible.

From Audrey's observations, they were in a basement car park. There were concrete walls and sturdy pillars. A dull green sign read EXIT. The presence of heavily armed men stationed around the floor was a reminder that they were not free to go.

A tall, well-built black woman appeared from the set of elevators – she was cheerful and welcoming. She ushered the women towards the elevators, speaking to them in both English and Spanish. They stopped on the tenth floor, the doors opening onto a small reception area where they were handed grey sweatpants and T-shirts, and clean underwear to change into.

"My name is Petra; I will oversee you from now on. These are the rules, so listen up.

"You will be inducted into the factory tomorrow and start work the following day. You will work every day except Sunday, when you will be taken to a church service and can have the rest of the day off.

"You cannot leave this building at any time unless escorted by me, and you will be transported to and from work.

"In this building, you will share accommodation. You will be fed and well paid, and for those who choose to, I will arrange to send money back home to your families. I will open a bank account for you.

"The owner of the factory owns this building, and the only people living here are his workers from the factory. There are other crews on different floors, but you must not communicate with them; they will work different shifts. This is a twenty-four-hour operation.

"My apartment is first on the right, apartment 1001. You can ask me questions at any time. I will answer as honestly as I can.

"The owner of the company will not tolerate any behaviour that does not please him. You will not be able to discuss the nature of your work with anyone outside of your work crew, only me.

"The penalty for disobeying me or any of the rules will result in your immediate death. Do I need to repeat this? If you try to run away, we will find you and you will be made an example of in front of the other girls by being publicly executed."

Petra met each one of the women's gazes, her kind, welcoming face wore a sharp look now. "Any questions?"

Audrey put her hand up, "Will we have to sleep with the owner?"

"No," said Petra. All the women sighed with relief.

Petra laughed for the first time and said, "Only if you want to."

Petra had one more piece of advice. "You must all be friends; it will be easier for you if we all get along and share any problems."

Petra paired them all off, putting Audrey with the little Arab girl who had stopped crying over the last hour. Their apartment was 1002 across the hall from Petra's.

Audrey couldn't believe how beautiful the apartment was. It had two queen-size beds, a bathroom and a small lounge and kitchenette with coffee and a few necessities. There was a TV in both rooms and the bathroom. A huge window with a view of the harbour dominated one wall.

She bundled the little Arab girl into the bathroom and pointed to the shower. "You go first, get all cleaned up, and I will go next."

For the first time, the Arab girl spoke. "My name is Maryam."

Audrey wandered around the apartment, deep in thought, while she waited for the bathroom. After suffering a lifetime of abuse, Audrey knew this set-up couldn't be as good as it appeared; things didn't usually go that well for her. This surely wasn't going to last. She would take each day as it comes. Perhaps she could save enough money and escape one day.

A short time later, Petra knocked on the door. She came to see if the girls needed anything and had brought them some pizzas for dinner and some ice cream for dessert. The main reason for her visit was that she had some concerns about Maryam.

She sat Audrey and Maryam down. "Tomorrow, you will be inducted into the factory. There is a rule that you may not be comfortable with, Maryam; you will not be permitted to wear clothing while you work.

"The truth is, you will be packaging cocaine, not sugar. The owner does not permit clothing for many reasons: theft, it sticks to clothing in the heat, and the owner just likes to look. You will be able to wear the standard underwear that we provide and a face mask.

"The penalty for breaking the rules, as I said before, will be death. If you even think of trying to escape this building at any time, you will be made an example of in front of the entire workforce, so please don't make me give that order.

"I will leave you now to think this through, you are no use to us if you can't follow the rules. Remember, your own family doesn't want you; they sold you. We are your family now.

"You have an early start tomorrow, so I suggest you get some sleep."

Maryam started crying again. Through her tears, she told Audrey how she came to be here. "In my country, women have no rights. They are seen and not heard; their use is to have babies for rich husbands who already have many wives. I have not been able to produce a child, and because my husband's head wife despised me, she accused me of showing my face to a man from another household. They stoned me publicly with rocks and sold me into slavery. Even my own mother and sisters refused to talk to me.

"I have come from a very privileged life, with fine clothing and food. From a culture where it is a sin to show your face, let alone your body, how am I going to cope tomorrow?"

Audrey had no response. Her better judgement told her she must not get attached to this girl. She was a survivor, and if it meant keeping to herself to survive, she would. On the other hand, she had been shown kindness in her lifetime, which saved her life.

"Getting naked with a whole bunch of women is going to be far easier than getting naked with a whole bunch of men poking different things up your vagina," said Audrey. "If you want to live, and maybe one day get out of here, I suggest you grow a pair of balls and get on with it."

Audrey already knew what she had to do. She would work hard and get the respect of Petra and the owner and work her way up the ladder if there was one.

The next morning, Petra woke them all at 6 am. They had one hour to shower and get ready for their work induction. They would have breakfast at the factory.

The girls were shuffled into the lift, which took them down to the same basement they had arrived in the night before. From there, a van collected them to take them to the factory. Audrey found it exciting and couldn't wait to see her new place of work.

The factory was bustling. First, they were taken to the canteen where they could help themselves to an array of different foods. This was where they would have breakfast, lunch, and dinner while they were at work. After breakfast, the girls were all given their own lockers. In the locker was a pair of cotton briefs and a face mask. They were told to get changed while Petra waited.

Maryam initially refused to take her top off, which was met with an angry command from Petra. She reminded the girls that any breaking of the rules would result in being hacked to death with a machete in front of everyone. Petra pointed to a blood-stained marking on the floor to push her point home.

Audrey took the lead and sternly told Maryam to decide, "Live or die! This is your life now." Maryam reluctantly removed her top.

Inside the next room was a row of ladies of all shapes and sizes and colours, all in their little undies and masks. They were weighing and packaging piles of white powder, each package was sealed with a gold sticker with the embossed logo 'PH'. The women, covered in white dust, worked like clockwork. Other women collected the packages and took them to another area. Above the women on walkways high in the roof were armed men, always moving, always watching, backed up by cameras from all angles.

Today, the new girls were buddied up with the ladies in front of them. After about ten packages, the work became second nature. Audrey could do this all day; she still couldn't believe it was so easy. Surely reality would strike soon.

—

Five years later and Audrey was the pit boss of her own crew of girls.

During that time, she had witnessed the demise of Maryam, who was hacked to death with a machete as an example to the others for not following the rules. Audrey didn't have any emotions left to feel for Maryam's death; it was all just business to her. Girls were shot at point-blank range next to her; she didn't even flinch. When she considered Maryam's death, she wondered if it was suicide. Maryam just never got over her situation.

Petra and Audrey had become good friends. Along with a couple of the other floor leaders, from time to time, they had the luxury of mingling with the crew of guards that managed Paulo's security. Audrey wasn't looking for love, but the night Angelo had directed her towards the tall white boy, something in her heart softened.

He had a funny accent and was a bit shy, and he smelt nice. He was interesting, he had travelled, and he had a family that he loved to talk about; she was in a dream, just hanging on to his every word. Most of all, his touch was gentle.

Since the first night they met, Audrey and Joseph had spent very little time together, but he told her he had a plan. "I can't share the details, but I need you to trust me and be prepared to leave instantly if I call for you. You may not even have time to pack. More importantly, you can't tell anyone."

They both knew if they were found out, the result would be death.

She trusted him, and her gut told her he was her ticket out of here.

Ship-Shape

Doug and Joseph had been working day and night on the ship. There had been a change of plan with the accommodation quarters now that extra passengers had to be considered; five people, including Raphael and a limited crew. Everyone would have to pull their weight. Not to mention the growing shopping list that Doug needed to complete his master plan.

The engineer was the key to the success of the trip; no expense had been spared on the maintenance of the huge diesel engines that drove the ship. It wasn't going to be the fastest trip, but the ship needed to chug along at a reasonable speed to not draw the attention of the authorities.

Finding the right engineer came from a surprising quarter; it was a genius idea of Paulo's. Paulo had put the word out to his associates and found a German backpacker who was currently serving a long prison sentence in the Modelo Prison in Bogotá on drug charges and attempted manslaughter; a drug deal gone bad. He wasn't getting out any time soon, and with no financial backing from his family and no means of legal support from his government, the German was never going to leave that prison alive. Paulo did a deal with the prison governor, and Doug and Joseph made the secret undercover journey to Bogotá to collect him.

Ansel was malnourished and covered in what looked like sores, but on closer inspection, they were stab wounds. Almost all his teeth were missing, and he was naked except for a pair of oversized underpants, having had most of his clothing either beaten off him or stolen, and he stunk like vomit. Doug handed the envelope of cash to the governor and demanded that he arrange to hose Ansel down before they transported him anywhere. Doug sent Joseph down the street to buy some clothing.

Ansel was frightened, not only of Doug but of anyone who came near him, curling up in a ball to protect himself. Doug questioned his mental ability to perform the role of ship's engineer, but time was running out, and he was out of ideas. Doug had found another candidate on an earlier search but had decided on another use for him, so this had to be the guy.

Ansel's head had been shaved before they left the prison due to a lice infestation, and he was now sporting a pair of blue industrial overalls; he looked like a new man already. Doug directed his questions directly to Ansel when they were in the car, away from the prison.

Ansel, through spit gushing out his mouth from missing teeth, suddenly burst into life about his engineering skills and experience. He had been working on a cargo carrier, which was how he got to Colombia in the first place. Doug knew he had his man.

The next thing Ansel said was, "I'm hungry."

They stopped for food, then Ansel slept the rest of the way in the back seat of the car. Once they got back to the ship, Doug set Ansel up in the engine room with his own quarters. In the meantime, Doug posted full-time guards to make sure he didn't escape. Ansel had promised to do whatever he was asked. If it got him out of Colombia alive, he'd be loyal, no questions asked.

Over the next seventy-two hours, Ansel had to choose his team from the pool of workers who had prepared the ship for sailing. Due to the nature of the trip, everyone would have to pitch in to keep the crew numbers low.

The paint job was completed, and all the modifications to support a crane to lower goods overboard had also been finished. There were still several safety items and things that they would need for a quick escape if the authorities managed to board the ship while at sea.

Doug had Edith book plane flights in their own names on an international carrier as a backup.

—

There had been good, constructive dialogue between Raphael's father and Raphael. To date, Raphael had been helpful and positive about the progress. He had hinted about being released from his prison, but understood the process. As predicted, recordings from Raphael's room revealed that some information had been passed to Angelo.

Paulo's health was rapidly declining. Henry and Joseph took shifts covering his bedside during the day. Doug kept the nights for himself. He had set up a bed next to Paulo's, and they talked for hours before the morphine took hold of Paulo's brain, and he drifted off to sleep. Doug intended to take Paulo with him on the ship and bury him at sea. One thing Doug knew for sure, he couldn't leave him behind or finish him off as Paulo once suggested.

The morning before they were due to set sail, Paulo took his last breath with his old mate Doug by his side, the morphine pump clicking away, the gold rings long ago too big for those frail hands, were now on the chain around Doug's neck.

As planned, Paulo's body was being prepared by his own funeral company and was to be flown to Doug's funeral director in Australia for a proper funeral when Doug returned. Paulo hadn't held back on any of the arrangements, and in true Paulo style, the coffin was solid gold, and the weight meant logistics to transport it to Australia had been difficult. Paulo had hired a Boeing cargo plane to transport his coffin and his body to Australia.

Between moments of overwhelming grief at his bereavement, Henry gave the professional moving company last orders to pack the entire house up for shipping to Australia to Joseph's house, where it was decided Henry would live out his final years in retirement.

Busted

The ship had set sail just after dawn from the Port of Buenaventura. As arranged, it would make its way to the Golfo de Panamá and make passage through the Panama Canal until it reached the Port of Colon, on the other side of the Canal. Here, it would add to its current cargo of three thousand kilos of cocaine, the three thousand kilos of methamphetamine from Raphael's end of the arrangement, all packaged and ready for its new market in Europe, then on to Asia and the Pacific. Raphael's father, Hector, would be waiting at Colon and oversee the transfer of goods.

Raphael had been placed on board in a purpose-built holding facility below deck. His relocation was carried out by Doug and Joseph under the cover of darkness. They had covered Raphael's head in a hood and made him wear a long coat so as not to expose his identity or the handcuffs if they were accidentally discovered.

As arranged, once out at sea on the passage across the Atlantic to Senegal, Raphael would be able to roam freely around the ship. In the meantime, he had enough provisions and comfortable quarters.

Angelo was given strict instructions not to communicate with him or let any of the crew know who the captive was, at least until they had left the Port of Colon.

Doug had given Angelo the task of ship's manager and captain at sea. Although he had a pilot to sail the ship, he was still in charge and still seen as the captain. Angelo was able to take a few of his most trusted men with him, along with a crew made up from the Indian shipbuilders.

Arrangements had changed at the last minute with the death of Paulo, so Doug and Joseph had not boarded the ship, which had annoyed Angelo, but he seemed satisfied that he had Raphael incarcerated below deck as his bargaining tool.

With all things considered, the weather holding and the volume of boat traffic in the canal, it should take eight or nine days to reach Colon.

—

The Port of Colon was busy. Colon is a very dangerous city and rarely on the tourist itinerary. The cargo carrier ship that Angelo captained had been painted and named the same as a Maersk shipping line ship, so it didn't draw any additional attention. Detailed down to flying the US flag, everything looked in order.

With a backlog of one hundred and one vessels in port on any given day and the waiting time to load and unload normally taking four days, it had taken a lot of negotiation and bribes to get a slot with a minimal waiting time. Even Paulo's influence had little impact. Then Hector Garcia stomped his feet, and the ship was given clearance, and the containers were loaded immediately. Some were empty, some carrying the drugs, all in an effort to throw off the DEA or pirates if they got wind of it.

The ship had barely left sight of the Venezuelan coastline when the engine drone of a Chinook helicopter drew closer, the dull thud vibrating the air. As it flew a course in their direction, the sound intensified. There was no doubt it was heading for the ship. Coming up behind it was a US Coast Guard ship, its speed making its approach fast. It had been following in stealth mode, going undetected from radar and sight, hiding in the shadow of another cargo cruiser, so had remained unseen.

The loudspeaker from the helicopter overhead blared orders to surrender the ship at once. The voice coming over the ship's radio from the coastguard was also directing the ship to stop immediately. Men from elite tactical forces dropped onto the deck from long ropes hanging from the helicopter.

The nervous ship's pilot looked towards Angelo for guidance; there was no sign of worry or panic on Angelo's face. He calmly told the pilot to instruct the engine room to stop the engines and gave the order to drop the anchor. His wry smile gave it away.

As the tactical force's leader, Leroy entered the bridge to stand in front of Angelo. The two men grasped each other's hands in a firm handshake, slapping each other on the back as they did so.

"You'll get a commendation from the President himself for this, mate. You've been a long time undercover, I bet you thought we were never coming."

Both men looked pleased with themselves.

Angelo puffed out his chest. He had dreamed of this moment for a long time. "Garcia's brat is down in the cargo hold, locked in a room," boasted

Angelo. "He's probably dead by now. I never checked on him. Another filthy Mexican we won't miss anytime soon."

The coastguard ship had pulled alongside, and the DEA had already boarded. The ship's crew had been rounded up and sat handcuffed on the main deck in the hot sun. Someone from the DEA was filming the event for evidence, while others took fingerprints and checked identification.

Angelo and Leroy made their way down to the cargo hold with the keys for the locked room. In the corner of the room was a figure, curled up in a ball with the hood over his head. He was still handcuffed, but he had managed to loosen the rope that tied the hood tight around his neck. Angelo nudged him with his boot. A strangled Mexican voice pleaded for water. Leroy tugged violently at the hood and removed it from his head. Both men stood in shock, staring in disbelief. This was not Raphael Garcia!

Leroy ordered his men to open the shipping containers, both he and Angelo frantically digging through the first container themselves. The blocks of one-kilo squares were neatly stacked in wrapped blocks of twelve, all carrying the gold identification sticker of Paulo Hernandez. The other container was stacked in a similar fashion with blocks of methamphetamine; wax sealed with the name Garcia imprinted into the wax. They looked the part, but they were all fake; sugar in some, baking soda in the others.

Leroy got on the radio immediately to confirm that the flights to Australia had been stopped, and that the airport was under lockdown, also ensuring that Paulo's estate was being surrounded and searched. The radio chatter going backwards and forwards rapidly.

There was no sign of Doug, Joseph, Raphael, or Henry; they all appeared to have disappeared into thin air.

Angelo was humiliated. He could see the other men sniggering behind his back. He tried to explain to Leroy that his information had come directly from Raphael's own mouth. During the hours he had spent guarding him, Raphael had run his mouth off, bragging about his soon-to-be riches.

Leroy confirmed that the only other ships to leave the Golfo de Panamá in the last two weeks had all been legitimately accounted for, even the environmental 'Save the Planet' ship that had just left the Galapagos Islands.

When they arrested Hector Garcia trying to leave Colon airport, it was another Hector Garcia, not the father of Raphael. It was the ultimate 'sting'.

Ocean Breezes

Doug stood watch on the bridge, staring ahead at the Pacific Ocean before him. He was visualising his reunion with Jane, God, how he missed her.

As he looked to the left of the ship, he could see Joseph and Audrey walking hand in hand along the port side; they looked happy. It was a regular event for them to walk around the ship together, constantly talking. She was all right; Doug didn't pick up any bad vibes from her. But she was a broken soul, and there would be times when her demons would resurface. Joseph would have to be very thoughtful at those times, but he had a sensitive side; Doug wasn't that worried.

Raphael broke his thoughts as he entered the bridge and sat in the captain's chair, pretending to steer the ship, a cheeky grin on his face. Doug didn't mind him, all said and done, he was actually a nice kid once you peeled off a few layers.

Raphael had some fresh updates from his father. "It appears that the video recording of Angelo chopping off the head of a Mexican citizen has found its way onto the CNN breaking news feed, along with the bungled filming of the 'Great Cocaine Bust'," he said. "The tapes of the decapitation had been professionally edited. The man he chopped the head off was reported as being from a good Christian family, on an adventure holiday. He left behind a family of five with no means of income to support themselves."

Doug took the news in his stride, "How's Henry this morning?"

"He's in the kitchen cooking up a storm, but he's still pretty cut up about Uncle Paulo."

"How's our crazy German?"

"Oh, he's still crazy. This morning he's planning to do some fishing; that should be amusing to watch."

"Have you sorted out your connection when you get off the coast of New Zealand yet?"

"Well, all going to plan, my contact will bring a boat out past the twelve-mile mark, and I will start transferring half the crack to him."

"Are you one hundred per cent sure he's safe?" asked Doug.

"On my life. I met him years ago, we have done business before, he would never let me down or squeal."

"Let's go over the details again, it's important to plan and remember what I have taught you. Okay, so you remember the process once you get off the coast of Australia?"

"Yes, the boat will be met out past the twelve-mile mark by a Chinese fishing trawler. The GPS coordinates are in the ship's computer. They will take the rest of the cargo, and they will pay me for my part of the cargo in a foreign money transfer to my Avocado business back in Mexico."

Doug reassured him, "I give you my word, you can trust these people, I have been dealing with them for years. Tell me what the drill is if you get caught?"

"Sink the boat, if possible, use the explosives, if necessary, escape to the life rafts with no evidence. If my Kiwi connection gets caught, I will look after him financially, he will do the time, come out a rich man."

"And? You forgot one thing."

"Save all the passengers."

"What if you don't get caught?" asked Doug.

"I have the option to keep the ship as long as it goes undetected, but give the crew the option to leave. Give the German safe passage to anywhere in the world, just not back to Colombia," responded Raphael.

"I have paid them handsomely, so they will expect similar payment from you if they stay," replied Doug.

There was a long pause, then Raphael said, "It sounds like you are leaving this boat soon. Can I know the details?"

"Not really," said Doug, "I have no interest in this once I get to New Zealand. I was just doing a favour for a friend; he's dead now. I've fixed the bad blood. I've set you up in business."

"You're welcome to shift into Paulo's house once you return. I own it, but I wouldn't mind if someone saved me the maintenance bill every year."

"I would be honoured to take that offer up, my friend," replied Raphael, shaking Doug's hand.

"Believe it or not," Doug said, "I'm going to retire!"

The conversation on the bridge was broken by Henry entering with a big tray of bacon and eggs, salmon, and some fine champagne. Joseph and Audrey followed with plates and cutlery.

"We invited the *Germanski*. He's making his way up into the sunlight, the rest of the crew are eating in the galley."

Ansel appeared like a spring, bursting through the doors, covered in oil and grease, but he had managed to wash his hands at Henry's insistence. His big, gaping smile trying to light up the room with no teeth. He was always saying thank you; he was so grateful. There were never any scraps when Ansel was around. He ate like a dog that had been starved all its life. He had a great sense of humour and told amazing stories. This morning, he washed the stories down with his own bottle of champagne, as nobody wanted to share with him, in case they caught something from him.

Once they had all eaten Joseph took over the ship's controls again, he was teaching a young Indian national the finer workings of navigating a ship and how to read the GPS.

Ansel and Raphael went to inspect the engine room. Doug said it was important that once he owned the ship, Raphael knew as much about running the ship as Ansel in case of emergency. The key to running a big ship like this was the engineer and the engine. The entire engine system was new, so he was lucky in that respect, but without a happy engineer, things could turn bad in a hurry.

Doug took the opportunity to walk around the ship with Henry, time to let Paolo's loyal servant of so many years get some clean air and exercise while the weather was holding.

It was day eight at sea. After leaving Buenaventura, they had sailed to Acapulco to collect Raphael's cargo, bypassing the Galapagos Islands; too many tourists might want a picture of their ship, disguised as a Greenpeace ship, making an unscheduled appearance. They would have another six days, maximum, at sea at this pace with a tropical cyclone forecast in the next day or two. Which reminded Doug he would have to ensure the cargo was securely tied down and wouldn't shift in the rough sea.

Doug had already confirmed that Kane had landed in New Zealand and Edith had also confirmed that Paolo's body had arrived and was on ice at the funeral home, while the coffin was clearing customs, and she was trying to find a carrier that could pick up such a heavy item and deliver it to the farm.

Jane had sent her love, Orhan had been too emotional to talk on the phone but was happy his father was alive.

Alone At Sea

Raphael awoke to the gentle hum of the ship; a cold sweat came over him. For some reason, the ship was missing its normal noise, no kitchen noise, no crazy German banter. He looked at his watch: it was almost noon; he had slept through breakfast.

The last two days had been rough, gale force winds lashing the ship, it pitched and rolled in the huge seas. They were all exhausted; that might account for him sleeping so long. He felt lethargic, was it possible he had been drugged?

Raphael made his way to the bridge. The young Indian boy beamed up at him, "I'm the *capitan* now, sir. Mr Doug, he says to follow the GPS map, see," as he pointed to the computer screen. "Mr Doug said ship already know where to go."

Raphael tore back down the stairs to the private quarters. Everyone was gone. His heart pumping out of his chest, he ran and checked the cargo, it was still in place, untouched.

His heart still racing, he checked the life rafts, none were missing. How had they left the ship?

Raphael made his way to the engine room, Ansel was tinkering away with his fishing gear, his only concern was when was breakfast going to be served.

Ansel handed Raphael a sealed letter, it was from Doug, written in Spanish.

Doug wrote: *If you are reading this, then we have left, my friend. Remember the plan! If you get it right, you will be a rich man. This is your ship now, and these are your crew. Take control — the responsibility is now yours, make your father proud. We will meet again, I'm sure. Look after my house. Good luck.*

Raphael was shaking, not with anger but with fear of what lay ahead. He and Doug had gone over the plan a hundred times. It was his ship now; he would have to put his big boy pants on and grow some cojones. He didn't realise until now how much he had grown attached to Doug and his steadfastness. Yes, they would meet again, and he was confident Doug was now his friend.

Raphael found a crew member to start cooking breakfast for the crew. He went back to the bridge and studied the navigation path; all seemed in order.

The ship was just rounding the tip of New Zealand where the two oceans meet. He made a crucial phone call; everything was going to his plan.

Under the cover of darkness, the transfer to the first boat went as planned, five hundred kilos of meth were on its way to New Zealand, it had been a difficult transfer as the sea was rough. The instructions to his contact were to bury the first five hundred kilos along the coast in the sand dunes at various locations, then the second transfer of five hundred kilos was to meet with a campervan once it reached shore, then the boat was to come back for the third drop. It was Doug's idea not to put all their eggs in one basket just in case something went wrong.

Raphael knew something wasn't quite right when the third pick-up didn't arrive. They were creeping outside the time where the odds of remaining undetected were in their favour. If the authorities had now become aware of them it was dangerous to be out at sea this long. He decided to make the last drop and attached it to a buoy, not bothering to wait for the transfer boat to arrive. That's when he got a phone call from an Asian voice that simply said, "Abort," then hung up.

Raphael gave the order for the *capitan* to continue, no use waiting around, something must have gone wrong. He would find out in time how successful it had been. It was time to get back in the shipping lane and on to Australia to connect with the Chinese fishing trawler. This was a nerve-wracking business; he was definitely going to need a stiff drink.

Raphael now faced another twenty-five more days to head across the Tasman Sea; if the authorities were on to him, this is when it would happen. He was pretty sure he wasn't going to sleep a wink until that transfer had taken place. He would make sure he had a practice drill for the crew just in case, and he would check the explosives they had on board as their backup. How he wished he could talk to someone now; it was all just a waiting game with millions of dollars at stake.

Raphael's connection with the Chinese fishing trawler was easy with no complications. It was obvious that they were well-practised with the procedure. A good-looking businessman invited himself aboard and introduced himself. He was nice and polite. He gave direct orders to his crew, and they started to manually unload the containers. They were careful to make sure they separated Doug's cargo from Raphael's.

The ship was a hive of activity, Raphael wasn't sure where they all came from, but the flow of little Chinese men was continuous. The businessman confirmed with Raphael that the numbers stacked up and then shook his hand and left. As quickly as the trawler had pulled up alongside, it started to disappear into the distance.

Raphael stared in dumb silence at the sea in front of him, amazed at how fast the trawler had disappeared and relieved it was over.

The skipper interrupted him, "The boat is saying we are going back to Acapulco now Mr Raphael, okay?"

"Yes, very good. Let's celebrate. Call the German and tell him to come for a drink."

Raphael went to the galley. In the back of the chiller, he found a crate of Taittinger Champagne with a note on it. It read: *You're either celebrating or jumping overboard with a smiling face, hope it's the first one. Cheers D.* He had thought of everything.

Raphael would make no radio contact with land, his father, or his New Zealand contact while at sea; that was the plan, and he was following it. He would have to trust that the money would go into his account as Doug had promised.

Deep Water

They waited for the sleeping pills to take effect on Raphael. They couldn't take this final chance to get home if any complications arose. Raphael hadn't noticed while he consumed the meal Henry had made everyone.

Doug handed each person a survival suit, hand-tailored to fit each of them. They normally only came in bright red, but they needed to stay undercover so black suits had been made.

It was crucial that they jumped overboard while the engines were stopped to avoid being chewed up by the propellers. It was also crucial that the GPS coordinates were precise, plenty of hungry sharks out that far.

They were grateful for Ansel's understanding that they must leave him behind.

Doug took the precaution of tying everyone together, so they didn't drift apart. He had no idea how long they might be floating at sea before Kane arrived, and they hadn't picked the best night for it, the sea had churned up and the water temperature in June was very cold.

Once they had floated clear of the ship, Doug gave Ansel the signal with his torch. The ship rumbled back into life and onward, towards the tip of New Zealand.

Hours of walking around the deck had given Doug and Joseph time to prepare Audrey and Henry for what to expect in the water. It would be cold and extremely tough going, but they had to sit tight and wait. Doug wasn't going to let anyone die on his shift, and they had to stay focused on the end result.

—

Kane was nearing the GPS coordinate; he was yet to see any sign of life. He now had to factor in the flow of the current. Jane was keeping watch at the stern, Orhan at the port side and Wiremu on the starboard. It was a tense time with less moonlight than they'd expected, due to the weather conditions, making visibility difficult.

It was Audrey who heard the sound of the boat motor first. Through chattering teeth, she tried to tell Joseph but only managed to point in the direction of the sound.

Joseph flashed his torch in the general direction. Not long after, the flash came back, three short, one long. Joseph replied with one long and three short. They were about to be rescued from the depths of the black sea beneath them.

Wiremu and Kane helped haul their dead weights on board from the stern of the super yacht, none of them had any energy left to climb on board. Jane had blankets and oxygen ready, and the heat turned up in the ship's lounge. Once they were on board Kane returned to the controls and headed back to the harbour.

There was a long silence while Doug, Joseph, Audrey, and Henry caught their breath. They had been in the water for over an hour, any longer and Henry might not have made it. Jane had connected him to the oxygen mask.

"There better be some bloody booze on board," said Doug, as he wrapped his blanket around Jane and snuggled up to her; she always smelt nice. He could have kicked himself for ever leaving her.

He put Orhan under his other arm. Poor boy was so upset. "I'm home for good now, boy, you'll be okay."

Joseph and Audrey combined blankets, while Wiremu put a blanket around himself and Henry to warm Henry up.

Audrey introduced herself and added, "It's not your normal family, is it?" They all laughed. She felt totally at home and part of a family.

"We're heading for the Whangaroa Harbour," said Kane. "We'll stay on the boat for a couple of days, catch some fish, make it look like a family fishing trip. If there are any questions from the Ministry of Fisheries or police, old Sergeant Wiremu here should be able to take care of that."

"Oh, get it right! I'm Detective Wiremu now, bro," retorted Wiremu, eliciting more laughter.

"Once we anchor for the night, you seaweeds can warm up in the spa pool."

Jane served everyone drinks. Even Henry had recovered enough to ask for a large whisky, neat, no ice, he figured he was cold enough.

Kane warned them that Edith and Gay Kenny were flying over. They all laughed, good-naturedly mimicking Edith – the professional wailer was coming.

Doug made a toast, "To Paulo. Thank you for the yacht and thanked you for nearly getting us all killed!"

They spent the following days fishing and relaxing on the boat. They were never questioned by the authorities, although Wiremu had been called into work for an emergency briefing about a bungled meth shipment on Ninety Mile Beach. The numbers didn't quite add up, so it sounded like half of it was not found. The rest was a cluster-fuck.

There had been word from Mexico that the money transfer was confirmed. And Raphael had sent a cheeky selfie photo of himself on the balcony at the Buenaventura house with a glass of champagne in his hand.

Paulo's Funeral

It was decided that Paulo's body would be cremated. The funeral director had the foresight to remove the contents from Paulo's internal cavities when his body arrived. Doug would later keep half the ashes and Henry could keep the other half.

Paulo's last wishes were to have a lavish funeral with the gold coffin on display, lid closed.

There were hundreds of flowers tied with beautiful different coloured silks, lining the entrance and the room, to fulfil Paulo's wish that every guest took a bouquet home with them when they left.

The who's who of the underworld had jetted in from around the globe, along with members of the Catholic clergy, who had been massive benefactors of Paulo's donations for many years. Hollywood actors and government representatives from several countries were also guests.

Paulo had arranged for several framed portraits of himself to be displayed at the funeral. In each one he was dressed in a brightly coloured silk suit and his gold shoes.

A slide show of photo's played on a big screen, each with Paulo doing something adventurous, from playing golf to riding an ostrich or hiring a cruise ship for a joy ride. All depicting his charismatic character and his enthusiasm for life, while a choir of young boys sang beautiful hymns in the background as guests were ushered into seats in the chapel by brightly coloured drag queens.

All the guests received a gold-bound funeral programme including a list of charities that Paulo supported and a request that others follow in his footsteps.

A huge organ signalled that the service was about to start.

The priest gave a testimonial of Paulo's life, written by Paulo of course, starting with his first significant business venture as a young boy stealing the neighbours' eggs and selling them back to them, to his last day. Paulo's testimonial honoured Doug, without whom he would have died in the grimy little cell he had been imprisoned in, and he thanked him for his life.

There were funny moments and sad moments.

The priest asked if anyone would like to come to the front and share some words about Paulo.

Henry was the first to get up, supported by Audrey as he was still missing his employer and friend and still coping with grief. He introduced himself as Paulo's loyal servant and companion and acknowledged guests in the audience who were regular visitors to Paulo's many mansions.

Henry relayed a couple of disastrously funny stories where events had gone badly wrong, like the time Paulo bought a pair of hippopotamuses for his swimming pool and they decide to run amuck and escape. It ended in a police chase as they had killed the neighbour's dogs and nearly killed some neighbours.

He recalled the times Paulo would make Henry open parcels in case they contained bombs, and he joked about the times Paulo would come home and would completely forget that he had a body in the boot of his car until the chauffeur complained about the smell some days later.

Lastly, Henry took a deep breath, "I wish I had departed this earth first. I miss the little bugger every day." There wasn't a dry eye in the building. Audrey helped him from the stage back to his seat.

Hector Garcia went forward next; he announced that he was also attending on behalf of his son who couldn't make it as he was at sea but sent his regards. Hector was so funny in his delivery, starting with, "I hated the little bastard, he even fucked my ex-wife," he grinned, and everyone laughed. "But before he died, he did right by my son and my family, and for that I am grateful."

Hector also shared some funny stories, one of which brought the house down with laughter, "There was the time, a long time ago, Paulo bought a tattoo machine on a whim, and he got some dumb young Mexican fella very drunk and tattooed him for practice. He drew a crooked horse and thought it was a masterpiece!"

With that, Hector pulled up his sleeve and showed the room a terrible outline of a crooked horse, which simultaneously appeared on the big screen, the room roared with laughter. "That dumb Mexican was me," laughed Hector.

Many people got up to share their own entertaining stories, all agreeing that Paulo was a once-in-a-lifetime character who was one hundred per cent a better friend than an enemy.

When the priest stood to bring the proceedings to a close, he introduced Doug.

Doug walked to the front of the chapel to close the ceremony; he sensed a murmur from the crowd. He knew many people may have heard of him, but this was the first time most of them had seen him. He waited for silence to fall on the room.

He took a deep breath. "It's all been said. Here was a man who was hated by many and loved by a few. He was a generous man with a big heart and a wicked sense of humour. I keep thinking I see him in crowds or hear his voice or his laughter. Or is this one of his tricks, and I'll receive a cryptic message, and he will reappear again?

"But not this time. I held his hand while he took his last breath, dressed in his ridiculous pyjamas, the show pony to the last breath. I will miss you, my dear friend, and I will never forget you."

Doug finished off the proceedings with an invitation to guests to attend a function at his farm.

The Reading of The Will

Doug received word from Edith that a solicitor from Switzerland was trying to contact him regarding Paulo's estate. Edith had checked him out, and he was legitimate. The solicitor was even prepared to fly to Croatia, where Doug and Jane were currently living on their super yacht with Orhan, now Wiremu and his family had taken over the family farm in New Zealand. Elias needed to meet Doug in person as there were important documents that required signing. Doug agreed to meet with him.

He convinced Edith and the rest of the family to come for a visit at the same time. They could spend time on the yacht, and either Kane or Joseph could sail the yacht to another port for Doug and Jane. They were sick of Croatia now, and it was starting to get cold, so a good time to live it up somewhere else for a while. They had decided to live full-time on the yacht, travelling around the world. The only problem was that they didn't know how to sail it and relied on one of the boys to visit to relocate them.

Elias Keller arrived with his bags on wheels full of documents. A taxi had delivered him to the Split Harbour jetty. He was ridiculously overdressed for a Croatian summer. Although Elias was a bit travel-weary and overstimulated by the number of people on the yacht, he managed to retain a professional demeanour. Doug's family were loud, and in all honesty, Elias thought they looked a bit feral. He wasn't surprised that they were friends of the late Mr Hernandez.

Elias didn't want to stay with these people longer than he had to; his directive was to perform his purpose. He introduced himself as the representative of a law firm in Switzerland, whose primary business was to manage, protect and administer the many companies and enterprises around the world that previously belonged to Mr Paulo Hernandez, which now belonged solely to Mr Douglas Henderson. The portfolio was too large for just one person to manage, so his firm was hired to administer and invest where possible.

The first thing Elias did was hand Doug a sealed envelope. The wax seal had Paulo's stamp on it; it was unopened. Written instructions on the front in Paulo's writing said, *When the uptight prick fucks off open it,* Doug smirked, it was Paulo all over. Elias had not seen the humour in the writing and chose to ignore it.

The paperwork was a basic routine signing of documents, which Doug had Edith look over before he signed. The pages were endless. There was a catalogued list of properties, companies, assets, mines, and investments that were all to be given to Doug to do what he wanted with.

Elias suggested that Doug could quite possibly be one of the richest men in the world. Paulo had left him his entire estate with the only exception being a million-dollar bank account for Henry.

The signing of the paperwork took over an hour, then Elias, who was now perspiring with sweat, packed up his cases of files and left in the taxi that had waited for him all that time. Doug laughed and pointed out that he was paying for that taxi.

The family stood around in excitement, eager to see what the sealed envelope contained. Doug broke the seal on the envelope:

My dearest friend,

I'm like the gift that keeps on giving. I hope you haven't melted down that bloody coffin yet! Inside the lining on the sides of the coffin, engraved into the gold, are the GPS coordinates to the location of my millions of US dollars I have buried across Colombia. Inside, also, on the base of the coffin, are the coordinates of massive, underground, processed cocaine stores, also hidden across Colombia. If you talk to Henry, he will be able to confirm that this is true. It was too much for me to launder, so I buried it. You might have retired, but it's there for you or your sons to collect as you see fit. See you on the other side, amigo. Paulo XX.

"Fuck!" said Doug. "Where is that bloody coffin?"

"We dumped it in Joseph's back yard," said Edith. "We didn't know what else to do with it. We were going to turn it into a fishpond." The whole family burst into laughter.

"Well," said Doug, "I just inherited more money than I could ever spend in a lifetime, so if you boys want to go on a treasure hunt in Colombia, you're welcome."

     MICHELLE THOMPSON

The Wedding Gift

It was hot, unpleasant hot. Fields of dry brown dirt with only a few little plants for miles. Flies, desperate for any moisture, trying to get into the corners of your mouth and eyes.

It surprised Doug that anything grew here, but it did.

Women in dirty, past colourful sari tended the earth, so accustomed to the flies they no longer pushed them away. The women all had the same look, vacant faces devoid of emotion.

Intermittently, the women fought back the fear of punishment and looked up secretly from their garden duties to the tall white man standing like a tower at the edge of the field. Then they quickly looked away.

Doug thought he must be getting soft in his old age; he felt sorry for them.

Jane had the right idea. She was still in the van, happy in the air-conditioning.

Doug's visit to this unforgiving site had been months in the making. He could see the private detective he had hired in the distance frantically nodding and waving his arms in the air. Negotiations looked like they were going sour, but it was only the Indian way of communicating. Time wasn't on his side. If he didn't hurry up, Doug would step in.

Just then, Doug saw the envelope of money change hands; the agreed amount for an older female slave, $300 US dollars. The greedy farm owner spitting on his dirty hands and touching the money like it was a precious object, then spitting on his fingers again and wiping down the ends of his moustache.

This fat and somewhat filthy farm owner couldn't understand it. What would anyone want with an old dried-up one? He had plenty of young girls not yet reached puberty for sale, but no one normally came for the older ones.

Doug hated him straight away, wanted to punch him in his dirty little mouth.

The farm owner didn't make eye contact. He knew how this worked; he knew better. This big man had a power about him, a presence that made him sweat.

The private detective looked back at Doug and gave both thumbs-up. The deal was complete.

The dirty farmer produced a dirty whistle from secret folds in his robes. He began blowing it frantically while yelling and beckoning with his arm to a woman in the field. "Myra, Myra, get here. Do you hear me? Get here now."

He waved a cane stick in the air like a threat.

Myra, with head bowed, trudged in his direction. She hated him. What degrading deal had he just made to exploit her private places again?

He ordered her to kneel at his feet.

Doug had had enough; she was his now. He strode over to the kneeling woman, looked at the farmer's dirty little mouth and rat eyes, and his grubby turban, and told him to fuck off. The farmer scampered off like a wounded animal.

Doug waited until they were alone, then crouched down and showed Myra a photo. Without words or a sound, water flowed from her eyes, not like tears, more like someone had turned a tap on her face, the stream of water cutting a track through the encrusted dirt on her cheeks.

That was all the proof Doug needed.

He reached forward and gently helped her to her feet. He signalled Jane to bring a blanket.

Myra stood up and instantly ran away towards a little roofless mud hut on the edge of the field. She did this with such speed that she had returned before Jane had made it from the van with the blanket.

She handed Doug an old, well-worn Beehive brand matchbox, passing it to Doug like a precious gift in her open palms.

Doug took it. It was tattered and stained with years of dirt; he was careful as he opened it. Inside was a tiny pink ribbon with the name Audrey embroidered on it.

Myra spoke for the first time in Doug's presence. "Is she alive?"

"Very much so," replied Doug. "Get in the van or we'll be late for her wedding."

The End